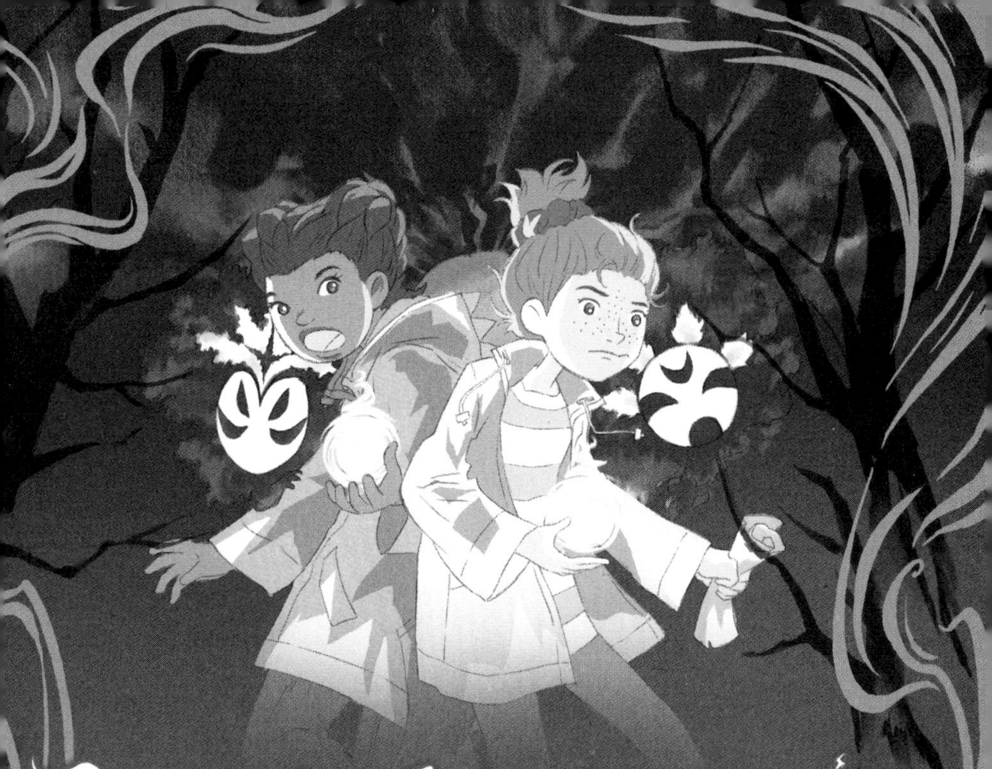

# The Weirn Books

## Be Wary of the Silent Woods

1

SVETLANA CHMAKOVA

JY

# The Weirn Books

## Be Wary of the Silent Woods 1

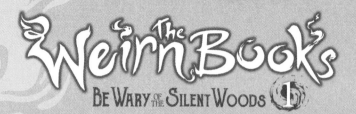

SVETLANA CHMAKOVA

Coloring assistants: Effie Lealand, Melissa McCommon
Inking assistants: Young Kim, Effie Lealand
Lettering: JuYoun Lee



JY
150 West 30th Street, 19th Floor
New York, NY 10001

Visit us at jyforkids.com
facebook.com/jyforkids • twitter.com/jyforkids
jyforkids.tumblr.com • instagram.com/jyforkids

First JY Edition: June 2020

JY is an imprint of Yen Press, LLC.
The JY name and logo are trademarks of Yen Press, LLC.

The publisher is not responsible for websites (or their content) that are not owned by the publisher.

Library of Congress Control Number: 2020936433

ISBNs: 978-1-975-31121-6 (hardcover)
978-1-975-31122-3 (paperback)
978-1-975-31120-9 (ebook)

10 9 8 7 6 5 4 3 2 1

LSC-C

Printed in the United States of America

# Table of Contents

# Chapter 1

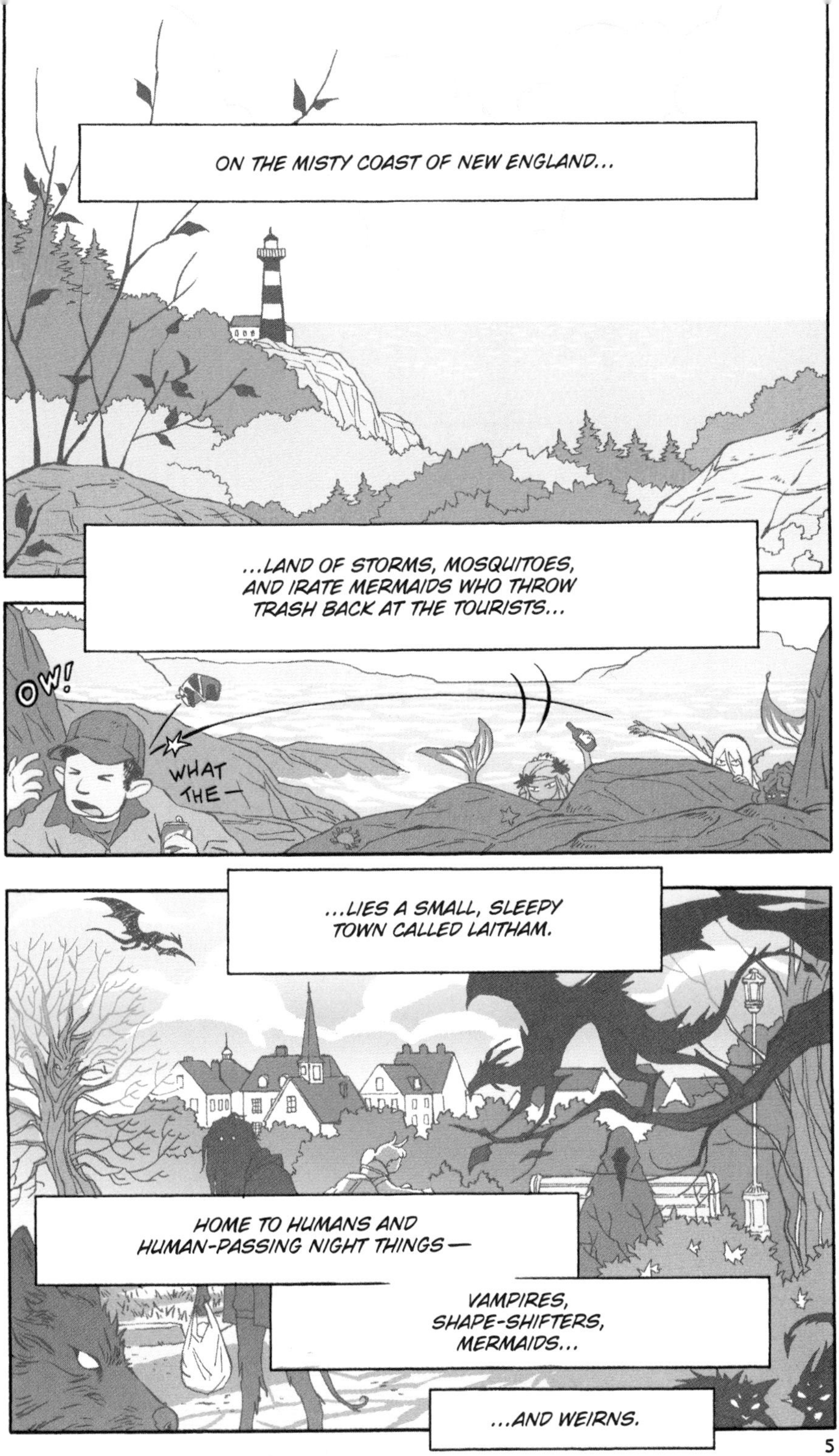
ON THE MISTY COAST OF NEW ENGLAND...
...LAND OF STORMS, MOSQUITOES, AND IRATE MERMAIDS WHO THROW TRASH BACK AT THE TOURISTS...
OW!
WHAT THE—
...LIES A SMALL, SLEEPY TOWN CALLED LAITHAM.
HOME TO HUMANS AND HUMAN-PASSING NIGHT THINGS—
VAMPIRES, SHAPE-SHIFTERS, MERMAIDS...
...AND WEIRNS.

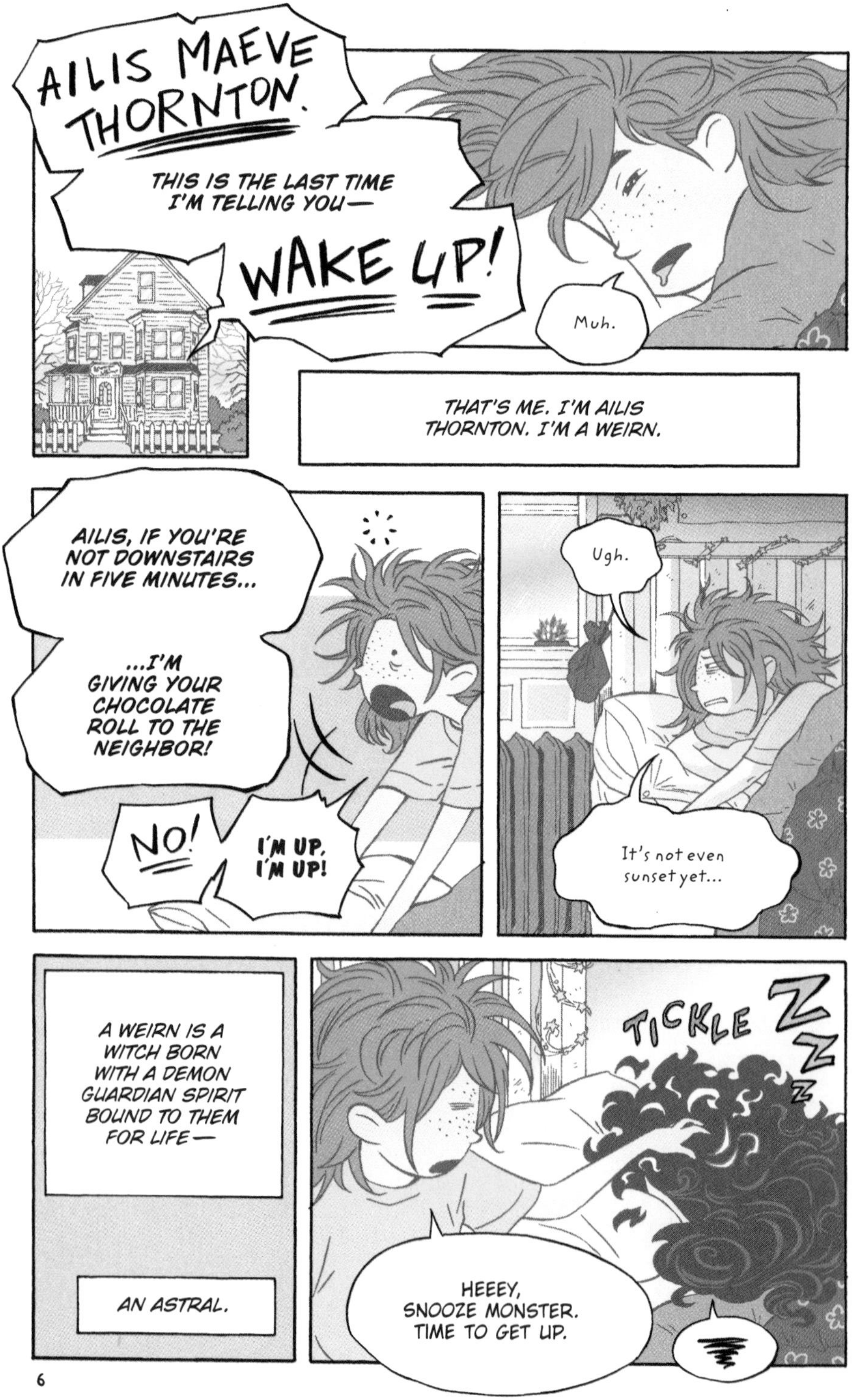
AILIS MAEVE THORNTON.
THIS IS THE LAST TIME I'M TELLING YOU—
WAKE UP!
Muh.
THAT'S ME. I'M AILIS THORNTON. I'M A WEIRN.
AILIS, IF YOU'RE NOT DOWNSTAIRS IN FIVE MINUTES...
...I'M GIVING YOUR CHOCOLATE ROLL TO THE NEIGHBOR!
NO!
I'M UP, I'M UP!
Ugh.
It's not even sunset yet...
A WEIRN IS A WITCH BORN WITH A DEMON GUARDIAN SPIRIT BOUND TO THEM FOR LIFE—
AN ASTRAL.
TICKLE
Z Z Z
HEEEY, SNOOZE MONSTER. TIME TO GET UP.

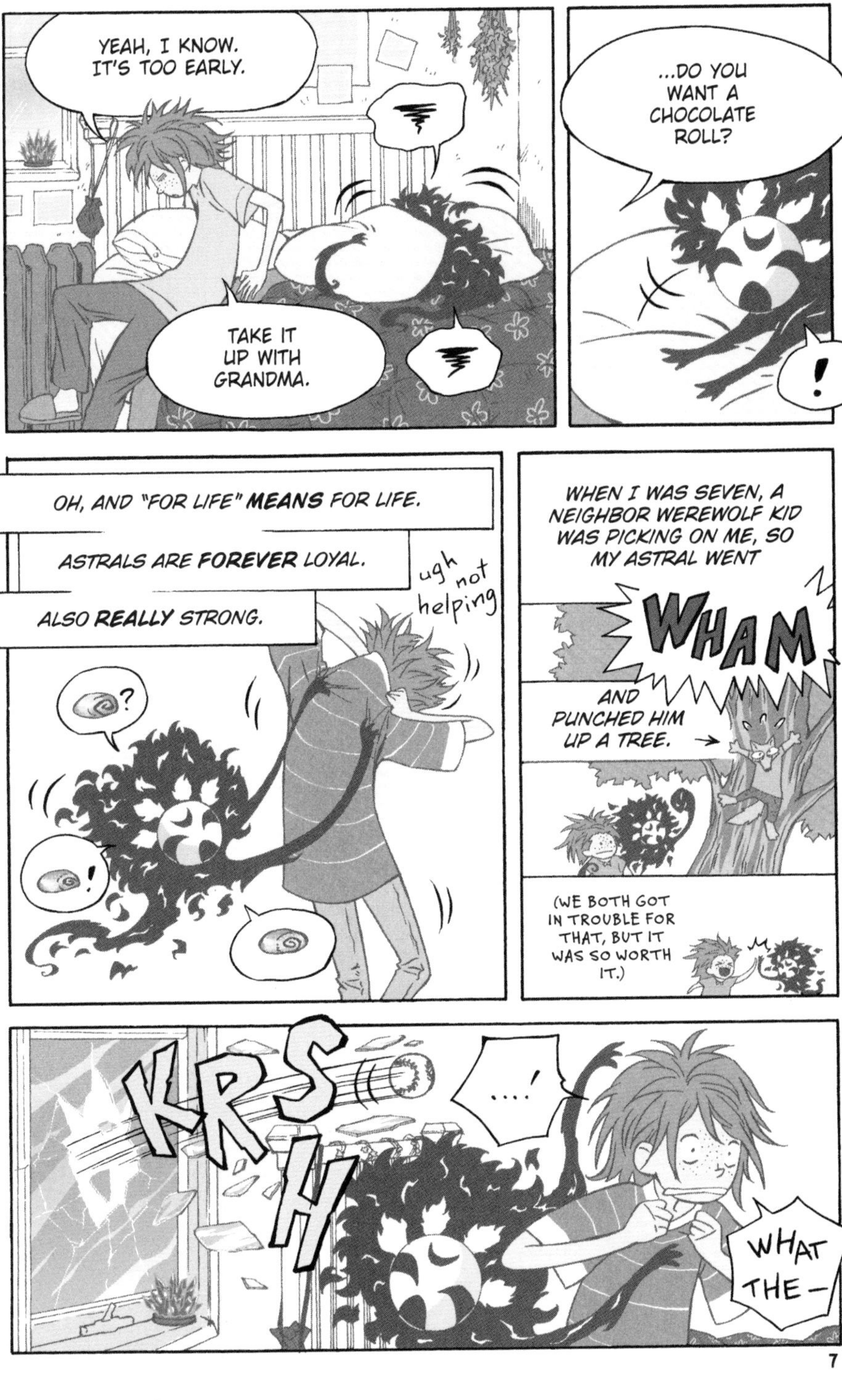

YEAH, I KNOW. IT'S TOO EARLY.
TAKE IT UP WITH GRANDMA.
...DO YOU WANT A CHOCOLATE ROLL?
!
OH, AND "FOR LIFE" MEANS FOR LIFE.
ASTRALS ARE FOREVER LOYAL.
ALSO REALLY STRONG.
ugh not helping
?
!
WHEN I WAS SEVEN, A NEIGHBOR WEREWOLF KID WAS PICKING ON ME, SO MY ASTRAL WENT
WHAM
AND PUNCHED HIM UP A TREE.
(WE BOTH GOT IN TROUBLE FOR THAT, BUT IT WAS SO WORTH IT.)
KRSH
....!
WHAT THE—

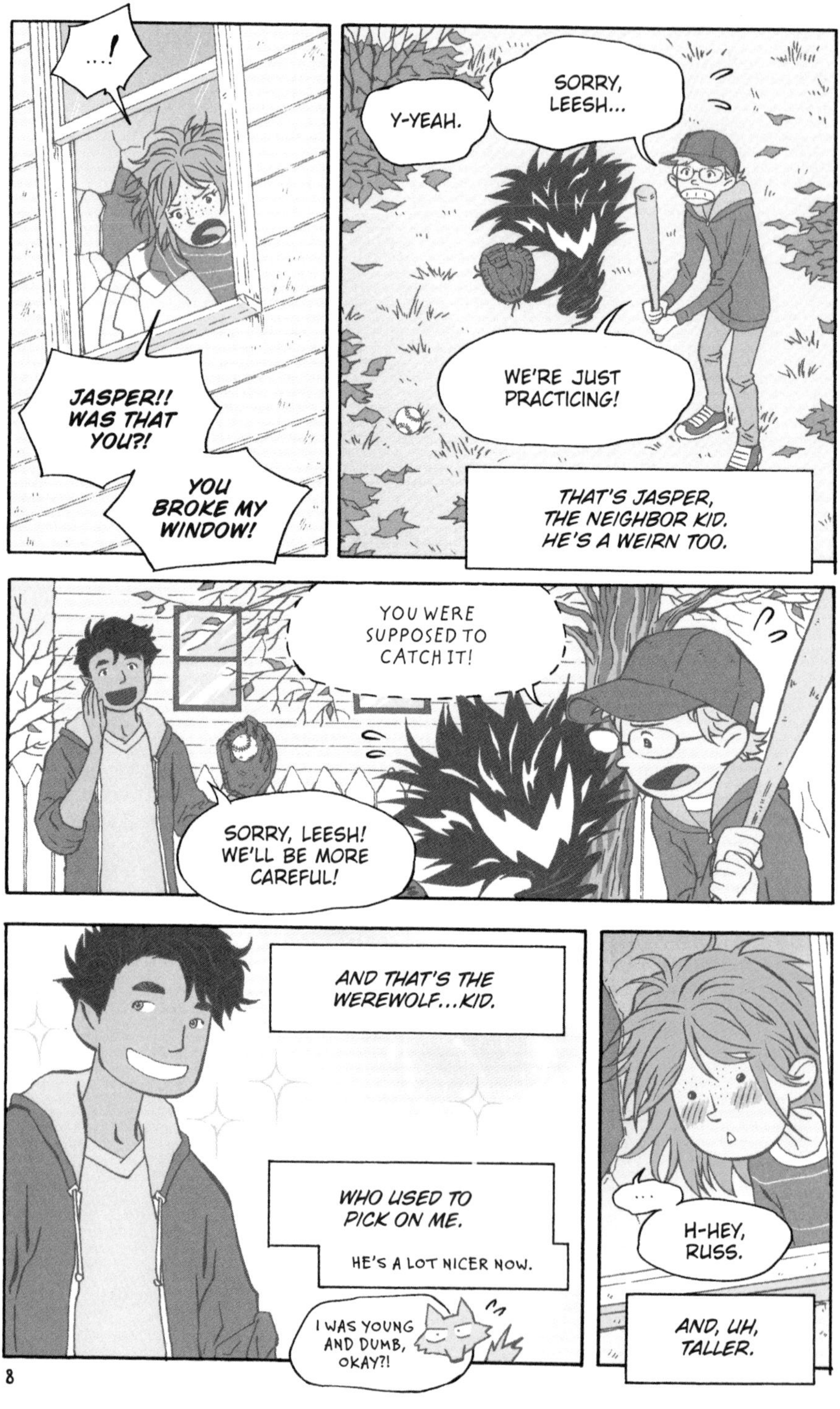
...!
JASPER!! WAS THAT YOU?!
YOU BROKE MY WINDOW!
SORRY, LEESH...
Y-YEAH.
WE'RE JUST PRACTICING!
THAT'S JASPER, THE NEIGHBOR KID. HE'S A WEIRN TOO.
YOU WERE SUPPOSED TO CATCH IT!
SORRY, LEESH! WE'LL BE MORE CAREFUL!
AND THAT'S THE WEREWOLF...KID.
WHO USED TO PICK ON ME.
HE'S A LOT NICER NOW.
I WAS YOUNG AND DUMB, OKAY?!
...
H-HEY, RUSS.
AND, UH, TALLER.

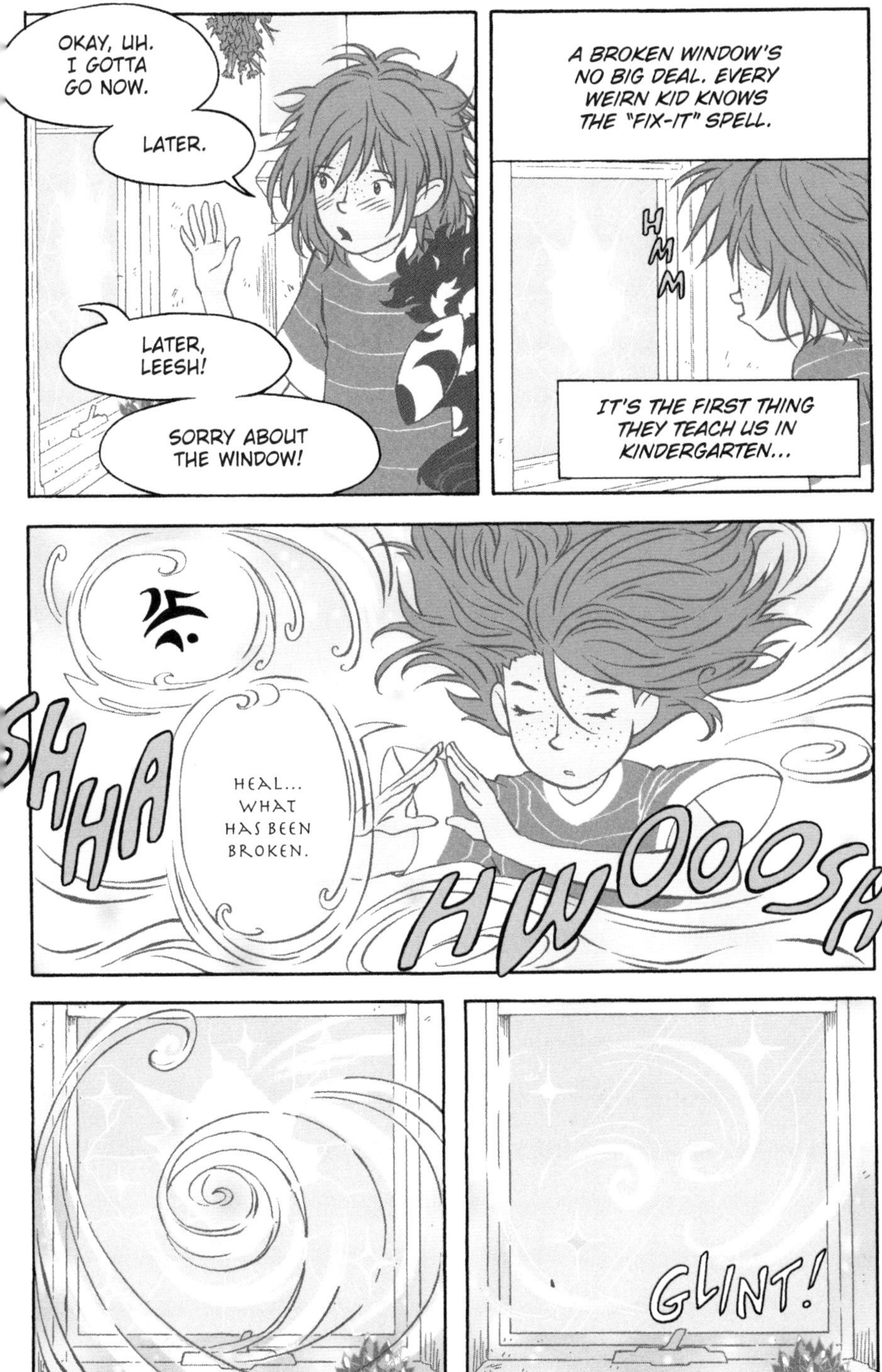
OKAY, UH. I GOTTA GO NOW.
LATER.
LATER, LEESH!
SORRY ABOUT THE WINDOW!
A BROKEN WINDOW'S NO BIG DEAL. EVERY WEIRN KID KNOWS THE "FIX-IT" SPELL.
HMM
IT'S THE FIRST THING THEY TEACH US IN KINDERGARTEN...
SHHA
HEAL... WHAT HAS BEEN BROKEN.
HWOOOSH
GLINT!

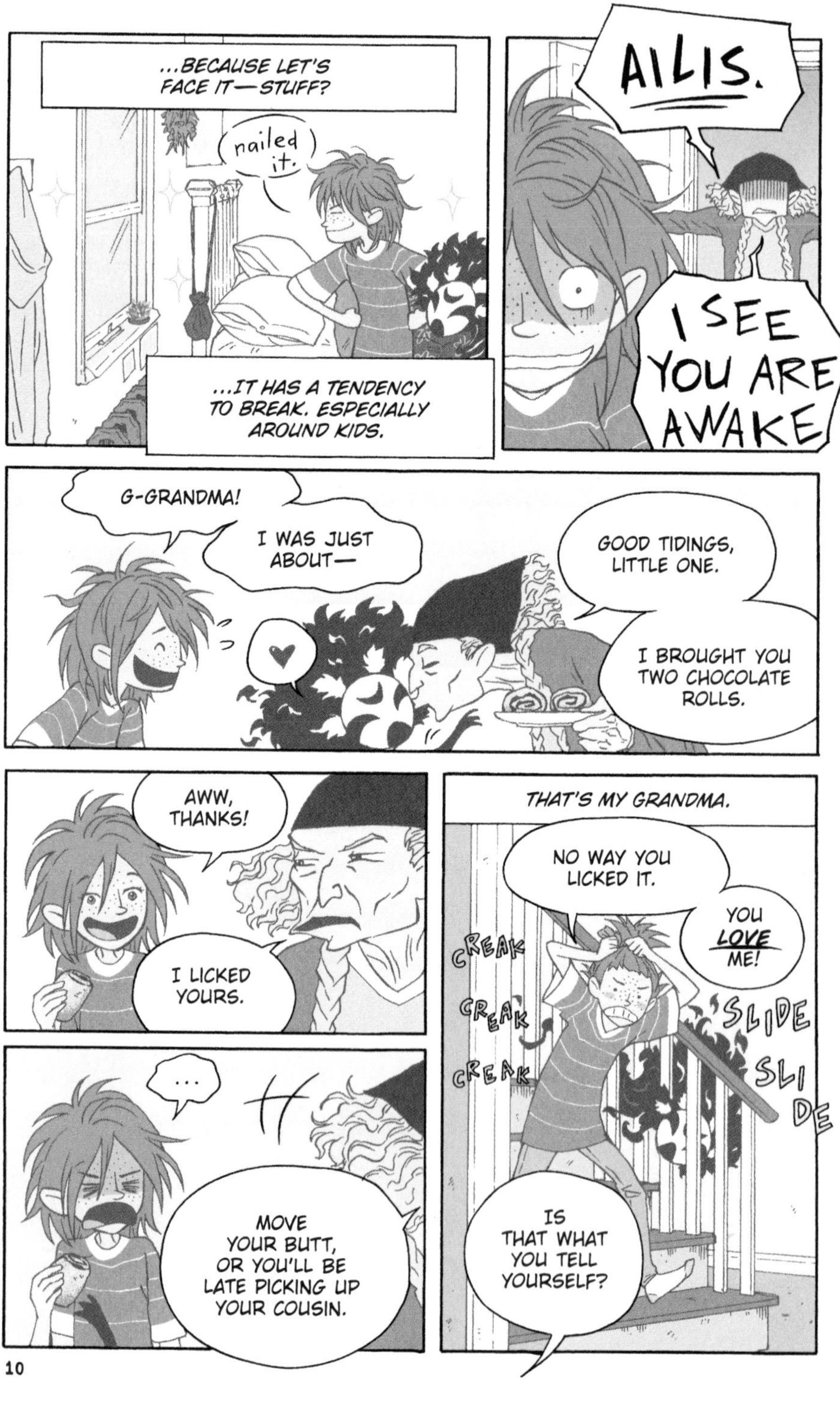
...BECAUSE LET'S FACE IT—STUFF?
nailed it.
...IT HAS A TENDENCY TO BREAK. ESPECIALLY AROUND KIDS.
AILIS.
I SEE YOU ARE AWAKE
G-GRANDMA!
I WAS JUST ABOUT—
GOOD TIDINGS, LITTLE ONE.
I BROUGHT YOU TWO CHOCOLATE ROLLS.
AWW, THANKS!
I LICKED YOURS.
THAT'S MY GRANDMA.
NO WAY YOU LICKED IT.
YOU LOVE ME!
CREAK
CREAK
CREAK
SLIDE
SLIDE
...
MOVE YOUR BUTT, OR YOU'LL BE LATE PICKING UP YOUR COUSIN.
IS THAT WHAT YOU TELL YOURSELF?

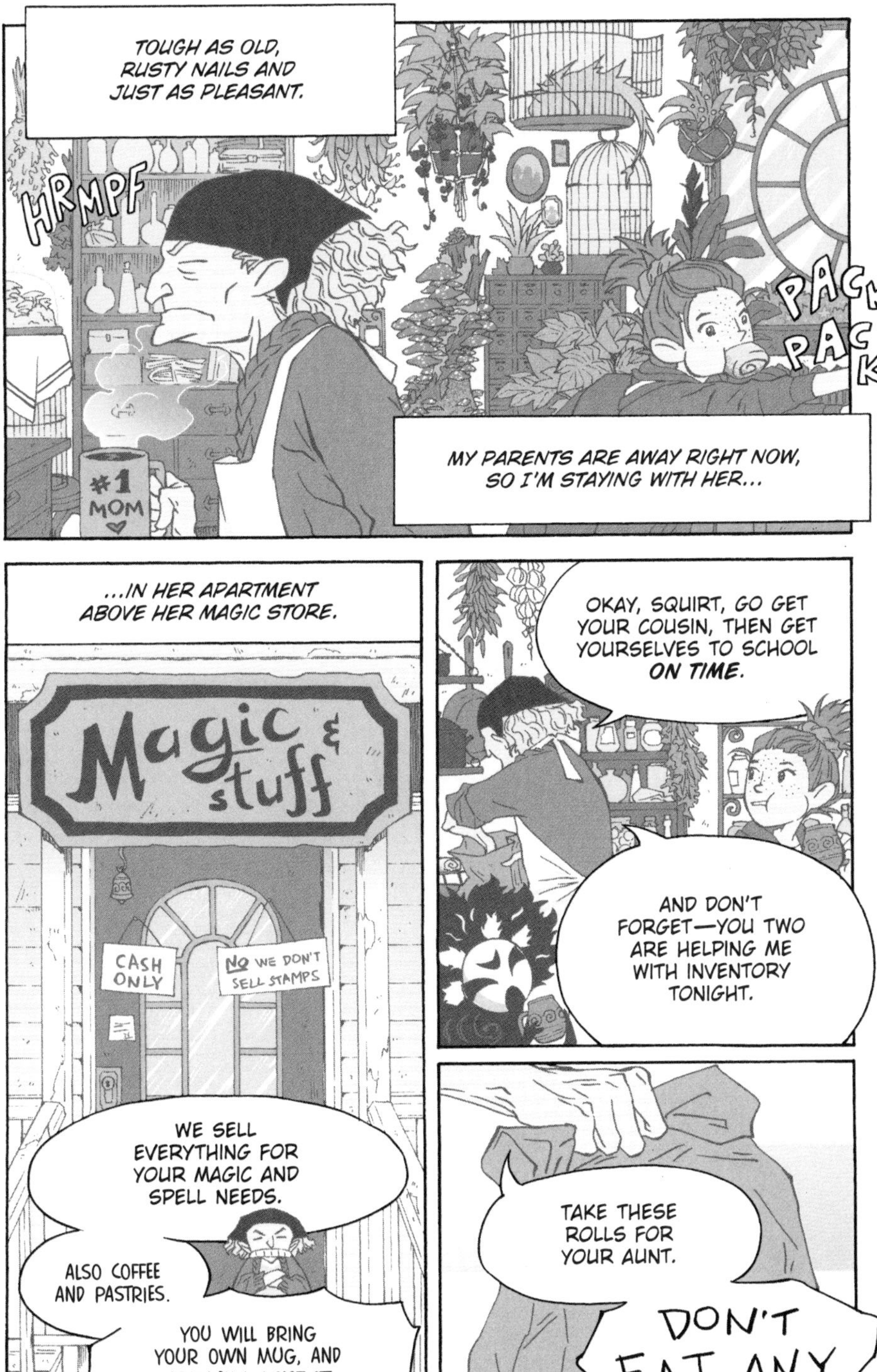
TOUGH AS OLD, RUSTY NAILS AND JUST AS PLEASANT.
HRMPF
PACK PACK
#1 MOM
MY PARENTS ARE AWAY RIGHT NOW, SO I'M STAYING WITH HER...
...IN HER APARTMENT ABOVE HER MAGIC STORE.
Magic & stuff
CASH ONLY
NO WE DON'T SELL STAMPS
WE SELL EVERYTHING FOR YOUR MAGIC AND SPELL NEEDS.
ALSO COFFEE AND PASTRIES.
YOU WILL BRING YOUR OWN MUG, AND **YOU WILL LIKE IT**.
OKAY, SQUIRT, GO GET YOUR COUSIN, THEN GET YOURSELVES TO SCHOOL **ON TIME**.
AND DON'T FORGET—YOU TWO ARE HELPING ME WITH INVENTORY TONIGHT.
TAKE THESE ROLLS FOR YOUR AUNT.
DON'T EAT ANY.

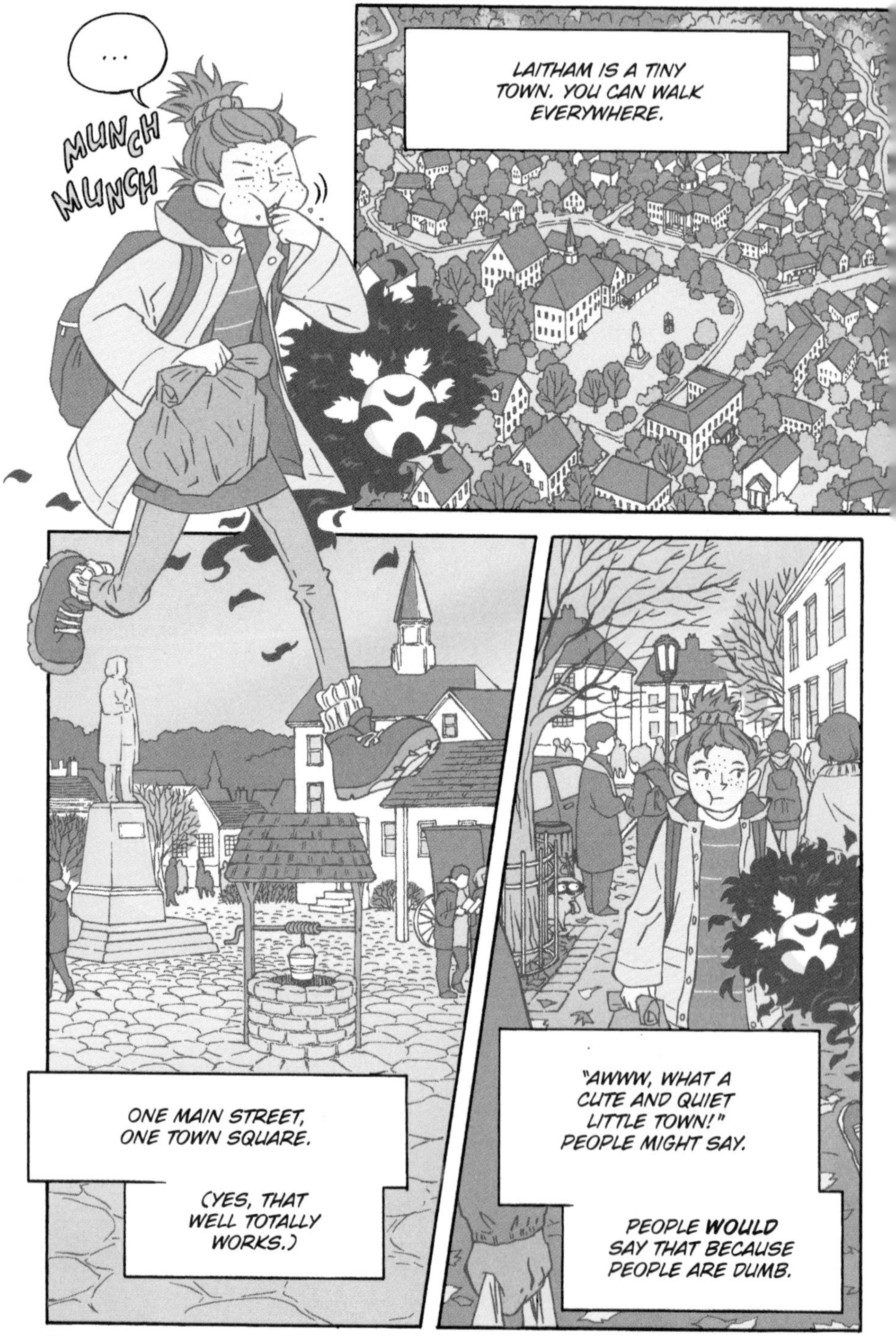
...
MUNCH MUNCH
LAITHAM IS A TINY TOWN. YOU CAN WALK EVERYWHERE.
ONE MAIN STREET, ONE TOWN SQUARE.
(YES, THAT WELL TOTALLY WORKS.)
"AWWW, WHAT A CUTE AND QUIET LITTLE TOWN!" PEOPLE MIGHT SAY.
PEOPLE **WOULD** SAY THAT BECAUSE PEOPLE ARE DUMB.

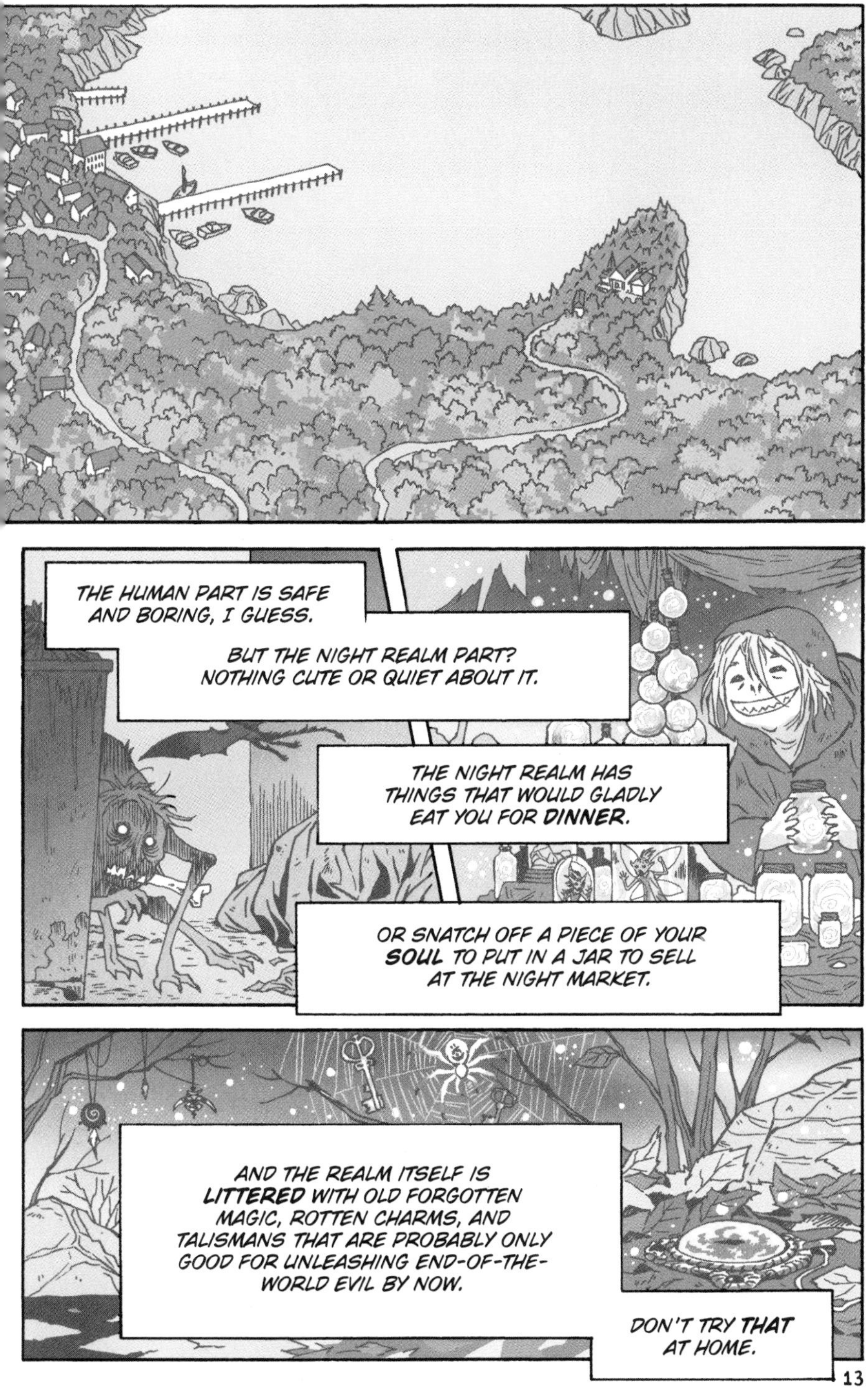
THE HUMAN PART IS SAFE AND BORING, I GUESS.
BUT THE NIGHT REALM PART? NOTHING CUTE OR QUIET ABOUT IT.
THE NIGHT REALM HAS THINGS THAT WOULD GLADLY EAT YOU FOR DINNER.
OR SNATCH OFF A PIECE OF YOUR SOUL TO PUT IN A JAR TO SELL AT THE NIGHT MARKET.
AND THE REALM ITSELF IS LITTERED WITH OLD FORGOTTEN MAGIC, ROTTEN CHARMS, AND TALISMANS THAT ARE PROBABLY ONLY GOOD FOR UNLEASHING END-OF-THE-WORLD EVIL BY NOW.
DON'T TRY THAT AT HOME.

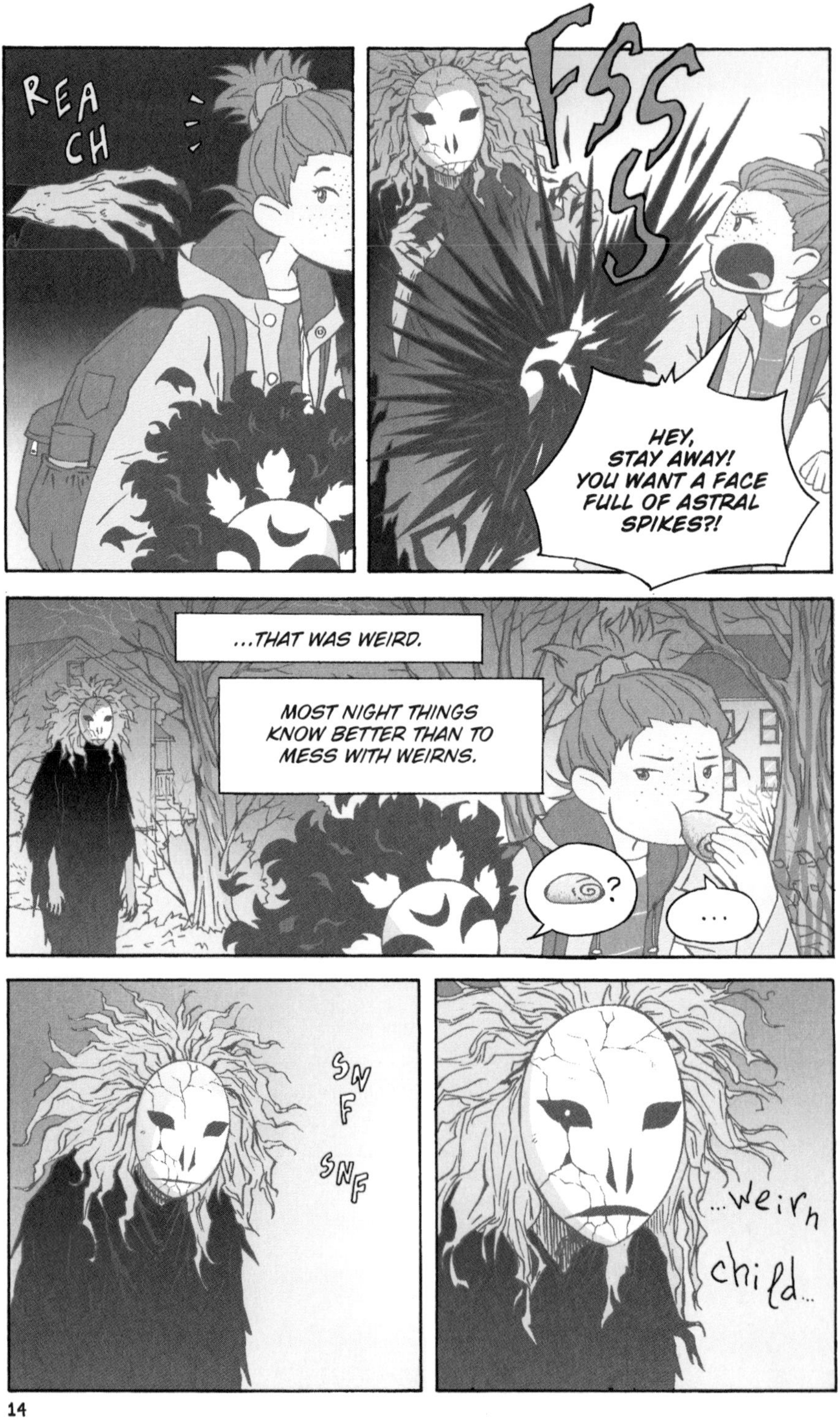
REACH
FSSS
HEY, STAY AWAY! YOU WANT A FACE FULL OF ASTRAL SPIKES?!
...THAT WAS WEIRD.
MOST NIGHT THINGS KNOW BETTER THAN TO MESS WITH WEIRNS.
?
...
SNF SNF
...weirn child...

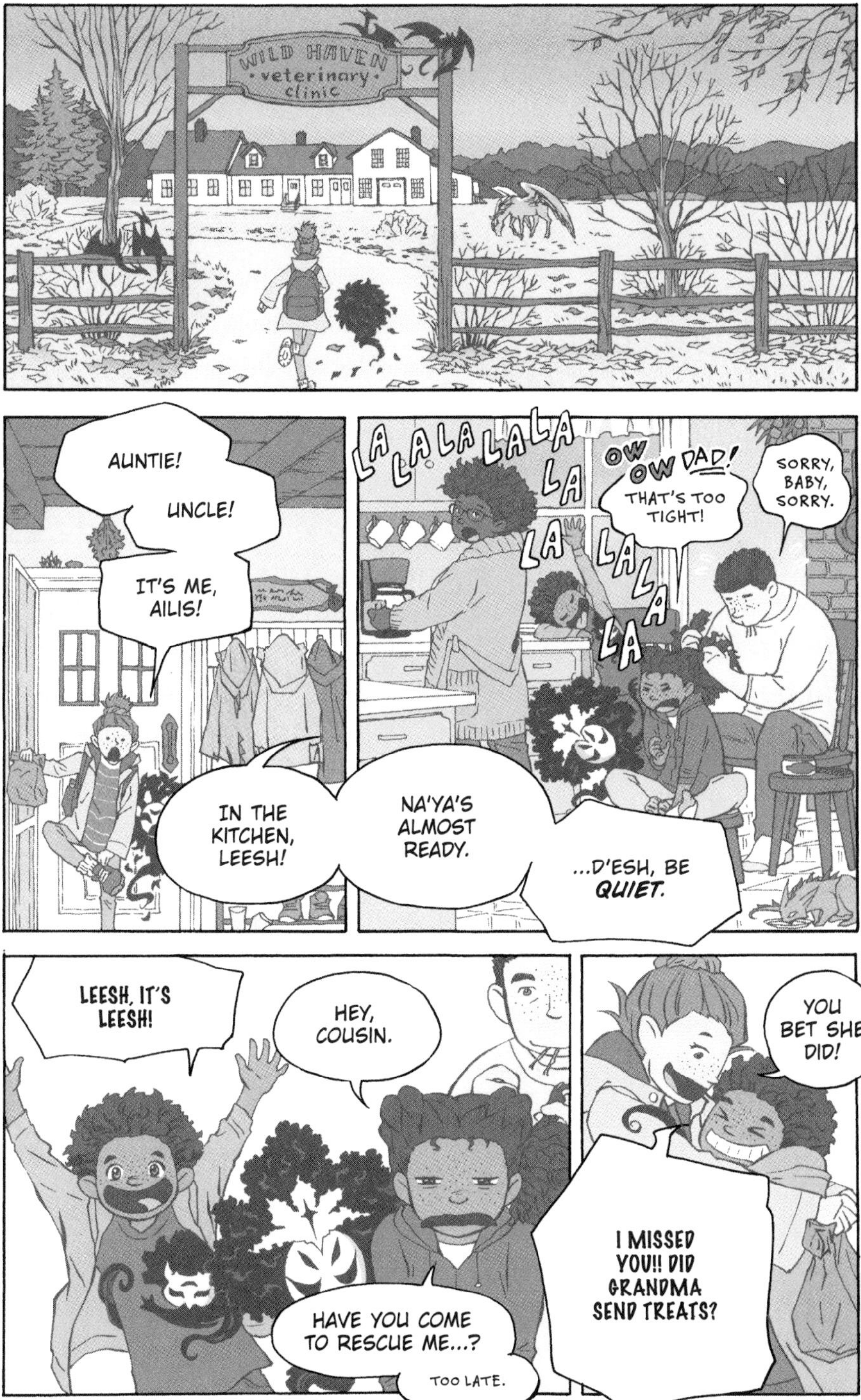
WILD HAVEN
•veterinary•
clinic
AUNTIE!
UNCLE!
IT'S ME, AILIS!
LA LA LA LA LA LA LA LA LA LA LA LA
OW OW DAD! THAT'S TOO TIGHT!
SORRY, BABY, SORRY.
IN THE KITCHEN, LEESH!
NA'YA'S ALMOST READY.
...D'ESH, BE QUIET.
LEESH, IT'S LEESH!
HEY, COUSIN.
HAVE YOU COME TO RESCUE ME...?
TOO LATE.
I MISSED YOU!! DID GRANDMA SEND TREATS?
YOU BET SHE DID!

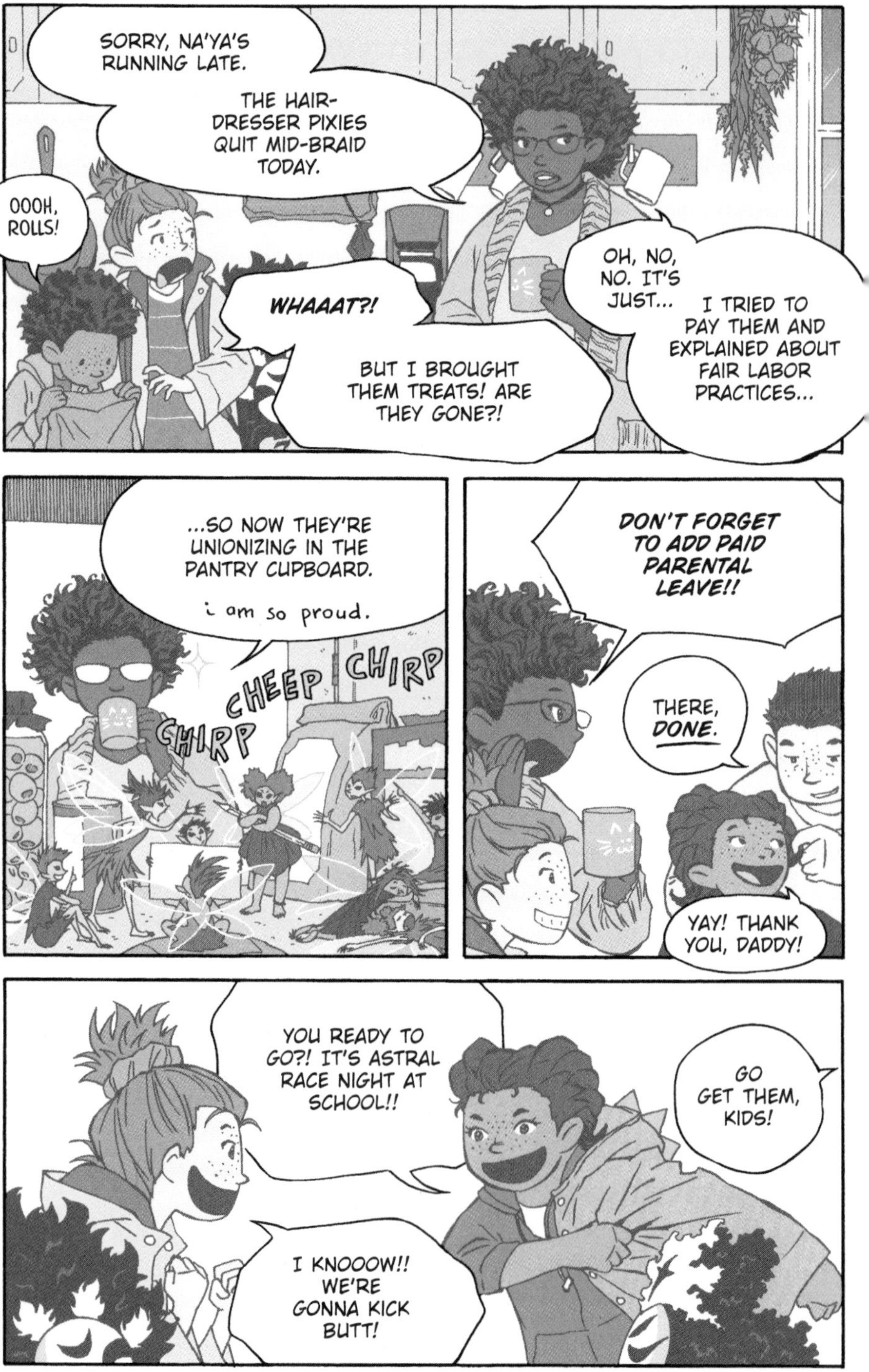
SORRY, NA'YA'S RUNNING LATE.
THE HAIR-DRESSER PIXIES QUIT MID-BRAID TODAY.
OOOH, ROLLS!
WHAAAT?!
BUT I BROUGHT THEM TREATS! ARE THEY GONE?!
OH, NO, NO. IT'S JUST...
I TRIED TO PAY THEM AND EXPLAINED ABOUT FAIR LABOR PRACTICES...
...SO NOW THEY'RE UNIONIZING IN THE PANTRY CUPBOARD.
i am so proud.
CHIRP
CHEEP
CHIRP
DON'T FORGET TO ADD PAID PARENTAL LEAVE!!
THERE, DONE.
YAY! THANK YOU, DADDY!
YOU READY TO GO?! IT'S ASTRAL RACE NIGHT AT SCHOOL!!
GO GET THEM, KIDS!
I KNOOOW!! WE'RE GONNA KICK BUTT!

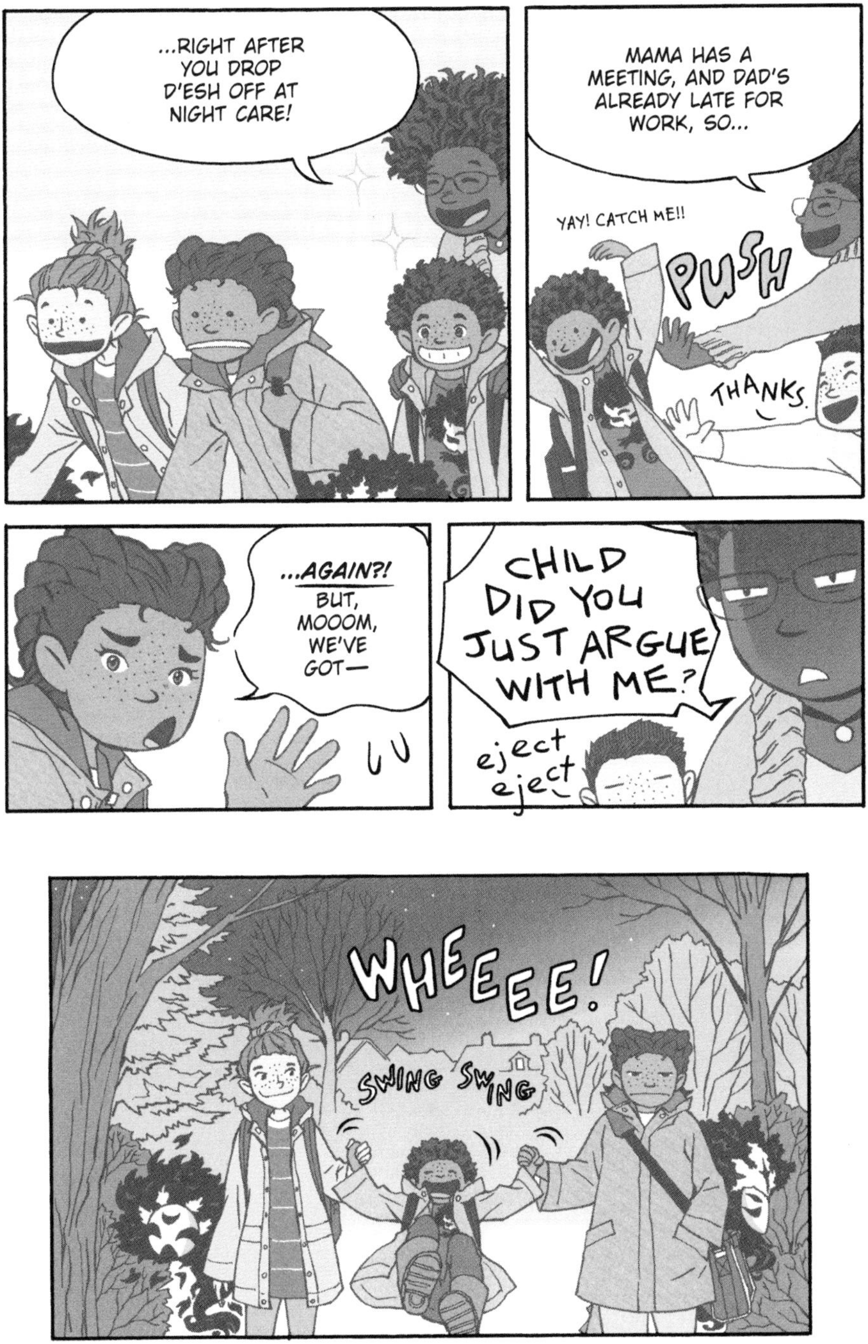
...RIGHT AFTER YOU DROP D'ESH OFF AT NIGHT CARE!
MAMA HAS A MEETING, AND DAD'S ALREADY LATE FOR WORK, SO...
YAY! CATCH ME!!
PUSH
THANKS
...AGAIN?! BUT, MOOOM, WE'VE GOT—
CHILD DID YOU JUST ARGUE WITH ME?
eject eject
WHEEEEE!
SWING SWING

SOOO...MEET MY COUSINS.

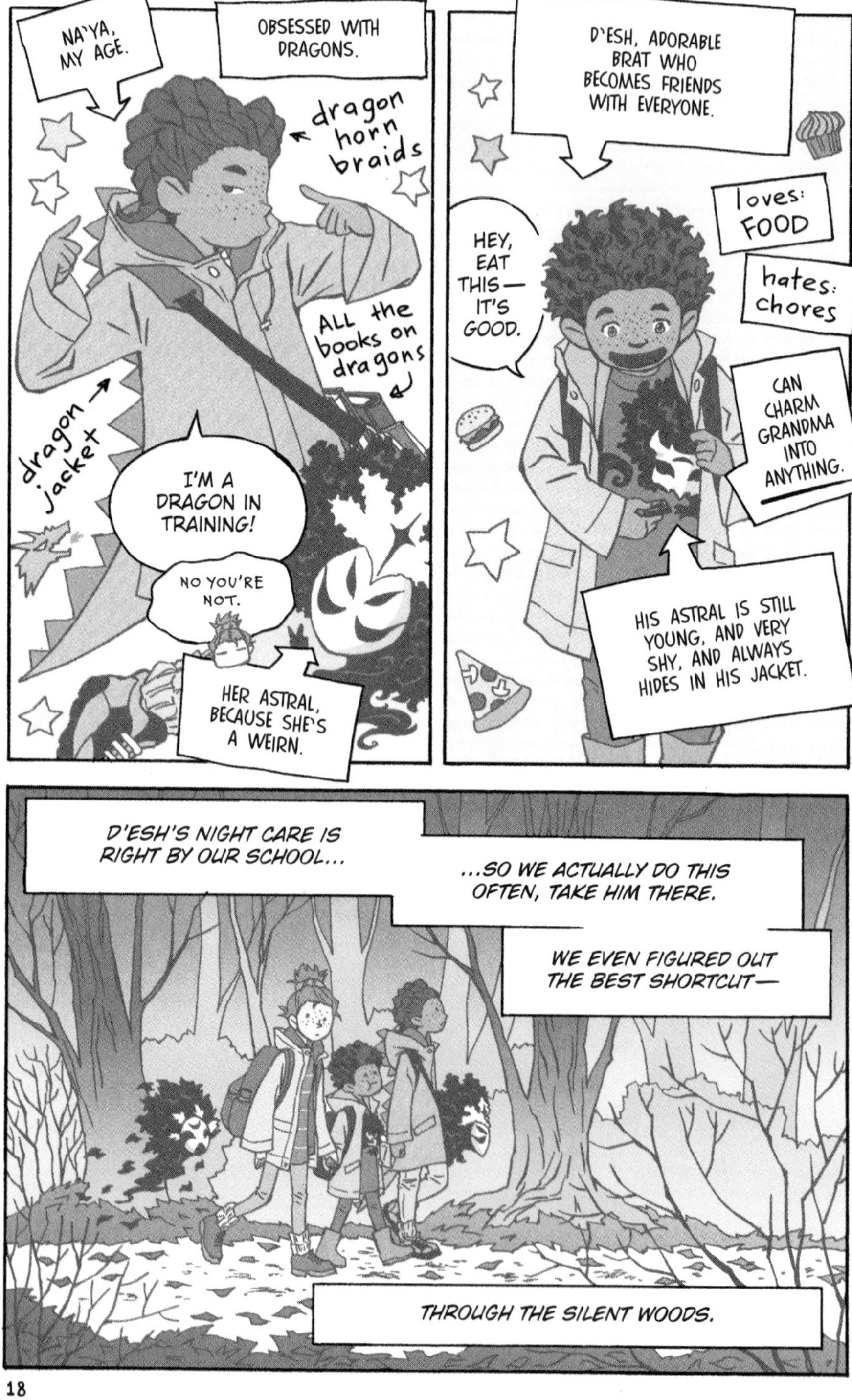
NA'YA, MY AGE.
OBSESSED WITH DRAGONS.
dragon horn braids
ALL the books on dragons
dragon jacket
I'M A DRAGON IN TRAINING!
NO YOU'RE NOT.
HER ASTRAL, BECAUSE SHE'S A WEIRN.
D'ESH, ADORABLE BRAT WHO BECOMES FRIENDS WITH EVERYONE.
HEY, EAT THIS— IT'S GOOD.
loves: FOOD
hates: chores
CAN CHARM GRANDMA INTO ANYTHING.
HIS ASTRAL IS STILL YOUNG, AND VERY SHY, AND ALWAYS HIDES IN HIS JACKET.
D'ESH'S NIGHT CARE IS RIGHT BY OUR SCHOOL...
...SO WE ACTUALLY DO THIS OFTEN, TAKE HIM THERE.
WE EVEN FIGURED OUT THE BEST SHORTCUT—
THROUGH THE SILENT WOODS.

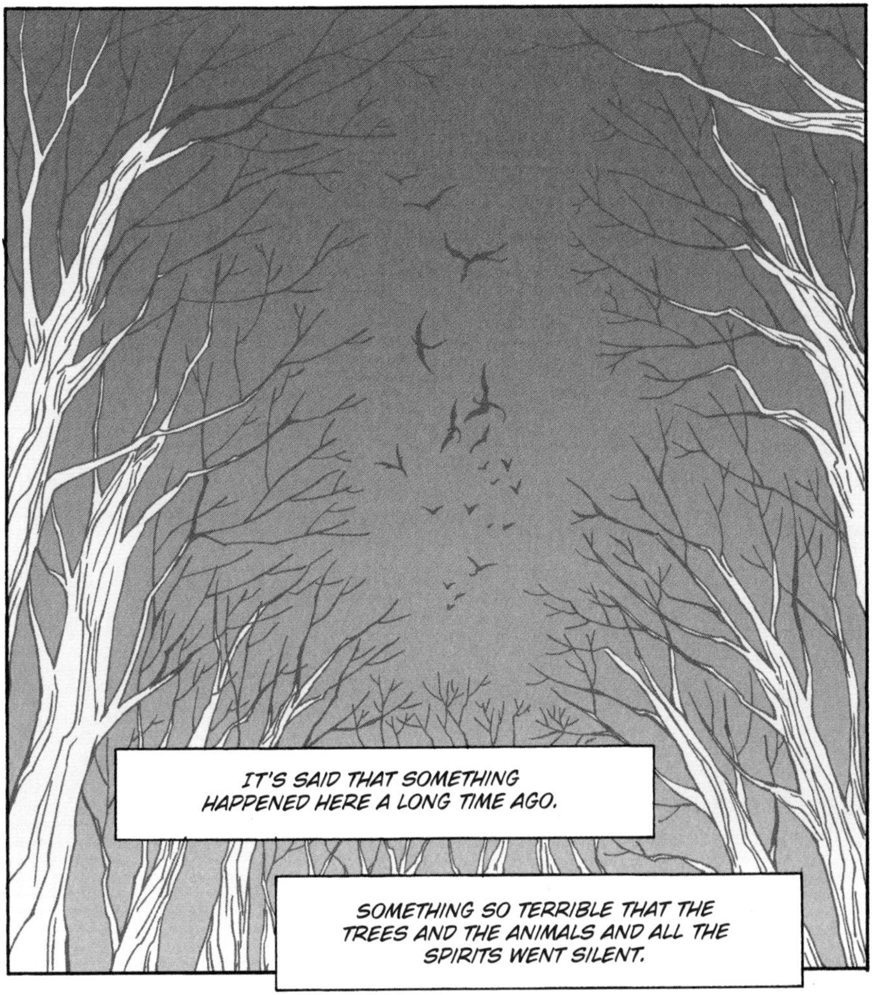
IT'S SAID THAT SOMETHING HAPPENED HERE A LONG TIME AGO.
SOMETHING SO TERRIBLE THAT THE TREES AND THE ANIMALS AND ALL THE SPIRITS WENT SILENT.

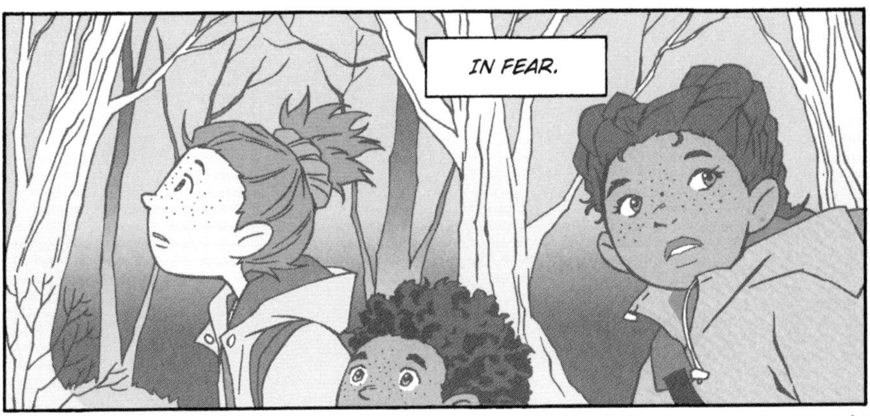
IN FEAR.

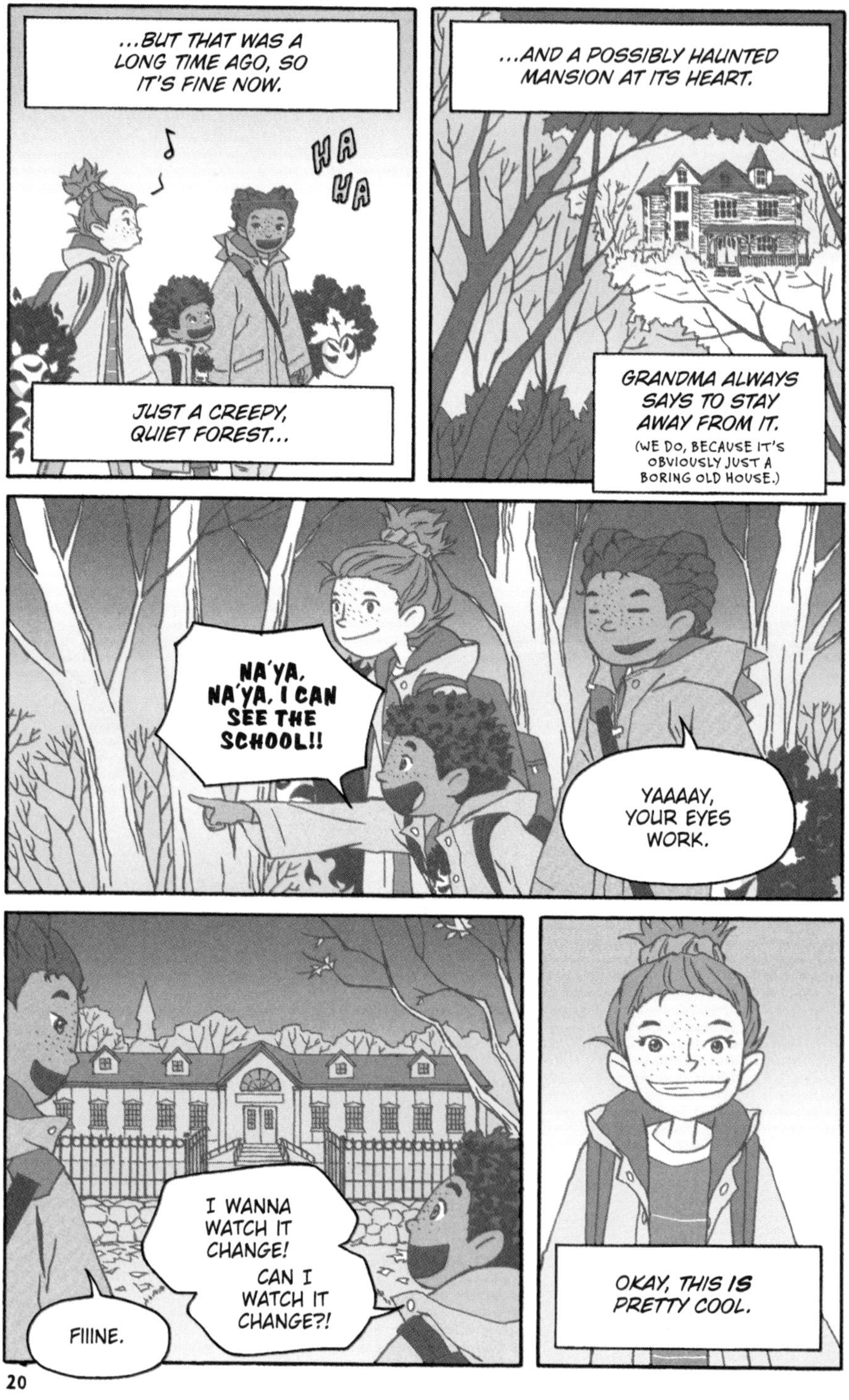
...BUT THAT WAS A LONG TIME AGO, SO IT'S FINE NOW.
HA HA
JUST A CREEPY, QUIET FOREST...
...AND A POSSIBLY HAUNTED MANSION AT ITS HEART.
GRANDMA ALWAYS SAYS TO STAY AWAY FROM IT.
(WE DO, BECAUSE IT'S OBVIOUSLY JUST A BORING OLD HOUSE.)
NA'YA, NA'YA, I CAN SEE THE SCHOOL!!
YAAAAY, YOUR EYES WORK.
I WANNA WATCH IT CHANGE!
CAN I WATCH IT CHANGE?!
FIIINE.
OKAY, THIS **IS** PRETTY COOL.

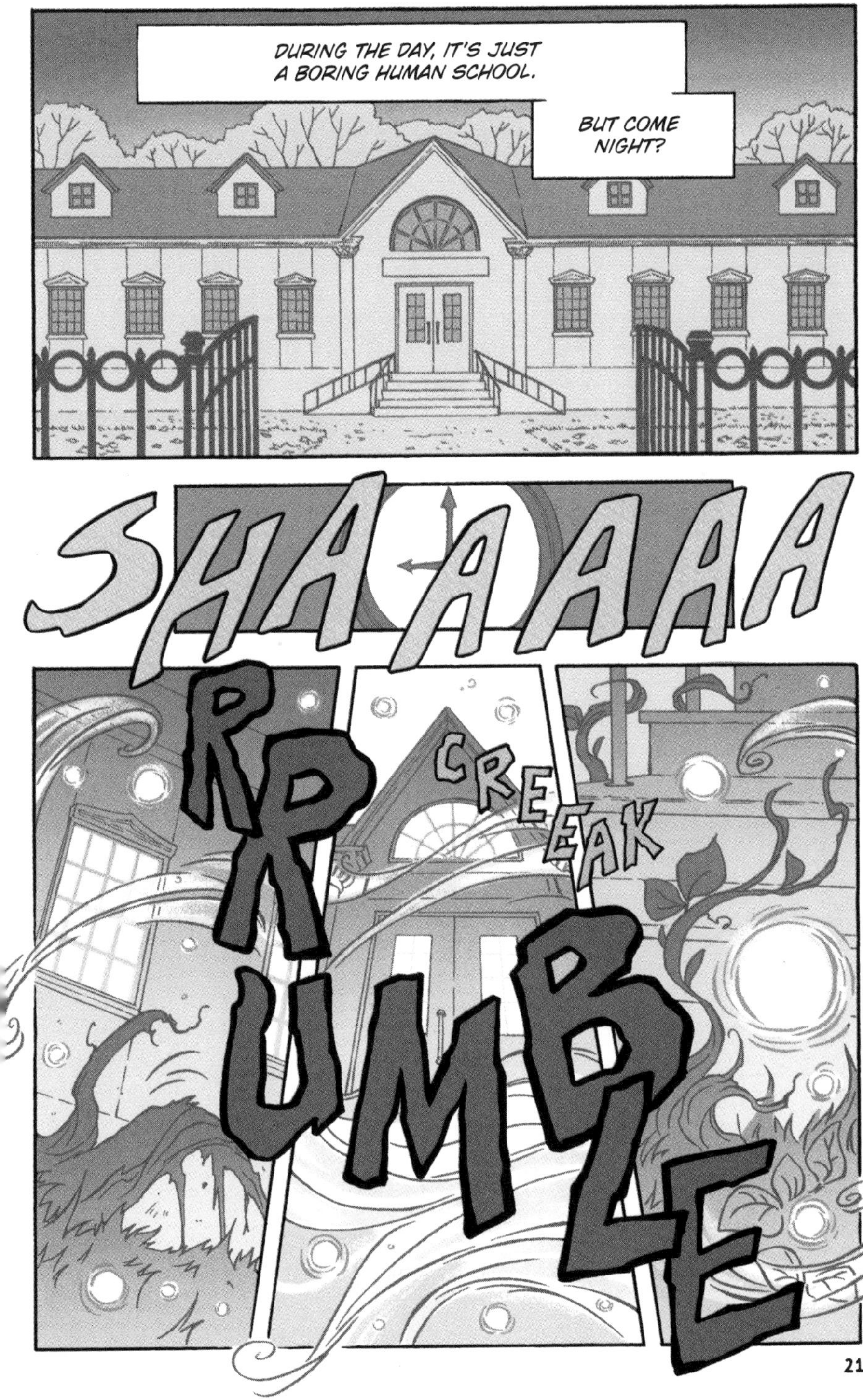
DURING THE DAY, IT'S JUST A BORING HUMAN SCHOOL.
BUT COME NIGHT?
SHAAAAAA
RRRUMBLE
CREEEAK

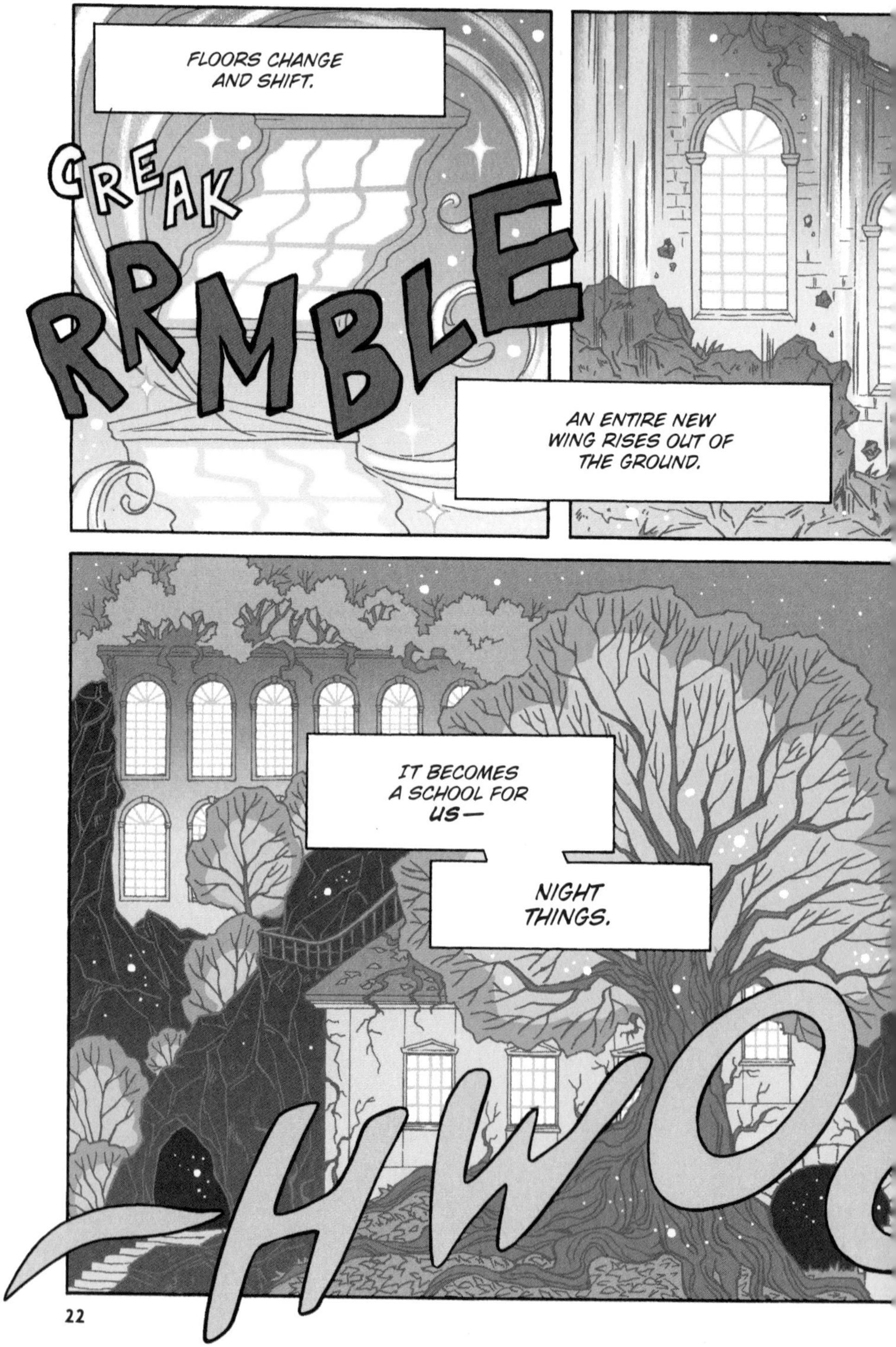

FLOORS CHANGE AND SHIFT.
CREAK
RRMBLE
AN ENTIRE NEW WING RISES OUT OF THE GROUND.
IT BECOMES A SCHOOL FOR US—
NIGHT THINGS.
HWOO

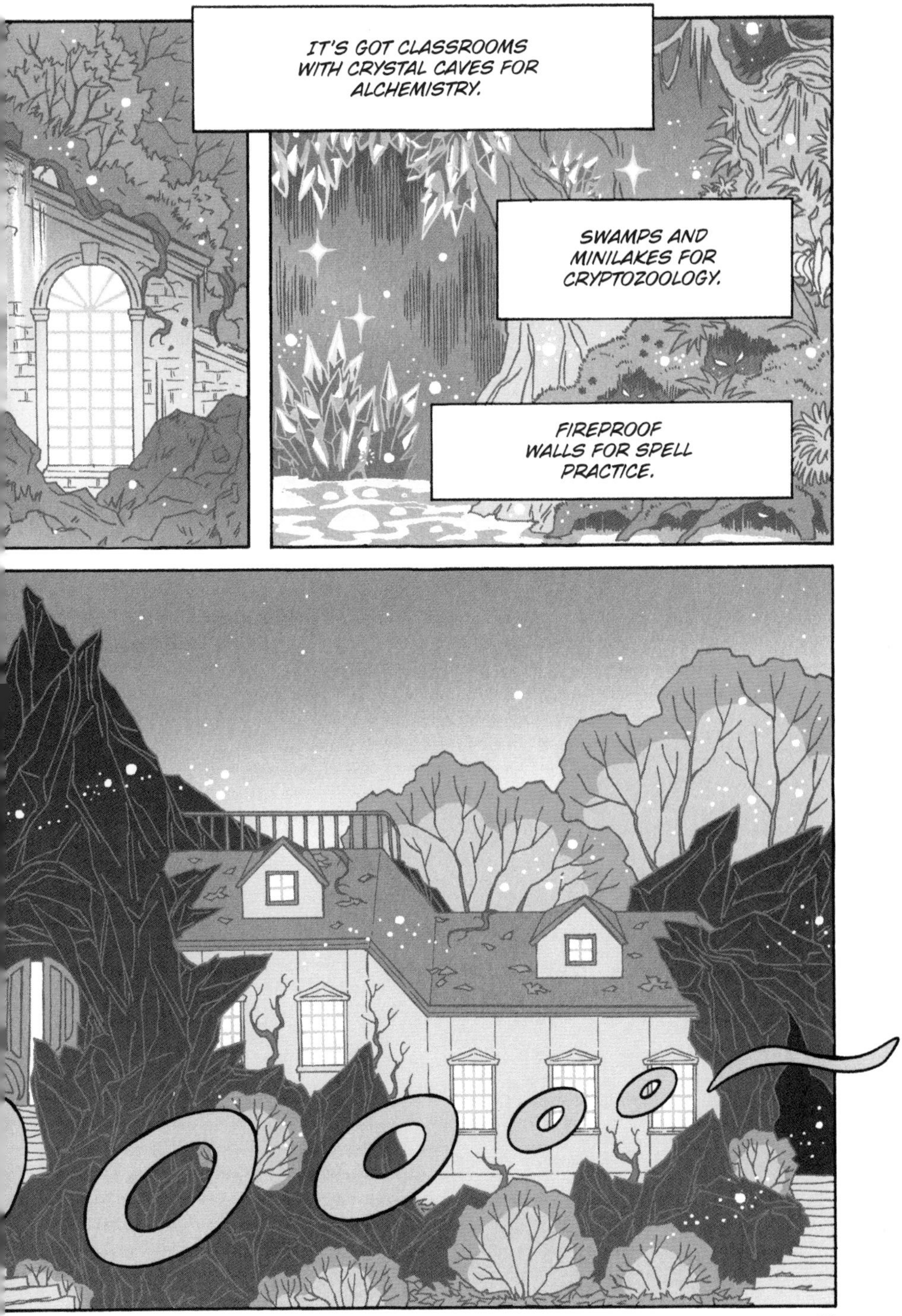
IT'S GOT CLASSROOMS WITH CRYSTAL CAVES FOR ALCHEMISTRY.
SWAMPS AND MINILAKES FOR CRYPTOZOOLOGY.
FIREPROOF WALLS FOR SPELL PRACTICE.

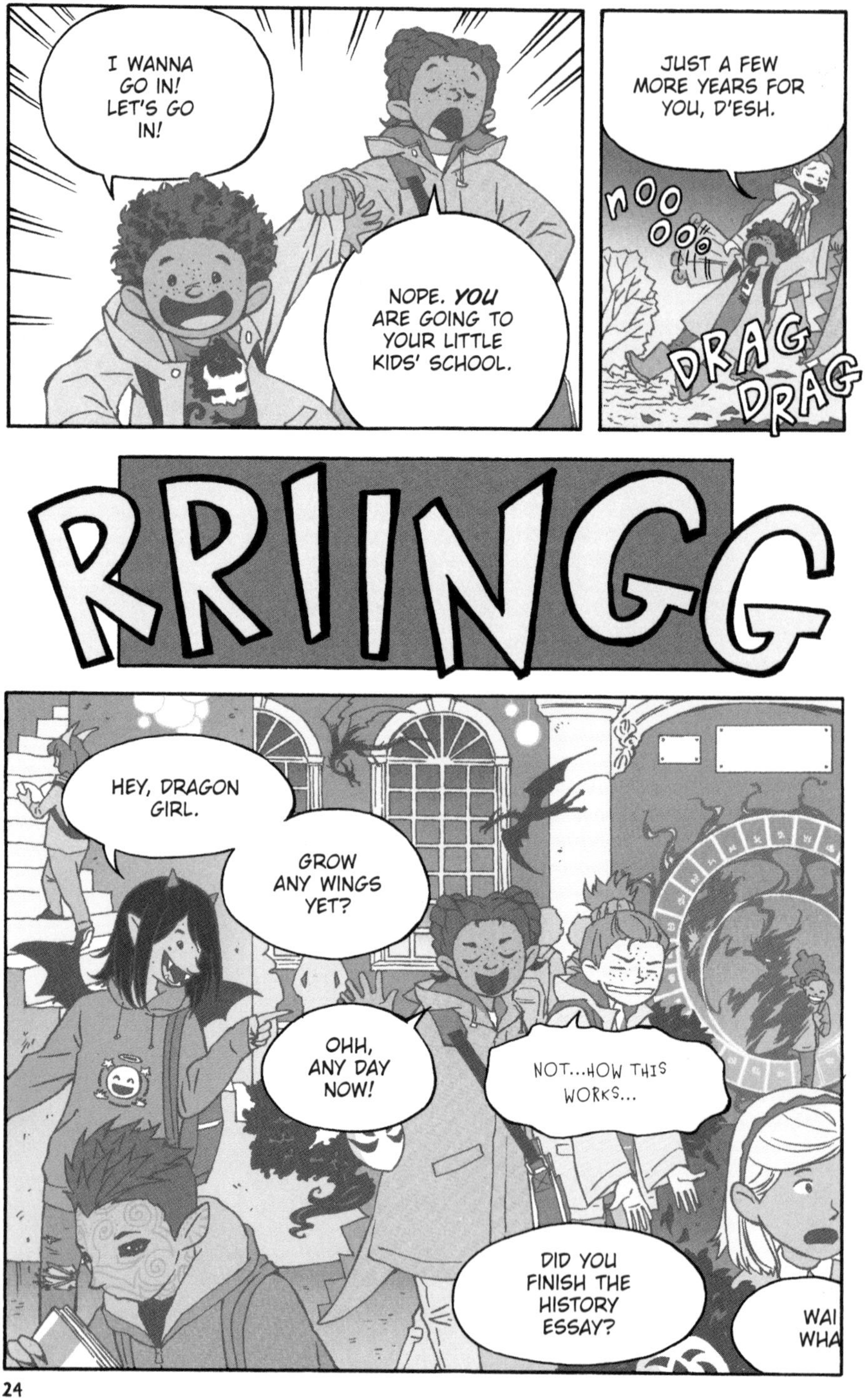
I WANNA GO IN! LET'S GO IN!
NOPE. YOU ARE GOING TO YOUR LITTLE KIDS' SCHOOL.
JUST A FEW MORE YEARS FOR YOU, D'ESH.
nooooo
DRAG DRAG
RRIINGG
HEY, DRAGON GIRL.
GROW ANY WINGS YET?
OHH, ANY DAY NOW!
NOT...HOW THIS WORKS...
DID YOU FINISH THE HISTORY ESSAY?
WAI WHA

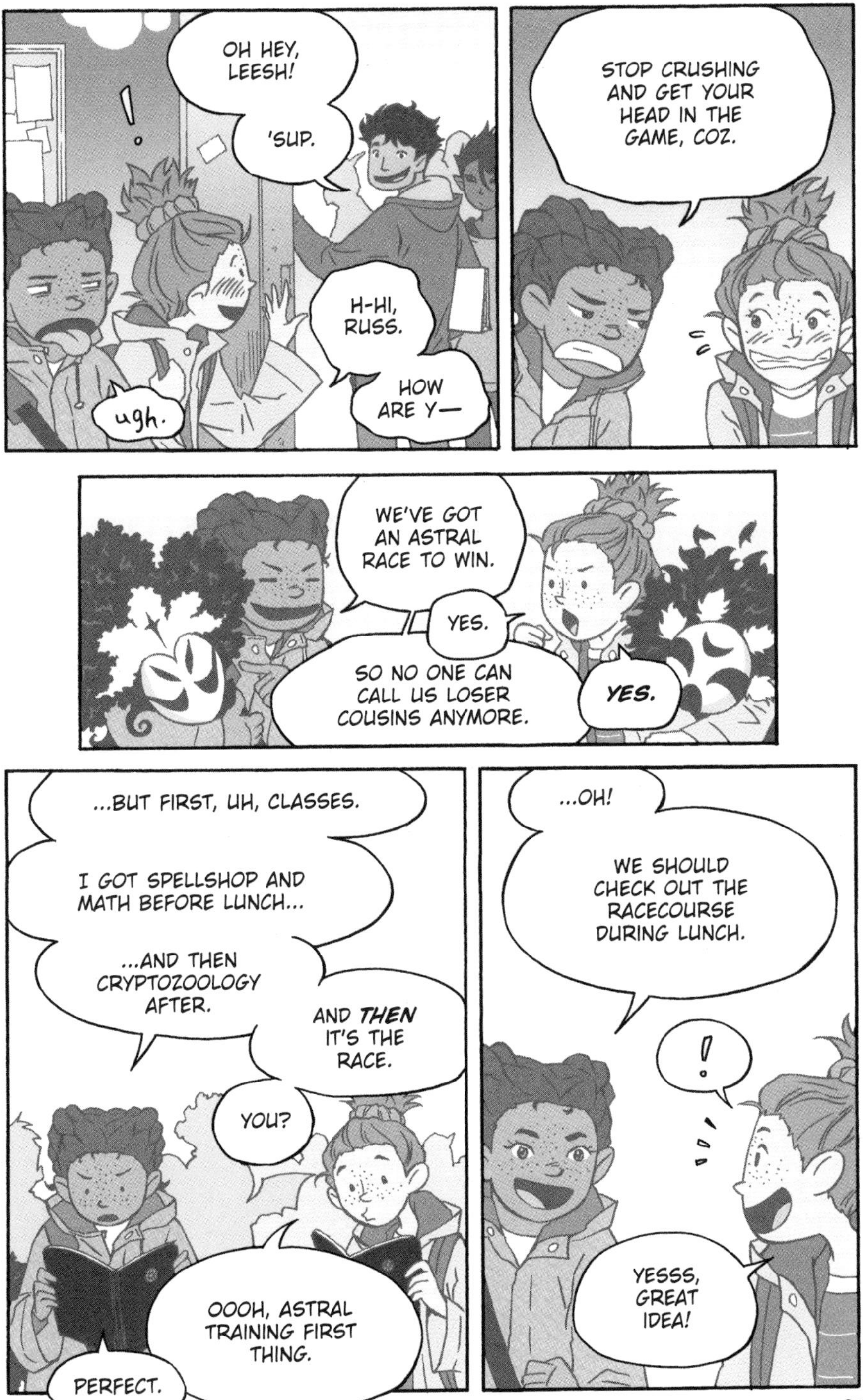
!
OH HEY, LEESH!
'SUP.
H-HI, RUSS.
HOW ARE Y—
ugh.
STOP CRUSHING AND GET YOUR HEAD IN THE GAME, COZ.
WE'VE GOT AN ASTRAL RACE TO WIN.
YES.
SO NO ONE CAN CALL US LOSER COUSINS ANYMORE.
YES.
...BUT FIRST, UH, CLASSES.
I GOT SPELLSHOP AND MATH BEFORE LUNCH...
...AND THEN CRYPTOZOOLOGY AFTER.
AND THEN IT'S THE RACE.
YOU?
OOOH, ASTRAL TRAINING FIRST THING.
PERFECT.
...OH!
WE SHOULD CHECK OUT THE RACECOURSE DURING LUNCH.
!
YESSS, GREAT IDEA!

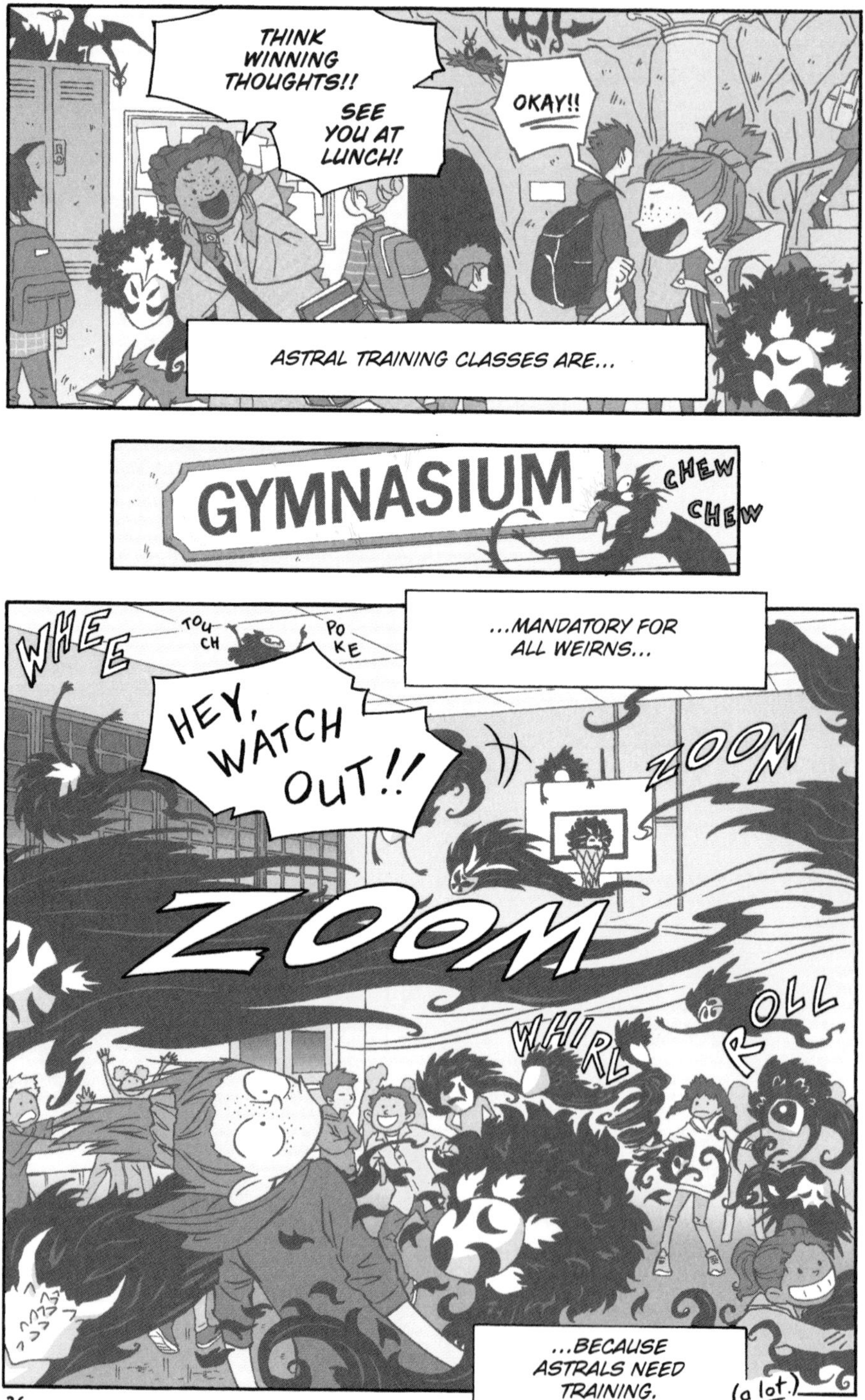
THINK WINNING THOUGHTS!!
SEE YOU AT LUNCH!
OKAY!!
ASTRAL TRAINING CLASSES ARE...
GYMNASIUM
CHEW CHEW
...MANDATORY FOR ALL WEIRNS...
WHEE
TOUCH
POKE
HEY, WATCH OUT!!
ZOOM
ZOOM
WHIRL
ROLL
...BECAUSE ASTRALS NEED TRAINING.
(a lot.)

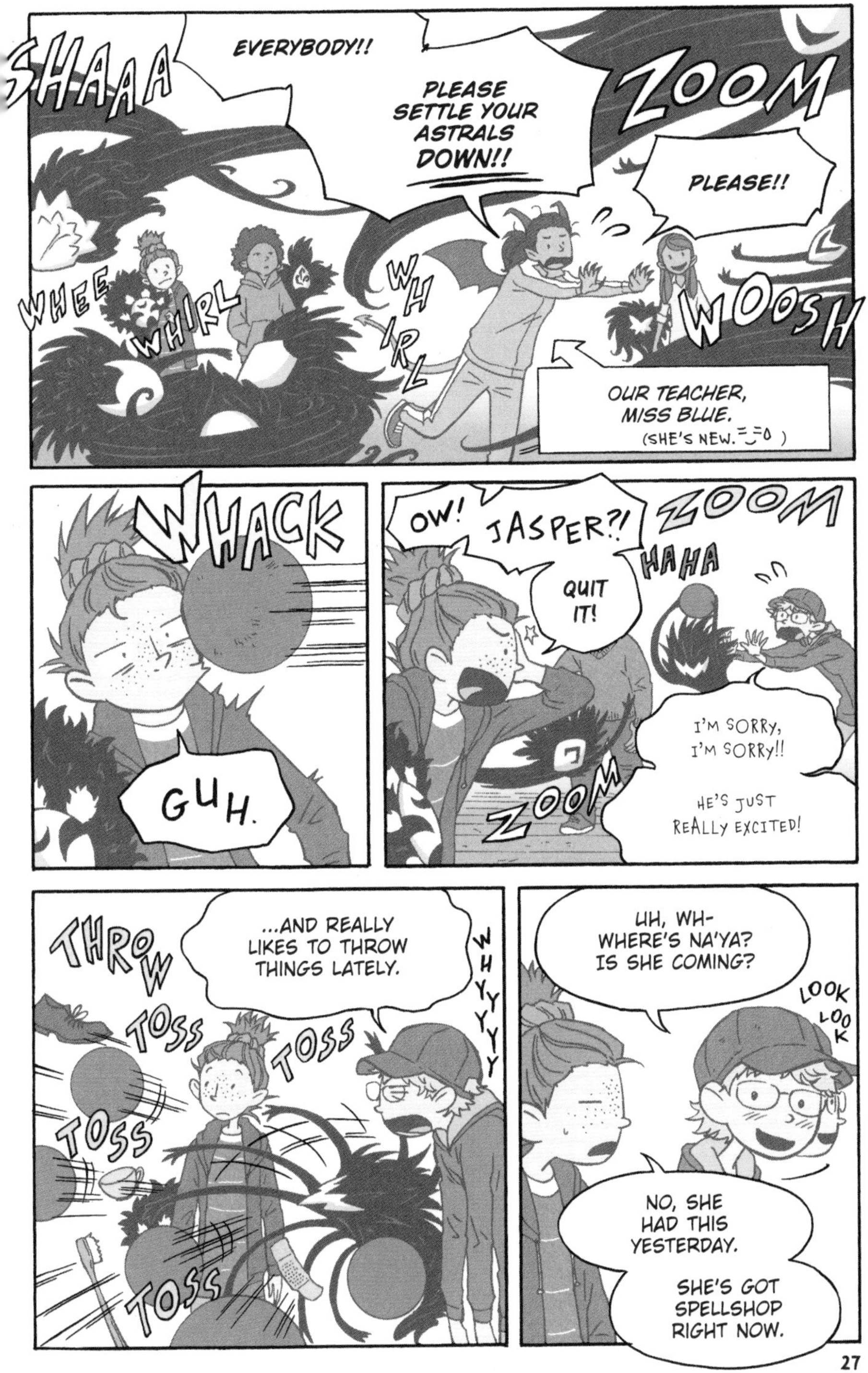
SHAAA
EVERYBODY!!
PLEASE SETTLE YOUR ASTRALS DOWN!!
ZOOM
PLEASE!!
WHEE
WHIRL
WHIRL
WOOSH
OUR TEACHER, MISS BLUE. (SHE'S NEW. =‿=0 )
WHACK
GUH.
OW!
JASPER?!
ZOOM
HAHA
QUIT IT!
I'M SORRY, I'M SORRY!!
HE'S JUST REALLY EXCITED!
ZOOM
THROW
...AND REALLY LIKES TO THROW THINGS LATELY.
WHYYYYY
TOSS
TOSS
TOSS
TOSS
UH, WH-WHERE'S NA'YA? IS SHE COMING?
LOOK LOOK
NO, SHE HAD THIS YESTERDAY.
SHE'S GOT SPELLSHOP RIGHT NOW.

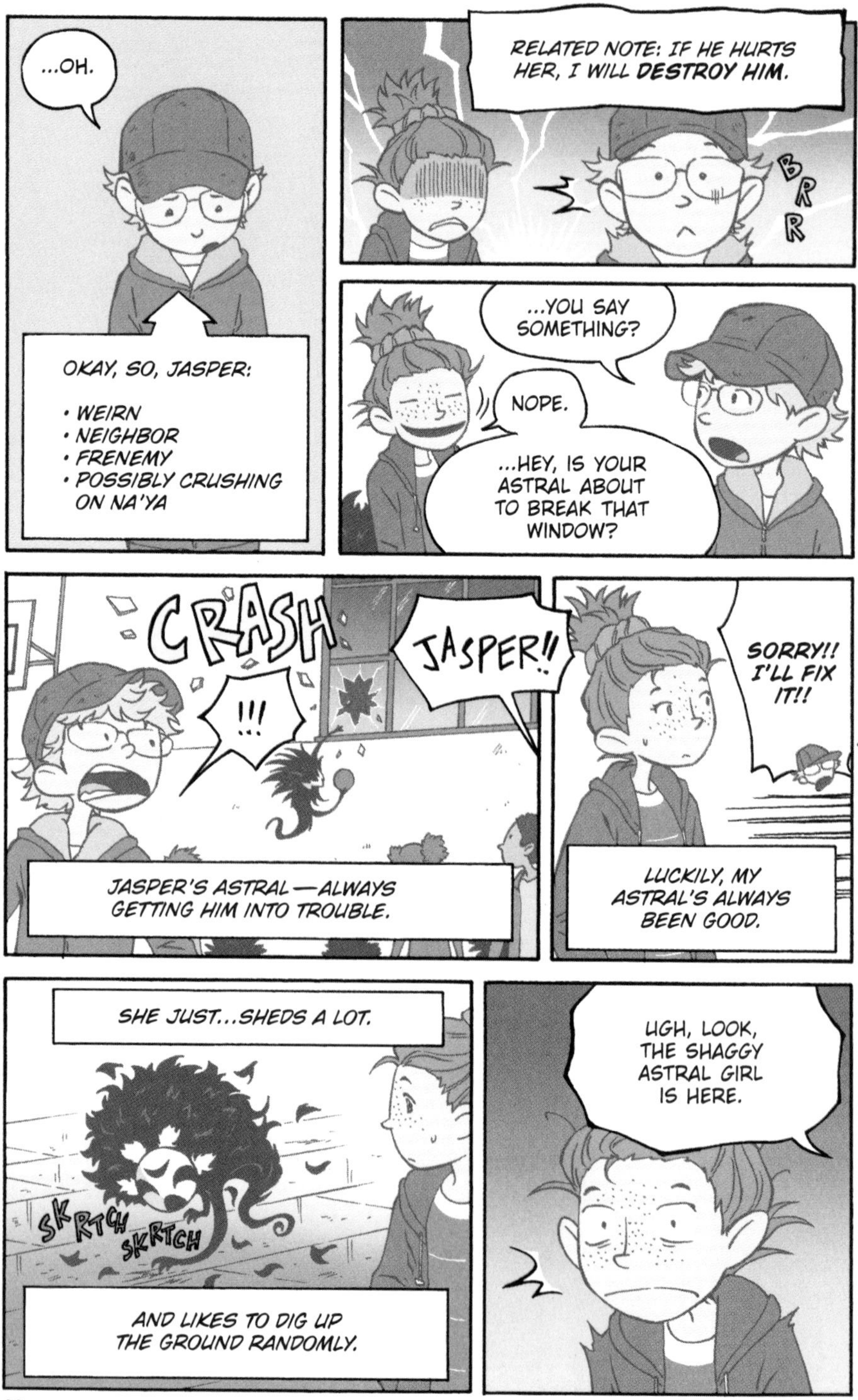
...OH.
OKAY, SO, JASPER:
• WEIRN
• NEIGHBOR
• FRENEMY
• POSSIBLY CRUSHING ON NA'YA
RELATED NOTE: IF HE HURTS HER, I WILL DESTROY HIM.
BRRR
...YOU SAY SOMETHING?
NOPE.
...HEY, IS YOUR ASTRAL ABOUT TO BREAK THAT WINDOW?
CRASH
!!!
JASPER!!
JASPER'S ASTRAL—ALWAYS GETTING HIM INTO TROUBLE.
SORRY!! I'LL FIX IT!!
LUCKILY, MY ASTRAL'S ALWAYS BEEN GOOD.
SHE JUST...SHEDS A LOT.
SKRTCH SKRTCH
AND LIKES TO DIG UP THE GROUND RANDOMLY.
UGH, LOOK, THE SHAGGY ASTRAL GIRL IS HERE.

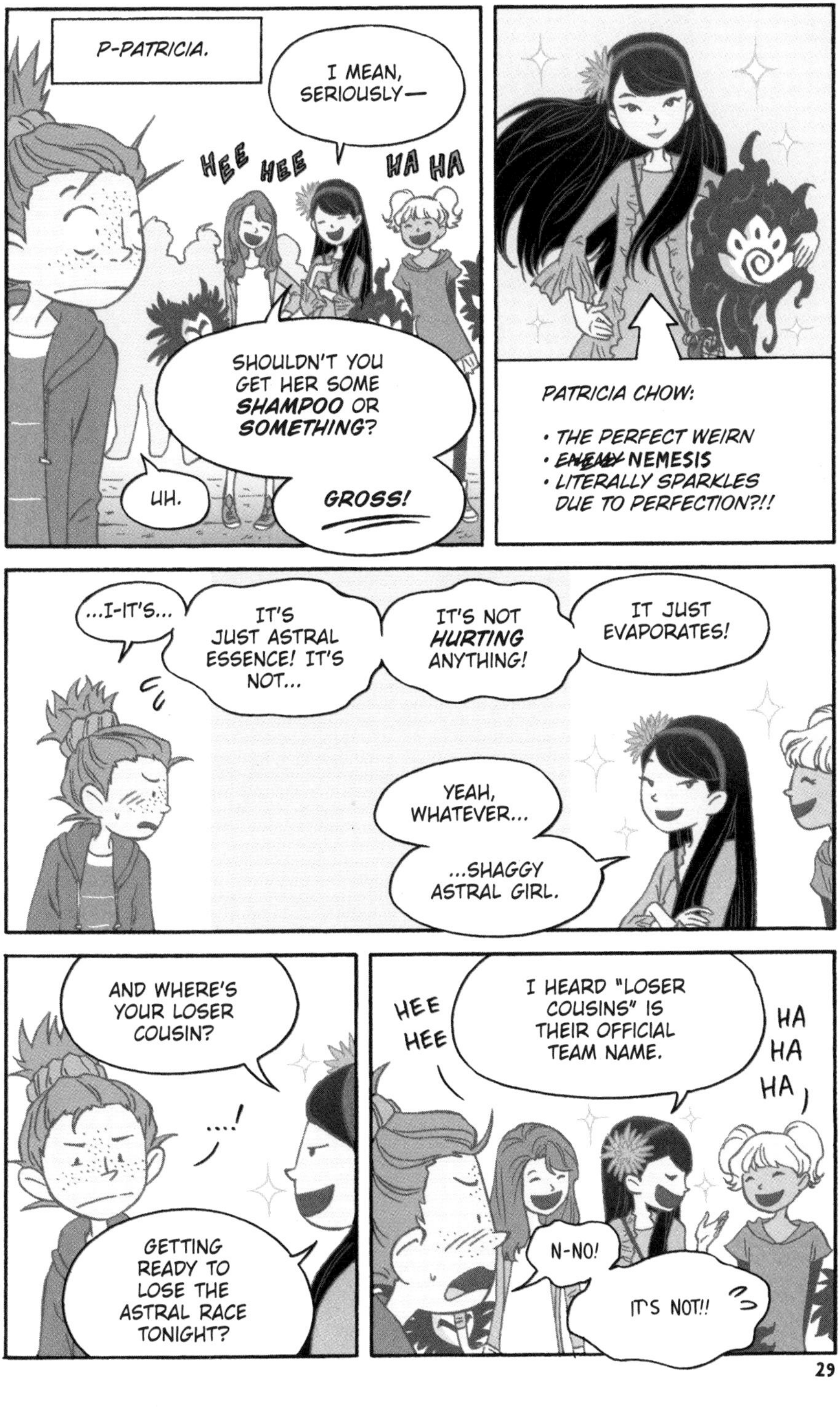
P-PATRICIA.
I MEAN, SERIOUSLY—
HEE HEE
HA HA
SHOULDN'T YOU GET HER SOME SHAMPOO OR SOMETHING?
UH.
GROSS!
PATRICIA CHOW:
• THE PERFECT WEIRN
• ~~ENEMY~~ NEMESIS
• LITERALLY SPARKLES DUE TO PERFECTION?!!
...I-IT'S...
IT'S JUST ASTRAL ESSENCE! IT'S NOT...
IT'S NOT HURTING ANYTHING!
IT JUST EVAPORATES!
YEAH, WHATEVER...
...SHAGGY ASTRAL GIRL.
AND WHERE'S YOUR LOSER COUSIN?
...!
GETTING READY TO LOSE THE ASTRAL RACE TONIGHT?
HEE HEE
I HEARD "LOSER COUSINS" IS THEIR OFFICIAL TEAM NAME.
HA HA HA
N-NO!
IT'S NOT!!

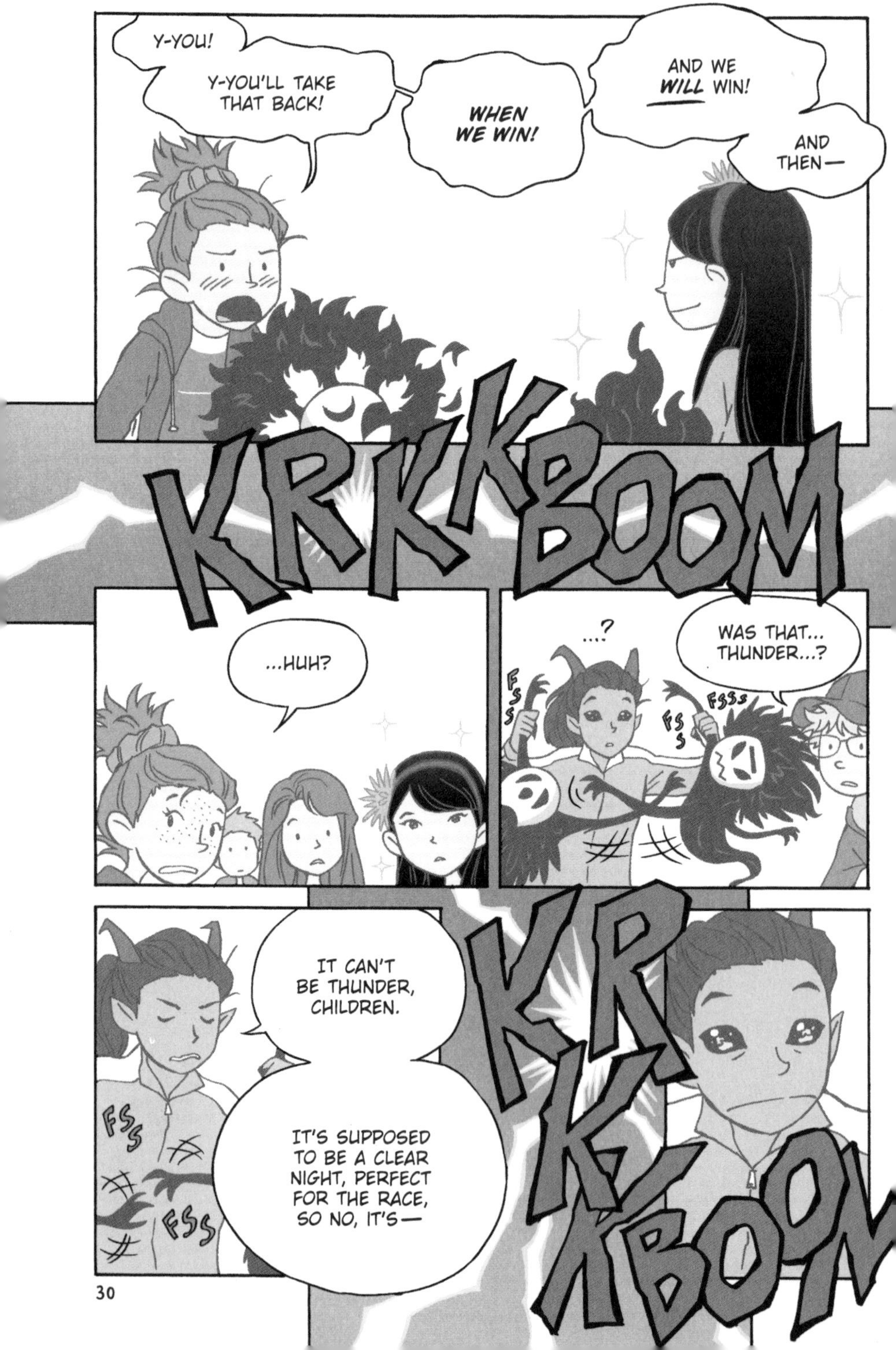
Y-YOU!
Y-YOU'LL TAKE THAT BACK!
WHEN WE WIN!
AND WE WILL WIN!
AND THEN—
KRKKBOOM
...HUH?
...?
WAS THAT... THUNDER...?
FSS
FSSS
FSS
IT CAN'T BE THUNDER, CHILDREN.
IT'S SUPPOSED TO BE A CLEAR NIGHT, PERFECT FOR THE RACE, SO NO, IT'S—
FSS
FSS
KRKKBOOM

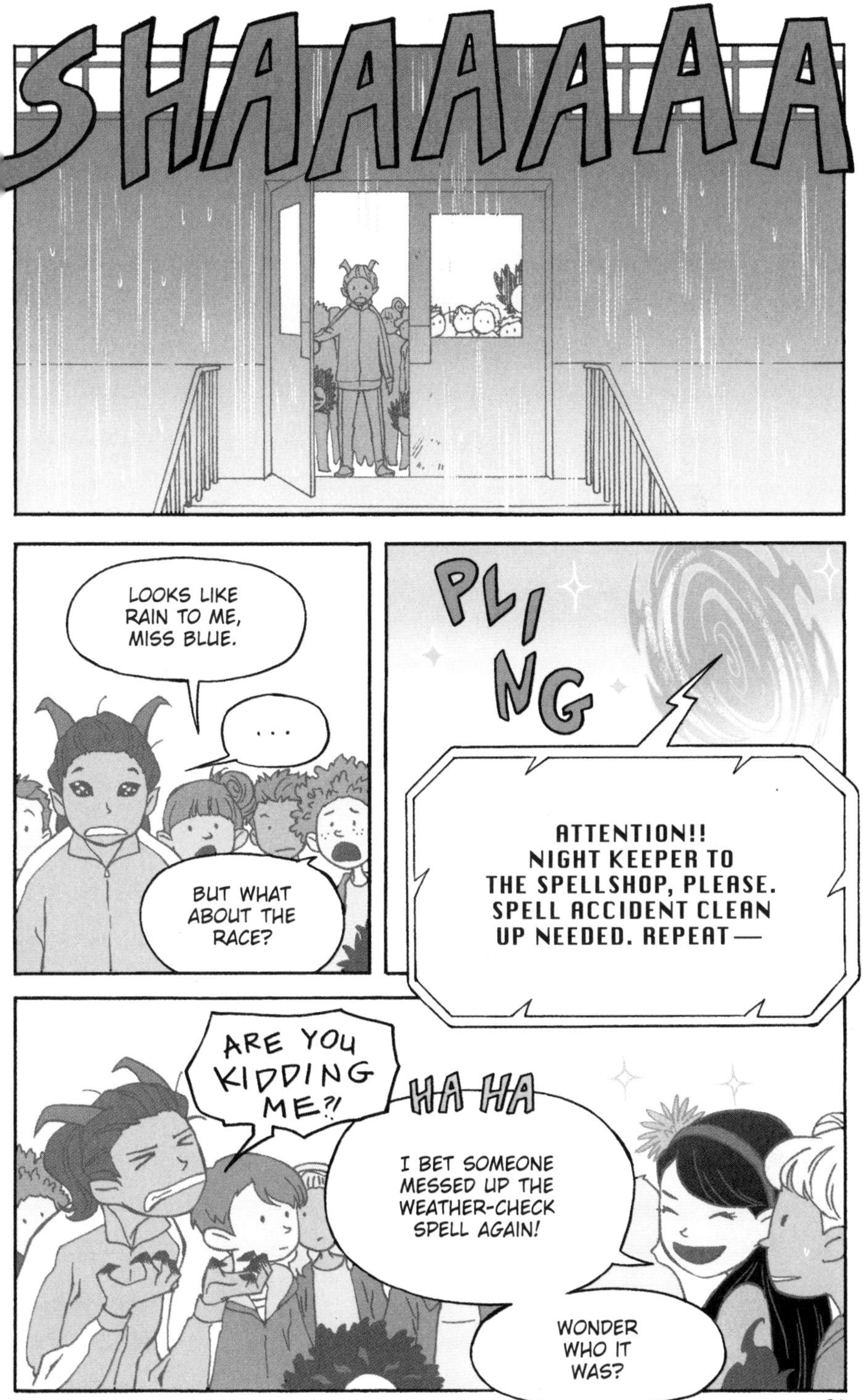
SHAAAAAA
LOOKS LIKE RAIN TO ME, MISS BLUE.
...
BUT WHAT ABOUT THE RACE?
PLING
ATTENTION!! NIGHT KEEPER TO THE SPELLSHOP, PLEASE. SPELL ACCIDENT CLEAN UP NEEDED. REPEAT—
ARE YOU KIDDING ME?!
HA HA
I BET SOMEONE MESSED UP THE WEATHER-CHECK SPELL AGAIN!
WONDER WHO IT WAS?

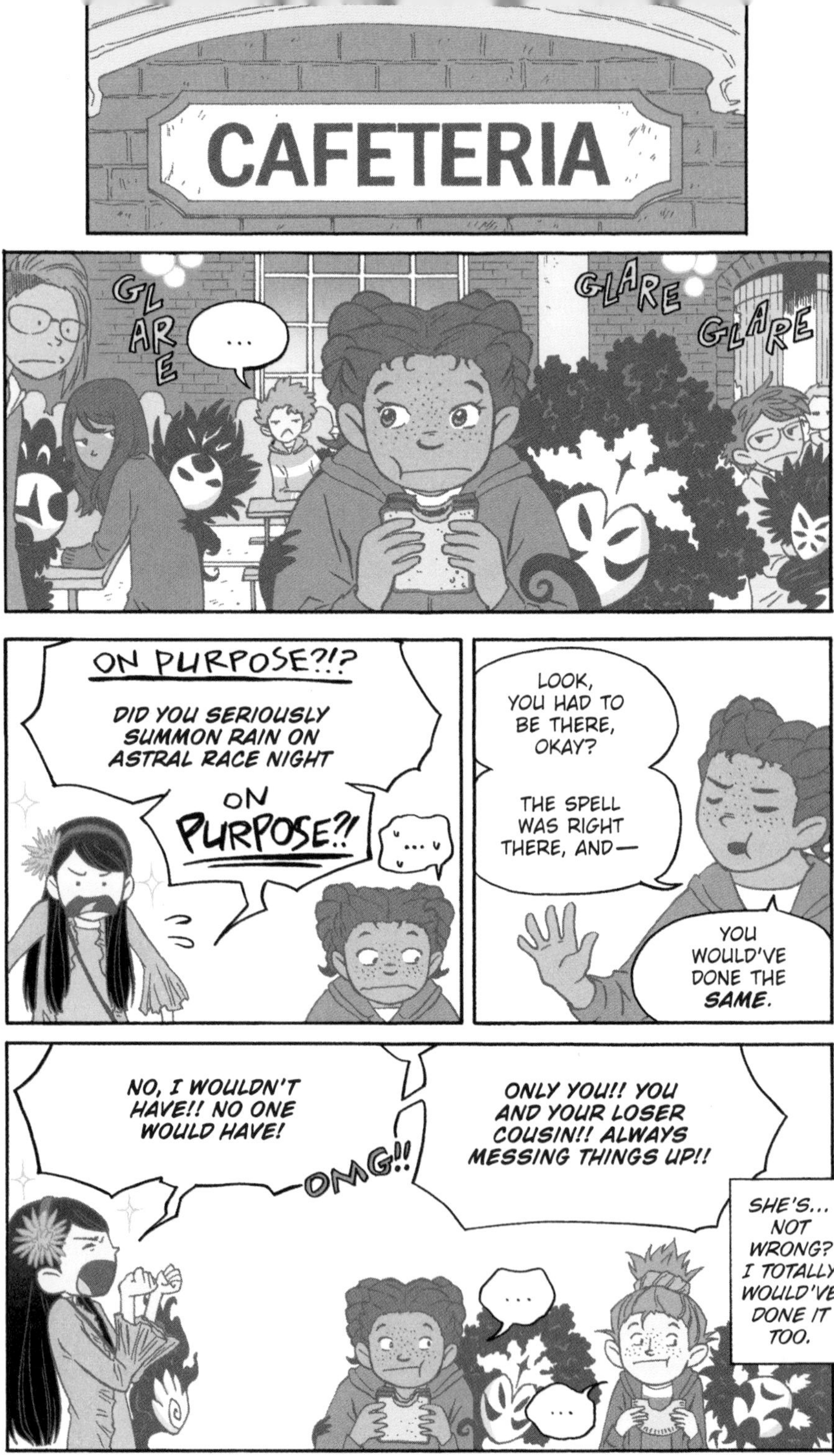
CAFETERIA
GLARE
...
GLARE
GLARE
ON PURPOSE?!?
DID YOU SERIOUSLY SUMMON RAIN ON ASTRAL RACE NIGHT
ON PURPOSE?!
...
LOOK, YOU HAD TO BE THERE, OKAY?
THE SPELL WAS RIGHT THERE, AND—
YOU WOULD'VE DONE THE SAME.
NO, I WOULDN'T HAVE!! NO ONE WOULD HAVE!
OMG!!
ONLY YOU!! YOU AND YOUR LOSER COUSIN!! ALWAYS MESSING THINGS UP!!
...
...
SHE'S... NOT WRONG? I TOTALLY WOULD'VE DONE IT TOO.

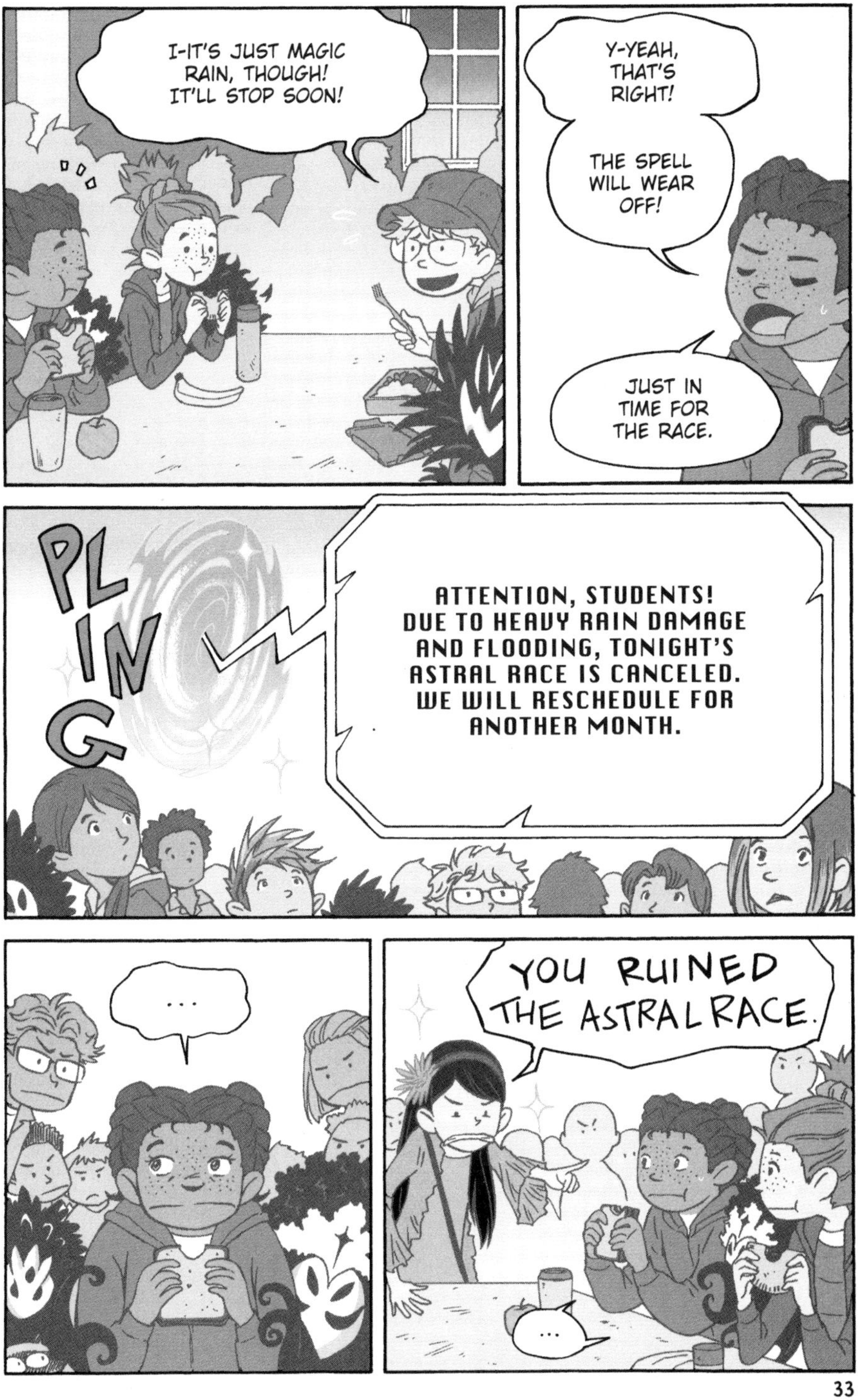
I-IT'S JUST MAGIC RAIN, THOUGH! IT'LL STOP SOON!
Y-YEAH, THAT'S RIGHT!
THE SPELL WILL WEAR OFF!
JUST IN TIME FOR THE RACE.
PLING
ATTENTION, STUDENTS! DUE TO HEAVY RAIN DAMAGE AND FLOODING, TONIGHT'S ASTRAL RACE IS CANCELED. WE WILL RESCHEDULE FOR ANOTHER MONTH.
...
YOU RUINED THE ASTRAL RACE.
...

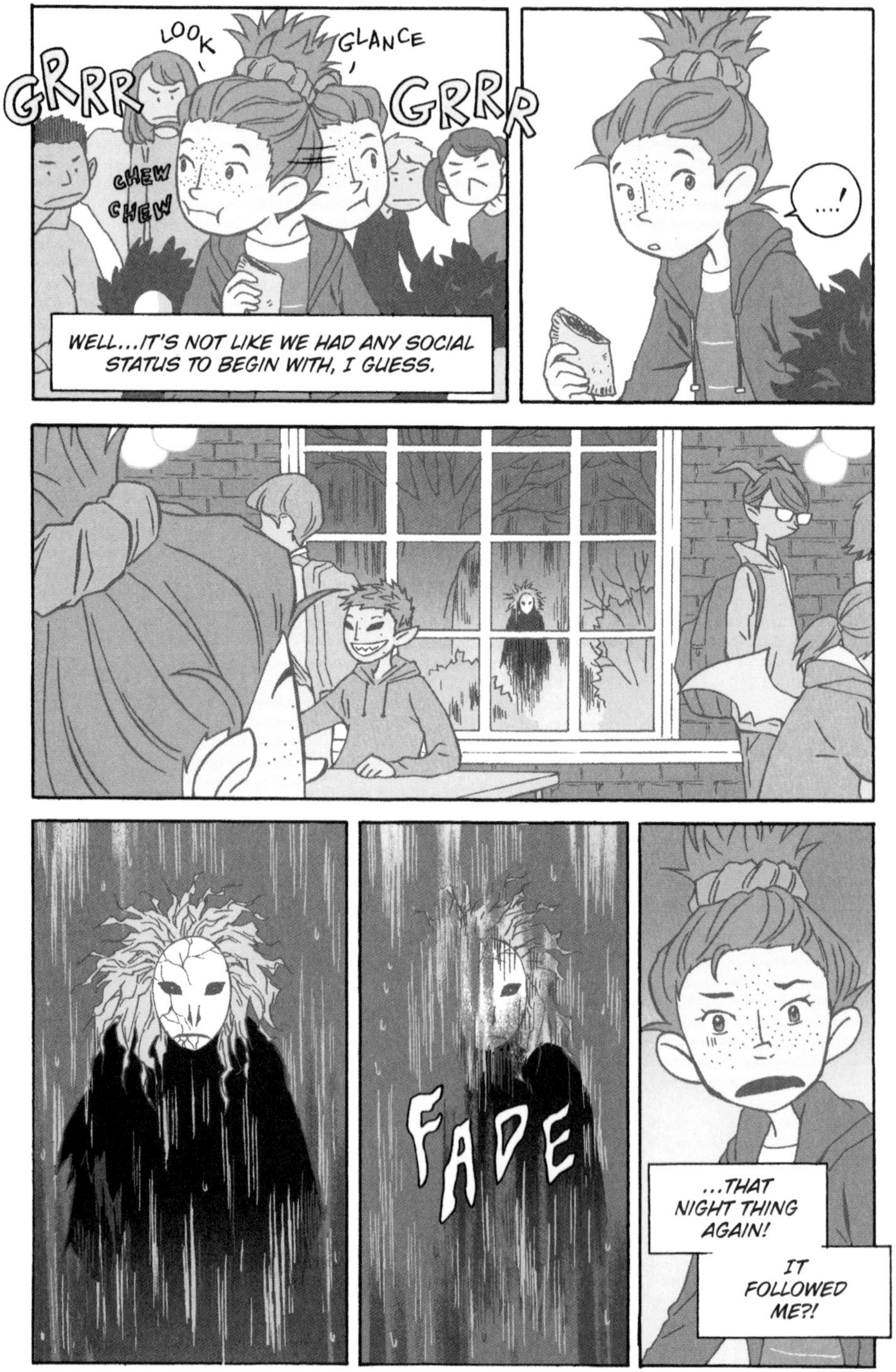
GRRR
LOOK
GLANCE
GRRR
CHEW
CHEW
WELL...IT'S NOT LIKE WE HAD ANY SOCIAL STATUS TO BEGIN WITH, I GUESS.
...!
FADE
...THAT NIGHT THING AGAIN!
IT FOLLOWED ME?!

# Chapter 2

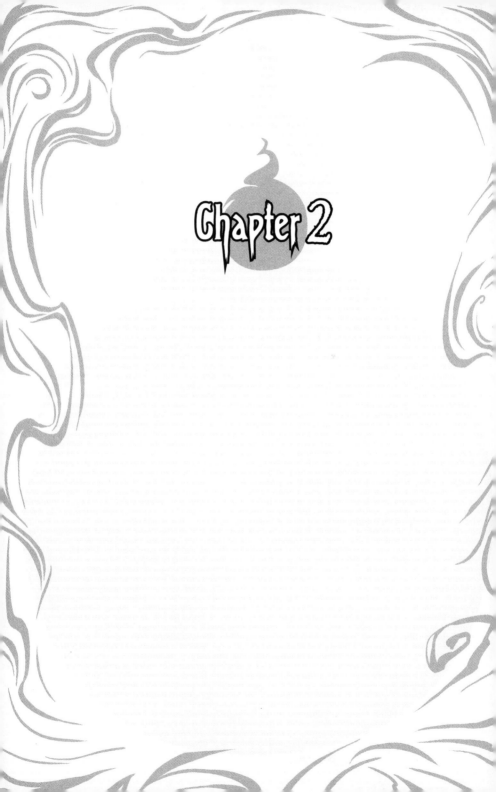

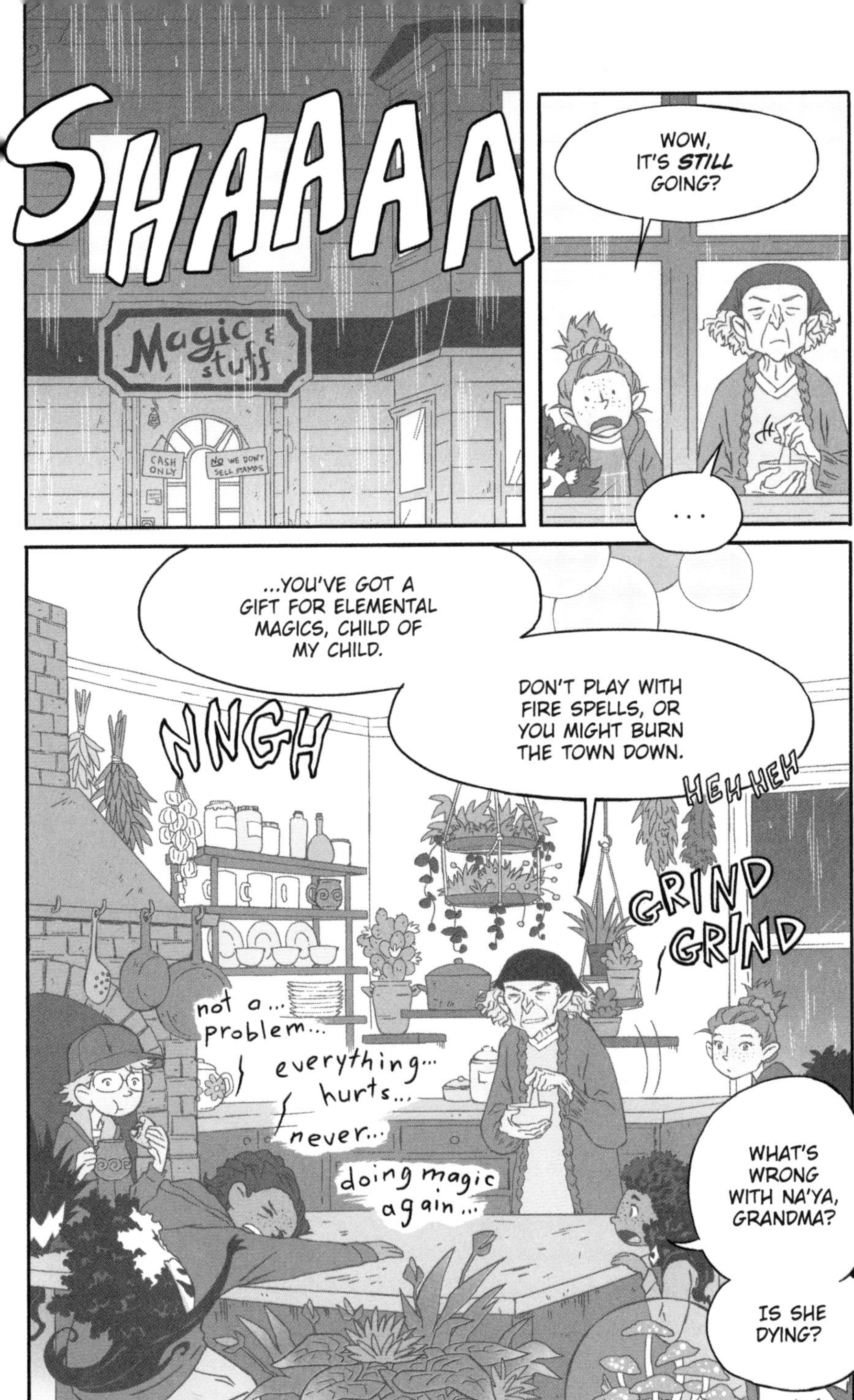
SHAAAA
Magic & stuff
CASH ONLY
NO WE DON'T SELL STAMPS
WOW, IT'S STILL GOING?
...
...YOU'VE GOT A GIFT FOR ELEMENTAL MAGICS, CHILD OF MY CHILD.
DON'T PLAY WITH FIRE SPELLS, OR YOU MIGHT BURN THE TOWN DOWN.
NNGH
HEH HEH
GRIND GRIND
not a... problem...
everything... hurts...
never...
doing magic again...
WHAT'S WRONG WITH NA'YA, GRANDMA?
IS SHE DYING?

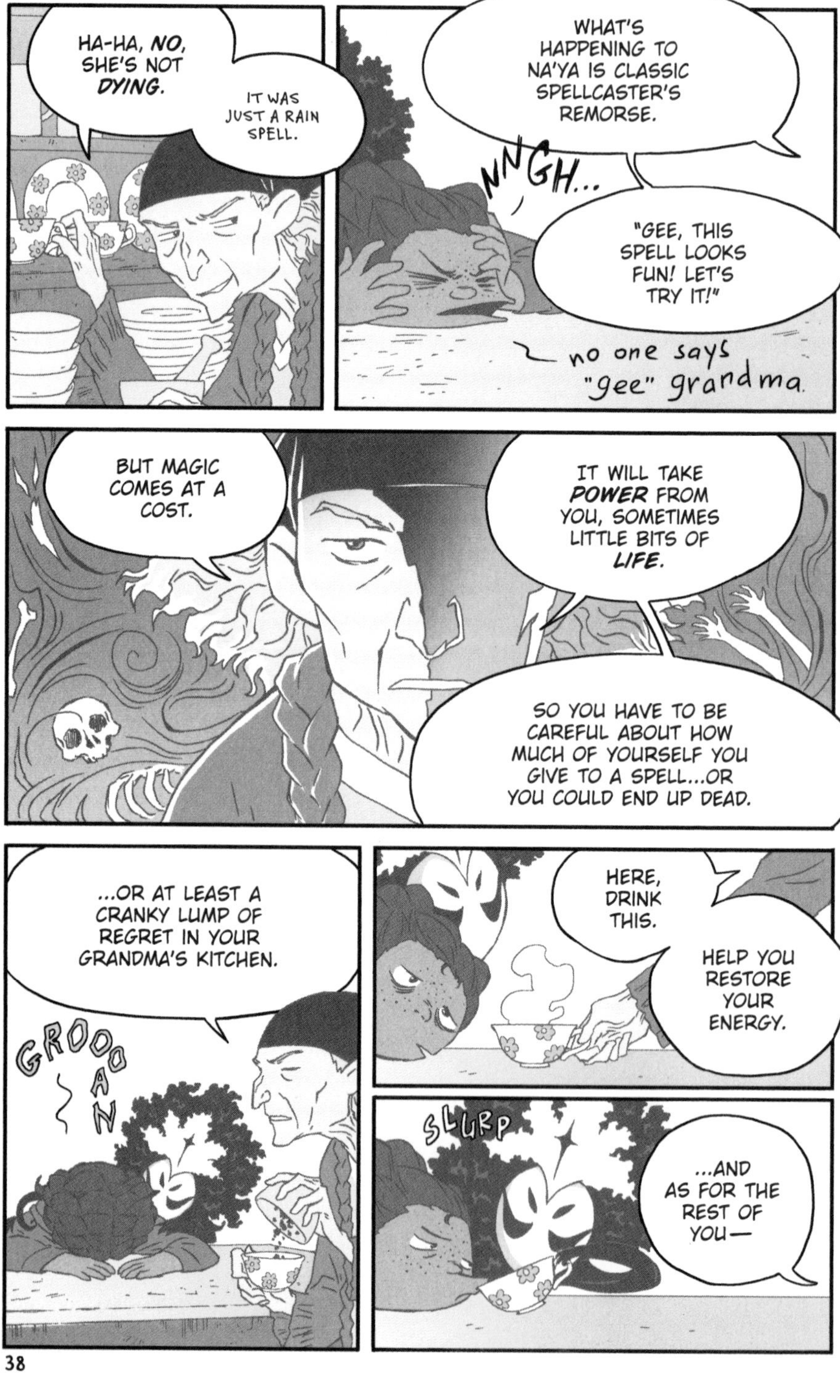
HA-HA, **NO**, SHE'S NOT **DYING**.
IT WAS JUST A RAIN SPELL.
WHAT'S HAPPENING TO NA'YA IS CLASSIC SPELLCASTER'S REMORSE.
NNGH...
"GEE, THIS SPELL LOOKS FUN! LET'S TRY IT!"
no one says "gee" grandma.
BUT MAGIC COMES AT A COST.
IT WILL TAKE **POWER** FROM YOU, SOMETIMES LITTLE BITS OF **LIFE**.
SO YOU HAVE TO BE CAREFUL ABOUT HOW MUCH OF YOURSELF YOU GIVE TO A SPELL...OR YOU COULD END UP DEAD.
...OR AT LEAST A CRANKY LUMP OF REGRET IN YOUR GRANDMA'S KITCHEN.
GROOOAN
HERE, DRINK THIS.
HELP YOU RESTORE YOUR ENERGY.
SLURP
...AND AS FOR THE REST OF YOU—

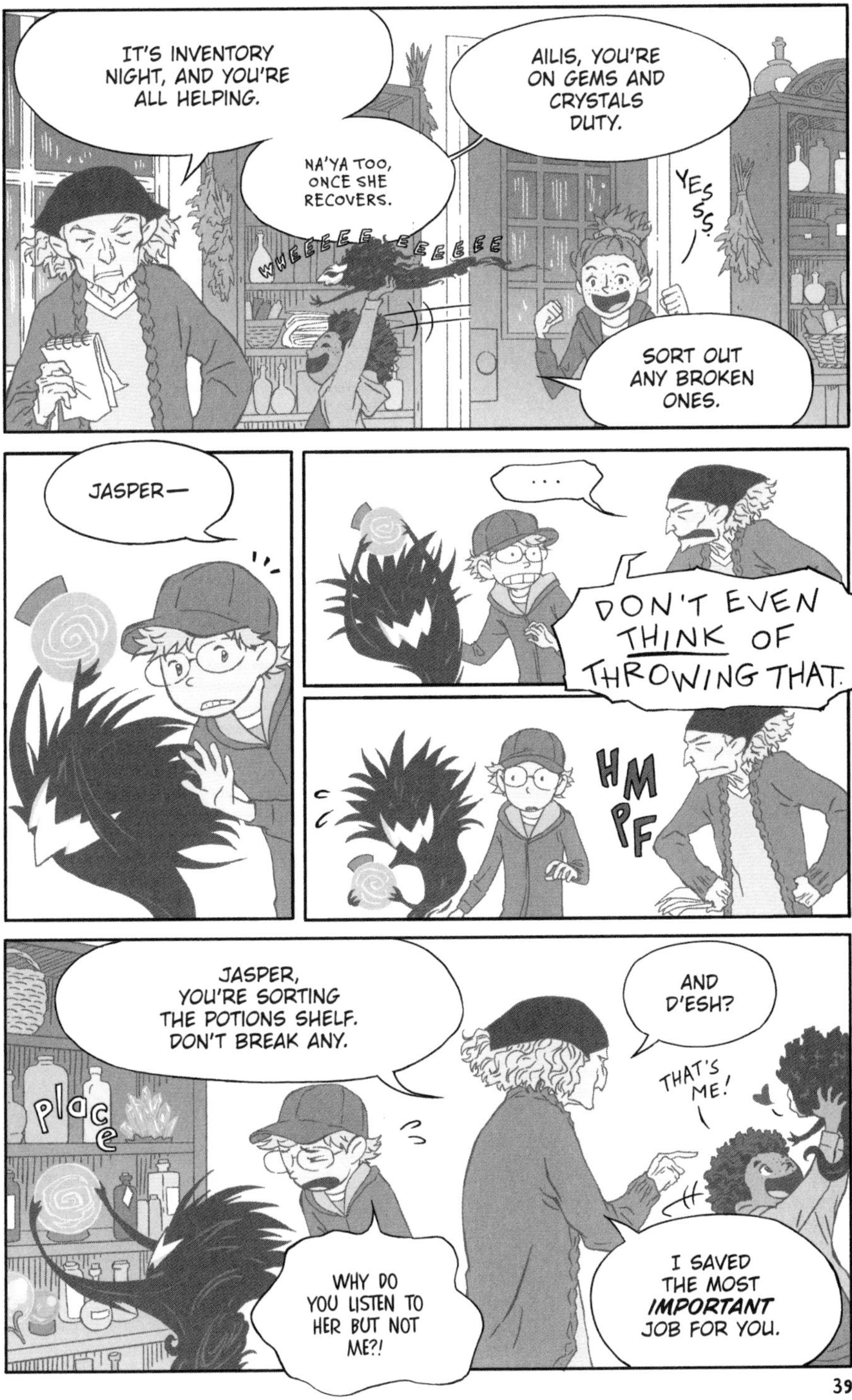
IT'S INVENTORY NIGHT, AND YOU'RE ALL HELPING.
NA'YA TOO, ONCE SHE RECOVERS.
AILIS, YOU'RE ON GEMS AND CRYSTALS DUTY.
WHEEEEEE EEEEEE
YESSS
SORT OUT ANY BROKEN ONES.
JASPER—
. . .
DON'T EVEN THINK OF THROWING THAT.
HMPF
JASPER, YOU'RE SORTING THE POTIONS SHELF. DON'T BREAK ANY.
AND D'ESH?
THAT'S ME!
place
WHY DO YOU LISTEN TO HER BUT NOT ME?!
I SAVED THE MOST ***IMPORTANT*** JOB FOR YOU.

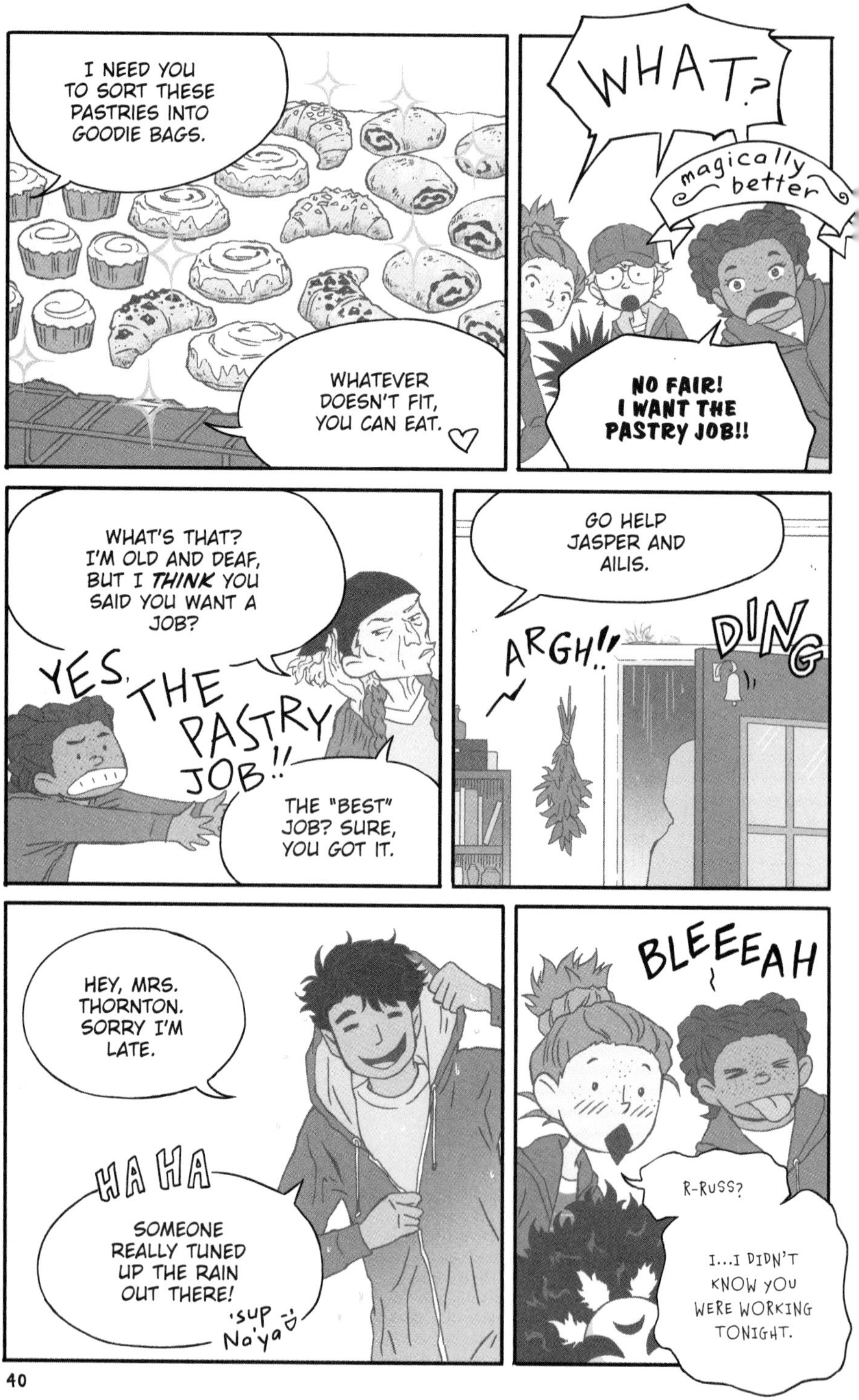
I NEED YOU TO SORT THESE PASTRIES INTO GOODIE BAGS.
WHATEVER DOESN'T FIT, YOU CAN EAT.
WHAT?
magically better
NO FAIR! I WANT THE PASTRY JOB!!
WHAT'S THAT? I'M OLD AND DEAF, BUT I THINK YOU SAID YOU WANT A JOB?
YES, THE PASTRY JOB!!
THE "BEST" JOB? SURE, YOU GOT IT.
GO HELP JASPER AND AILIS.
ARGH!!
DING
HEY, MRS. THORNTON. SORRY I'M LATE.
HA HA
SOMEONE REALLY TUNED UP THE RAIN OUT THERE!
'sup Na'ya
BLEEEAH
R-RUSS?
I...I DIDN'T KNOW YOU WERE WORKING TONIGHT.

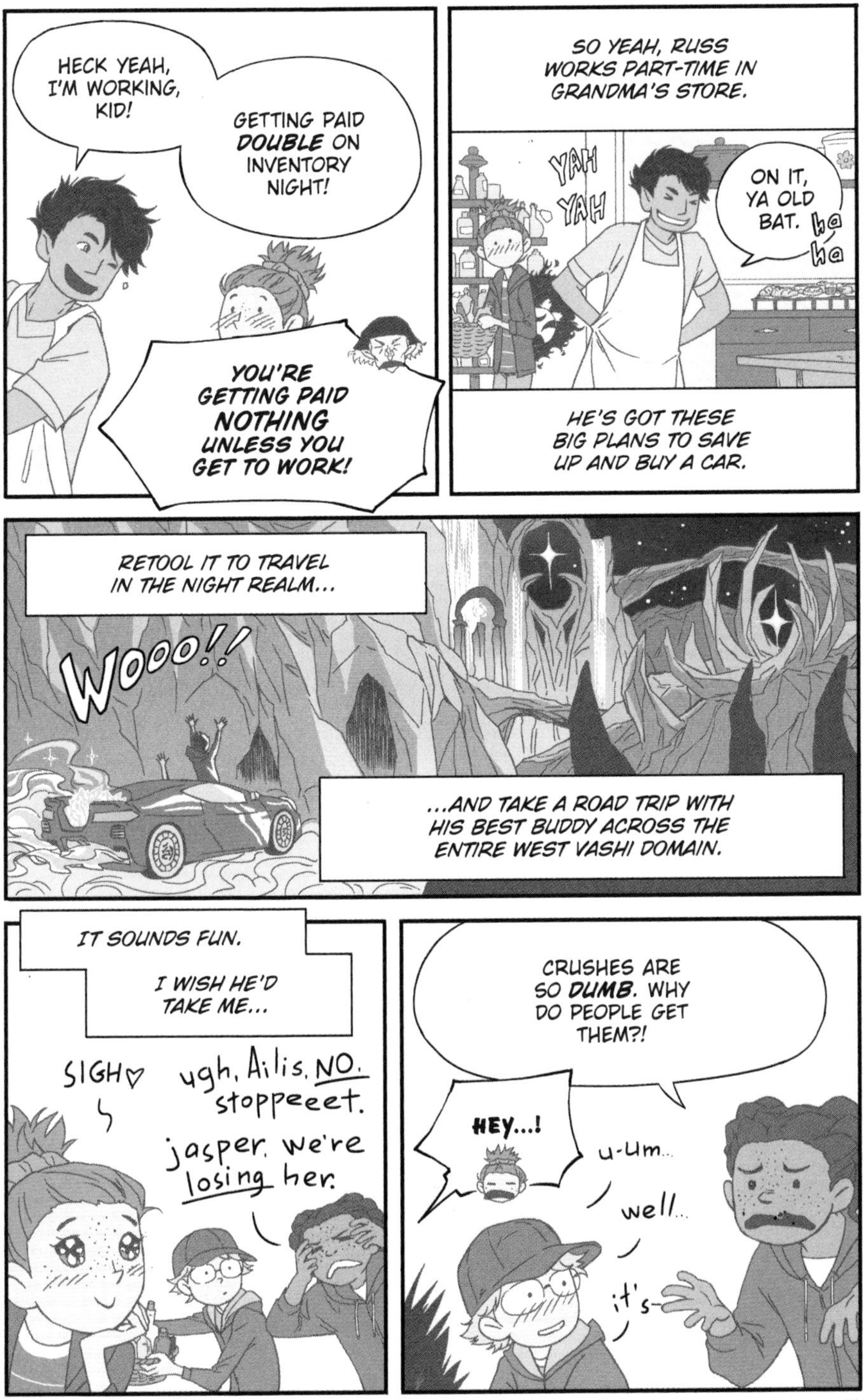

HECK YEAH, I'M WORKING, KID!
GETTING PAID DOUBLE ON INVENTORY NIGHT!
YOU'RE GETTING PAID NOTHING UNLESS YOU GET TO WORK!
SO YEAH, RUSS WORKS PART-TIME IN GRANDMA'S STORE.
YAH YAH
ON IT, YA OLD BAT. ha ha
HE'S GOT THESE BIG PLANS TO SAVE UP AND BUY A CAR.
RETOOL IT TO TRAVEL IN THE NIGHT REALM...
WOOO!!
...AND TAKE A ROAD TRIP WITH HIS BEST BUDDY ACROSS THE ENTIRE WEST VASHI DOMAIN.
IT SOUNDS FUN.
I WISH HE'D TAKE ME...
SIGH♡
ugh. Ailis. NO. stoppeeet.
jasper. we're losing her.
CRUSHES ARE SO DUMB. WHY DO PEOPLE GET THEM?!
HEY...!
u-um...
well...
it's-

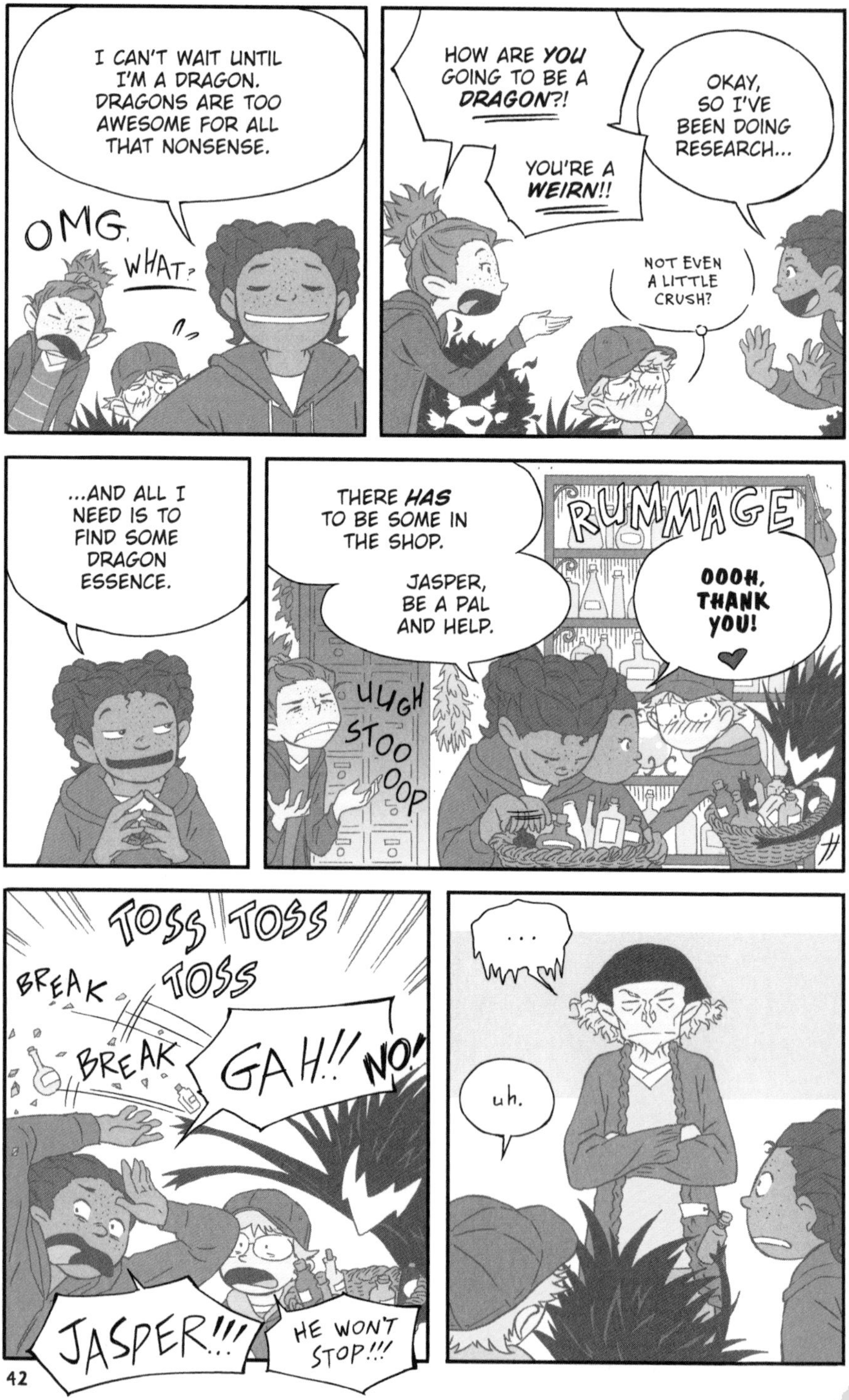
I CAN'T WAIT UNTIL I'M A DRAGON. DRAGONS ARE TOO AWESOME FOR ALL THAT NONSENSE.
OMG.
WHAT?
HOW ARE YOU GOING TO BE A DRAGON?!
YOU'RE A WEIRN!!
OKAY, SO I'VE BEEN DOING RESEARCH...
NOT EVEN A LITTLE CRUSH?
...AND ALL I NEED IS TO FIND SOME DRAGON ESSENCE.
THERE HAS TO BE SOME IN THE SHOP.
JASPER, BE A PAL AND HELP.
RUMMAGE
OOOH, THANK YOU!
UUGH
STOOOOOP
TOSS TOSS
BREAK
TOSS
BREAK
GAH!!
NO!
JASPER!!!
HE WON'T STOP!!!
...
uh.

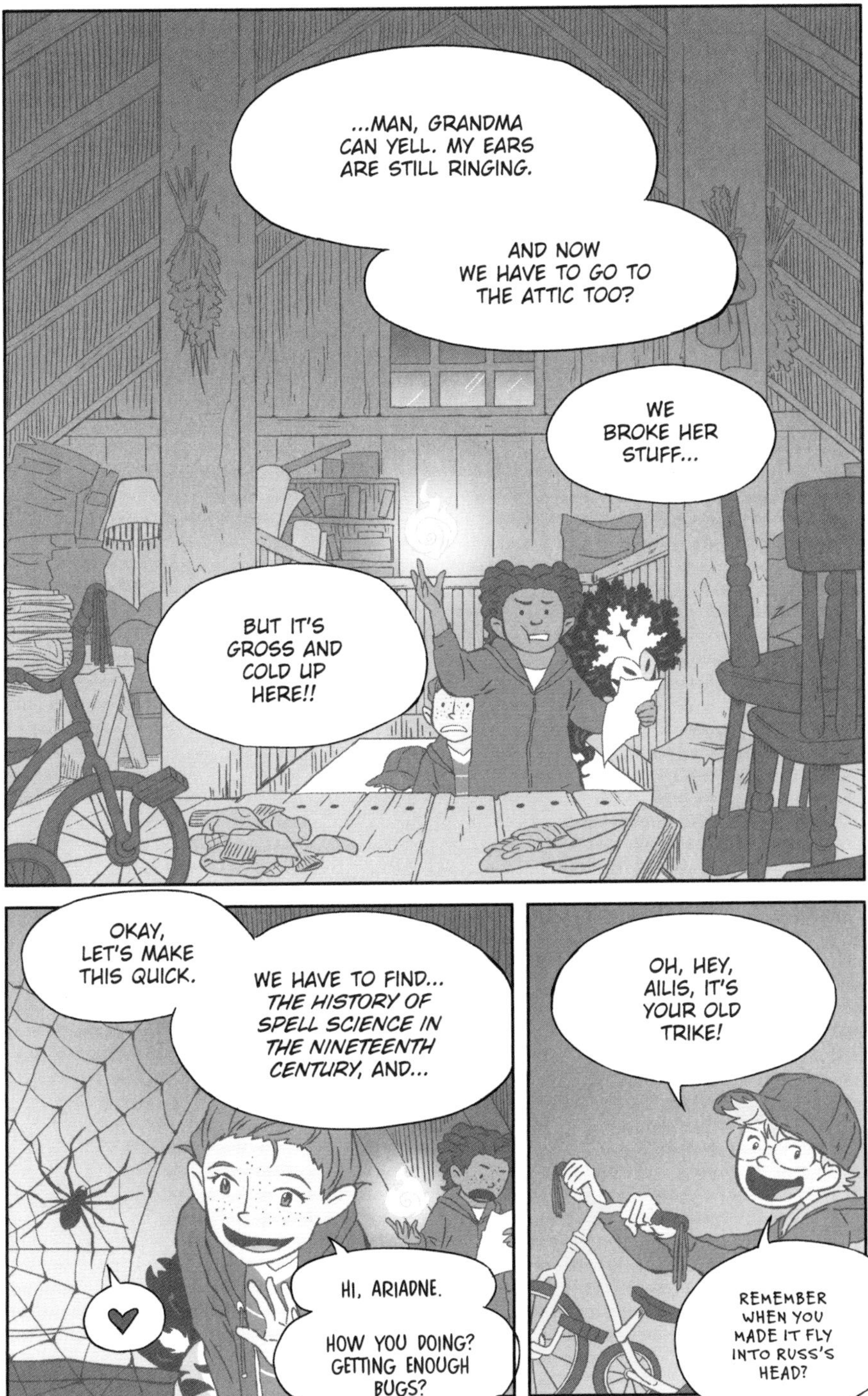
...MAN, GRANDMA CAN YELL. MY EARS ARE STILL RINGING.
AND NOW WE HAVE TO GO TO THE ATTIC TOO?
WE BROKE HER STUFF...
BUT IT'S GROSS AND COLD UP HERE!!
OKAY, LET'S MAKE THIS QUICK.
WE HAVE TO FIND... *THE HISTORY OF SPELL SCIENCE IN THE NINETEENTH CENTURY*, AND...
HI, ARIADNE.
HOW YOU DOING? GETTING ENOUGH BUGS?
OH, HEY, AILIS, IT'S YOUR OLD TRIKE!
REMEMBER WHEN YOU MADE IT FLY INTO RUSS'S HEAD?

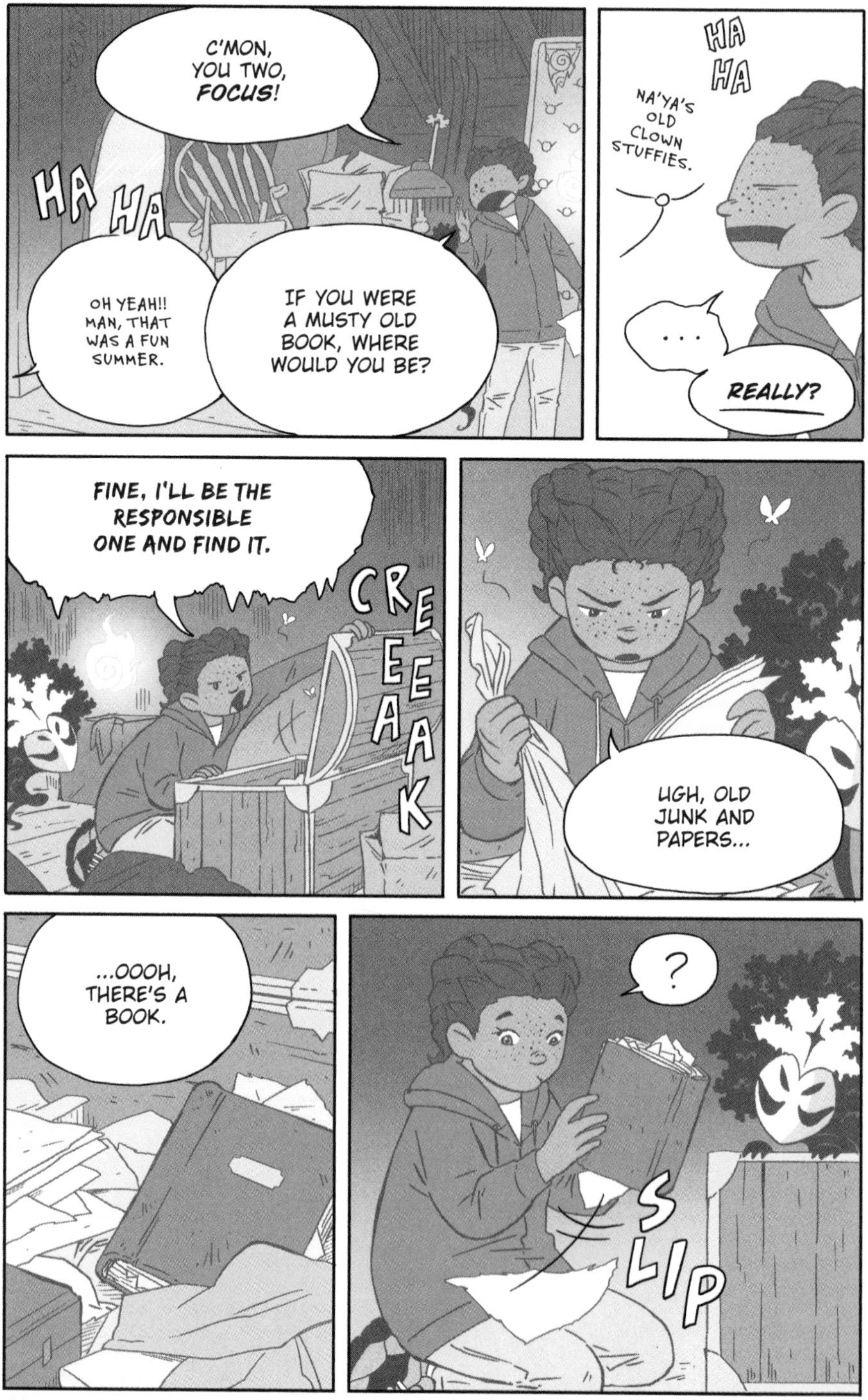
C'MON, YOU TWO, *FOCUS*!
HA HA
OH YEAH!! MAN, THAT WAS A FUN SUMMER.
IF YOU WERE A MUSTY OLD BOOK, WHERE WOULD YOU BE?
HA HA
NA'YA'S OLD CLOWN STUFFIES.
...
*REALLY?*
FINE, I'LL BE THE RESPONSIBLE ONE AND FIND IT.
CREEEAAK
UGH, OLD JUNK AND PAPERS...
...OOOH, THERE'S A BOOK.
?
SLIP

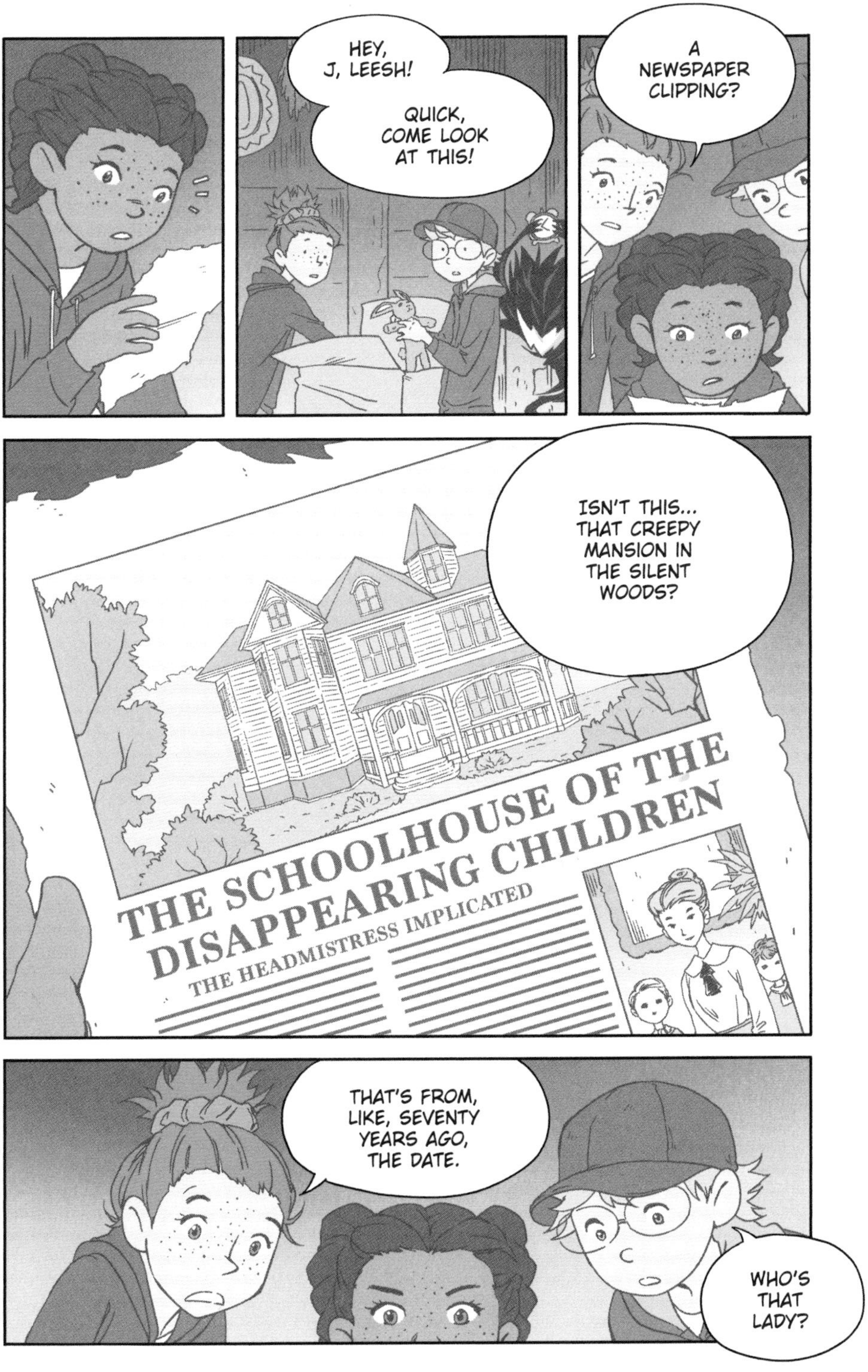
HEY, J, LEESH!
QUICK, COME LOOK AT THIS!
A NEWSPAPER CLIPPING?
ISN'T THIS... THAT CREEPY MANSION IN THE SILENT WOODS?
THE SCHOOLHOUSE OF THE DISAPPEARING CHILDREN
THE HEADMISTRESS IMPLICATED
THAT'S FROM, LIKE, SEVENTY YEARS AGO, THE DATE.
WHO'S THAT LADY?

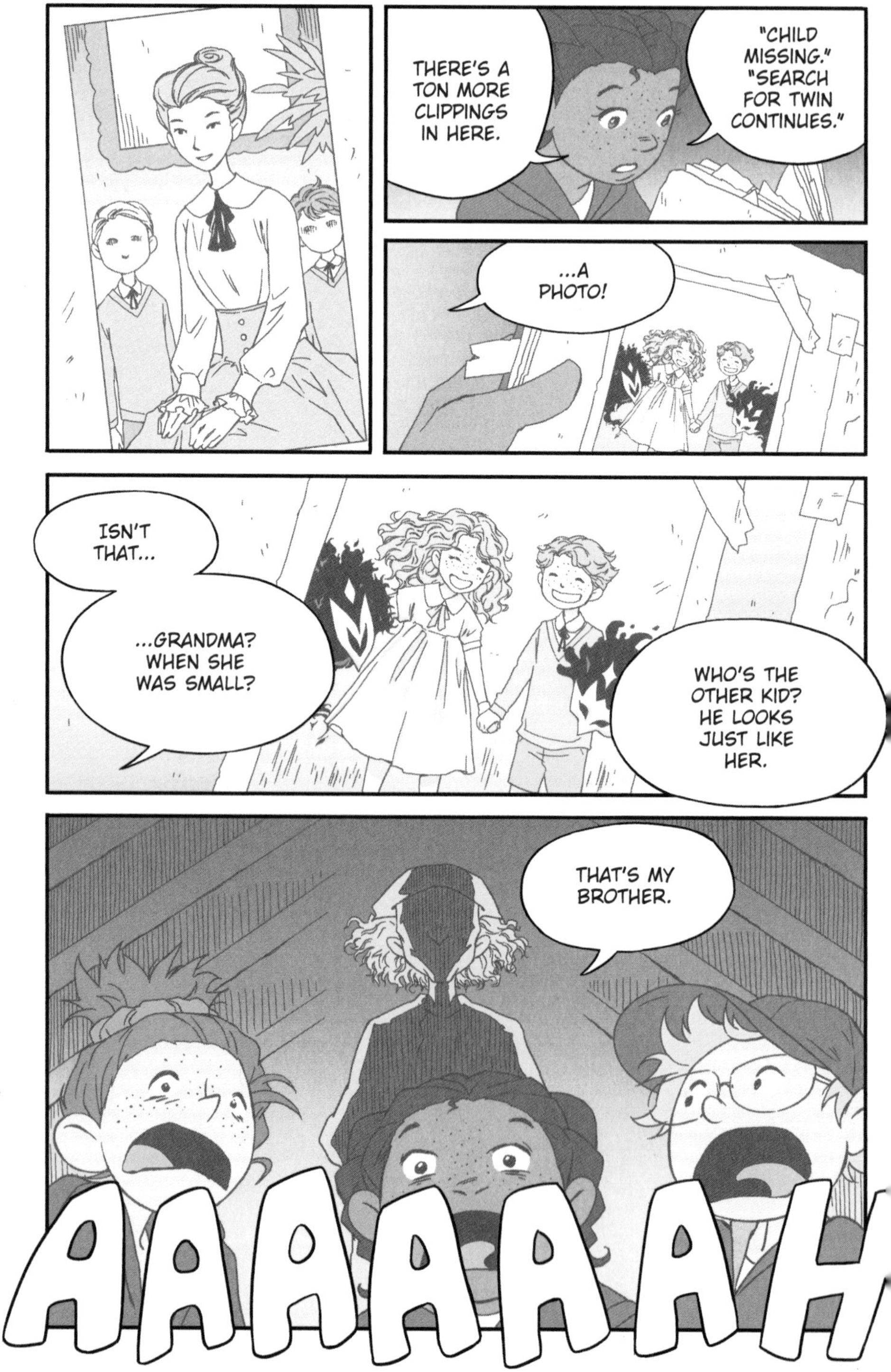
THERE'S A TON MORE CLIPPINGS IN HERE.
"CHILD MISSING." "SEARCH FOR TWIN CONTINUES."
...A PHOTO!
ISN'T THAT...
...GRANDMA? WHEN SHE WAS SMALL?
WHO'S THE OTHER KID? HE LOOKS JUST LIKE HER.
THAT'S MY BROTHER.
AAAAAAH

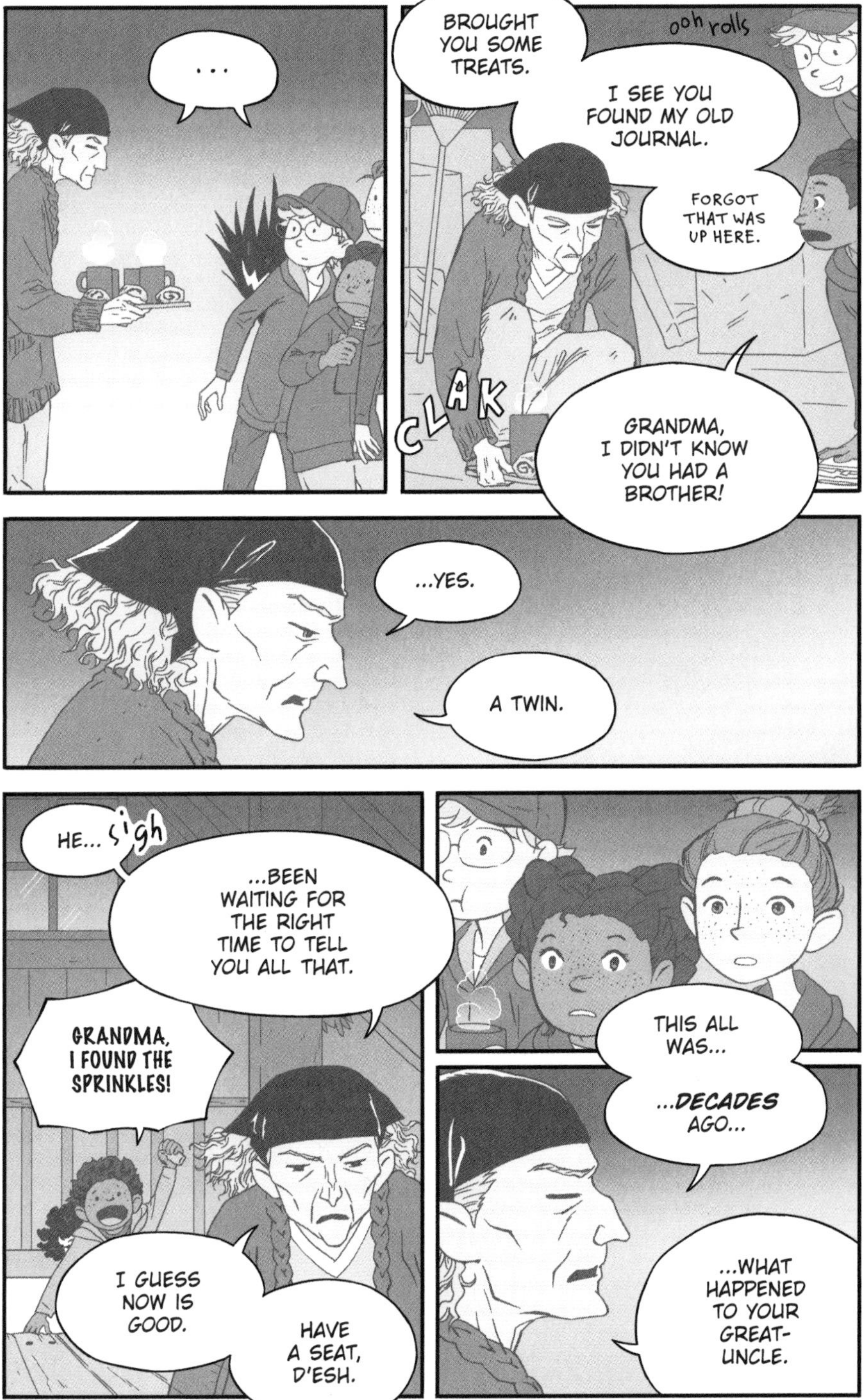
...
BROUGHT YOU SOME TREATS.
ooh rolls
I SEE YOU FOUND MY OLD JOURNAL.
FORGOT THAT WAS UP HERE.
CLAK
GRANDMA, I DIDN'T KNOW YOU HAD A BROTHER!
...YES.
A TWIN.
HE... sigh
...BEEN WAITING FOR THE RIGHT TIME TO TELL YOU ALL THAT.
GRANDMA, I FOUND THE SPRINKLES!
I GUESS NOW IS GOOD.
HAVE A SEAT, D'ESH.
THIS ALL WAS...
...DECADES AGO...
...WHAT HAPPENED TO YOUR GREAT-UNCLE.

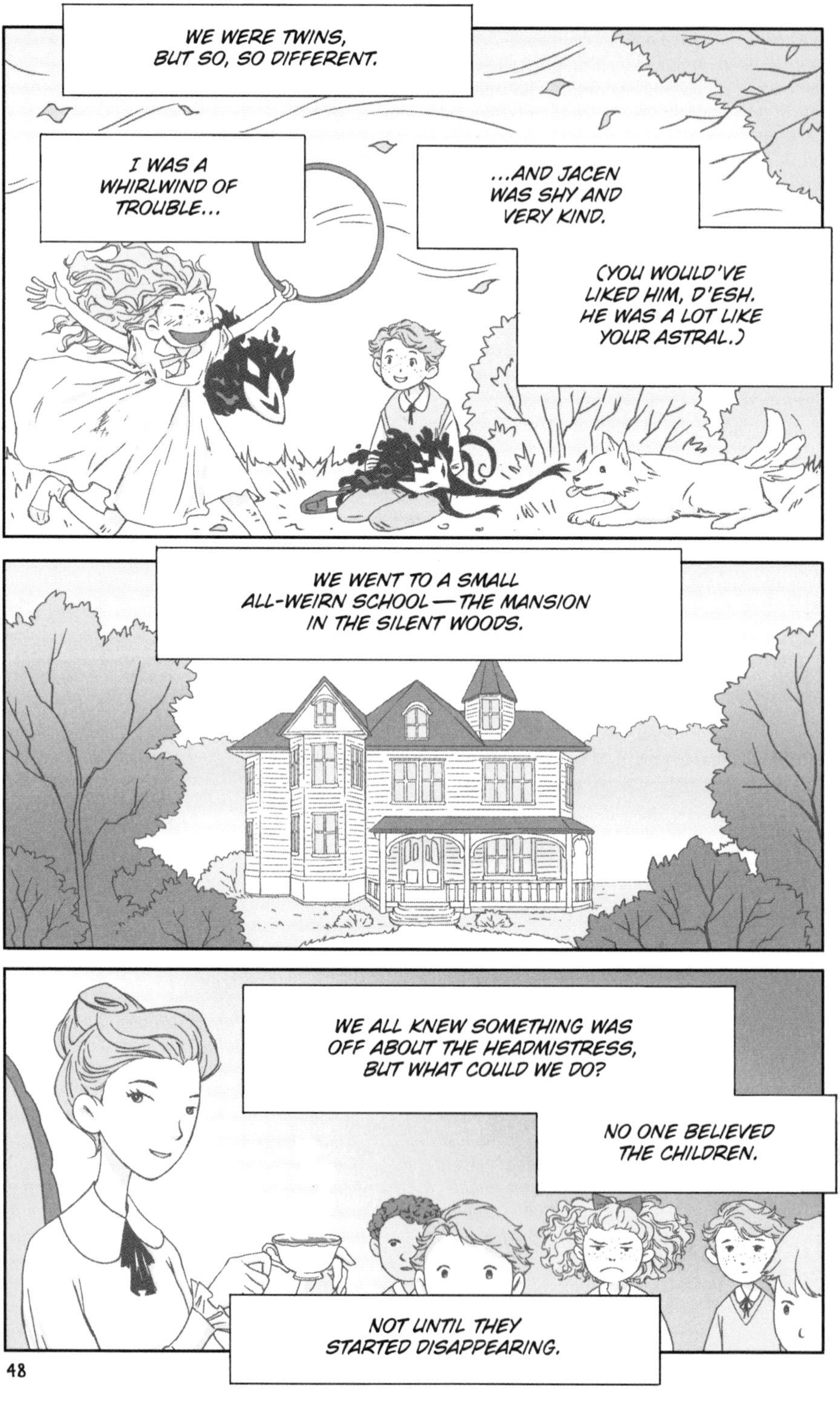
WE WERE TWINS, BUT SO, SO DIFFERENT.
I WAS A WHIRLWIND OF TROUBLE...
...AND JACEN WAS SHY AND VERY KIND.
(YOU WOULD'VE LIKED HIM, D'ESH. HE WAS A LOT LIKE YOUR ASTRAL.)
WE WENT TO A SMALL ALL-WEIRN SCHOOL—THE MANSION IN THE SILENT WOODS.
WE ALL KNEW SOMETHING WAS OFF ABOUT THE HEADMISTRESS, BUT WHAT COULD WE DO?
NO ONE BELIEVED THE CHILDREN.
NOT UNTIL THEY STARTED DISAPPEARING.

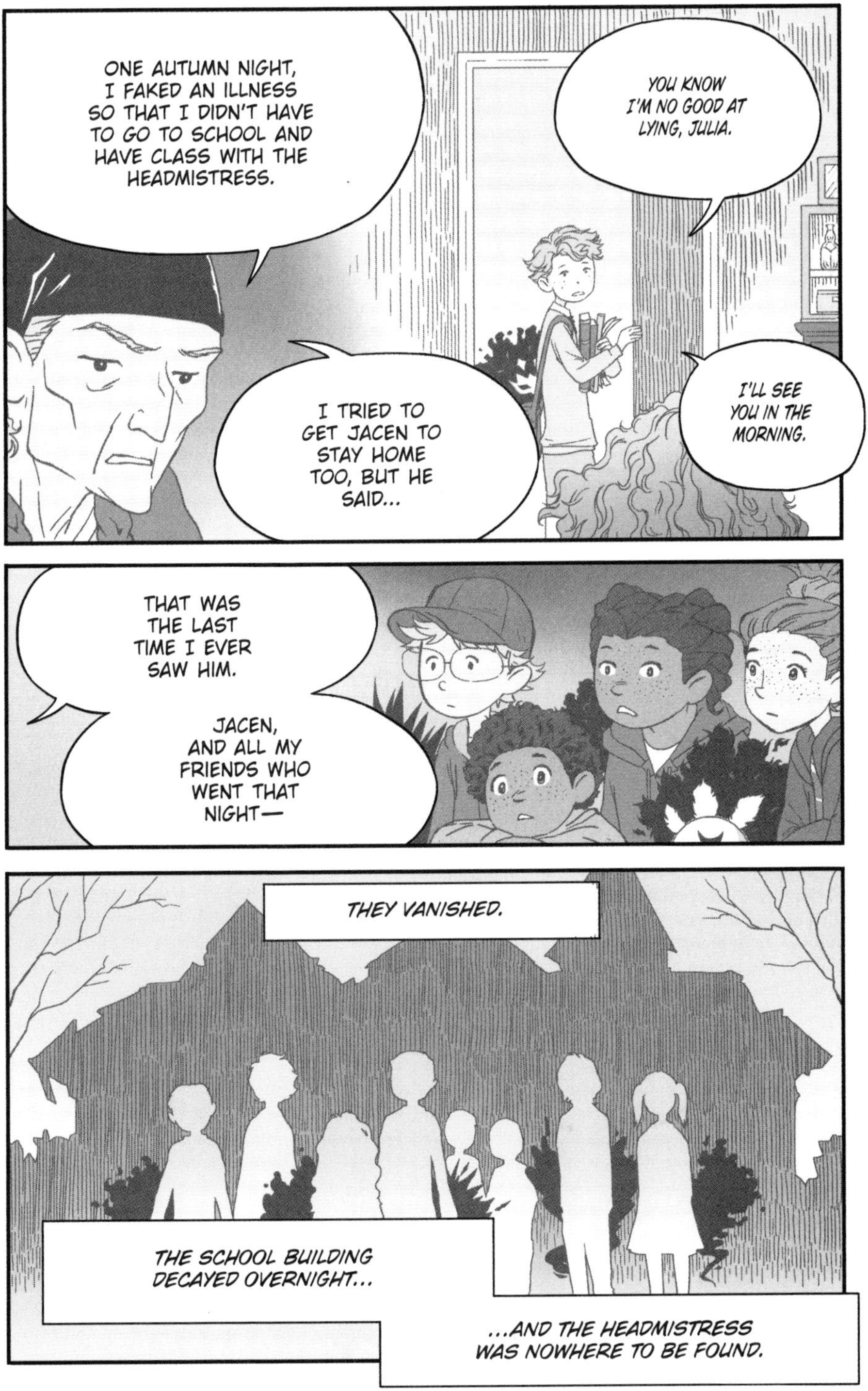
ONE AUTUMN NIGHT, I FAKED AN ILLNESS SO THAT I DIDN'T HAVE TO GO TO SCHOOL AND HAVE CLASS WITH THE HEADMISTRESS.
YOU KNOW I'M NO GOOD AT LYING, JULIA.
I TRIED TO GET JACEN TO STAY HOME TOO, BUT HE SAID...
I'LL SEE YOU IN THE MORNING.
THAT WAS THE LAST TIME I EVER SAW HIM.
JACEN, AND ALL MY FRIENDS WHO WENT THAT NIGHT—
THEY VANISHED.
THE SCHOOL BUILDING DECAYED OVERNIGHT...
...AND THE HEADMISTRESS WAS NOWHERE TO BE FOUND.

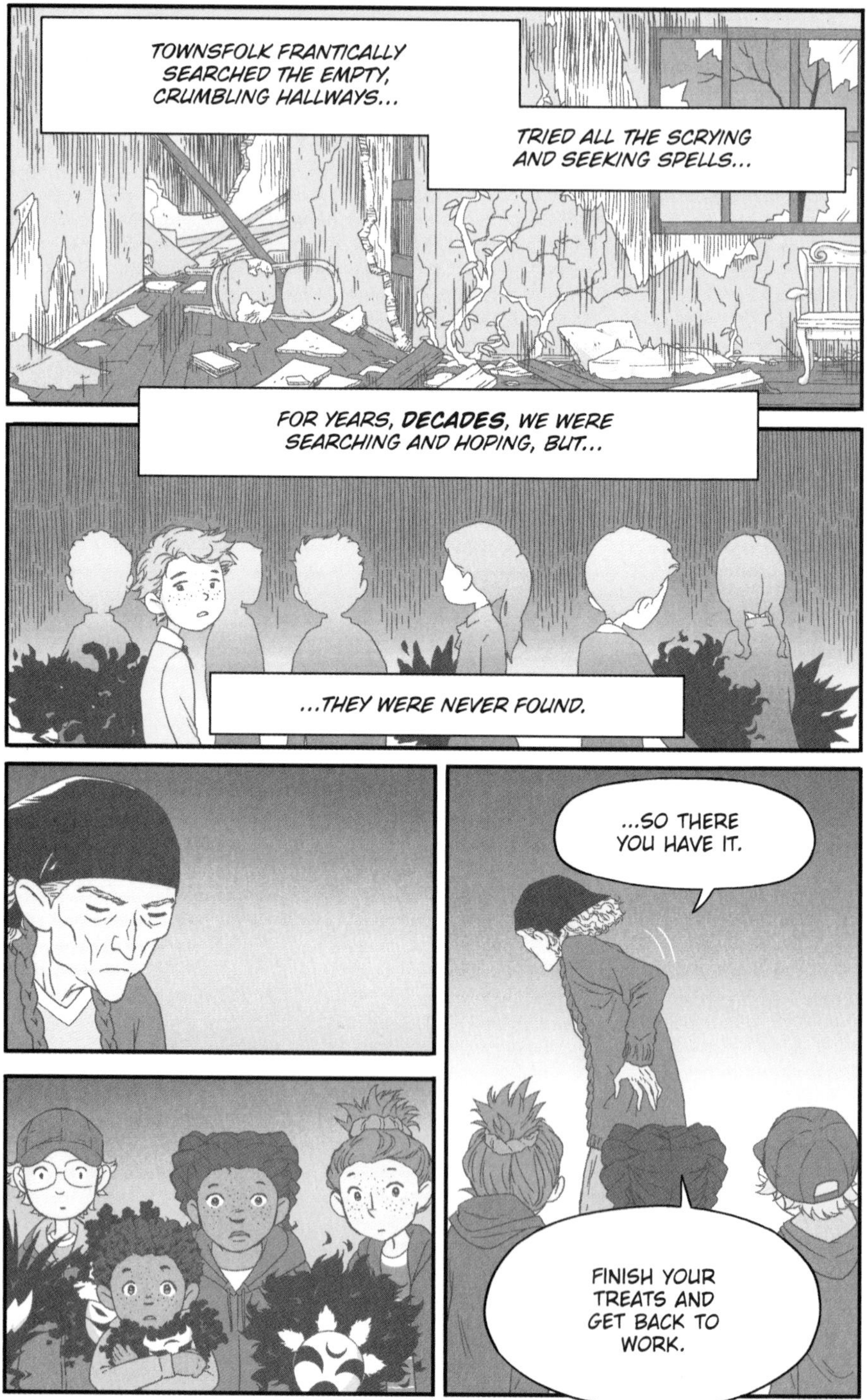
TOWNSFOLK FRANTICALLY SEARCHED THE EMPTY, CRUMBLING HALLWAYS...
TRIED ALL THE SCRYING AND SEEKING SPELLS...
FOR YEARS, **DECADES**, WE WERE SEARCHING AND HOPING, BUT...
...THEY WERE NEVER FOUND.
...SO THERE YOU HAVE IT.
FINISH YOUR TREATS AND GET BACK TO WORK.

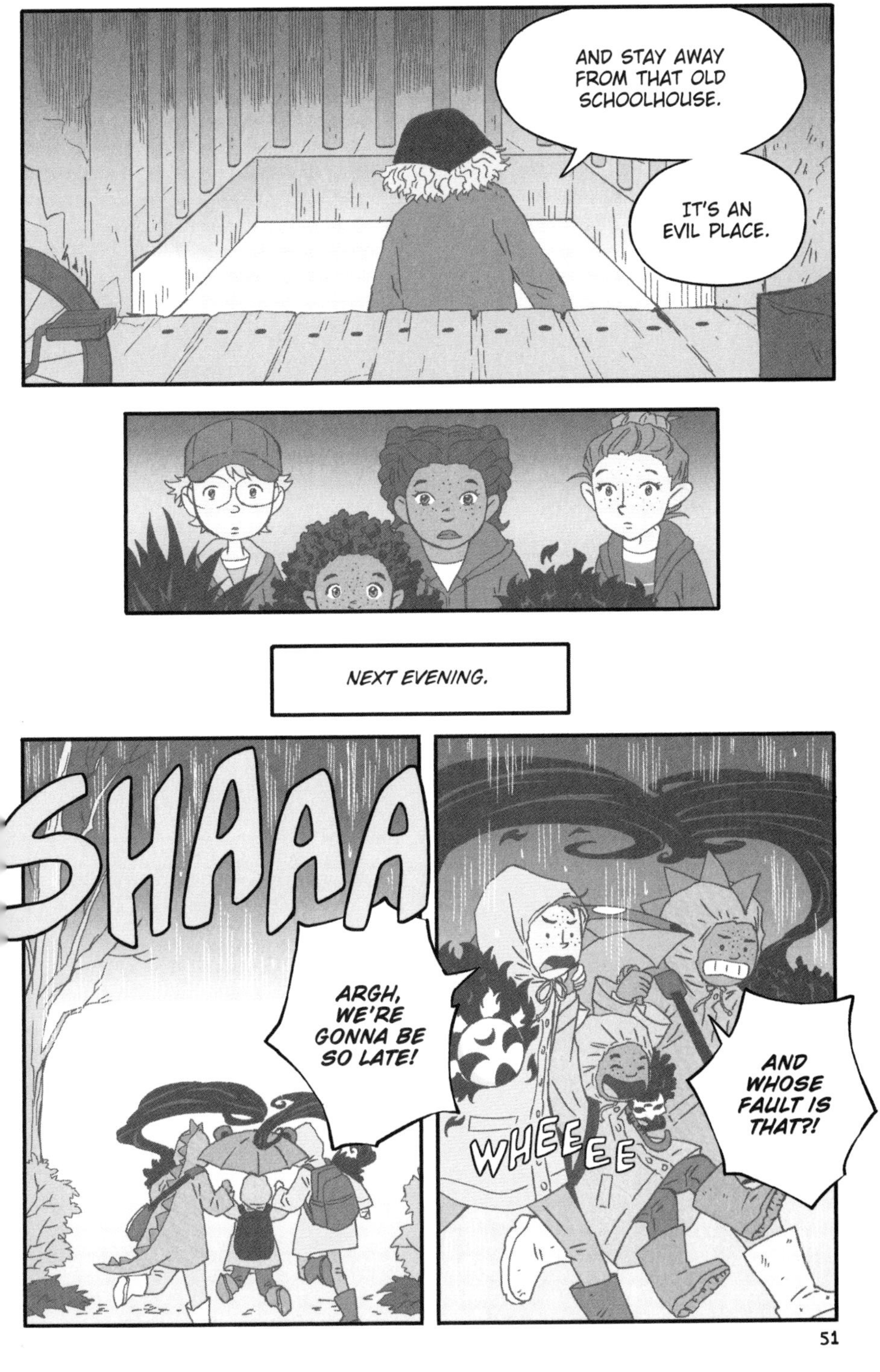
AND STAY AWAY FROM THAT OLD SCHOOLHOUSE.
IT'S AN EVIL PLACE.
NEXT EVENING.
SHAAA
ARGH, WE'RE GONNA BE SO LATE!
WHEEEEE
AND WHOSE FAULT IS THAT?!

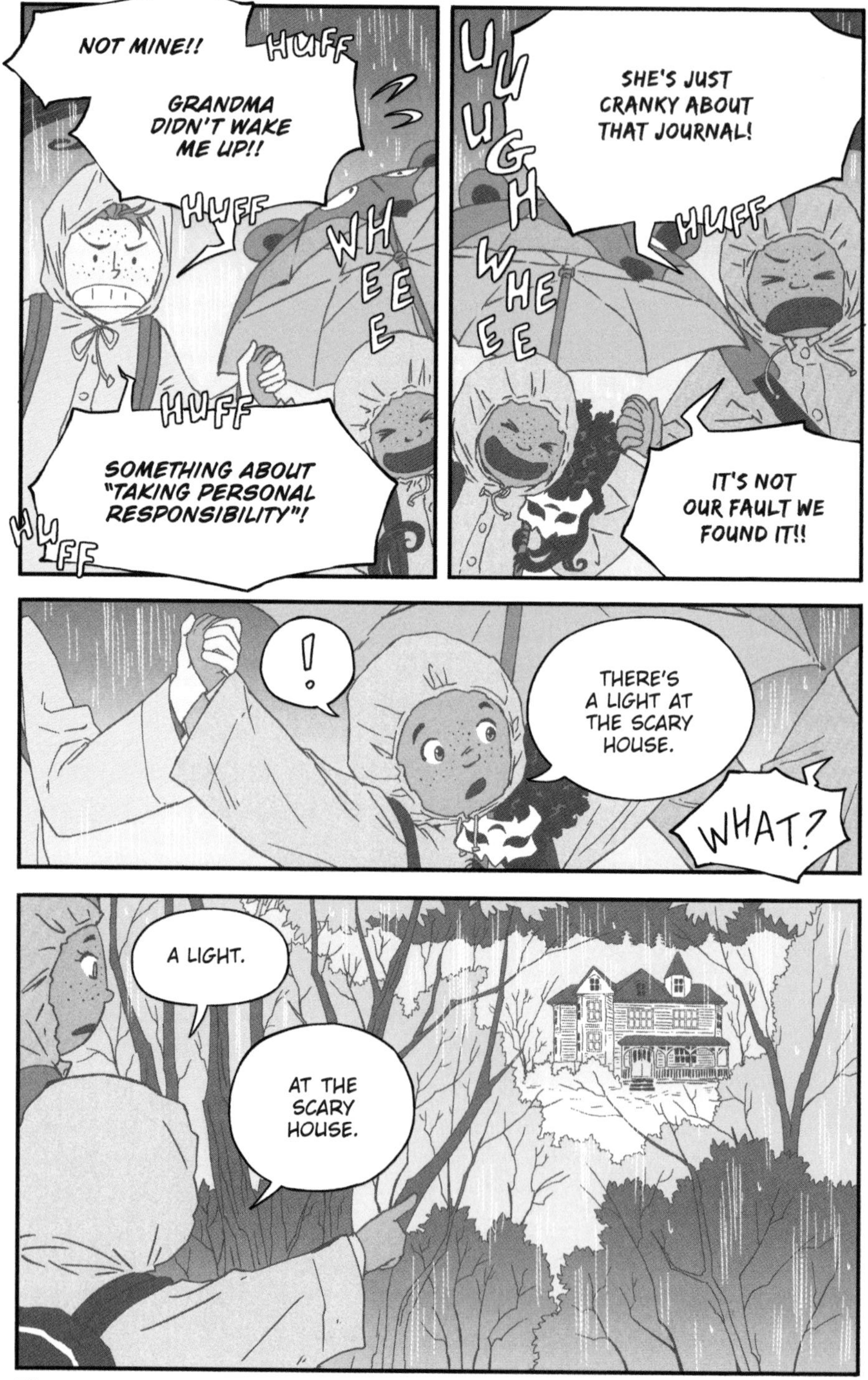
NOT MINE!!
HUFF
GRANDMA DIDN'T WAKE ME UP!!
HUFF
WHEEE
HUFF
SOMETHING ABOUT "TAKING PERSONAL RESPONSIBILITY"!
HUFF
UUUGH
SHE'S JUST CRANKY ABOUT THAT JOURNAL!
HUFF
WHEEE
IT'S NOT OUR FAULT WE FOUND IT!!
!
THERE'S A LIGHT AT THE SCARY HOUSE.
WHAT?
A LIGHT.
AT THE SCARY HOUSE.

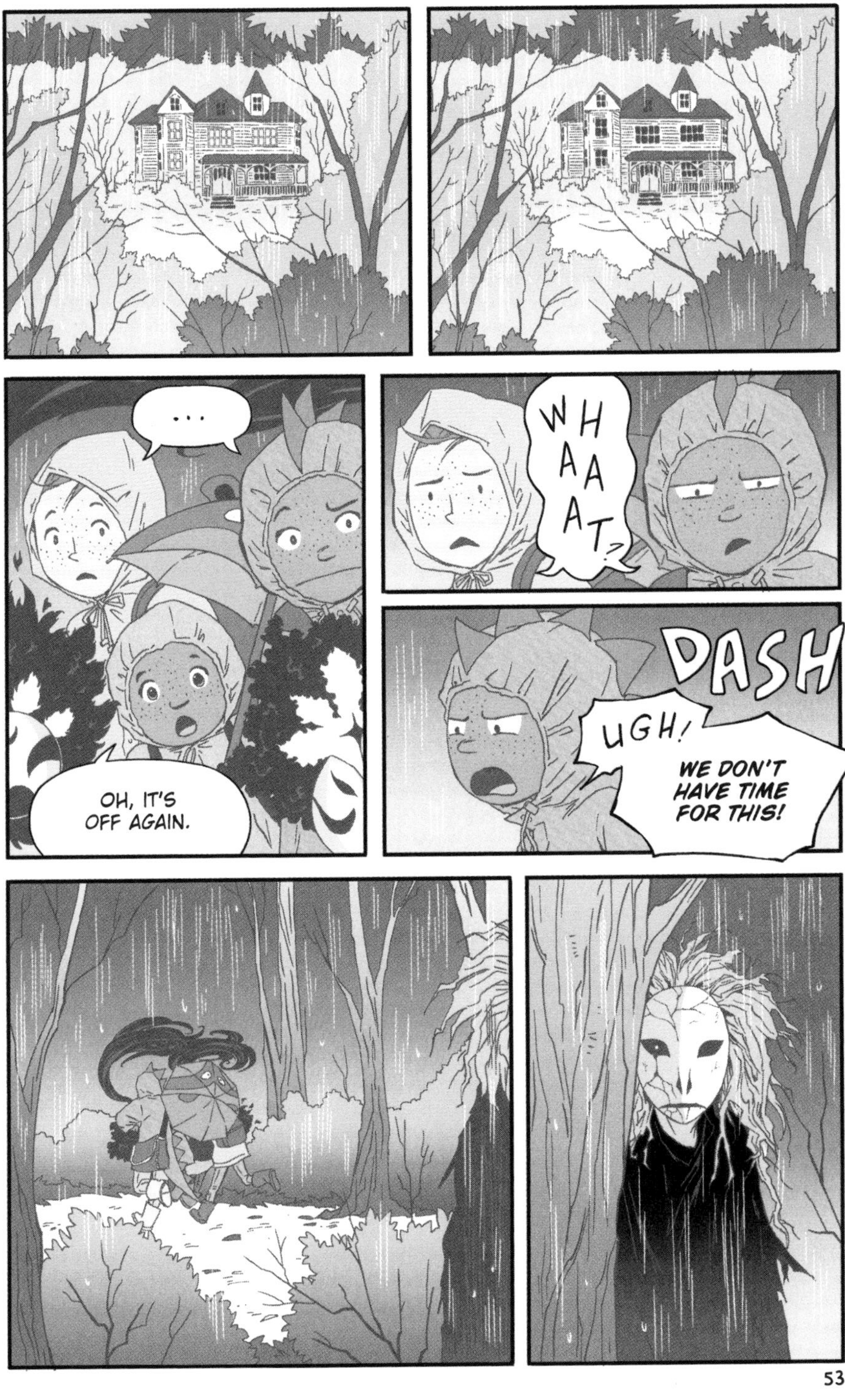
...
OH, IT'S OFF AGAIN.
WHAAAT?
DASH
UGH!
WE DON'T HAVE TIME FOR THIS!

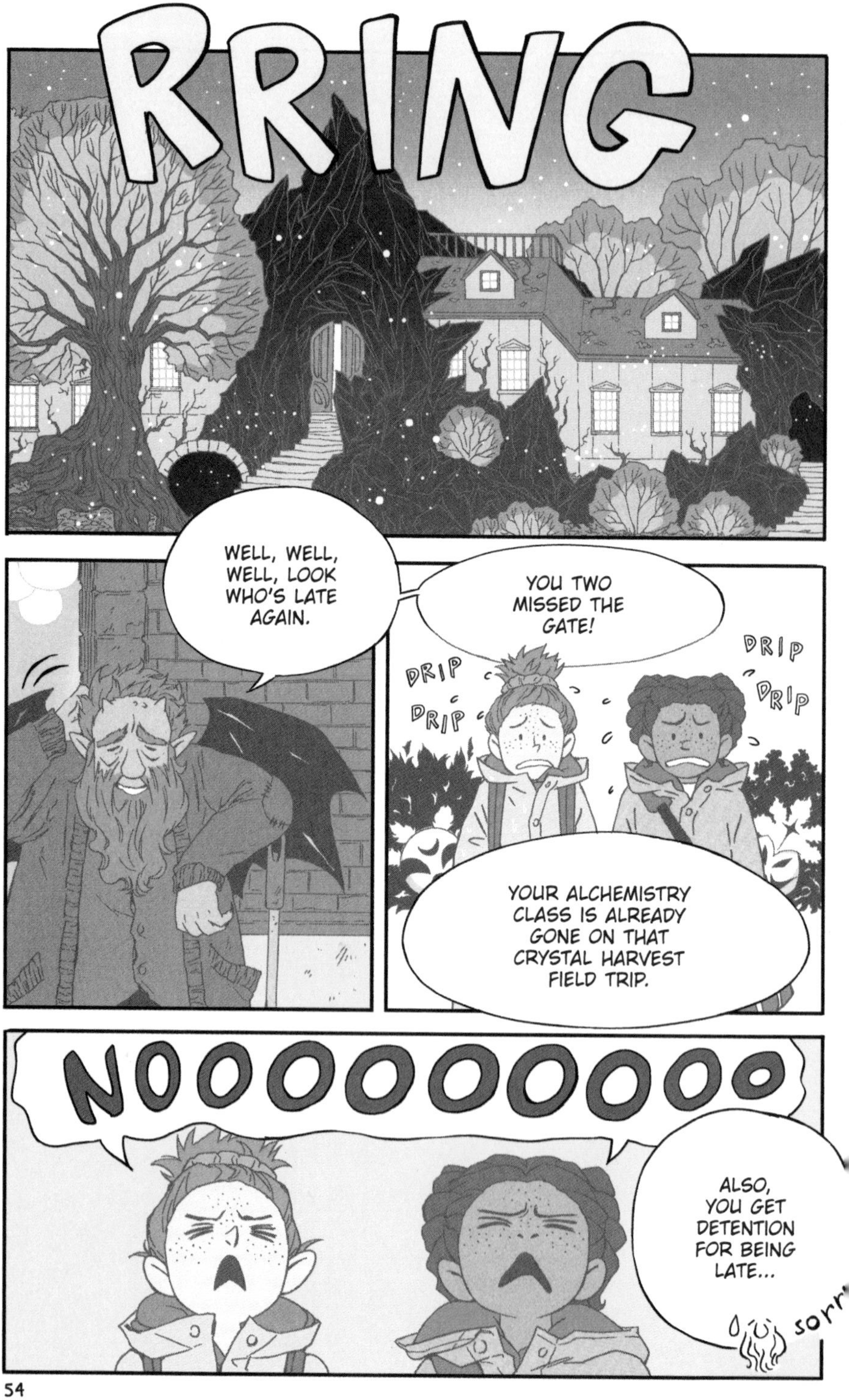
RRING
WELL, WELL, WELL, LOOK WHO'S LATE AGAIN.
YOU TWO MISSED THE GATE!
DRIP
DRIP
DRIP
DRIP
YOUR ALCHEMISTRY CLASS IS ALREADY GONE ON THAT CRYSTAL HARVEST FIELD TRIP.
NOOOOOOOOO
ALSO, YOU GET DETENTION FOR BEING LATE...

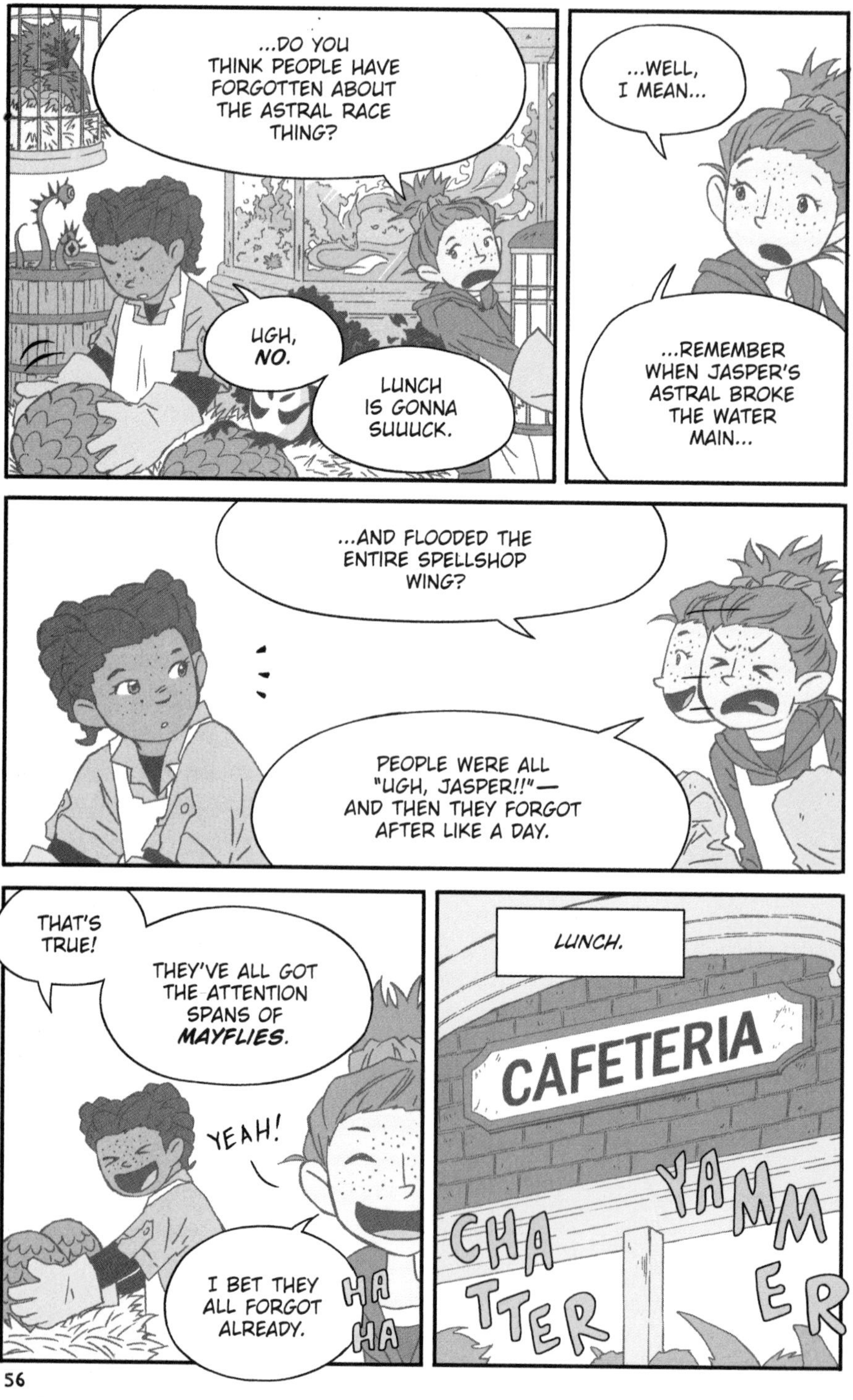
...DO YOU THINK PEOPLE HAVE FORGOTTEN ABOUT THE ASTRAL RACE THING?
UGH, **NO.**
LUNCH IS GONNA SUUUCK.
...WELL, I MEAN...
...REMEMBER WHEN JASPER'S ASTRAL BROKE THE WATER MAIN...
...AND FLOODED THE ENTIRE SPELLSHOP WING?
PEOPLE WERE ALL "UGH, JASPER!!"—AND THEN THEY FORGOT AFTER LIKE A DAY.
THAT'S TRUE!
THEY'VE ALL GOT THE ATTENTION SPANS OF ***MAYFLIES***.
YEAH!
I BET THEY ALL FORGOT ALREADY.
HA HA
*LUNCH.*
CAFETERIA
CHATTER
YAMMER

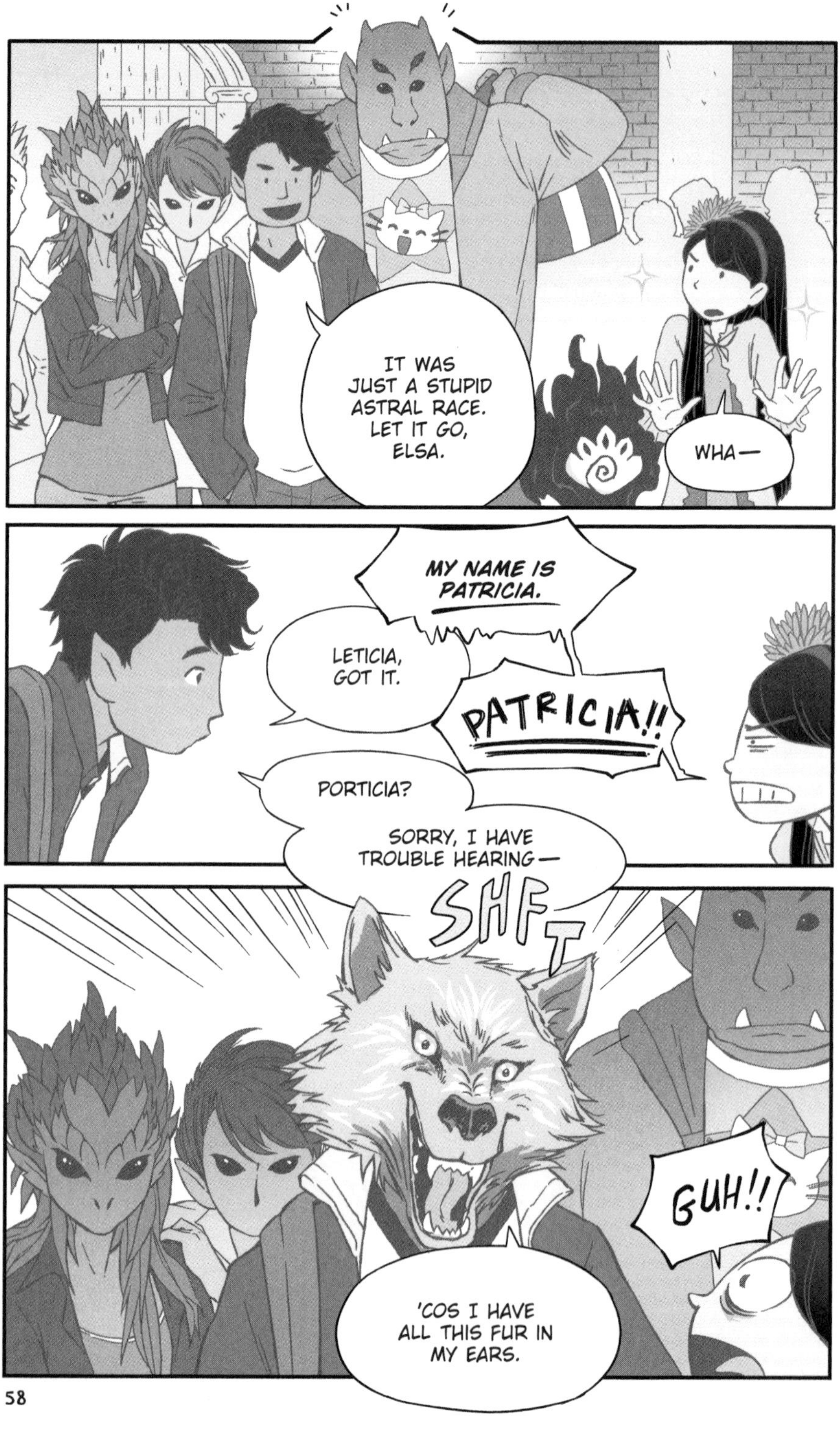
IT WAS JUST A STUPID ASTRAL RACE. LET IT GO, ELSA.
WHA—
MY NAME IS PATRICIA.
LETICIA, GOT IT.
PATRICIA!!
PORTICIA?
SORRY, I HAVE TROUBLE HEARING—
SHFT
GUH!!
'COS I HAVE ALL THIS FUR IN MY EARS.

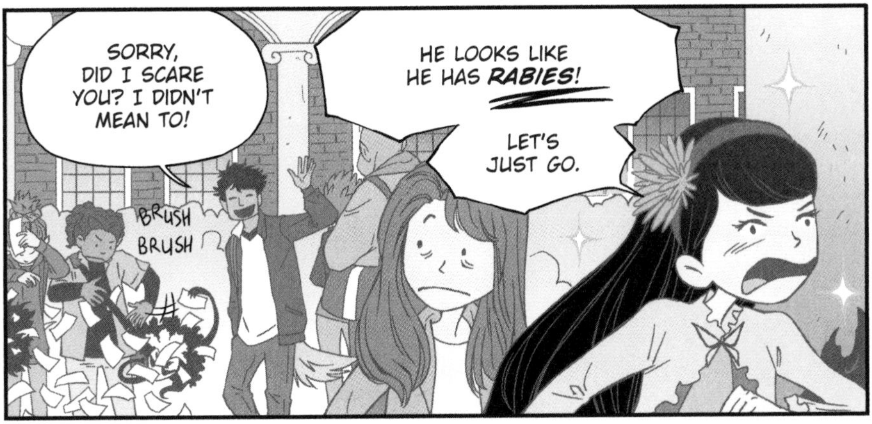
SORRY, DID I SCARE YOU? I DIDN'T MEAN TO!
BRUSH BRUSH
HE LOOKS LIKE HE HAS RABIES!
LET'S JUST GO.

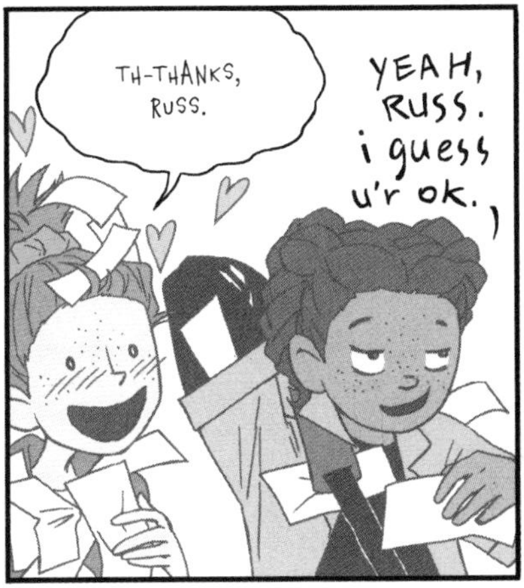
TH-THANKS, RUSS.
YEAH, RUSS. i guess u'r ok.

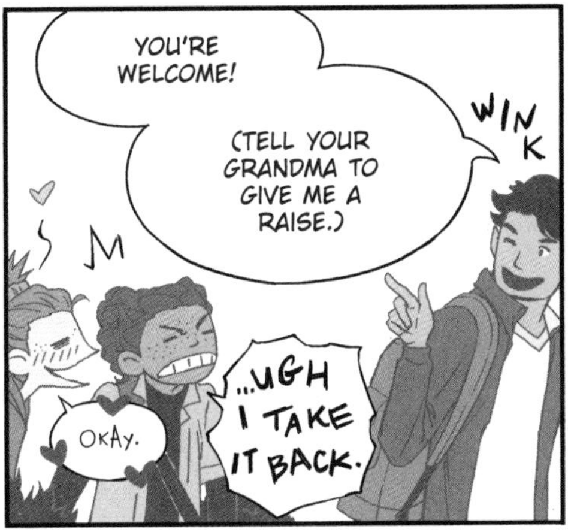
YOU'RE WELCOME!
(TELL YOUR GRANDMA TO GIVE ME A RAISE.)
WINK
OKAY.
...UGH I TAKE IT BACK.

*NEXT EVENING.*

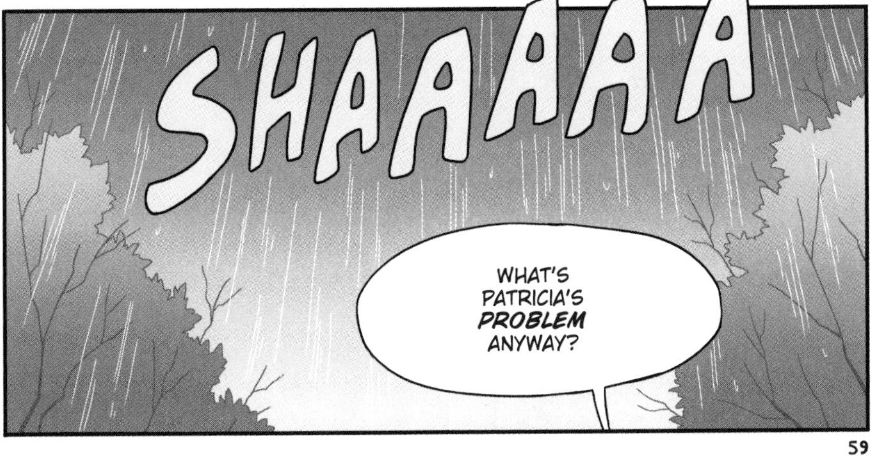
SHAAAAA
WHAT'S PATRICIA'S PROBLEM ANYWAY?

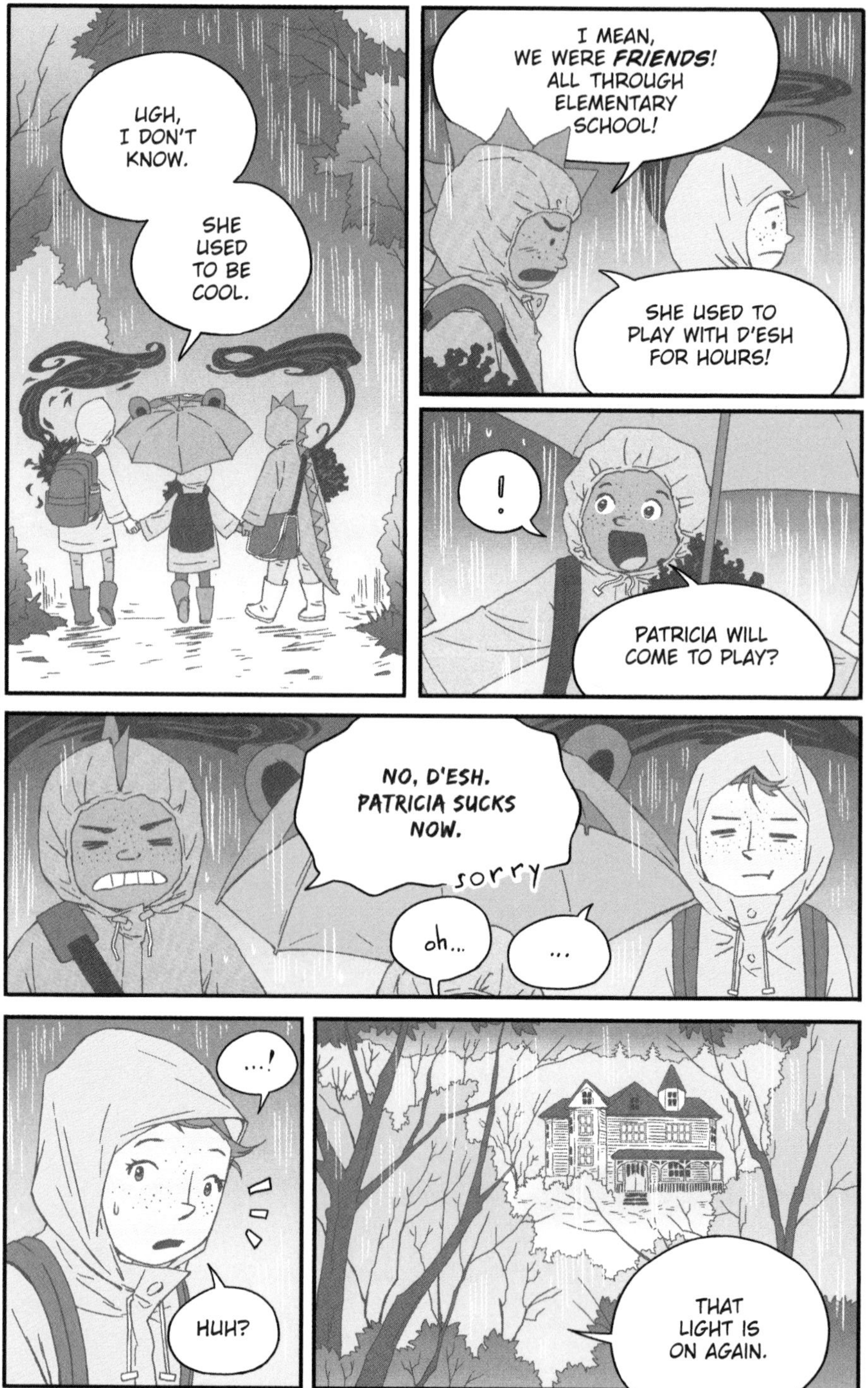
UGH, I DON'T KNOW.
SHE USED TO BE COOL.
I MEAN, WE WERE FRIENDS! ALL THROUGH ELEMENTARY SCHOOL!
SHE USED TO PLAY WITH D'ESH FOR HOURS!
!
PATRICIA WILL COME TO PLAY?
NO, D'ESH. PATRICIA SUCKS NOW.
sorry
oh...
...
...!
HUH?
THAT LIGHT IS ON AGAIN.

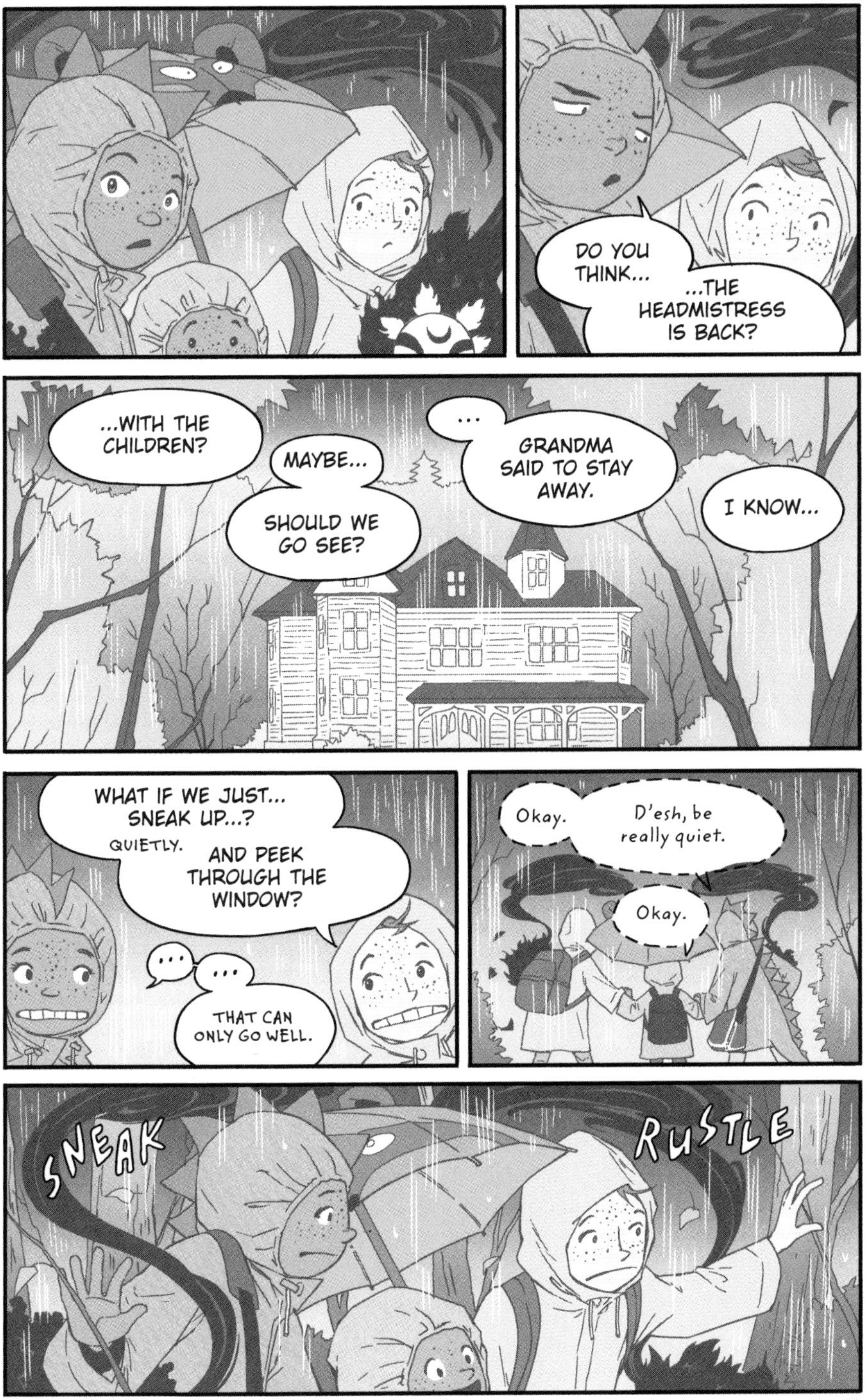
DO YOU THINK...
...THE HEADMISTRESS IS BACK?
...WITH THE CHILDREN?
MAYBE...
SHOULD WE GO SEE?
...
GRANDMA SAID TO STAY AWAY.
I KNOW...
WHAT IF WE JUST... SNEAK UP...?
QUIETLY.
AND PEEK THROUGH THE WINDOW?
...
...
THAT CAN ONLY GO WELL.
Okay.
D'esh, be really quiet.
Okay.
SNEAK
RUSTLE

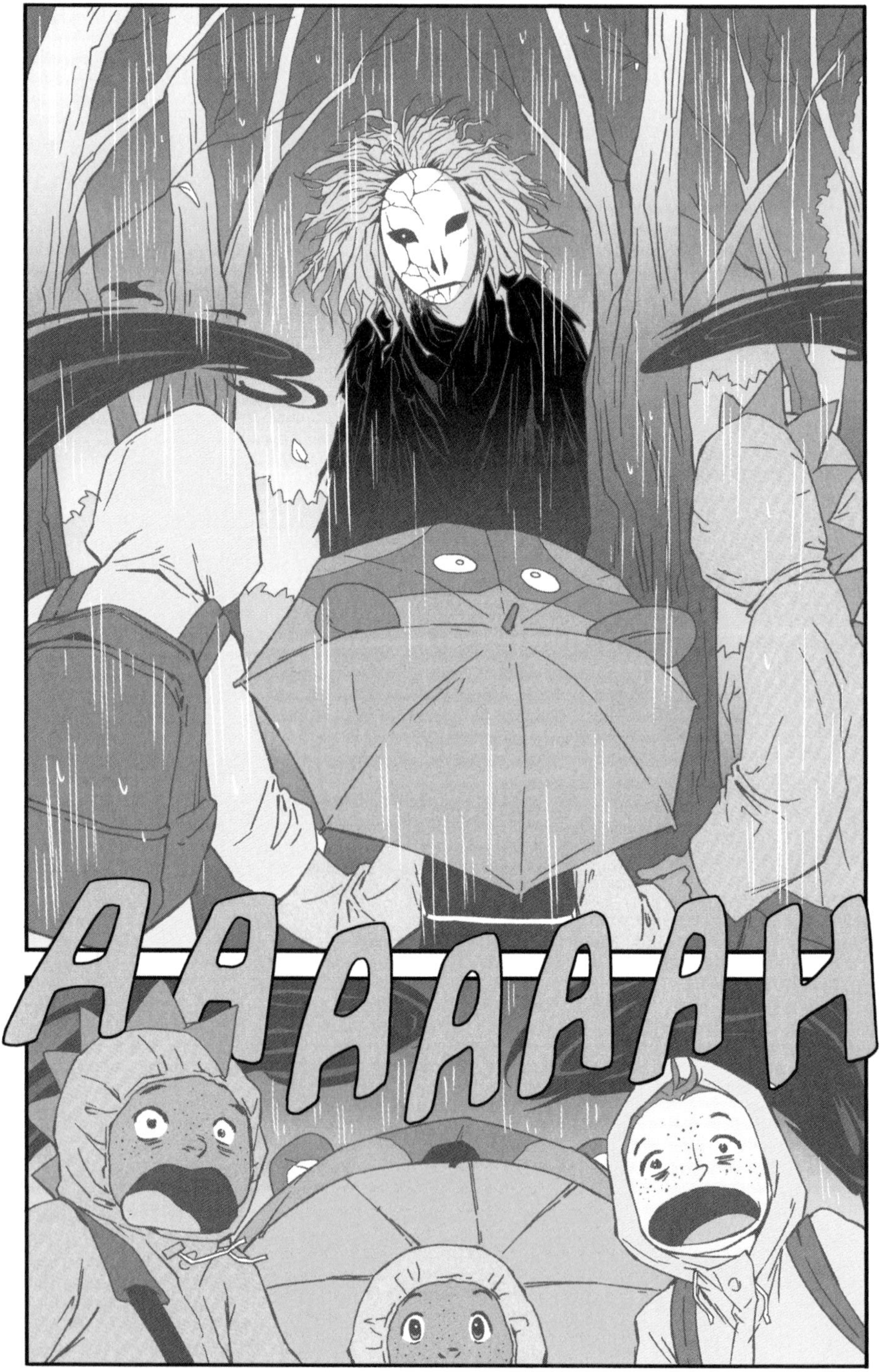
AAAAAAAH

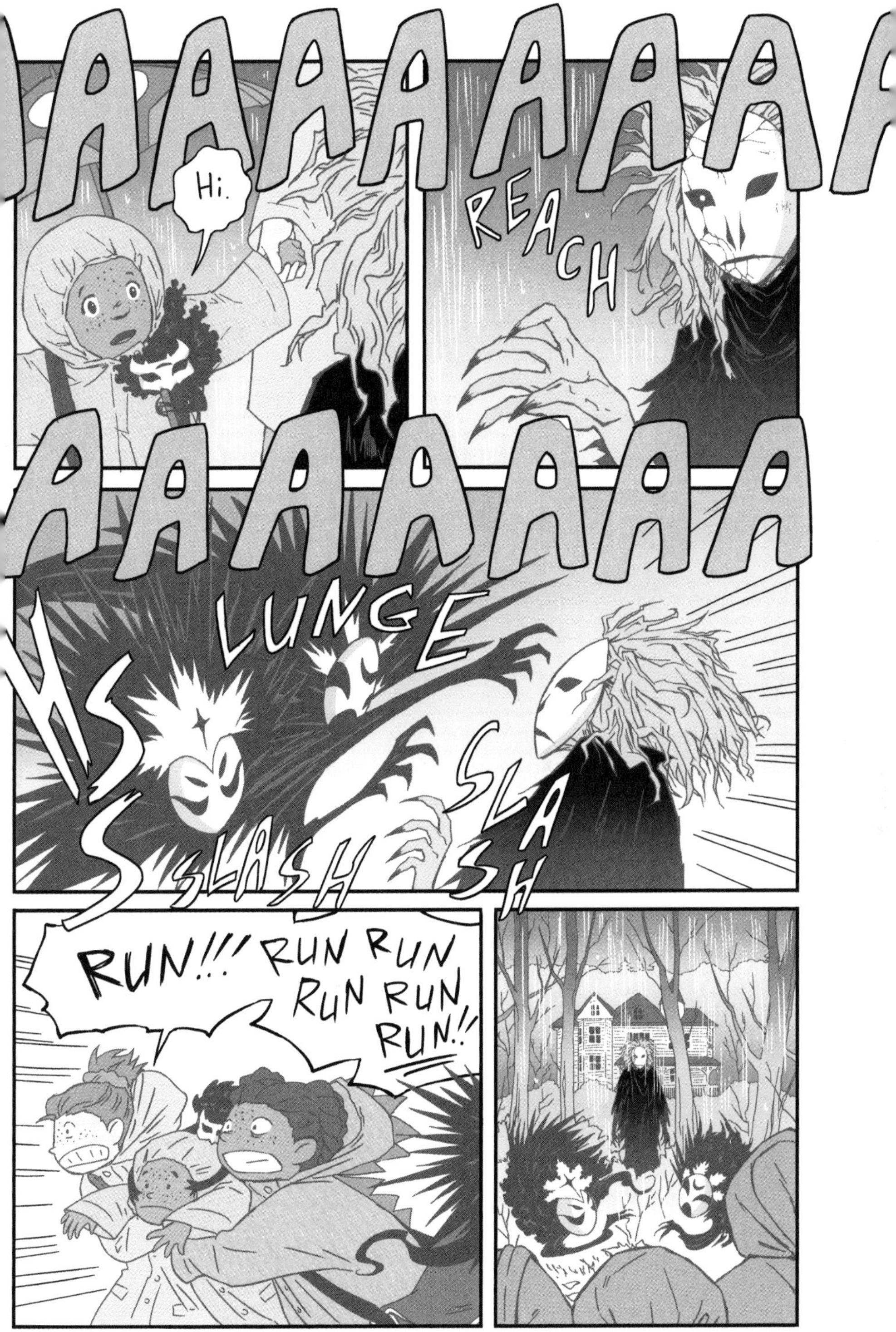
AAAAAAAAAAA
Hi.
REACH
AAAAAAAA
LUNGE
HSS
SLASH
SLASH
RUN!!!
RUN RUN RUN RUN RUN!!

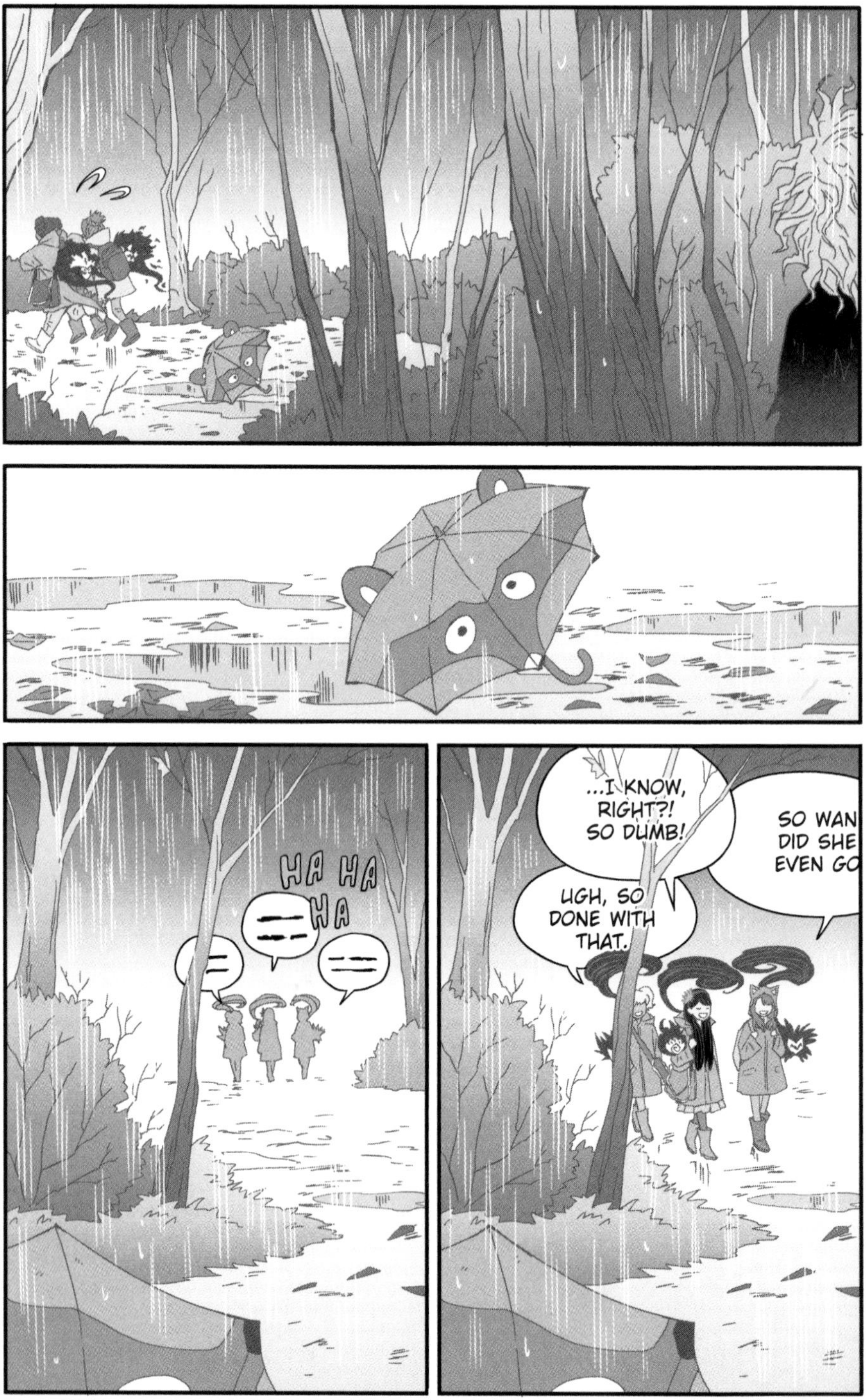
HA HA HA
...I KNOW, RIGHT?! SO DUMB!
UGH, SO DONE WITH THAT.
SO WAN DID SHE EVEN GO

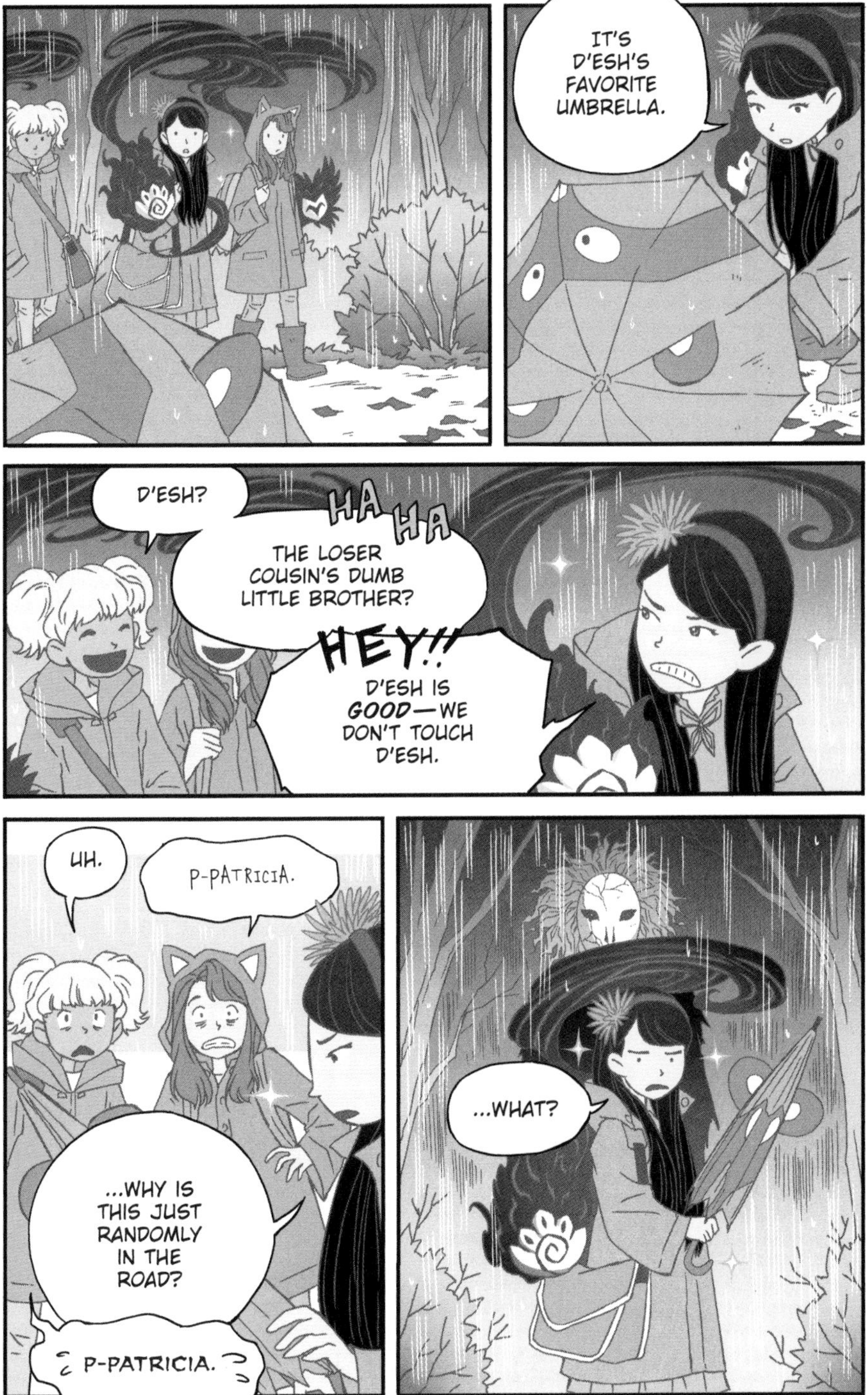
IT'S D'ESH'S FAVORITE UMBRELLA.
D'ESH?
HA HA
THE LOSER COUSIN'S DUMB LITTLE BROTHER?
HEY!!
D'ESH IS GOOD—WE DON'T TOUCH D'ESH.
UH.
P-PATRICIA.
...WHY IS THIS JUST RANDOMLY IN THE ROAD?
P-PATRICIA.
...WHAT?

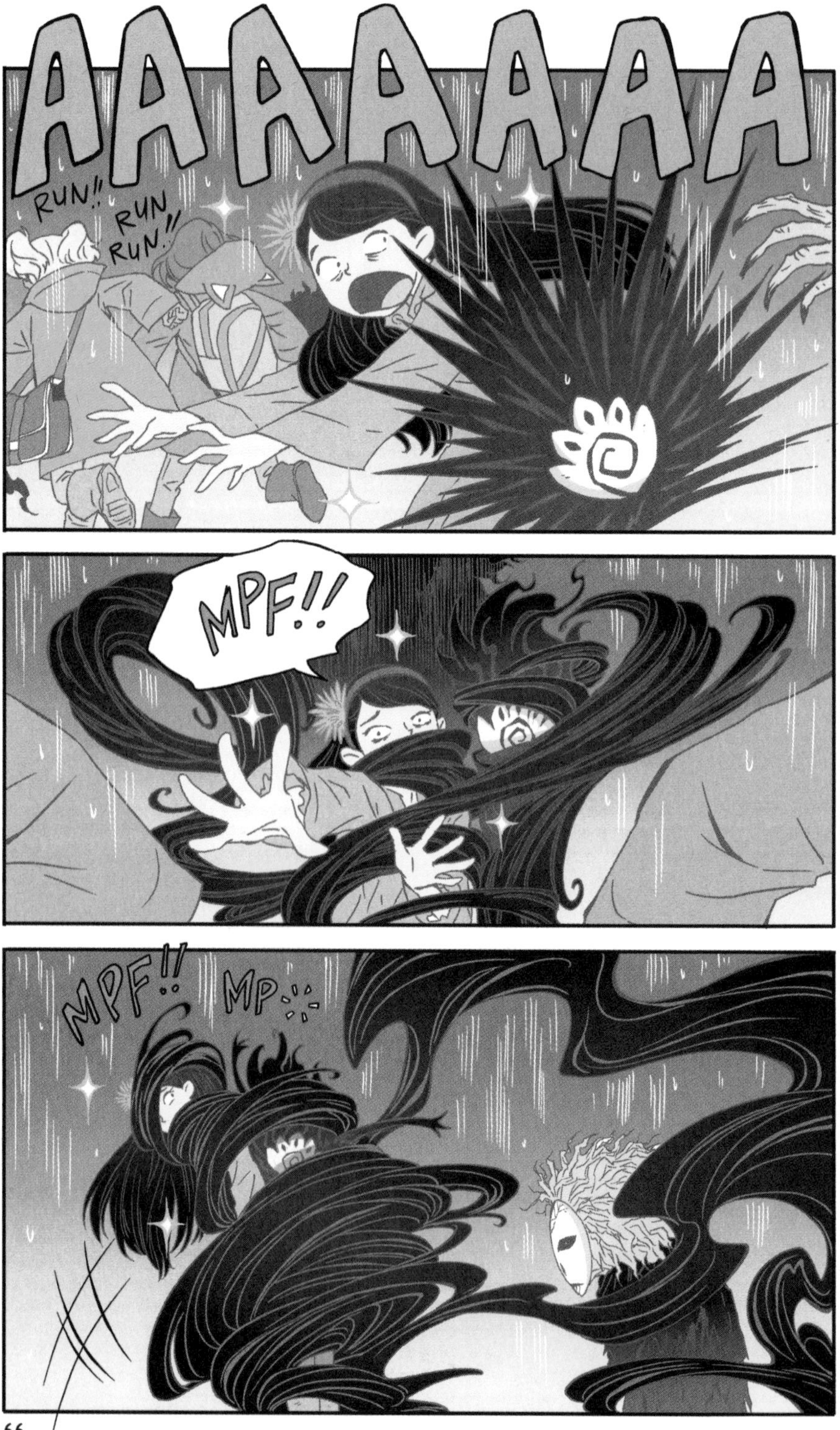
AAAAAAA
RUN!!
RUN RUN!!
MPF!!
MPF!!
MP...

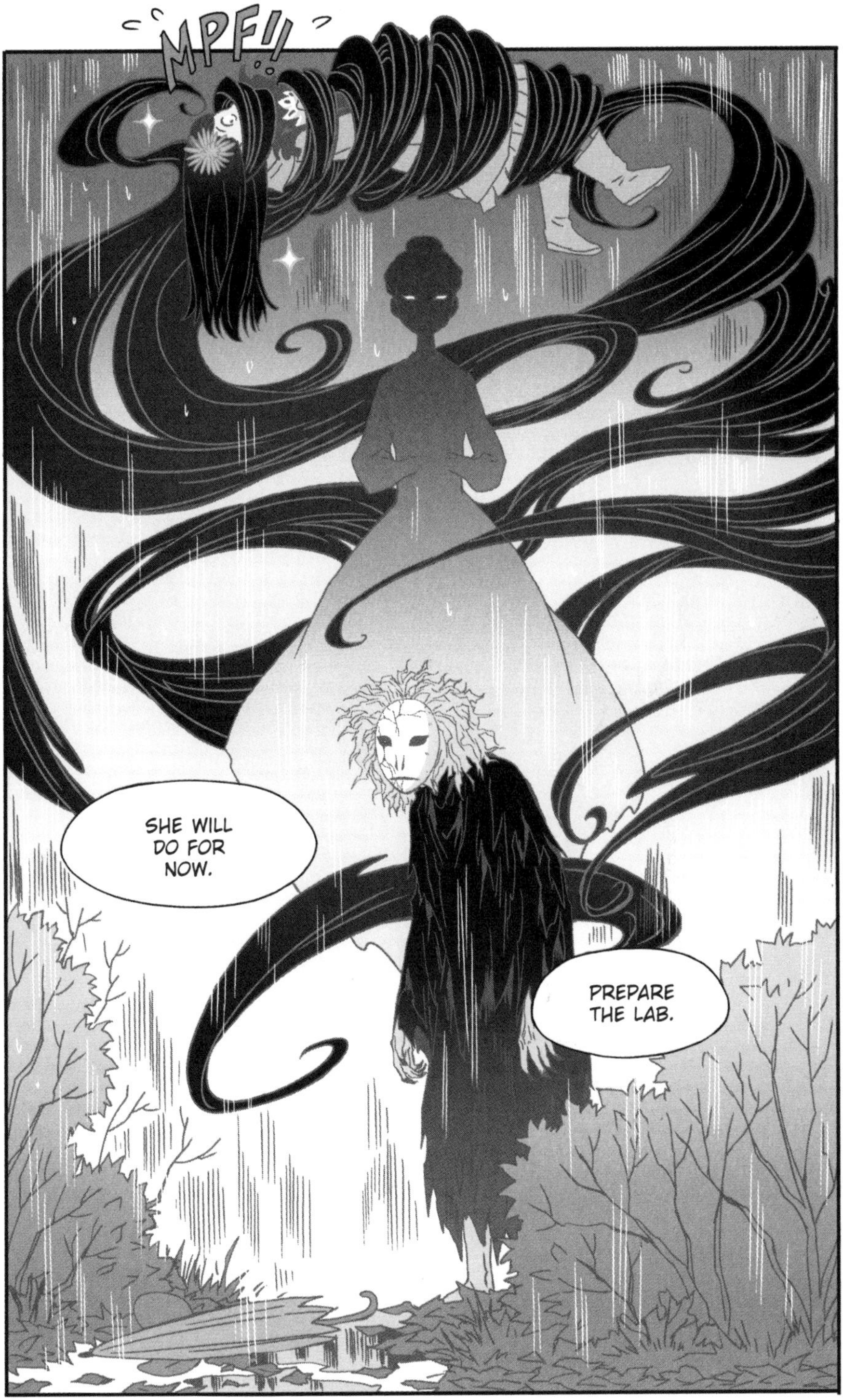
MPF!!
SHE WILL DO FOR NOW.
PREPARE THE LAB.

# Chapter 3

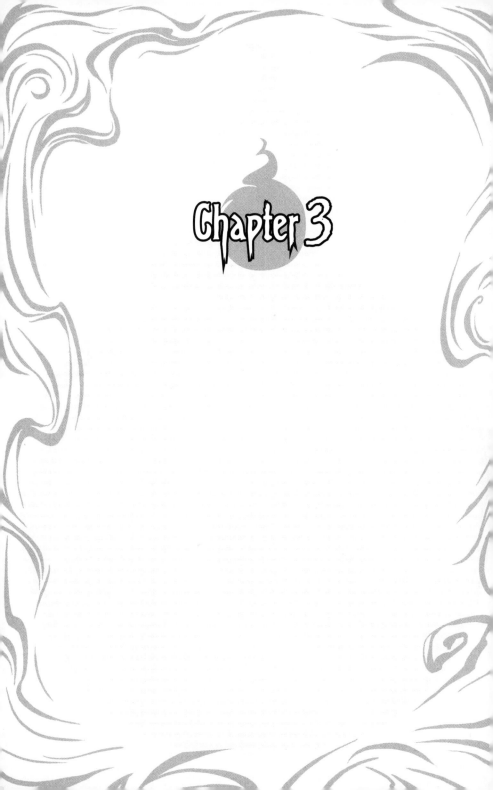

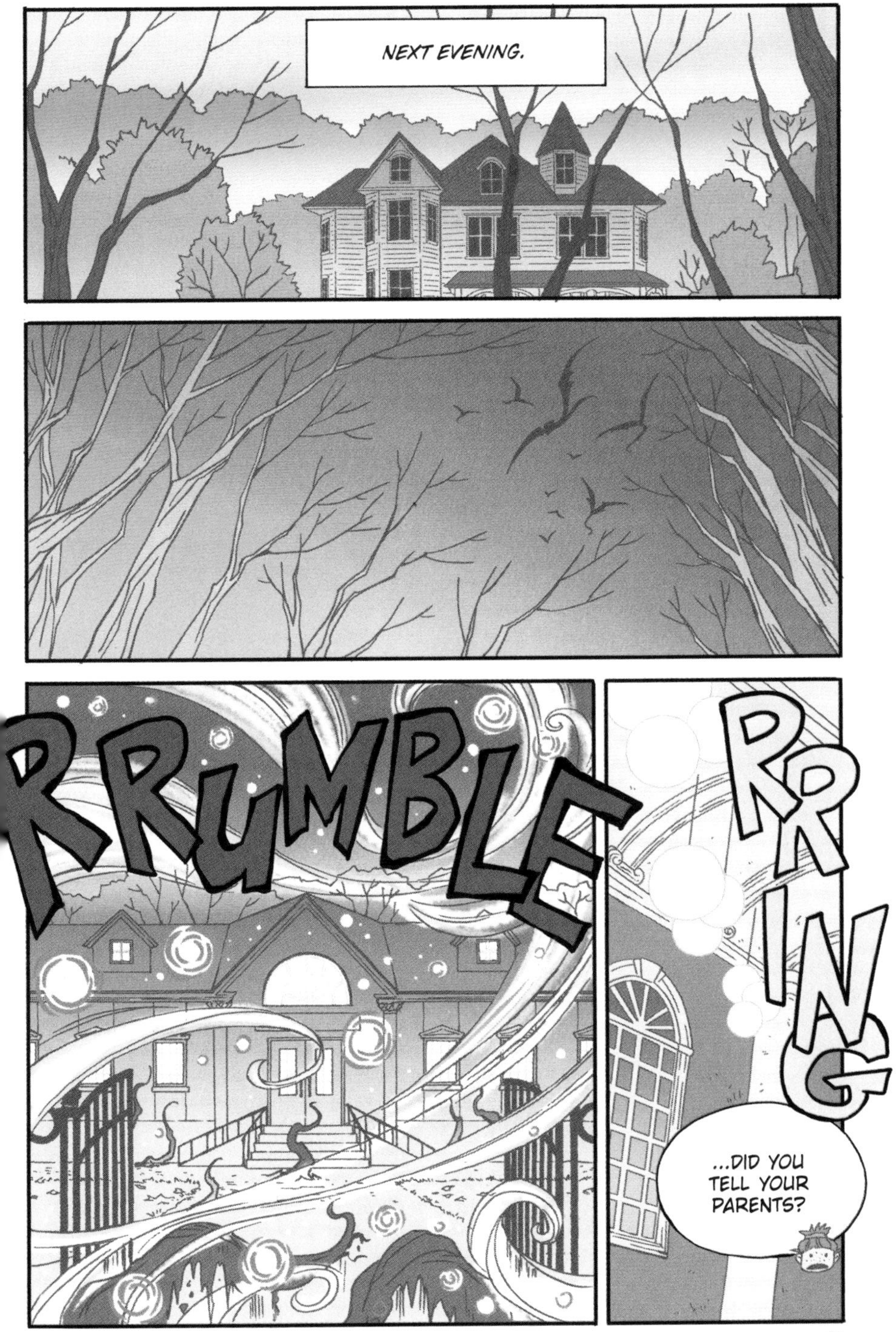
NEXT EVENING.
RRUMBLE
RRRING
...DID YOU TELL YOUR PARENTS?

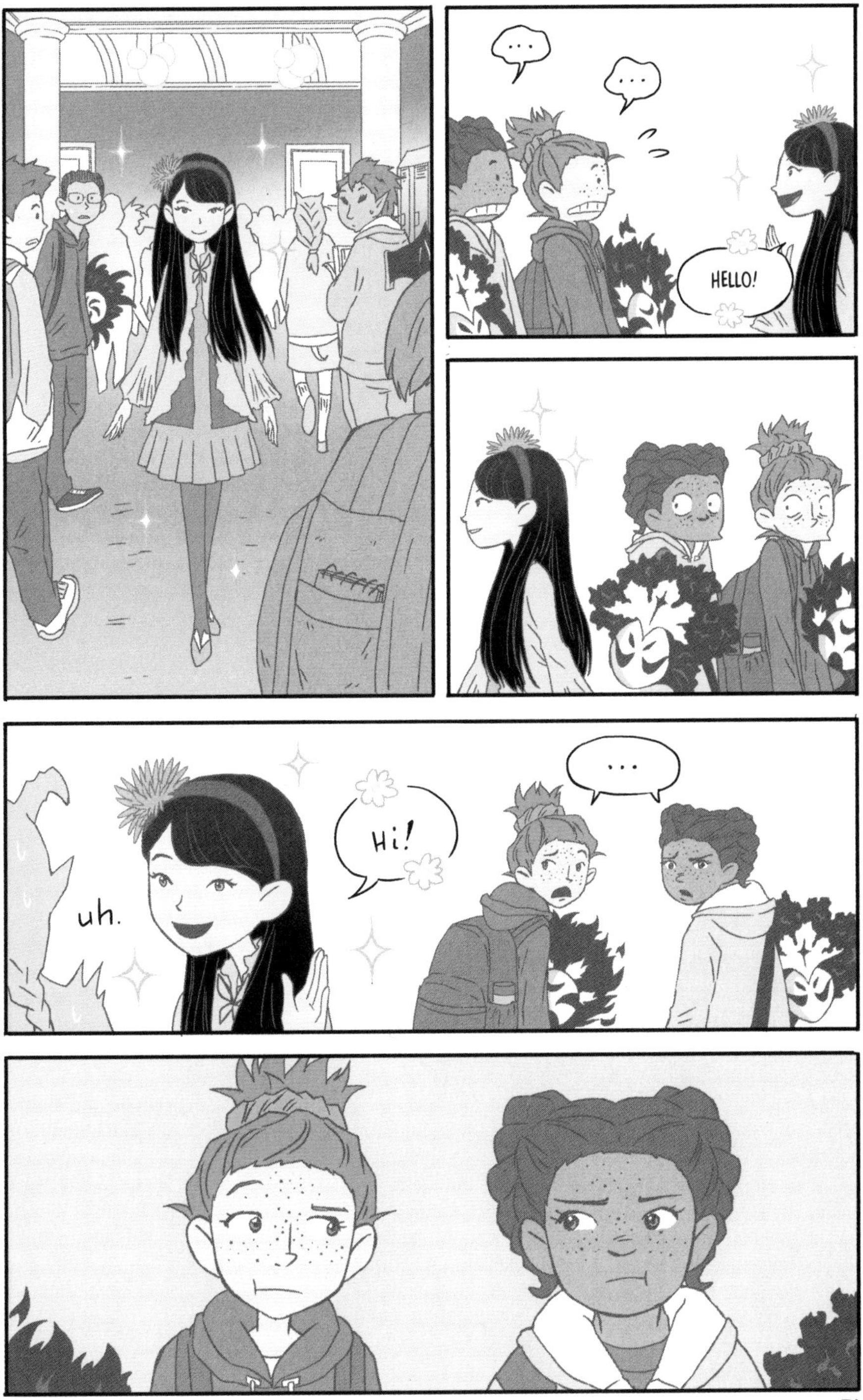
...
...
HELLO!
uh.
Hi!
...

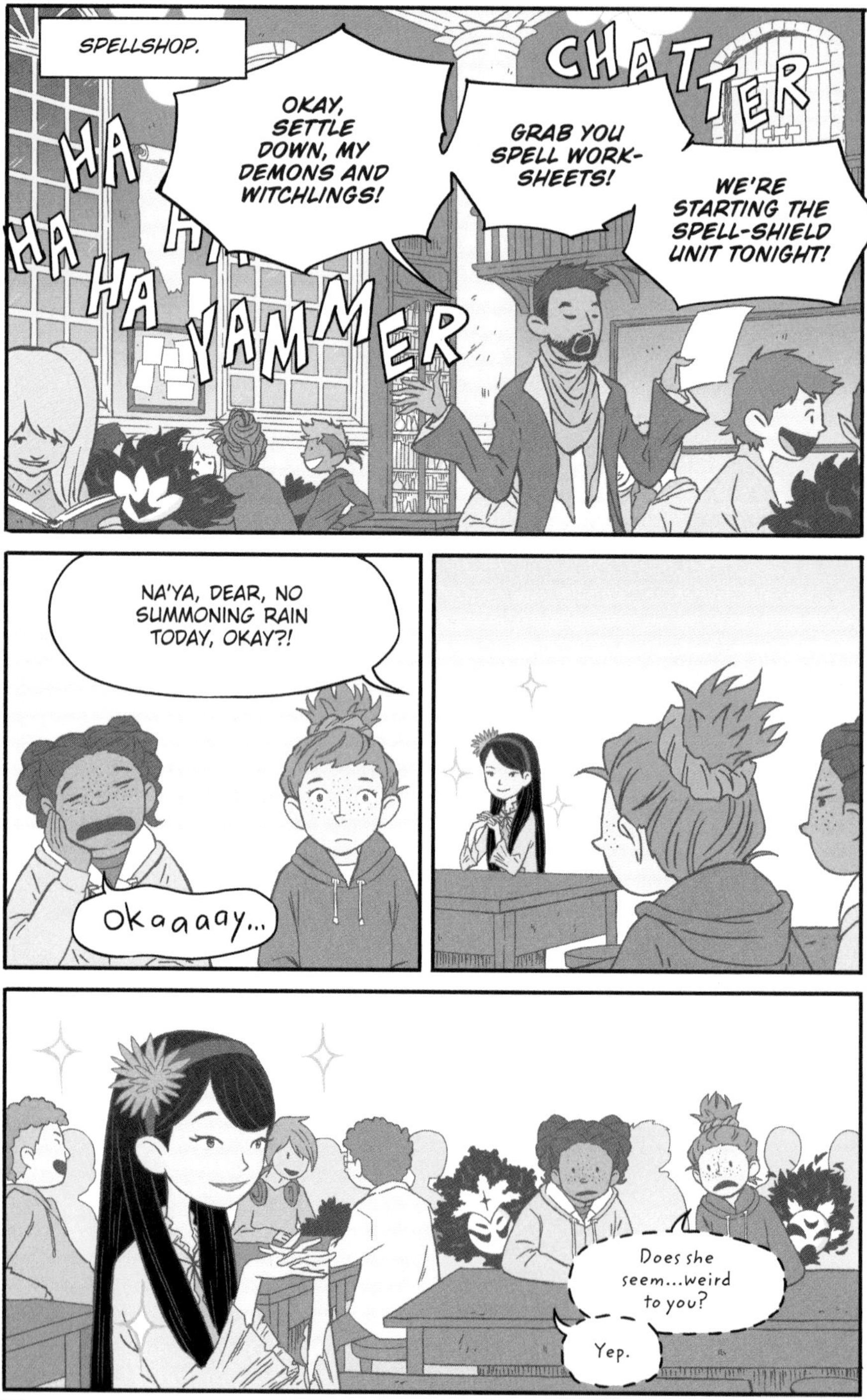
SPELLSHOP.
HA HA
HA
HA
CHATTER
YAMMER
OKAY, SETTLE DOWN, MY DEMONS AND WITCHLINGS!
GRAB YOU SPELL WORK-SHEETS!
WE'RE STARTING THE SPELL-SHIELD UNIT TONIGHT!
NA'YA, DEAR, NO SUMMONING RAIN TODAY, OKAY?!
Okaaaay...
Does she seem...weird to you?
Yep.

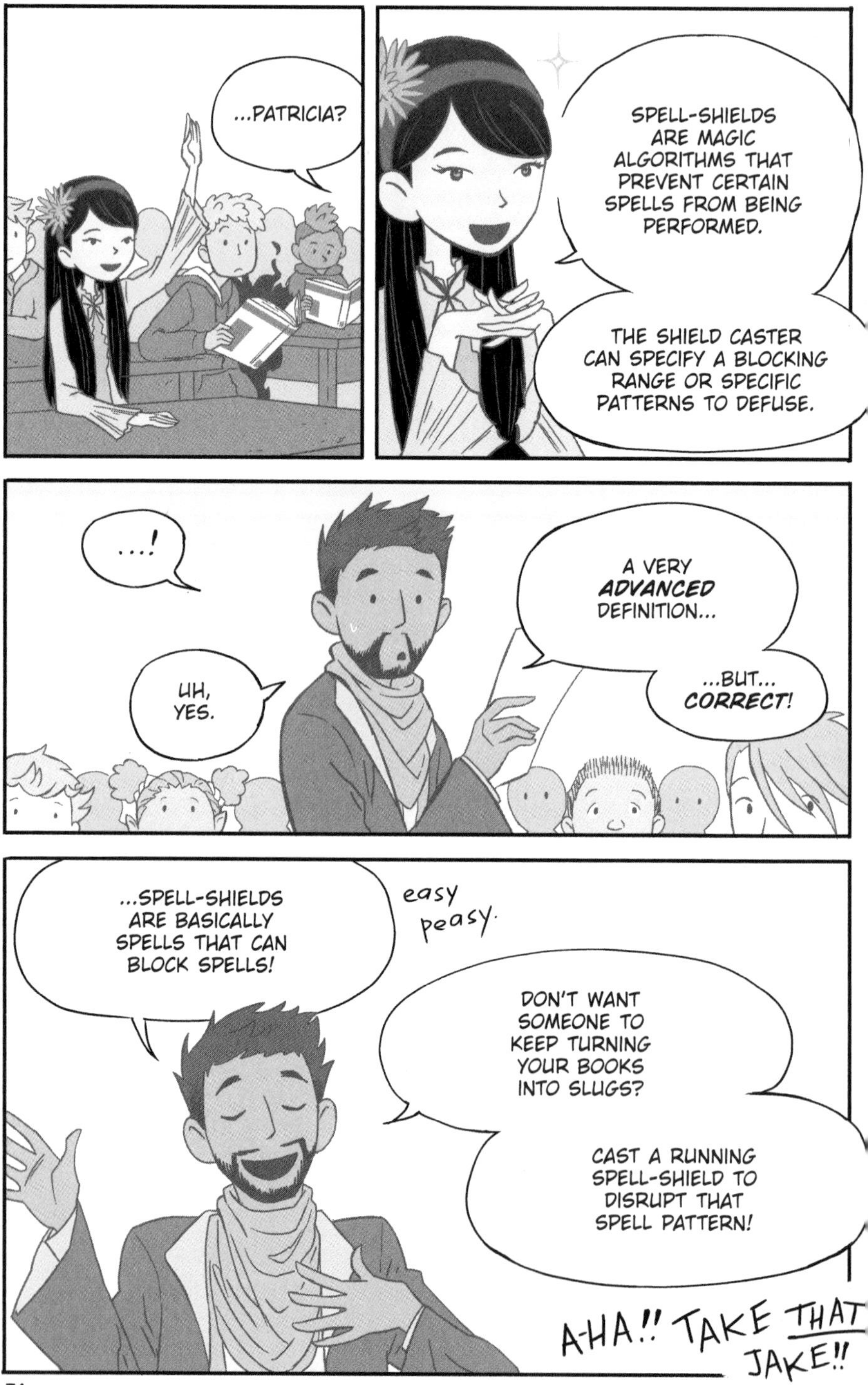
...PATRICIA?
SPELL-SHIELDS ARE MAGIC ALGORITHMS THAT PREVENT CERTAIN SPELLS FROM BEING PERFORMED.
THE SHIELD CASTER CAN SPECIFY A BLOCKING RANGE OR SPECIFIC PATTERNS TO DEFUSE.
...!
A VERY **ADVANCED** DEFINITION...
UH, YES.
...BUT... **CORRECT**!
...SPELL-SHIELDS ARE BASICALLY SPELLS THAT CAN BLOCK SPELLS!
easy peasy.
DON'T WANT SOMEONE TO KEEP TURNING YOUR BOOKS INTO SLUGS?
CAST A RUNNING SPELL-SHIELD TO DISRUPT THAT SPELL PATTERN!
A-HA!! TAKE THAT JAKE!!

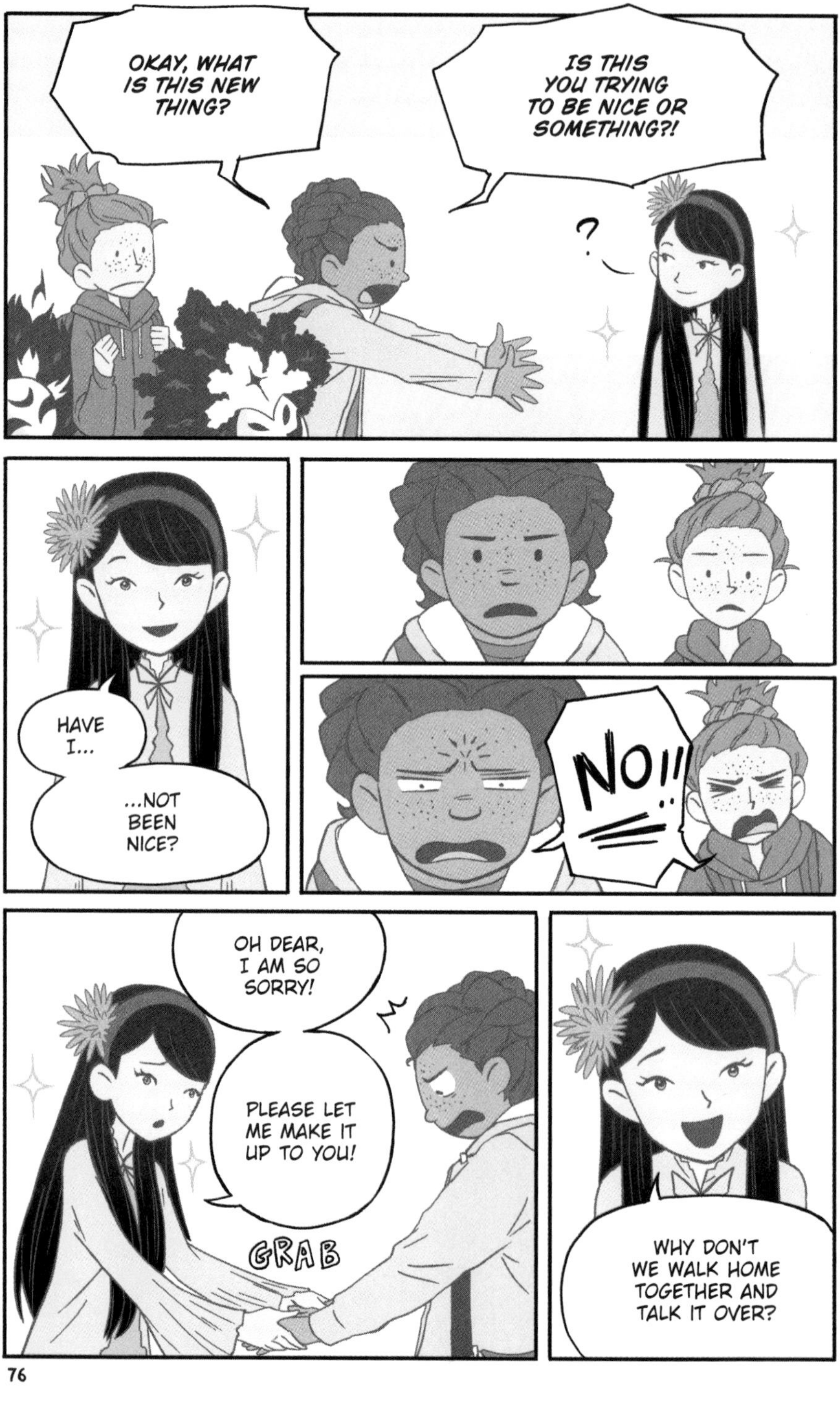
OKAY, WHAT IS THIS NEW THING?
IS THIS YOU TRYING TO BE NICE OR SOMETHING?!
?
HAVE I...
...NOT BEEN NICE?
NO!!
OH DEAR, I AM SO SORRY!
PLEASE LET ME MAKE IT UP TO YOU!
GRAB
WHY DON'T WE WALK HOME TOGETHER AND TALK IT OVER?

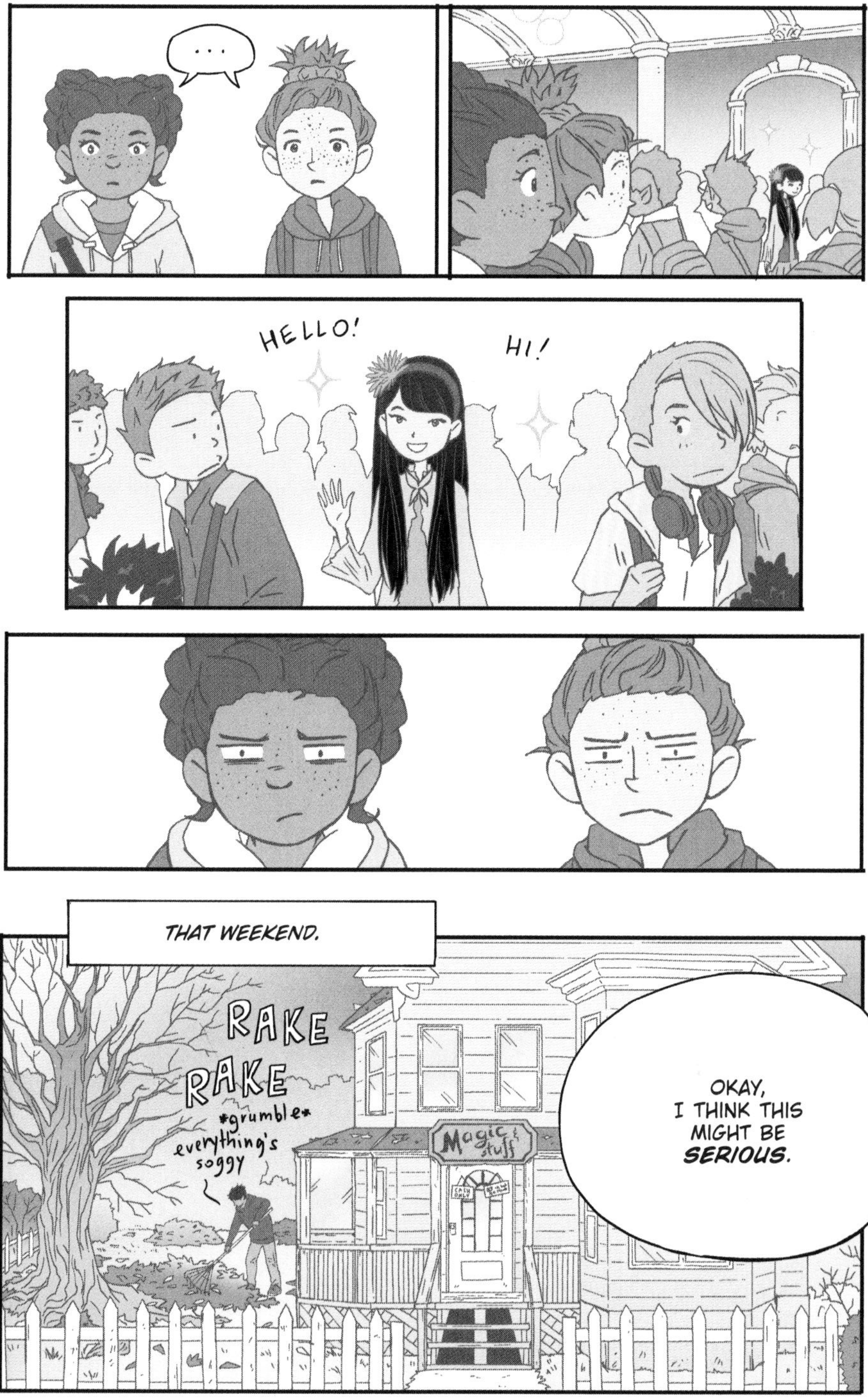
...
HELLO!
HI!
THAT WEEKEND.
RAKE
RAKE
*grumble*
everything's soggy
Magic & stuff
OKAY, I THINK THIS MIGHT BE ***SERIOUS.***

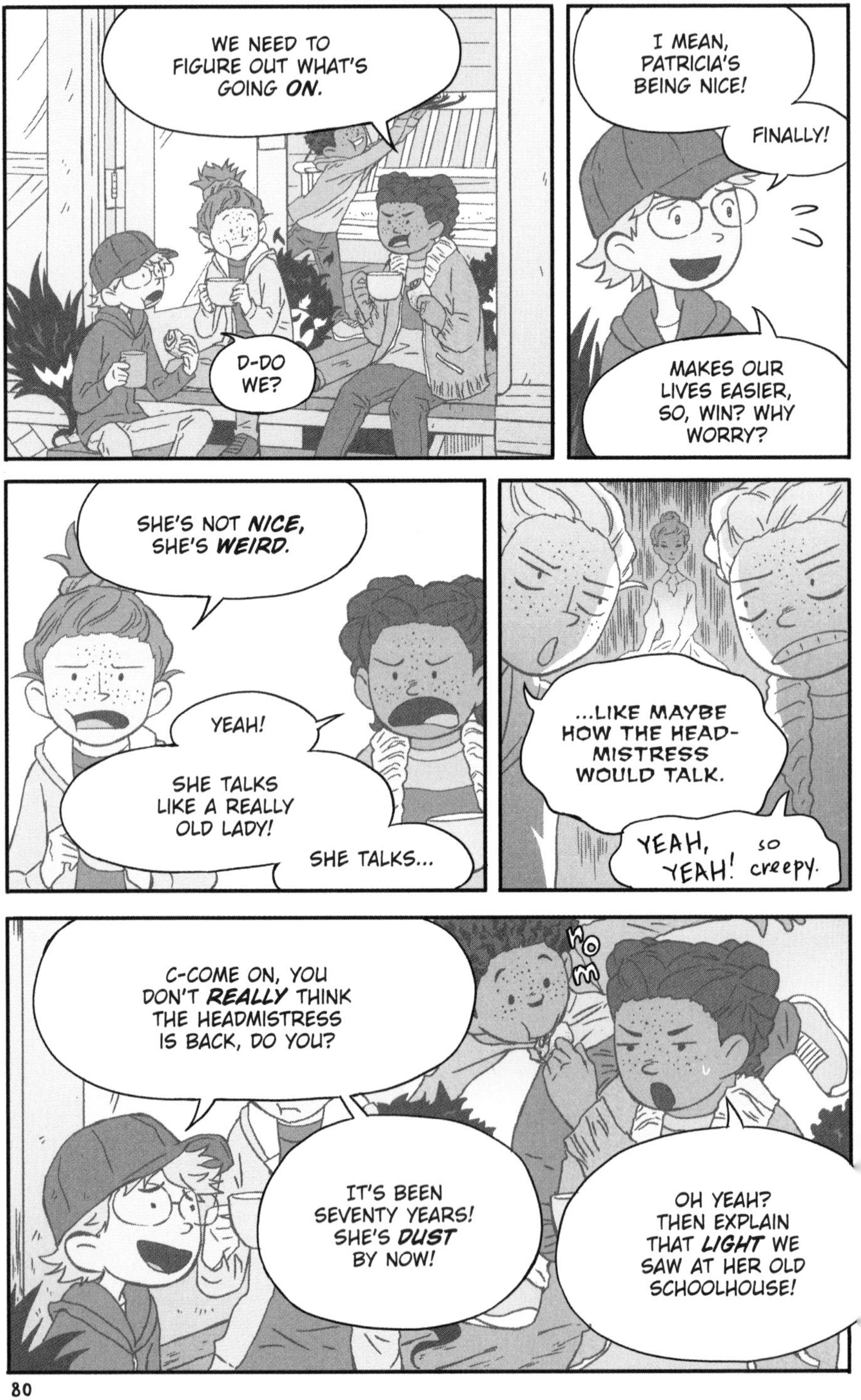
WE NEED TO FIGURE OUT WHAT'S GOING **ON**.
D-DO WE?
I MEAN, PATRICIA'S BEING NICE!
FINALLY!
MAKES OUR LIVES EASIER, SO, WIN? WHY WORRY?
SHE'S NOT ***NICE***, SHE'S ***WEIRD***.
YEAH!
SHE TALKS LIKE A REALLY OLD LADY!
SHE TALKS...
...LIKE MAYBE HOW THE HEAD-MISTRESS WOULD TALK.
YEAH, YEAH!
so creepy.
C-COME ON, YOU DON'T ***REALLY*** THINK THE HEADMISTRESS IS BACK, DO YOU?
nom
IT'S BEEN SEVENTY YEARS! SHE'S ***DUST*** BY NOW!
OH YEAH? THEN EXPLAIN THAT ***LIGHT*** WE SAW AT HER OLD SCHOOLHOUSE!

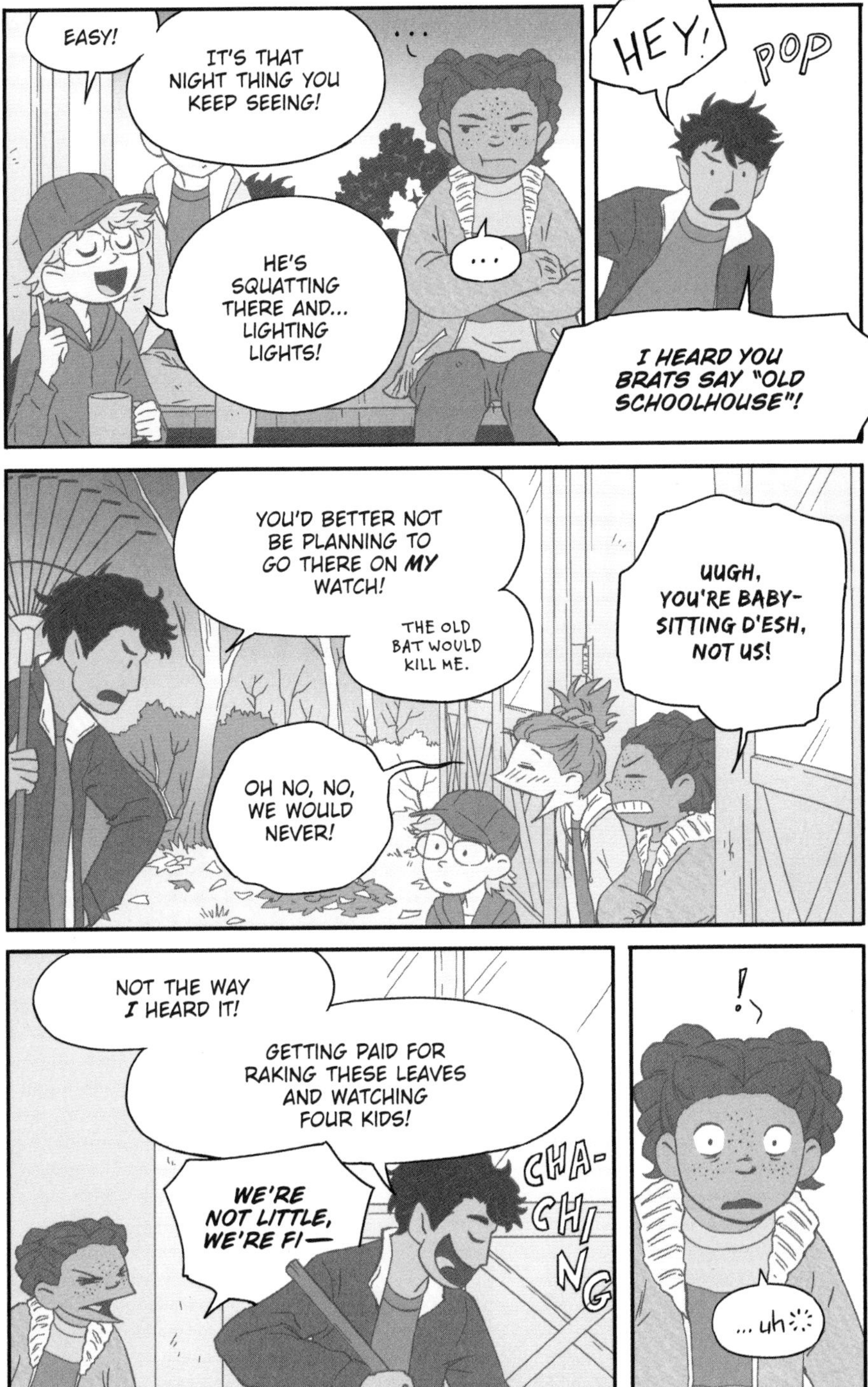
EASY!
IT'S THAT NIGHT THING YOU KEEP SEEING!
HE'S SQUATTING THERE AND... LIGHTING LIGHTS!
...
...
HEY!
POP
I HEARD YOU BRATS SAY "OLD SCHOOLHOUSE"!
YOU'D BETTER NOT BE PLANNING TO GO THERE ON MY WATCH!
THE OLD BAT WOULD KILL ME.
UUGH, YOU'RE BABY-SITTING D'ESH, NOT US!
OH NO, NO, WE WOULD NEVER!
NOT THE WAY I HEARD IT!
GETTING PAID FOR RAKING THESE LEAVES AND WATCHING FOUR KIDS!
WE'RE NOT LITTLE, WE'RE FI—
CHA-CHING
!
...uh

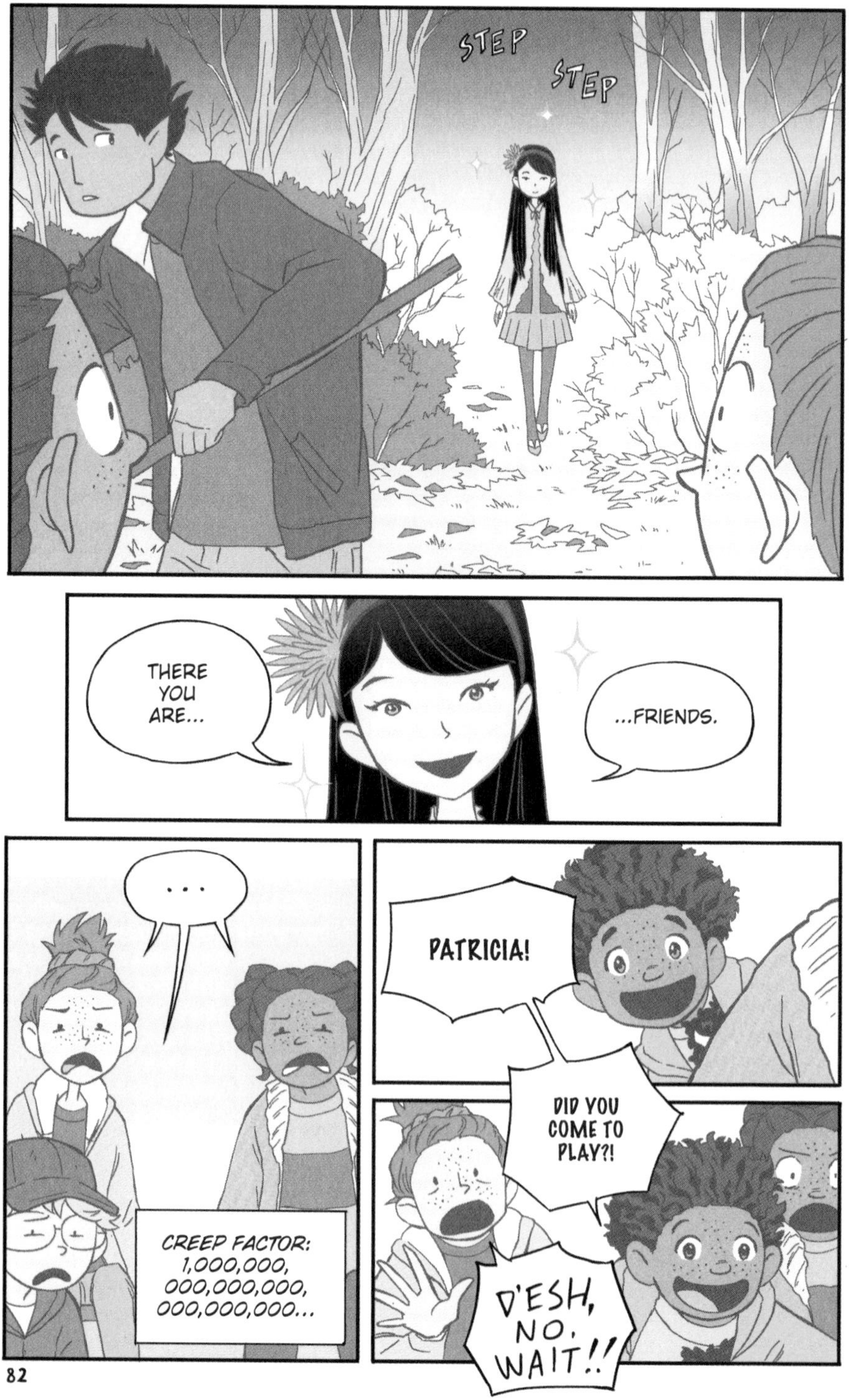
STEP
STEP
THERE YOU ARE...
...FRIENDS.
...
CREEP FACTOR: 1,000,000, 000,000,000, 000,000,000...
PATRICIA!
DID YOU COME TO PLAY?!
D'ESH, NO, WAIT!!

83

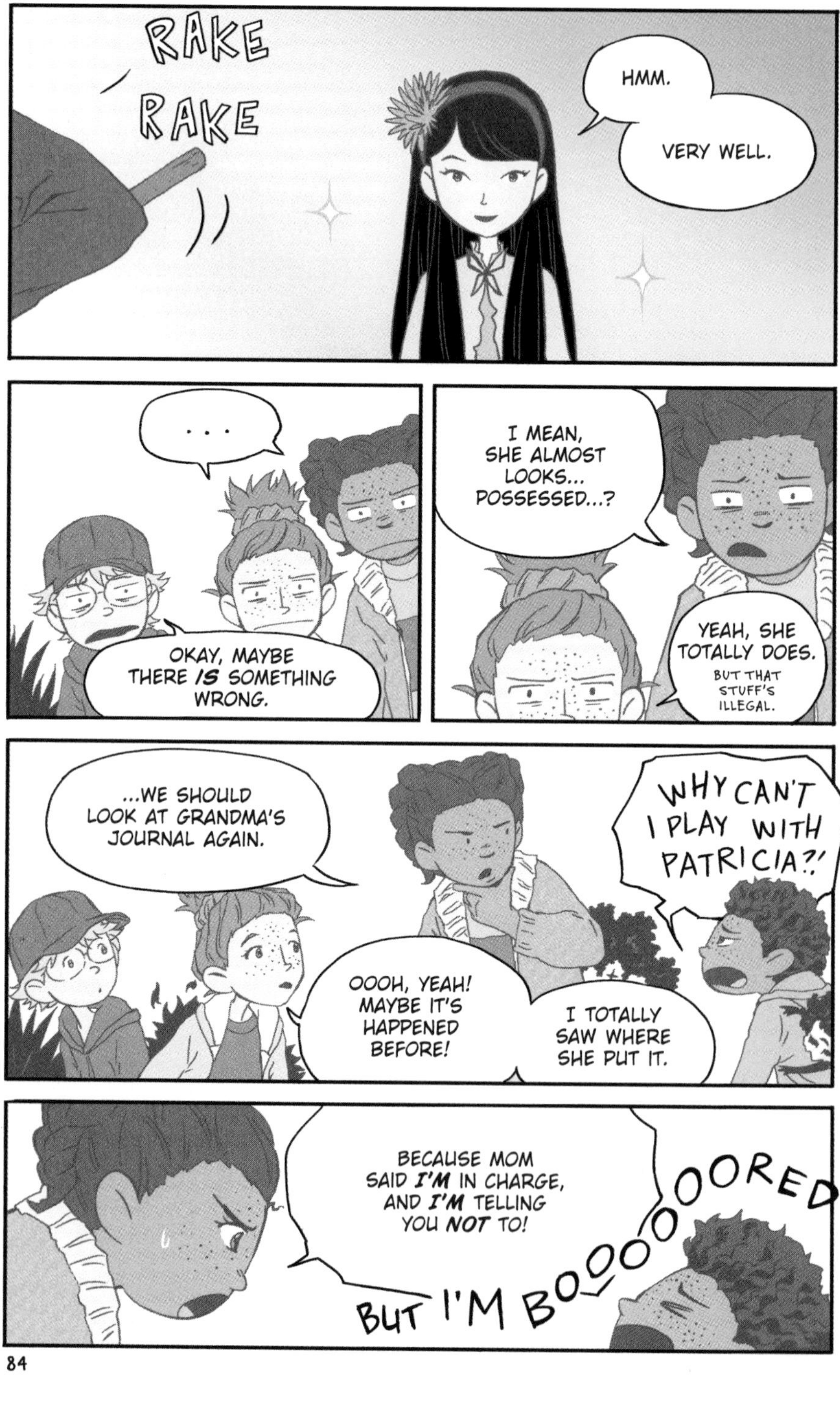
RAKE
RAKE
HMM.
VERY WELL.
...
OKAY, MAYBE THERE *IS* SOMETHING WRONG.
I MEAN, SHE ALMOST LOOKS... POSSESSED...?
YEAH, SHE TOTALLY DOES.
BUT THAT STUFF'S ILLEGAL.
...WE SHOULD LOOK AT GRANDMA'S JOURNAL AGAIN.
OOOH, YEAH! MAYBE IT'S HAPPENED BEFORE!
I TOTALLY SAW WHERE SHE PUT IT.
WHY CAN'T I PLAY WITH PATRICIA?!
BECAUSE MOM SAID ***I'M*** IN CHARGE, AND ***I'M*** TELLING YOU ***NOT*** TO!
BUT I'M BOOOOOOORED

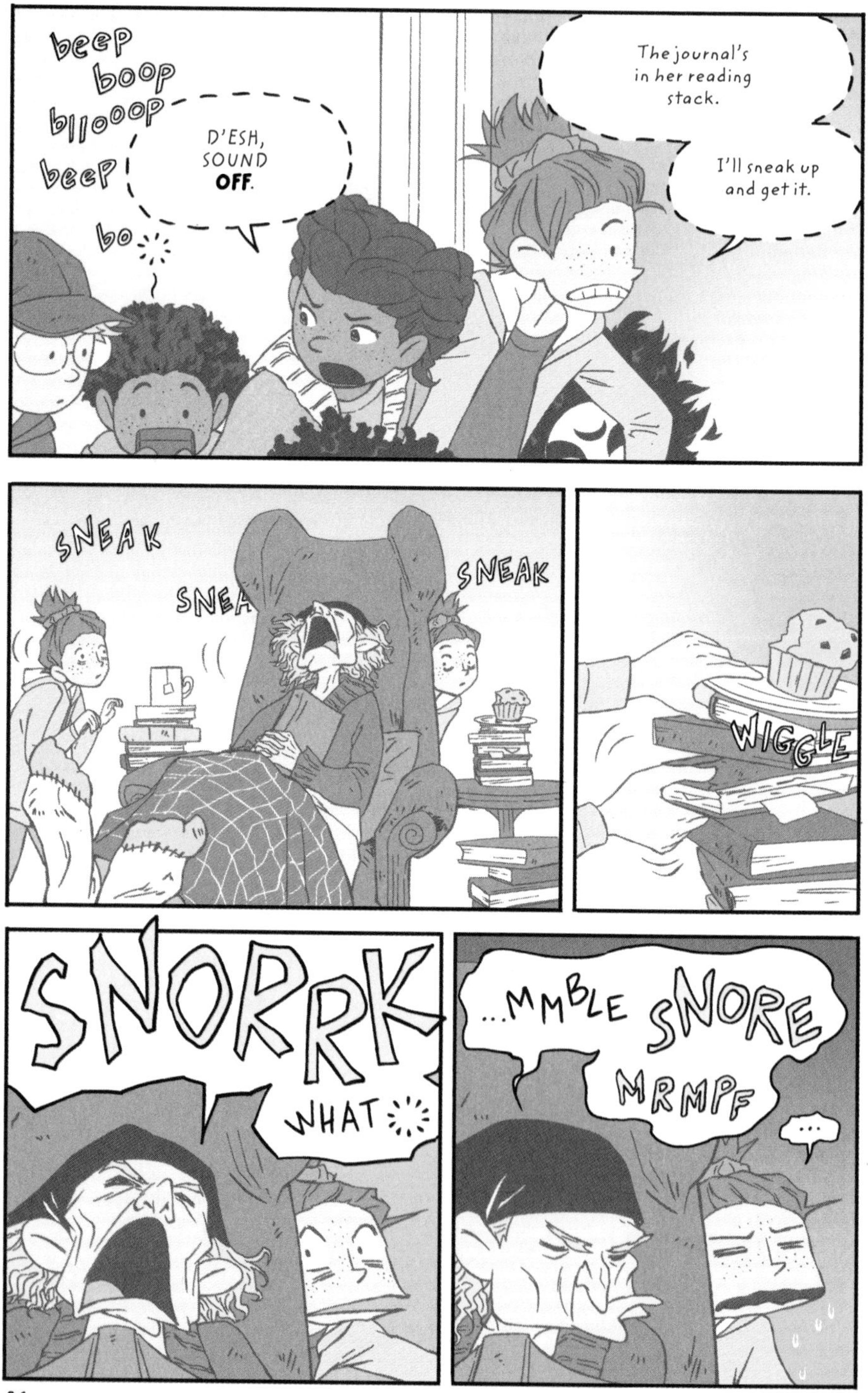
beep
boop
bllooop
beep
bo
D'ESH, SOUND **OFF**.
The journal's in her reading stack.
I'll sneak up and get it.
SNEAK
SNEAK
SNEAK
WIGGLE
SNORRK
WHAT
...MMBLE SNORE MRMPF
...

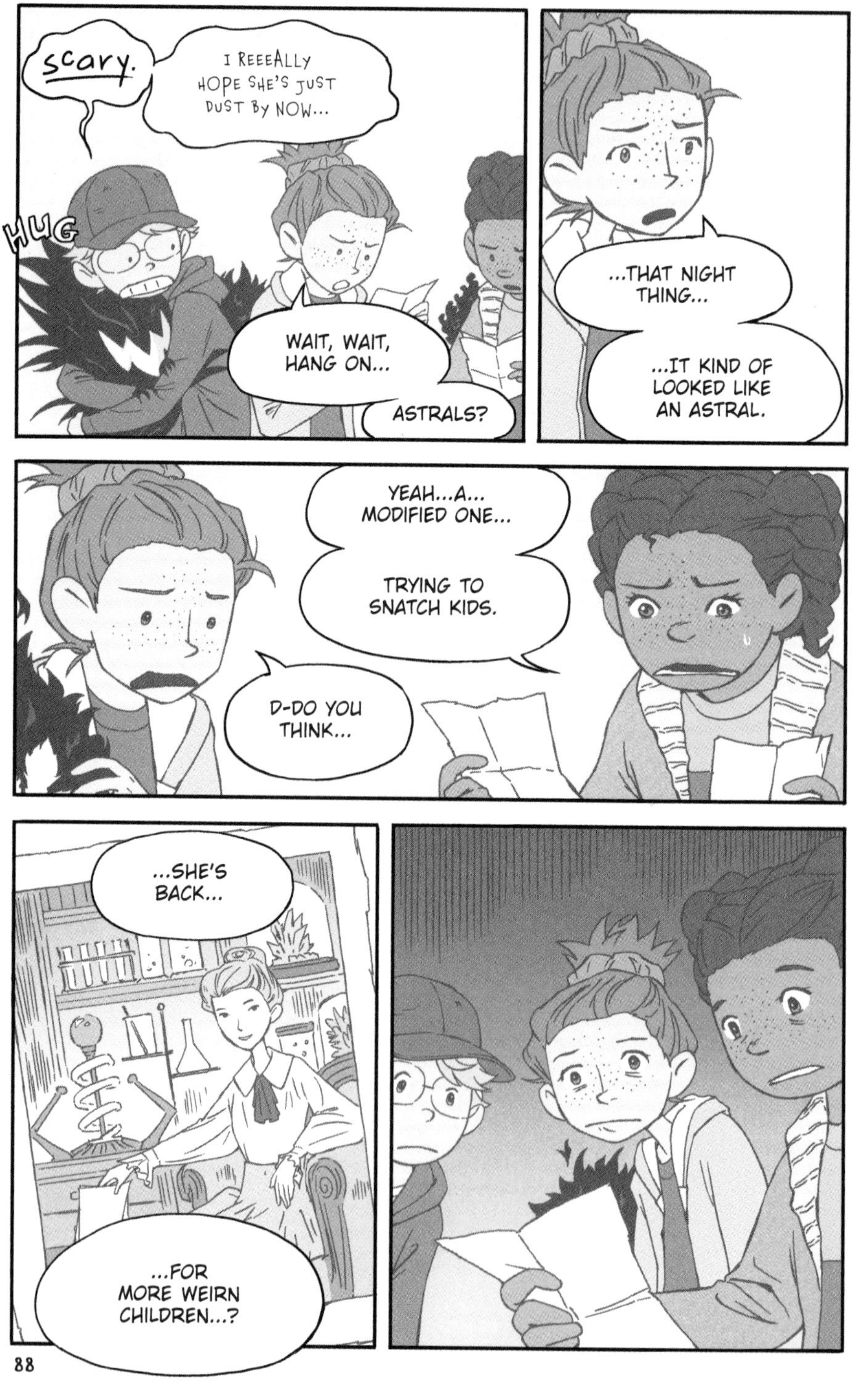
scary.
I REEEALLY HOPE SHE'S JUST DUST BY NOW...
HUG
WAIT, WAIT, HANG ON...
ASTRALS?
...THAT NIGHT THING...
...IT KIND OF LOOKED LIKE AN ASTRAL.
YEAH...A... MODIFIED ONE...
TRYING TO SNATCH KIDS.
D-DO YOU THINK...
...SHE'S BACK...
...FOR MORE WEIRN CHILDREN...?

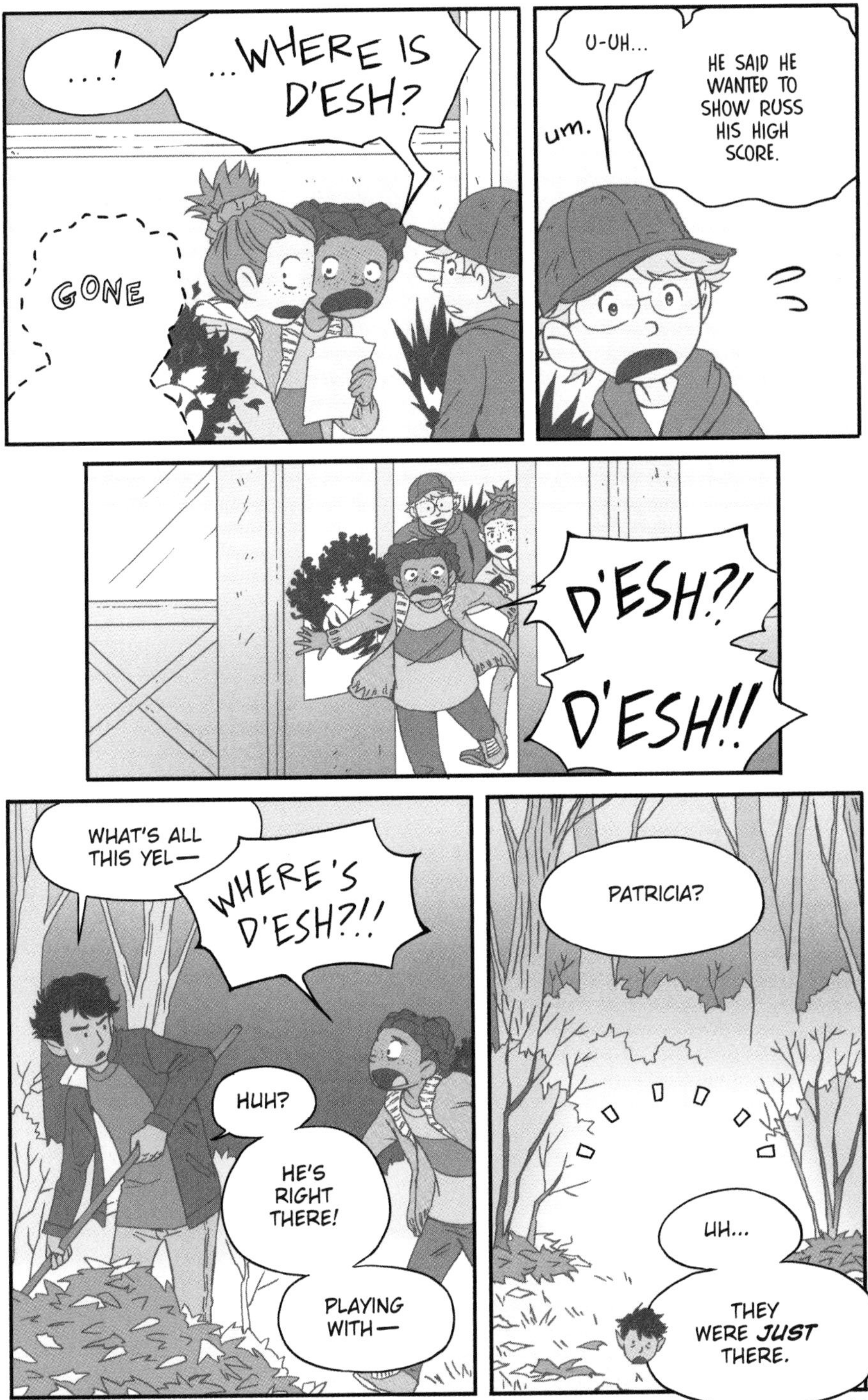
...!
...WHERE IS D'ESH?
GONE
U-UH...
um.
HE SAID HE WANTED TO SHOW RUSS HIS HIGH SCORE.
D'ESH?!
D'ESH!!
WHAT'S ALL THIS YEL—
WHERE'S D'ESH?!!
HUH?
HE'S RIGHT THERE!
PLAYING WITH—
PATRICIA?
UH...
THEY WERE *JUST* THERE.

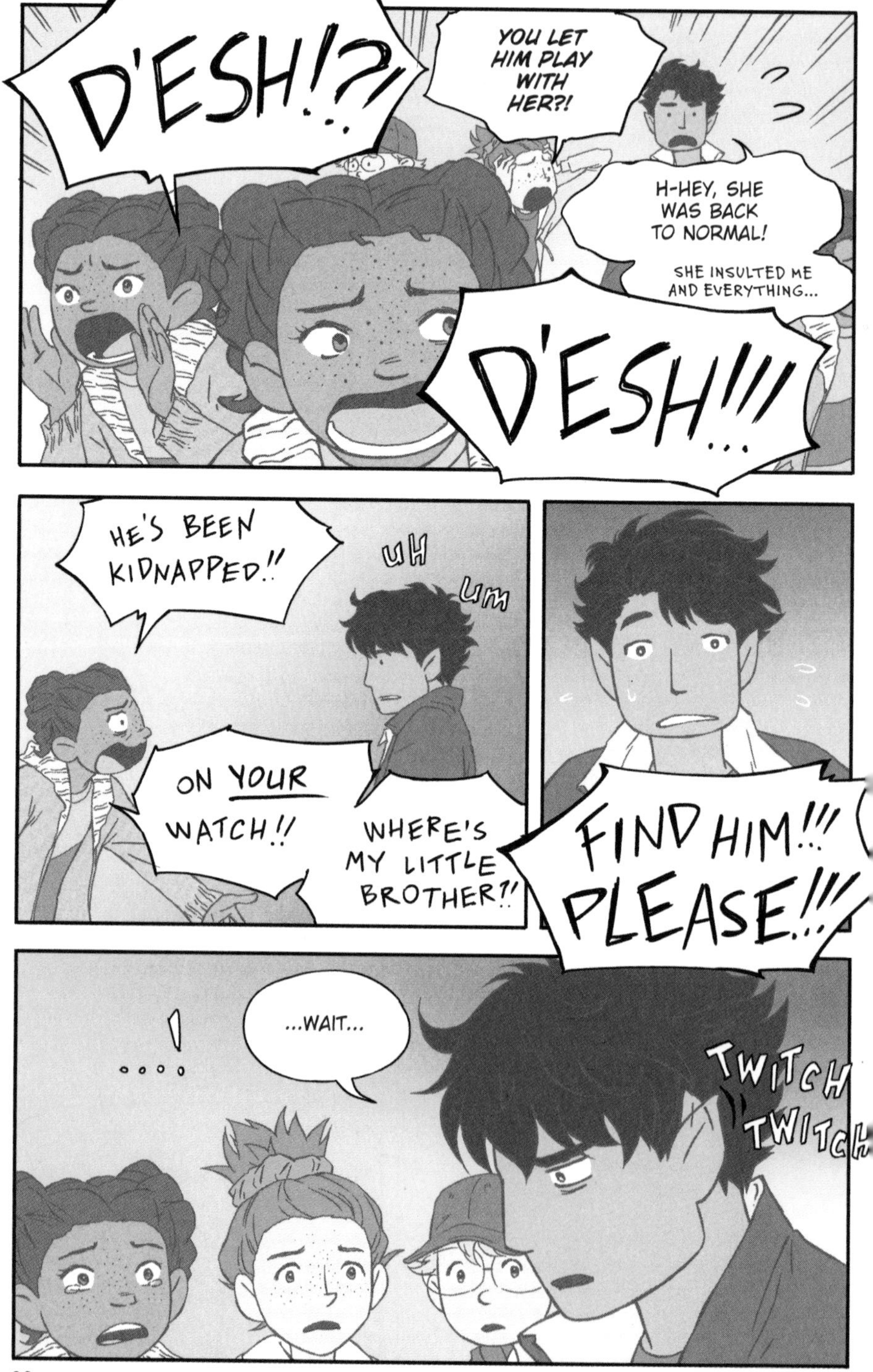
D'ESH!?!
YOU LET HIM PLAY WITH HER?!
H-HEY, SHE WAS BACK TO NORMAL!
SHE INSULTED ME AND EVERYTHING...
D'ESH!!!
HE'S BEEN KIDNAPPED!!
UH
UM
ON YOUR WATCH!!
WHERE'S MY LITTLE BROTHER?!
FIND HIM!!!
PLEASE!!!
!
....
...WAIT...
TWITCH
TWITCH

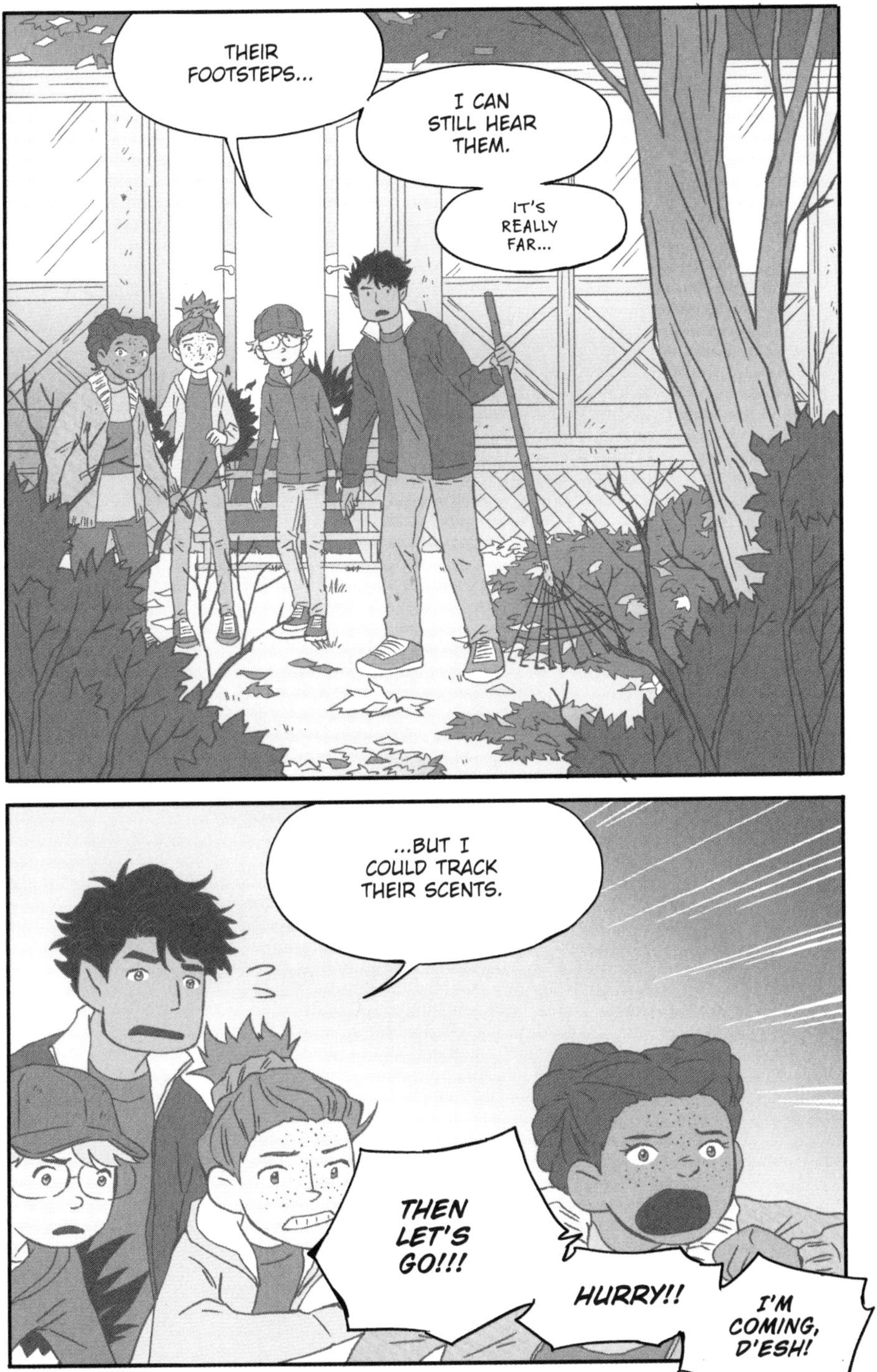
THEIR FOOTSTEPS...
I CAN STILL HEAR THEM.
IT'S REALLY FAR...
...BUT I COULD TRACK THEIR SCENTS.
THEN LET'S GO!!!
HURRY!!
I'M COMING, D'ESH!

Chapter 4

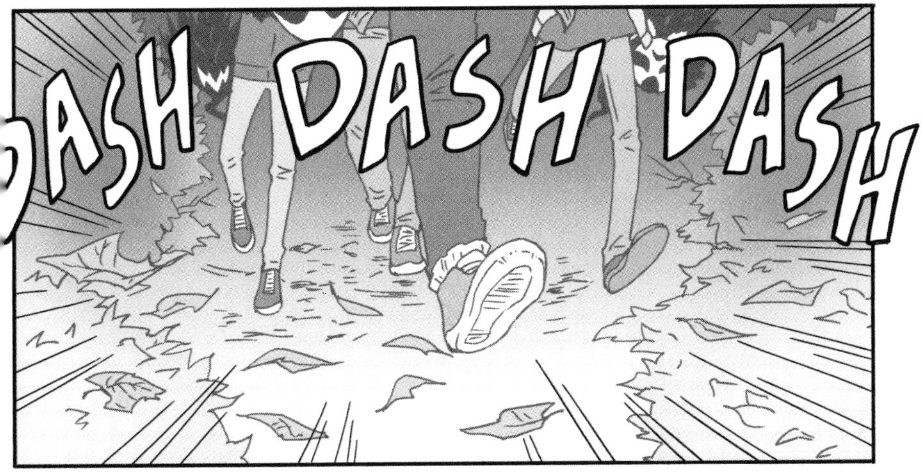
DASH DASH DASH

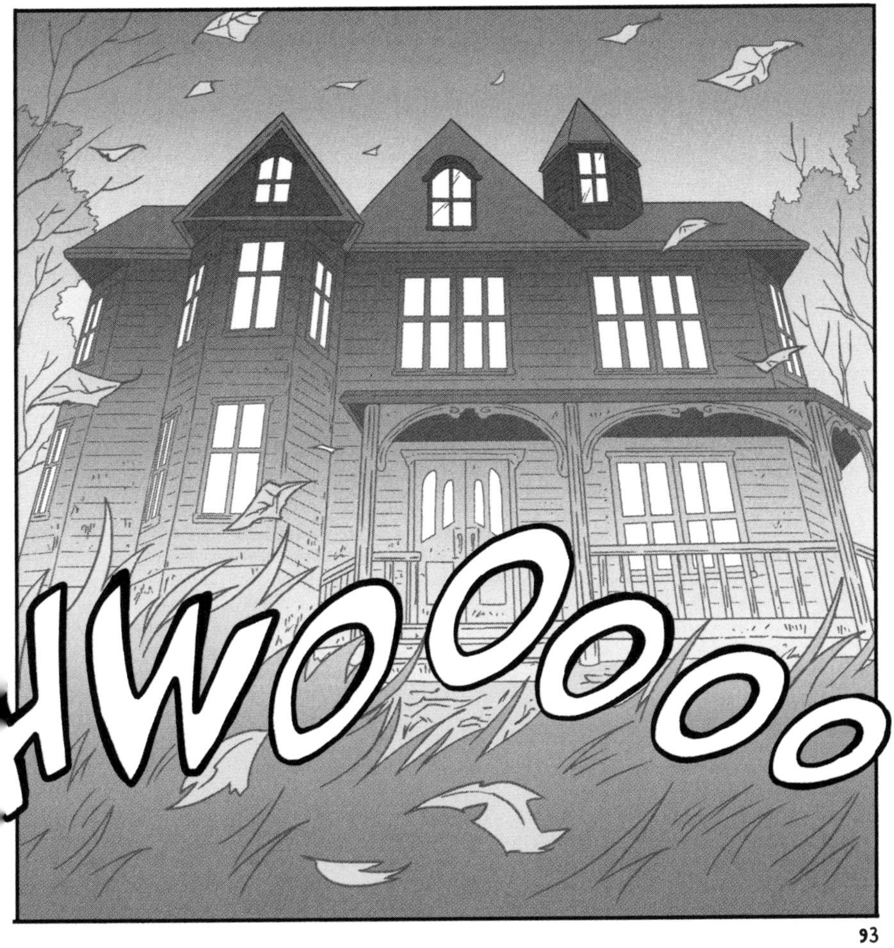
HWOOOOOO

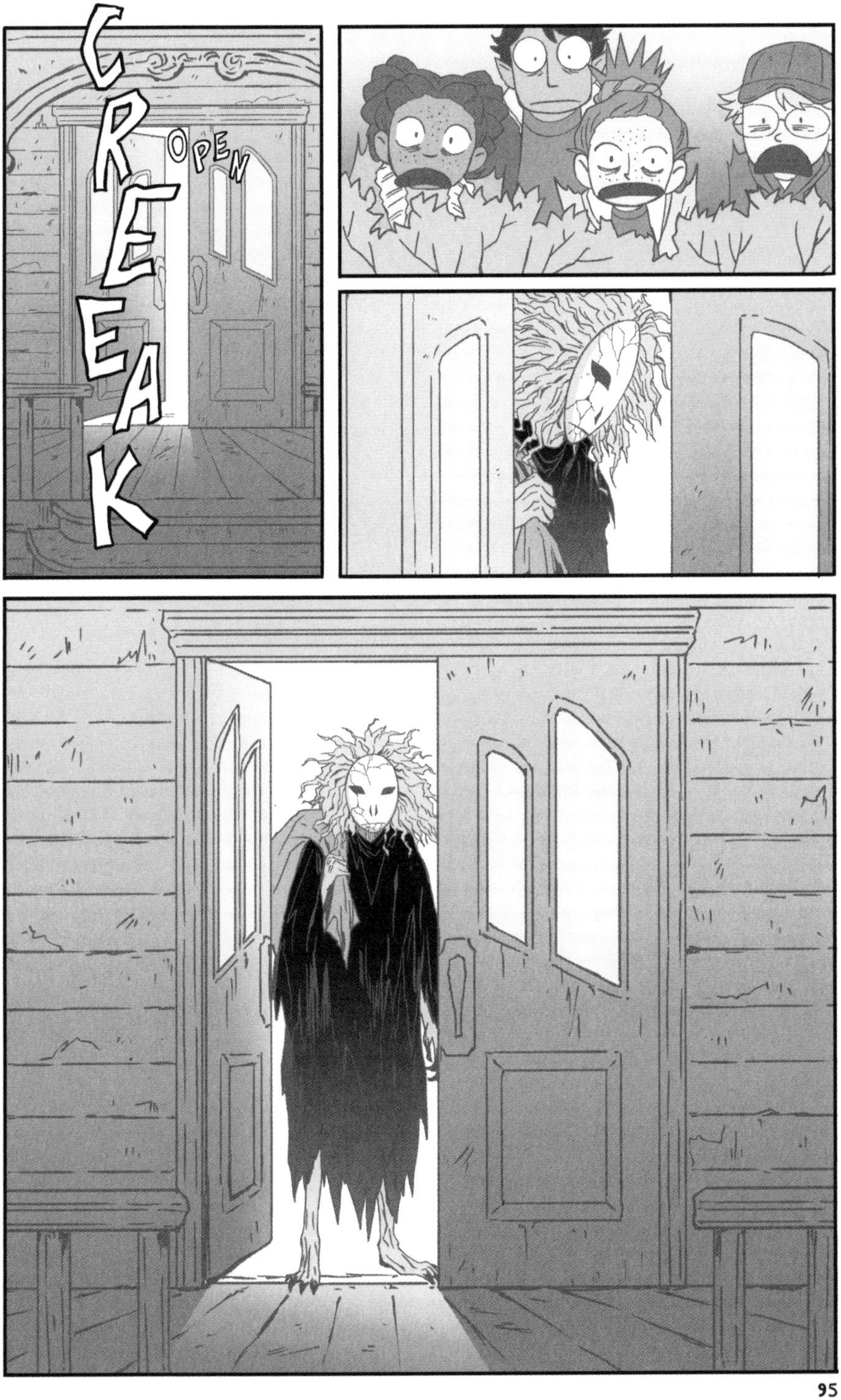
CREEAK
OPEN

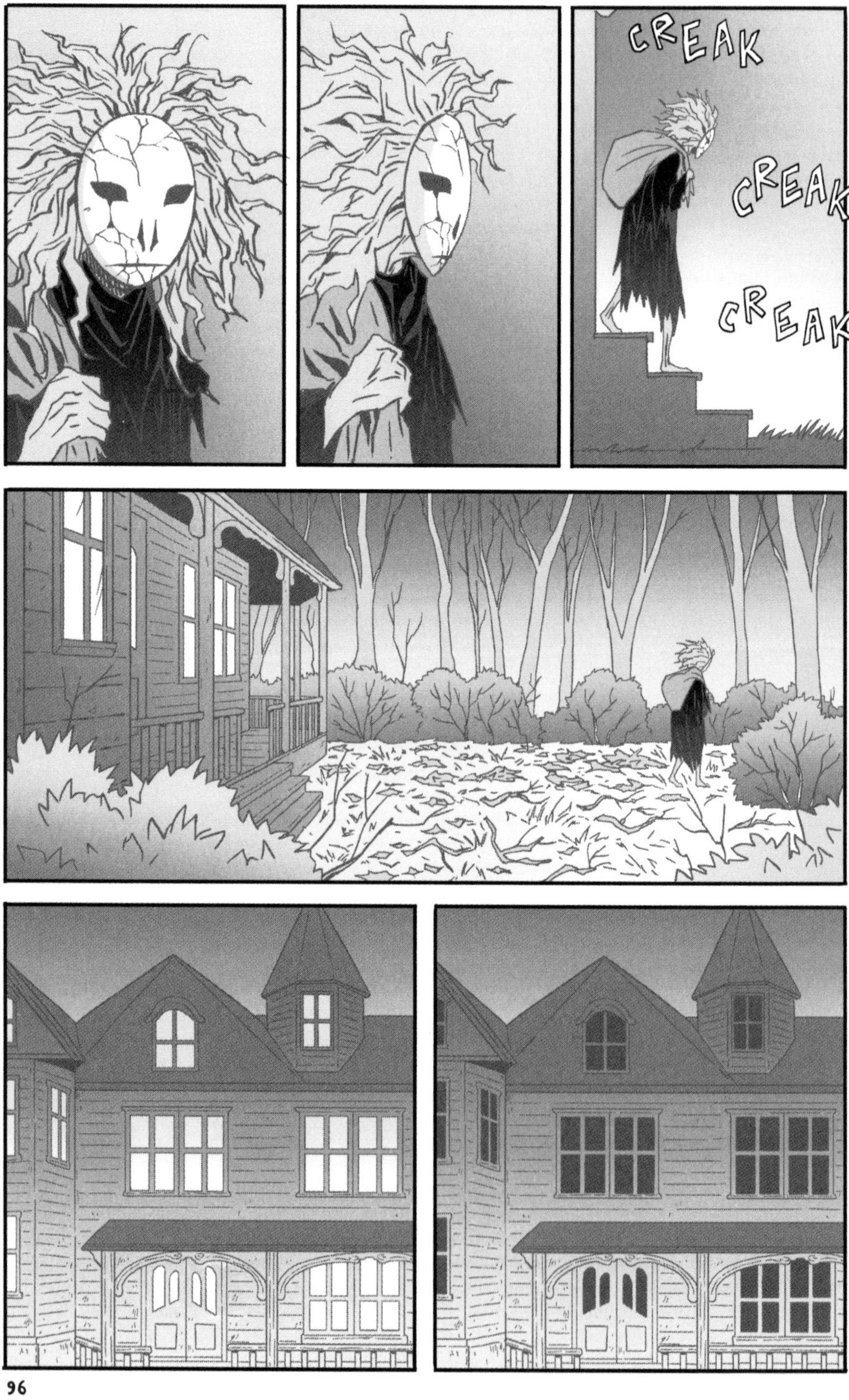
CREAK
CREAK
CREAK

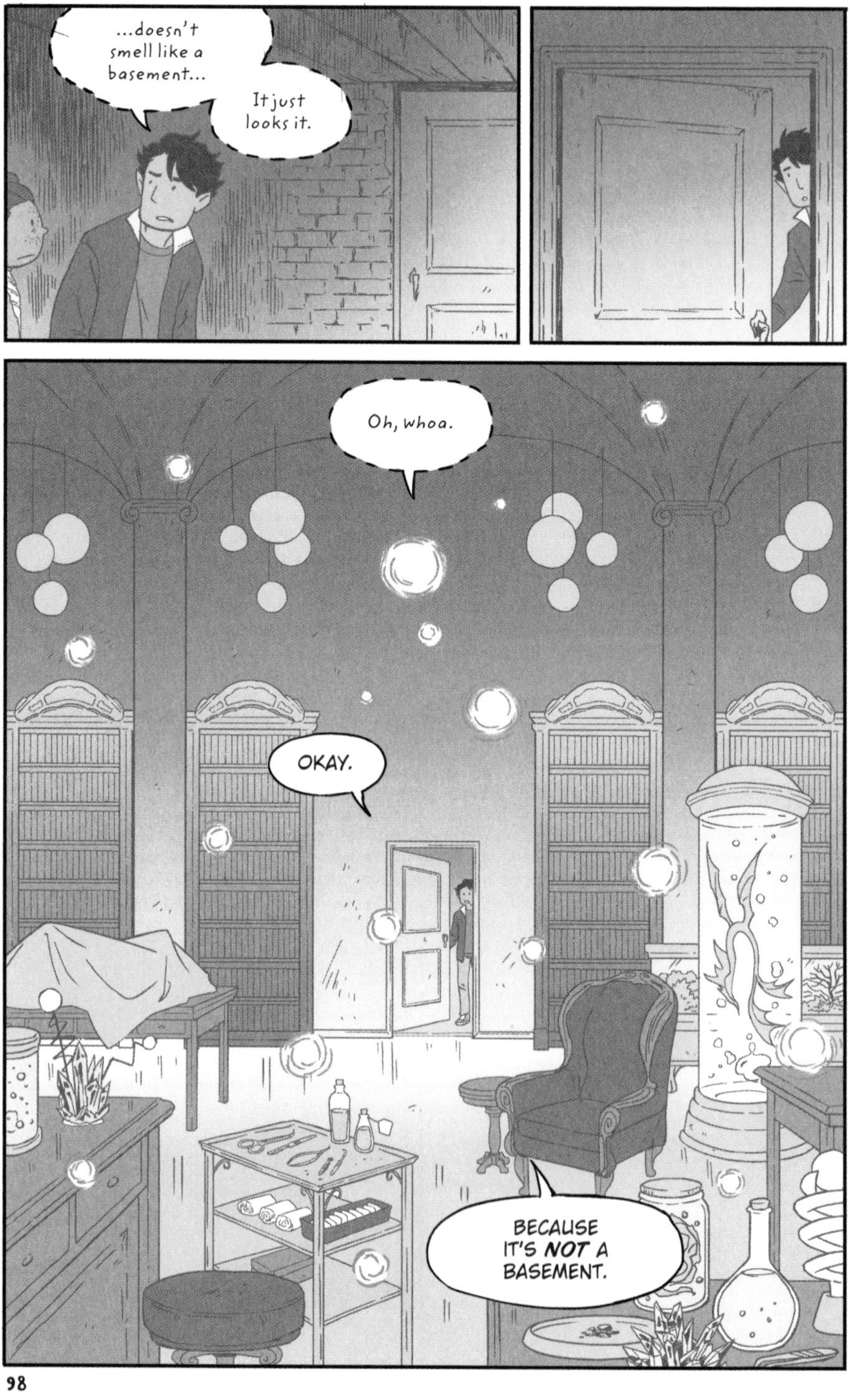
...doesn't smell like a basement...
It just looks it.
Oh, whoa.
OKAY.
BECAUSE IT'S ***NOT*** A BASEMENT.

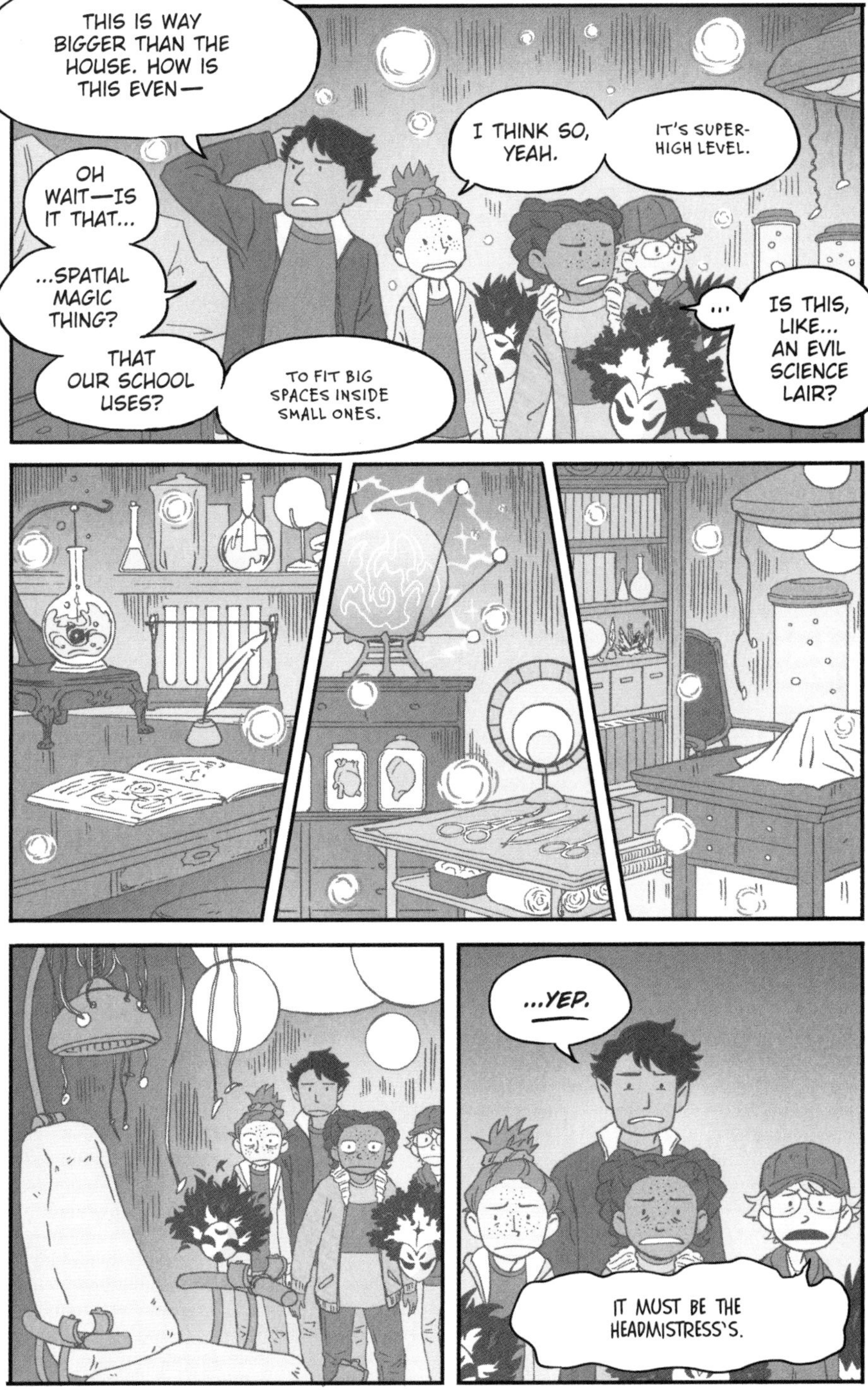
THIS IS WAY BIGGER THAN THE HOUSE. HOW IS THIS EVEN—
OH WAIT—IS IT THAT...
...SPATIAL MAGIC THING?
THAT OUR SCHOOL USES?
TO FIT BIG SPACES INSIDE SMALL ONES.
I THINK SO, YEAH.
IT'S SUPER-HIGH LEVEL.
...
IS THIS, LIKE... AN EVIL SCIENCE LAIR?
...YEP.
IT MUST BE THE HEADMISTRESS'S.

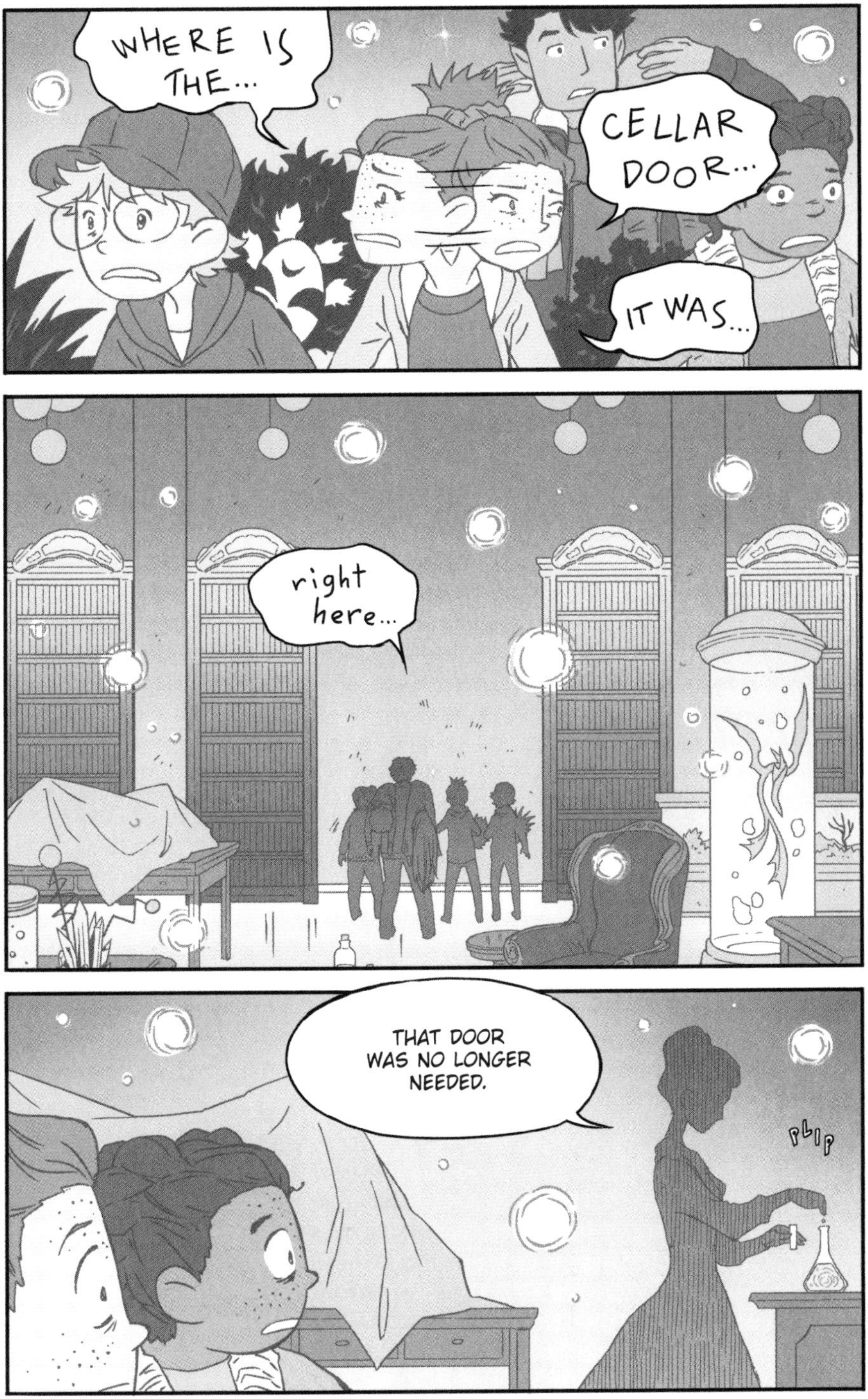
WHERE IS THE...
CELLAR DOOR...
IT WAS...
right here...
THAT DOOR WAS NO LONGER NEEDED.
PLIP

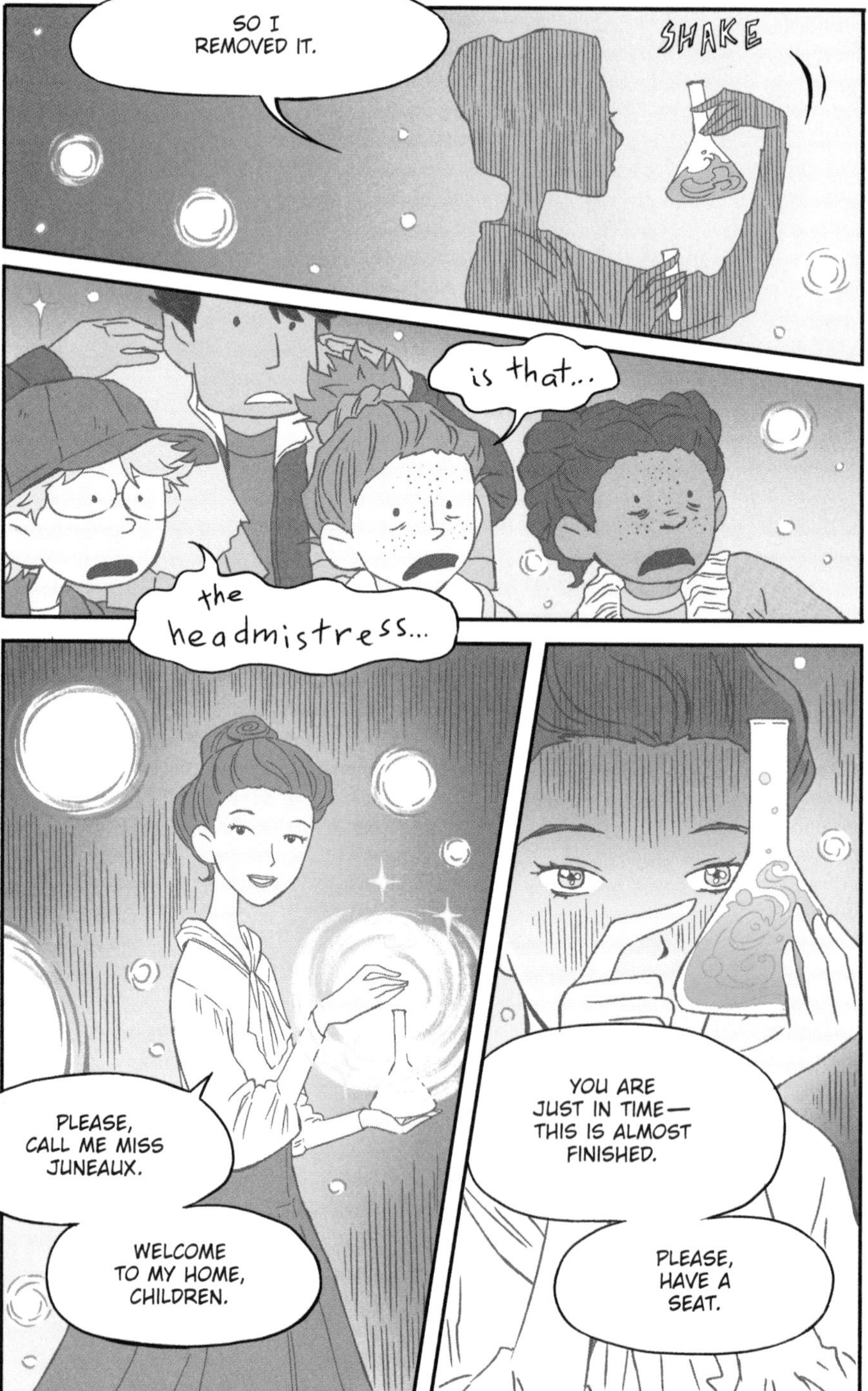

SO I REMOVED IT.
SHAKE
is that...
the headmistress...
PLEASE, CALL ME MISS JUNEAUX.
WELCOME TO MY HOME, CHILDREN.
YOU ARE JUST IN TIME— THIS IS ALMOST FINISHED.
PLEASE, HAVE A SEAT.

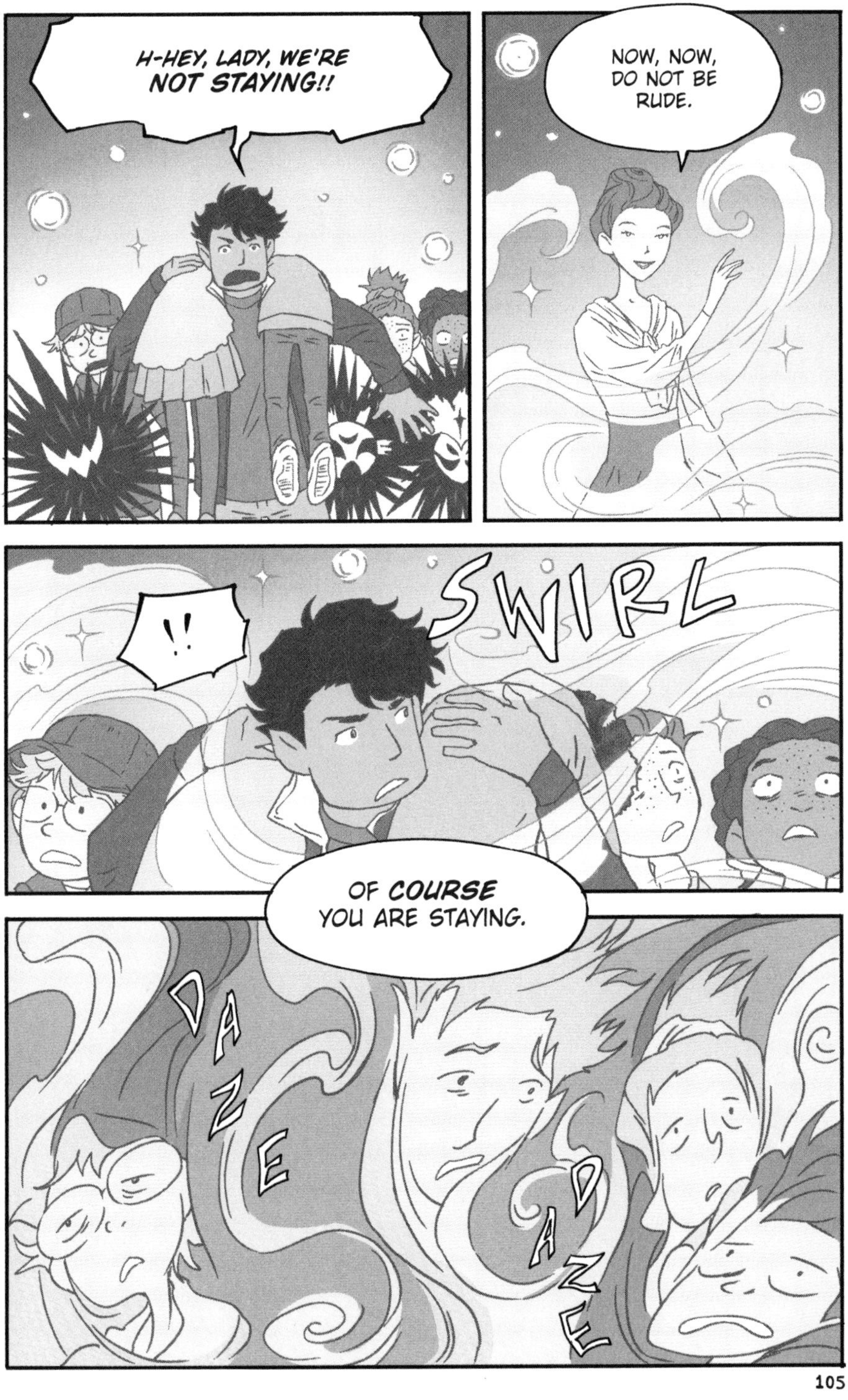
H-HEY, LADY, WE'RE NOT STAYING!!
NOW, NOW, DO NOT BE RUDE.
!!
SWIRL
OF COURSE YOU ARE STAYING.
DAZE
DAZE

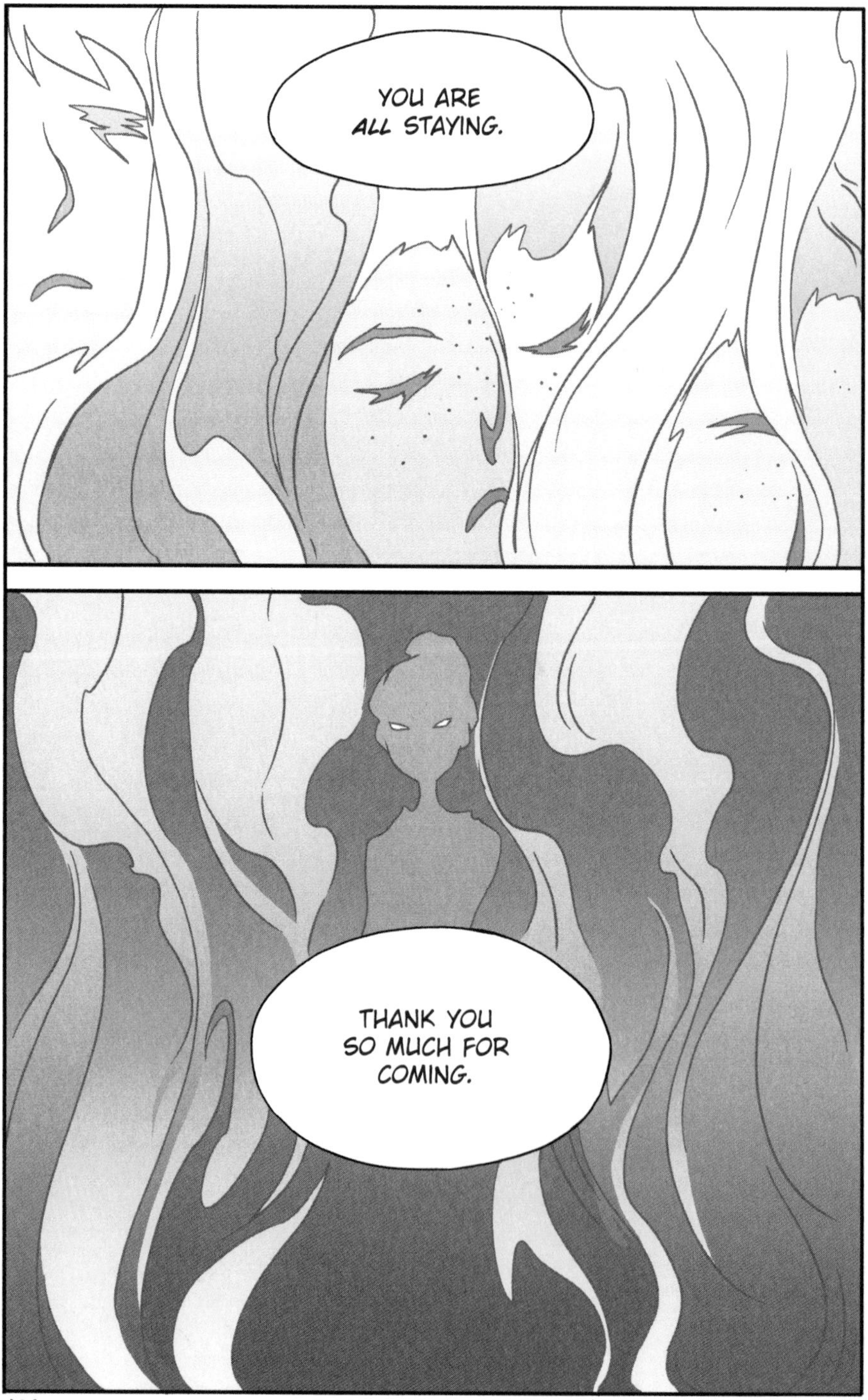
YOU ARE ALL STAYING.
THANK YOU SO MUCH FOR COMING.

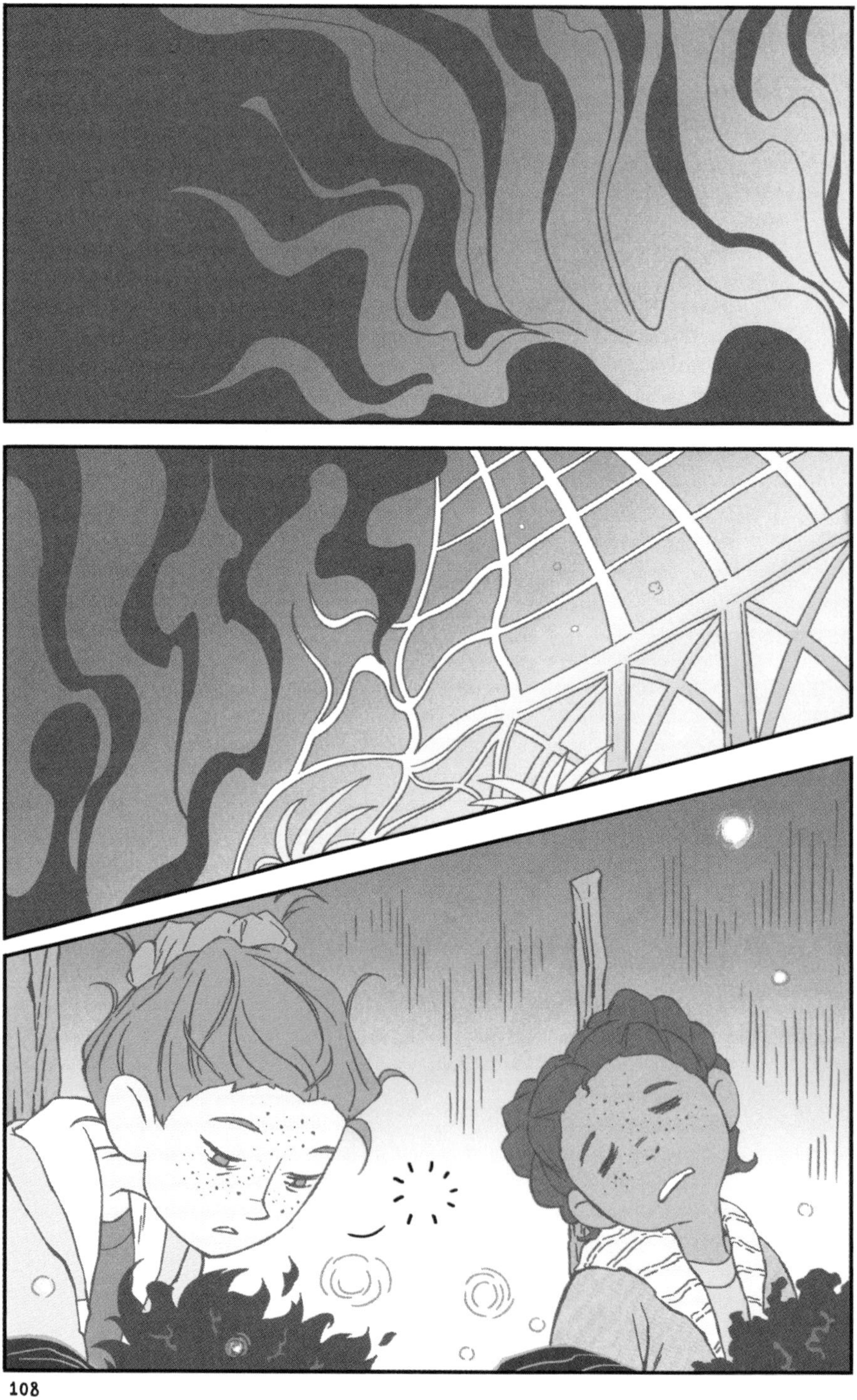

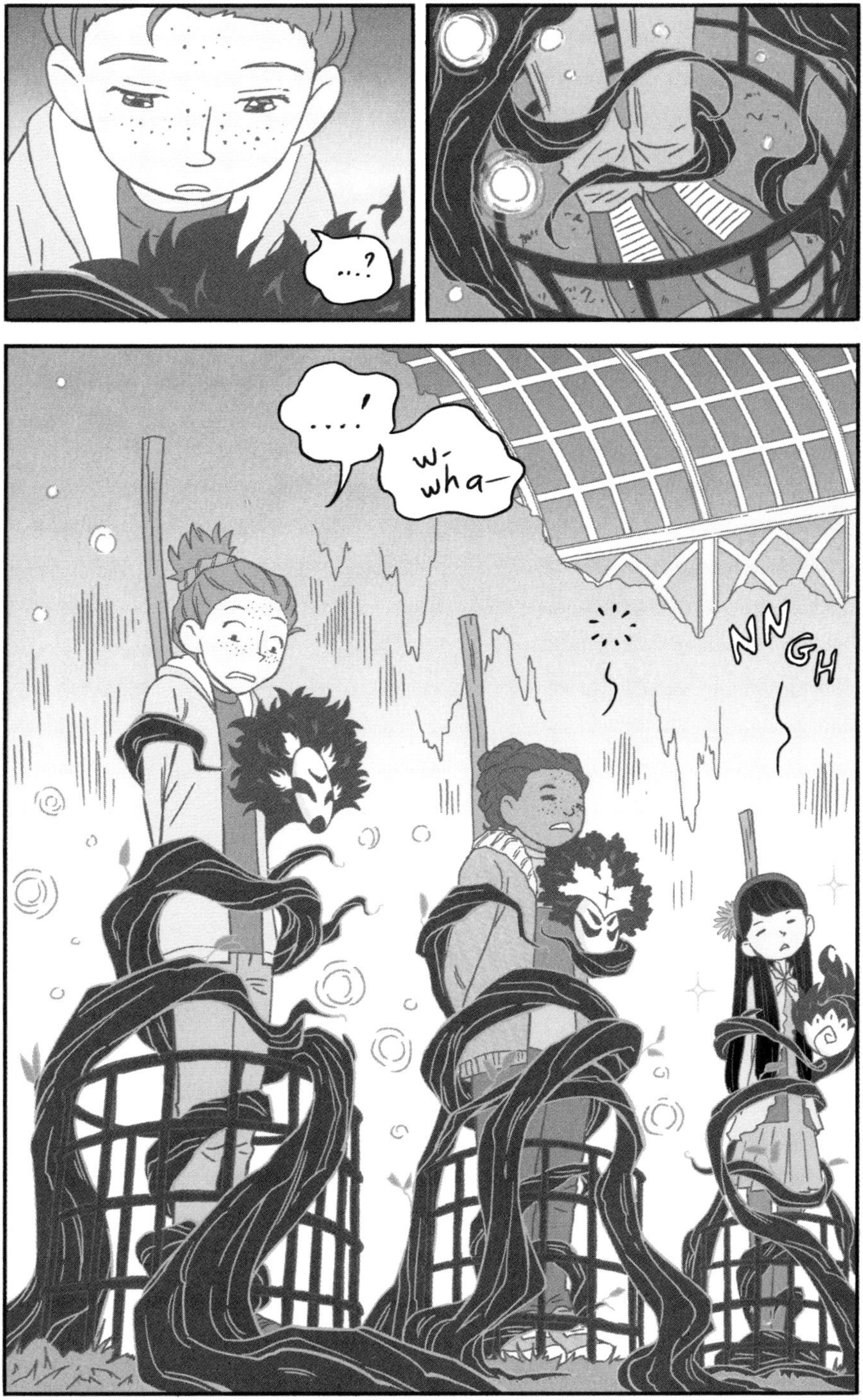
...?
...!
w-wha—
NNGH

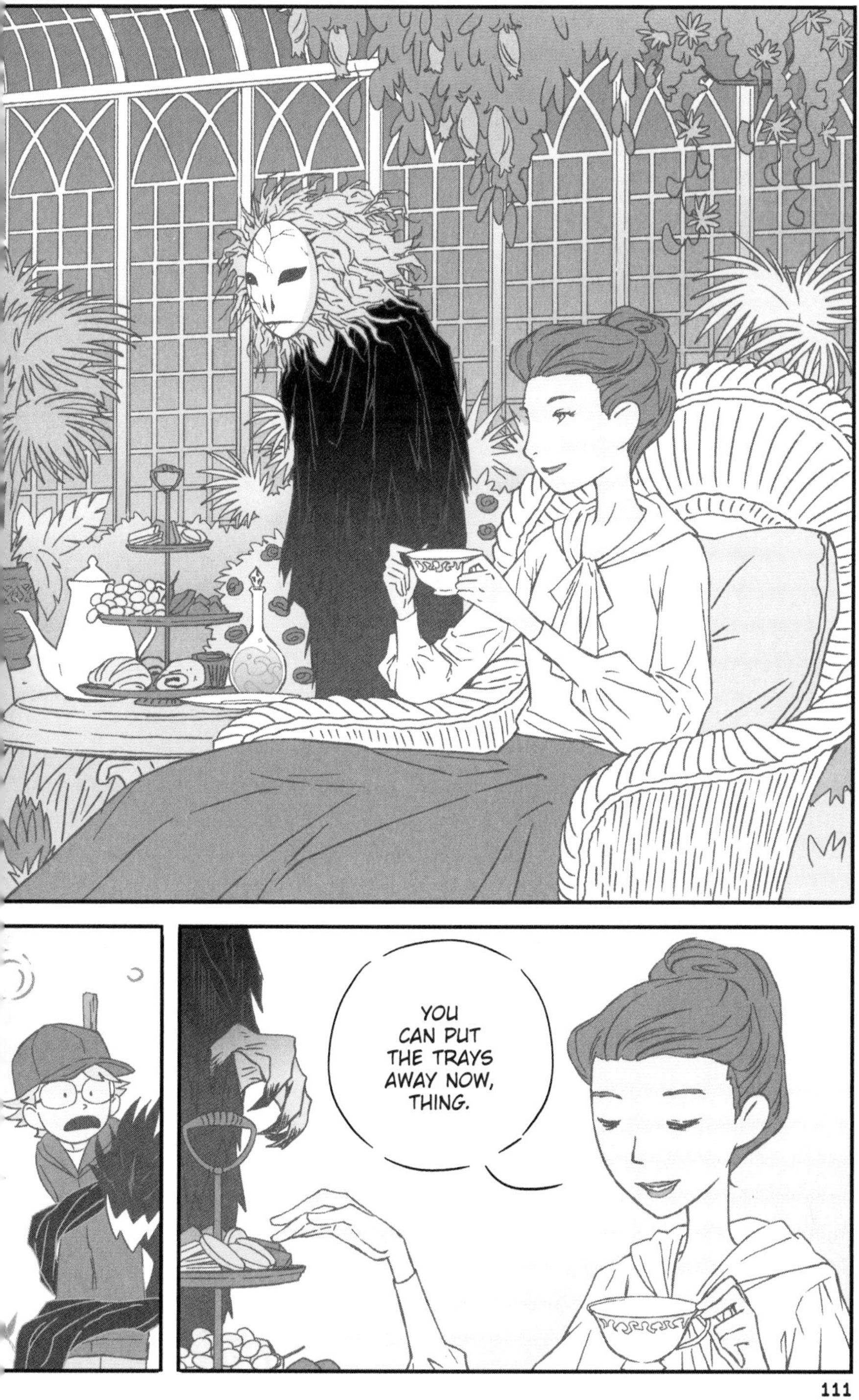
YOU CAN PUT THE TRAYS AWAY NOW, THING.

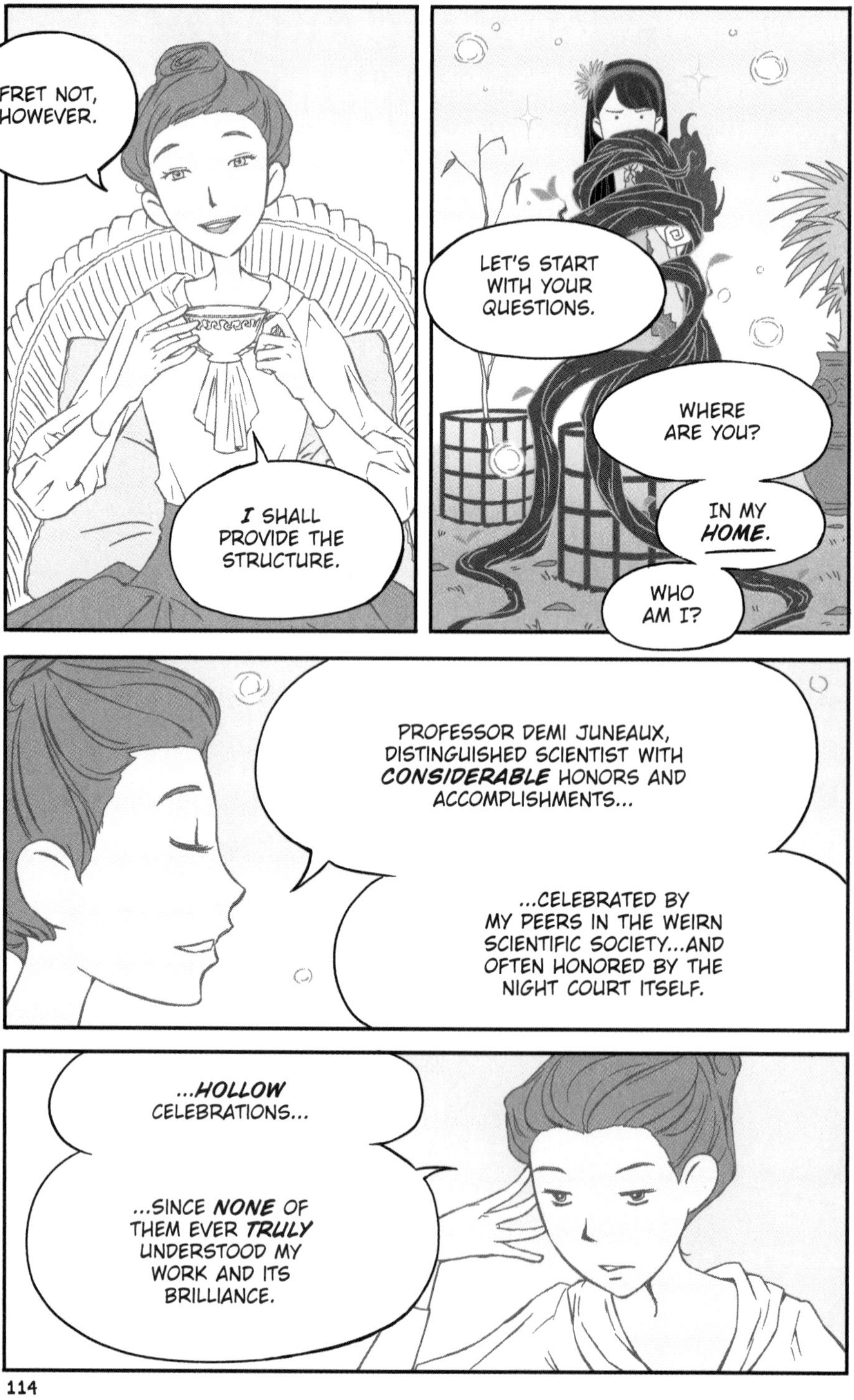
FRET NOT, HOWEVER.
I SHALL PROVIDE THE STRUCTURE.
LET'S START WITH YOUR QUESTIONS.
WHERE ARE YOU?
IN MY HOME.
WHO AM I?
PROFESSOR DEMI JUNEAUX, DISTINGUISHED SCIENTIST WITH CONSIDERABLE HONORS AND ACCOMPLISHMENTS...
...CELEBRATED BY MY PEERS IN THE WEIRN SCIENTIFIC SOCIETY...AND OFTEN HONORED BY THE NIGHT COURT ITSELF.
...HOLLOW CELEBRATIONS...
...SINCE NONE OF THEM EVER TRULY UNDERSTOOD MY WORK AND ITS BRILLIANCE.

115

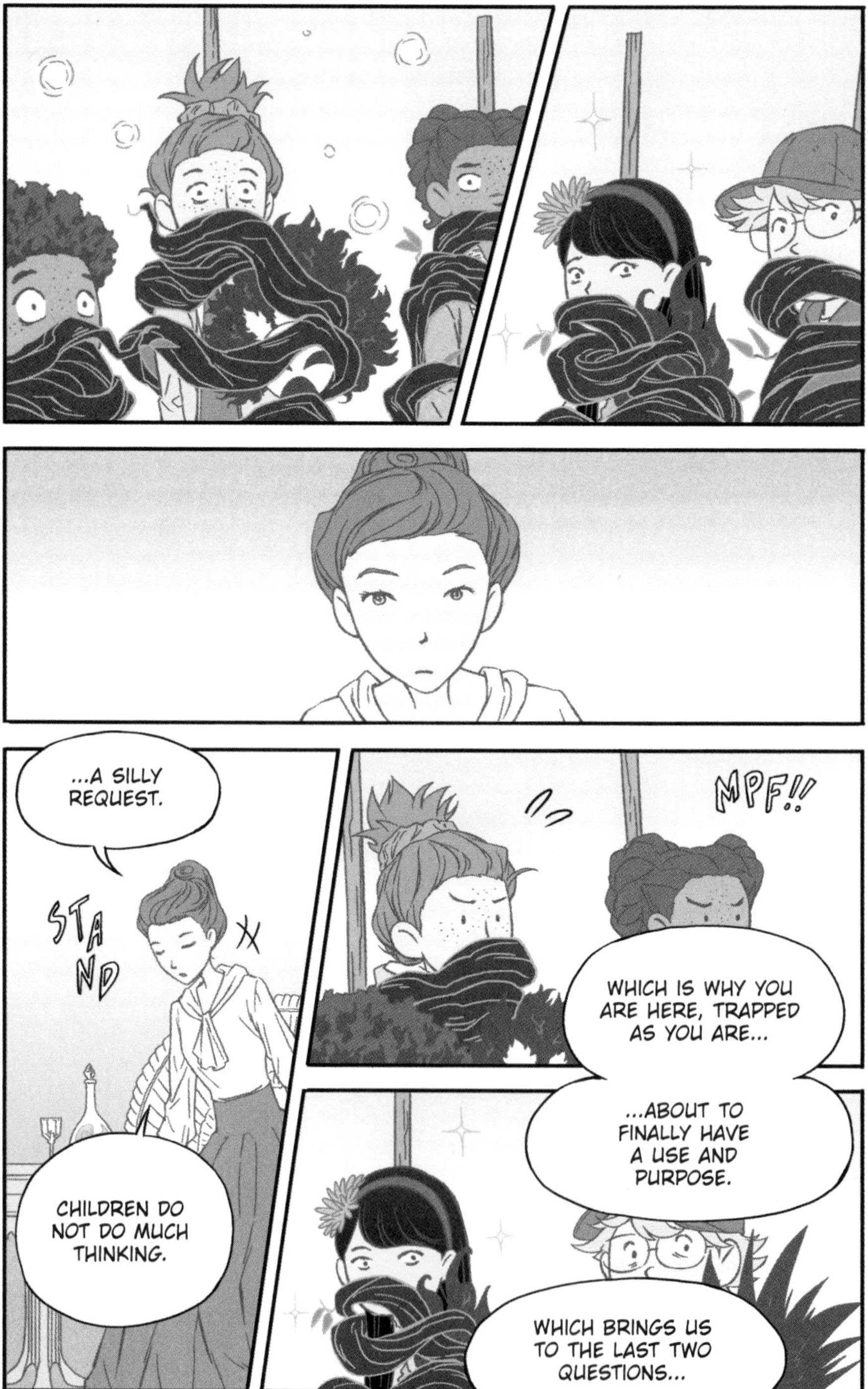
...A SILLY REQUEST.
STAND
CHILDREN DO NOT DO MUCH THINKING.
MPF!!
WHICH IS WHY YOU ARE HERE, TRAPPED AS YOU ARE...
...ABOUT TO FINALLY HAVE A USE AND PURPOSE.
WHICH BRINGS US TO THE LAST TWO QUESTIONS...

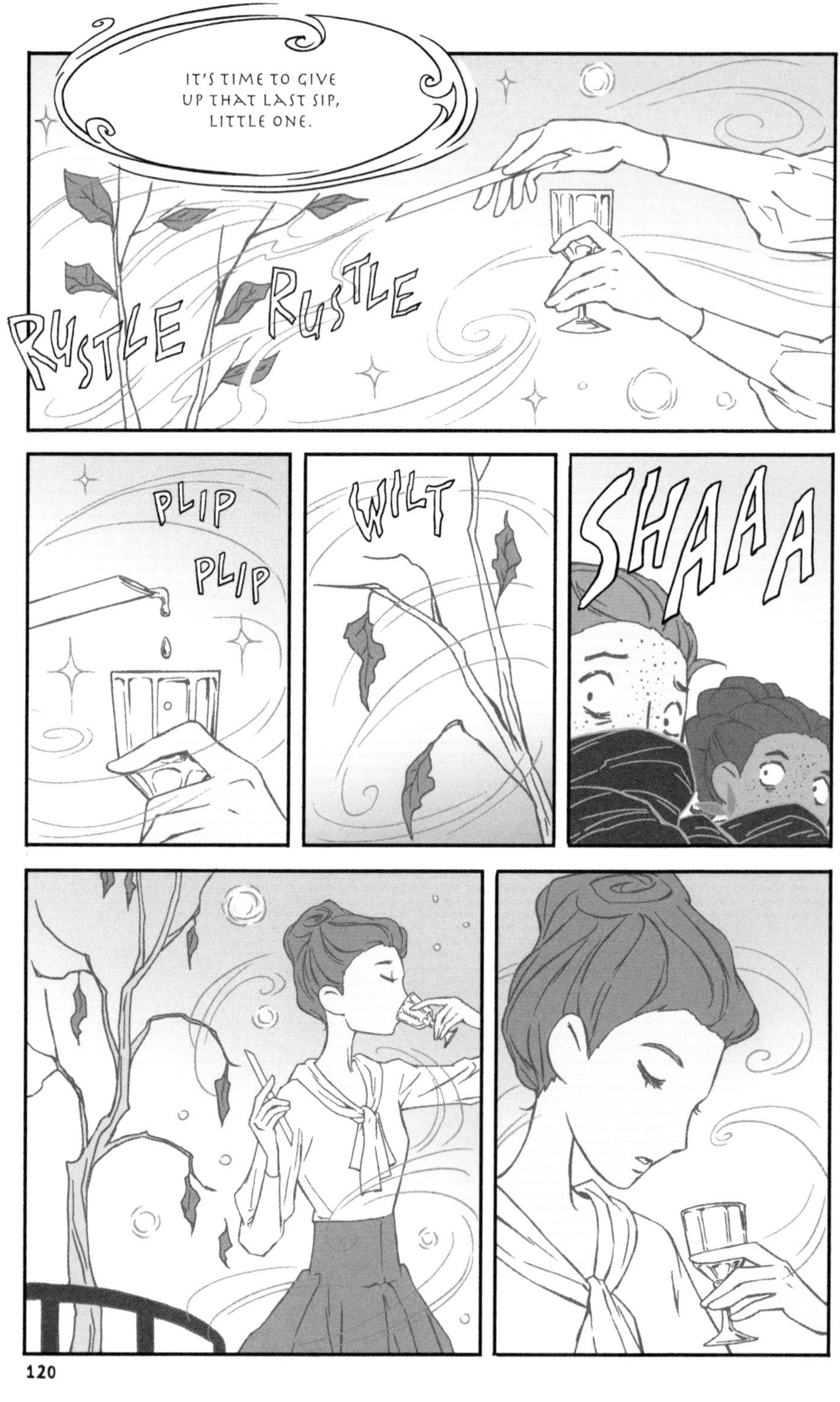
IT'S TIME TO GIVE UP THAT LAST SIP, LITTLE ONE.
RUSTLE RUSTLE
PLIP
PLIP
WILT
SHAAA

# Chapter 5

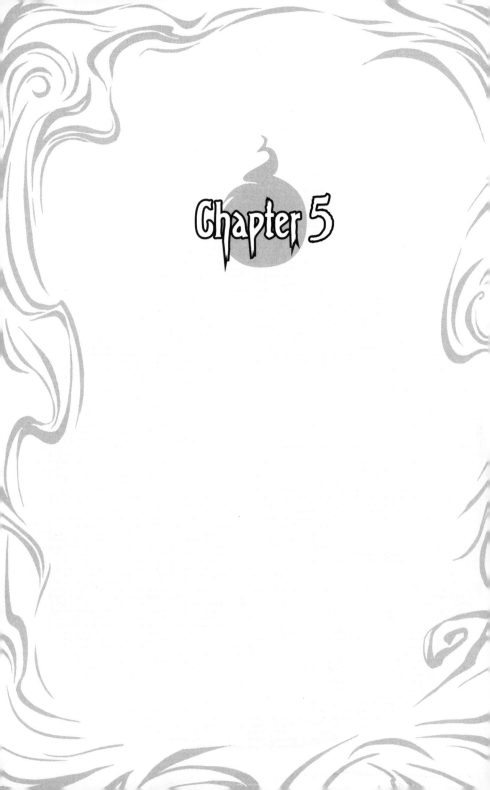

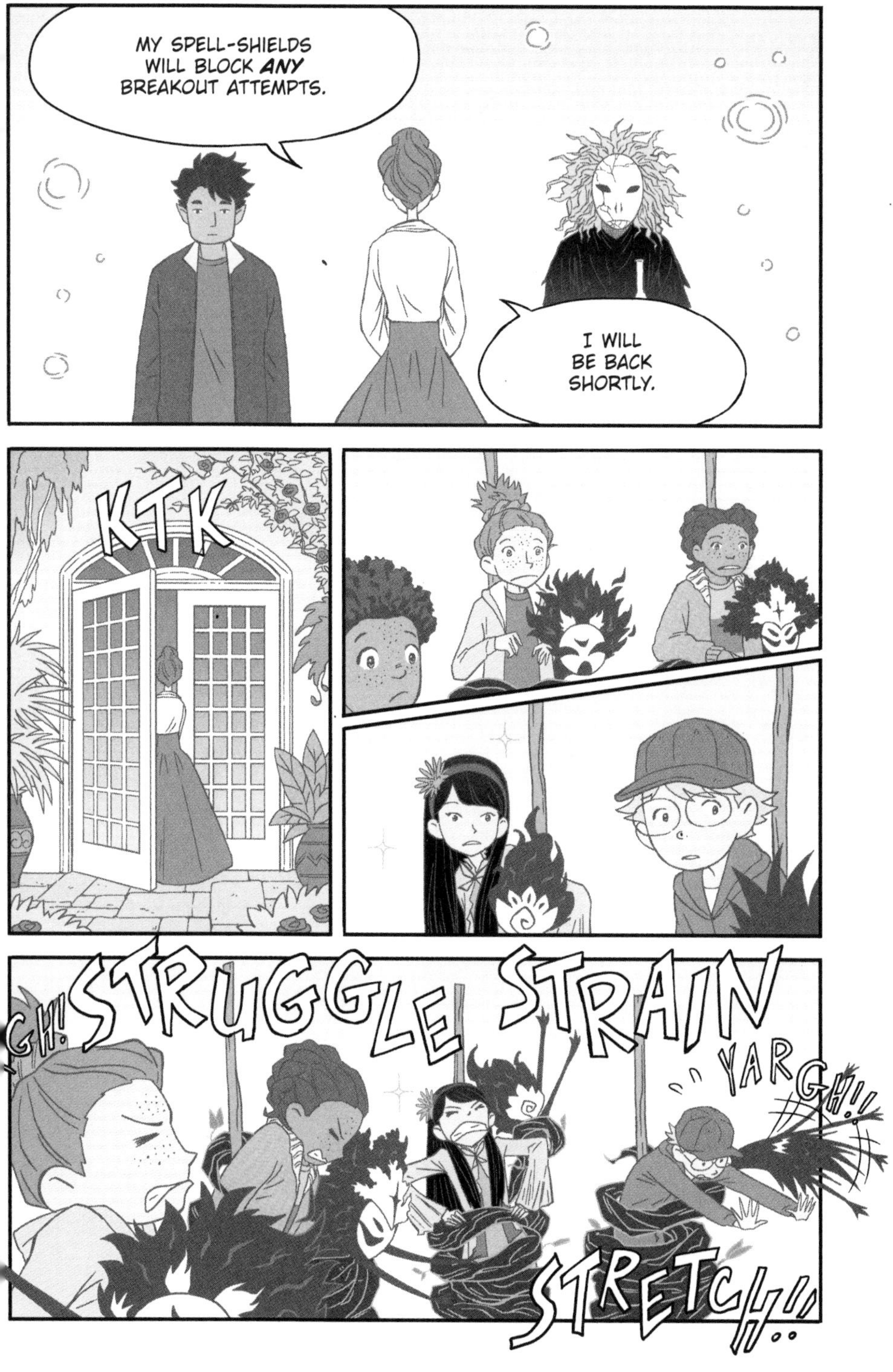
MY SPELL-SHIELDS WILL BLOCK ANY BREAKOUT ATTEMPTS.
I WILL BE BACK SHORTLY.
KTK
GH!
STRUGGLE
STRAIN
YARGH!!
STRETCH!!

139

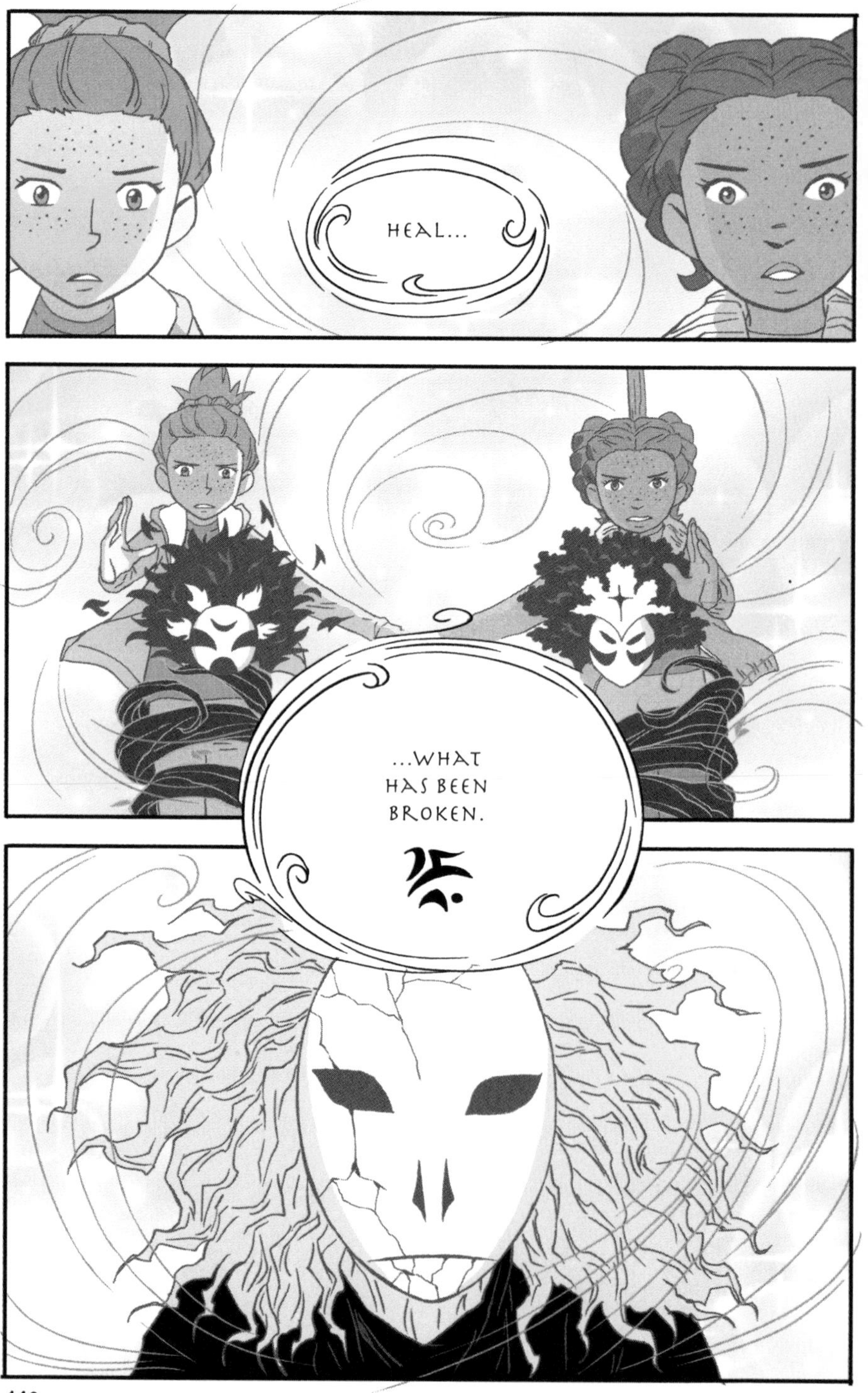
HEAL...
...WHAT HAS BEEN BROKEN.

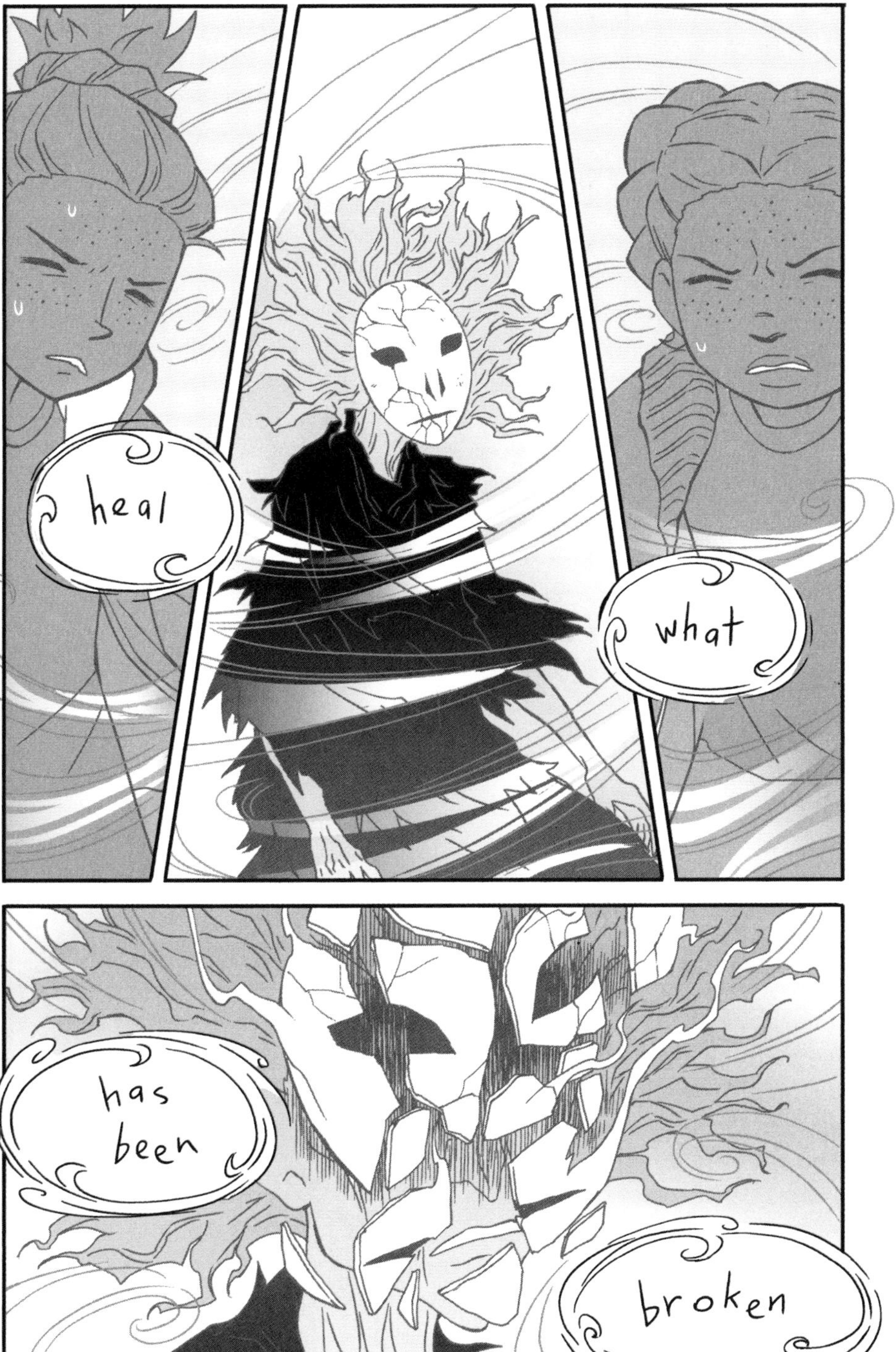
heal
what
has been
broken

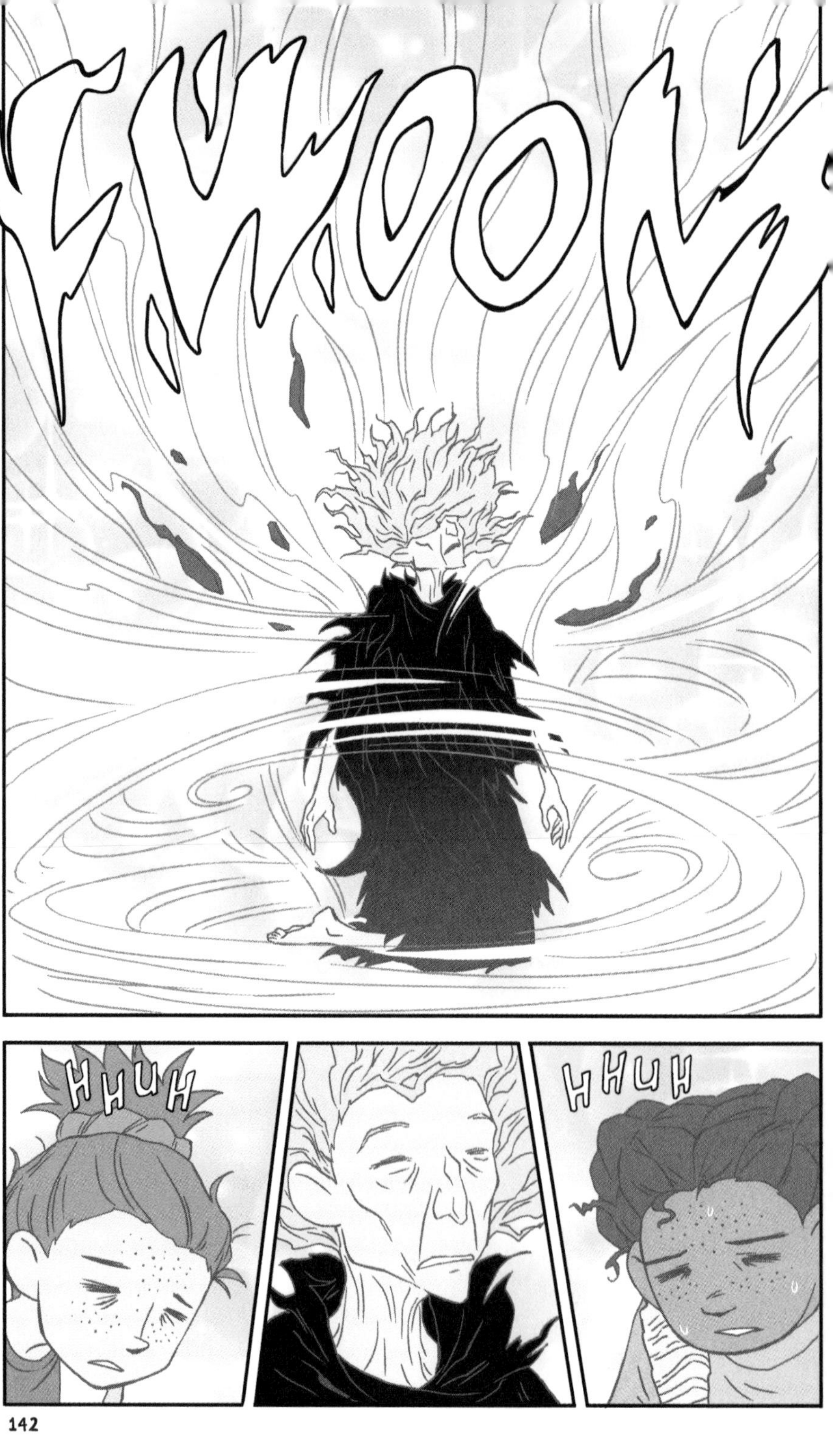
FWOOM
HHUH
HHUH

144

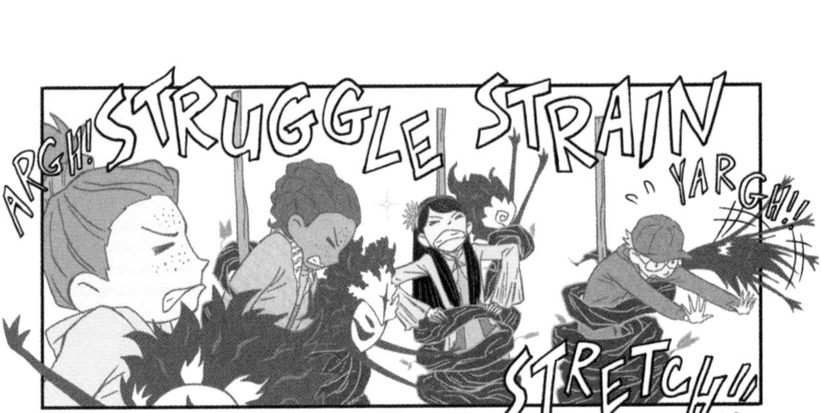
ARGH!
STRUGGLE STRAIN
YARGH!!
STRETCH!!

# Chapter 6

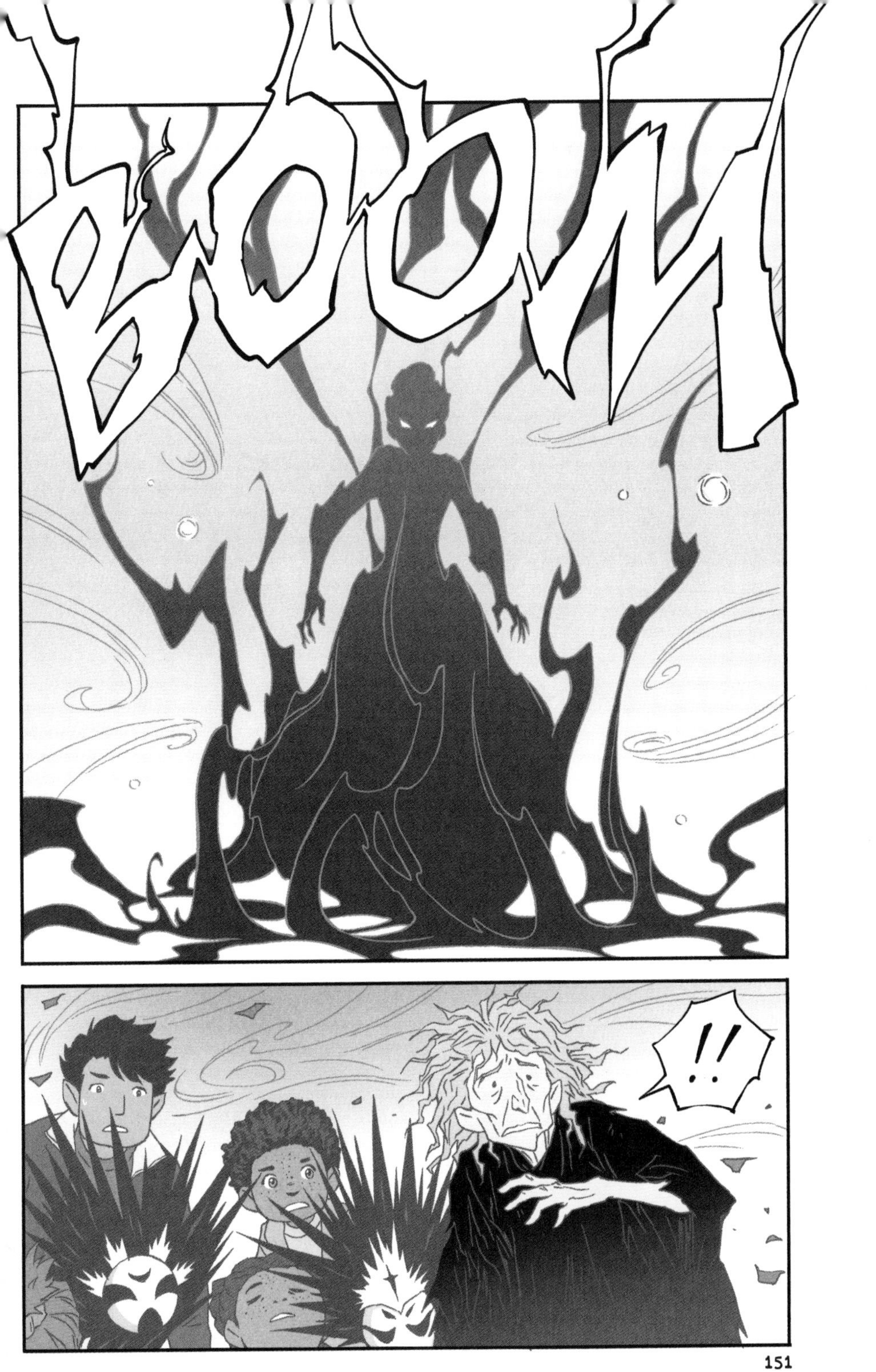
BOOM
!!

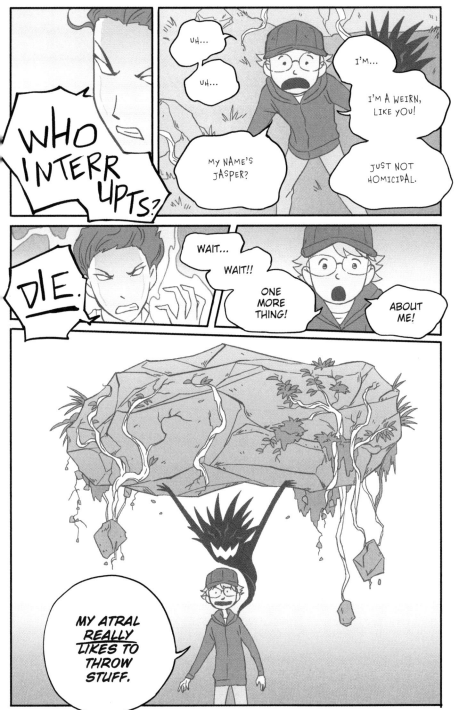

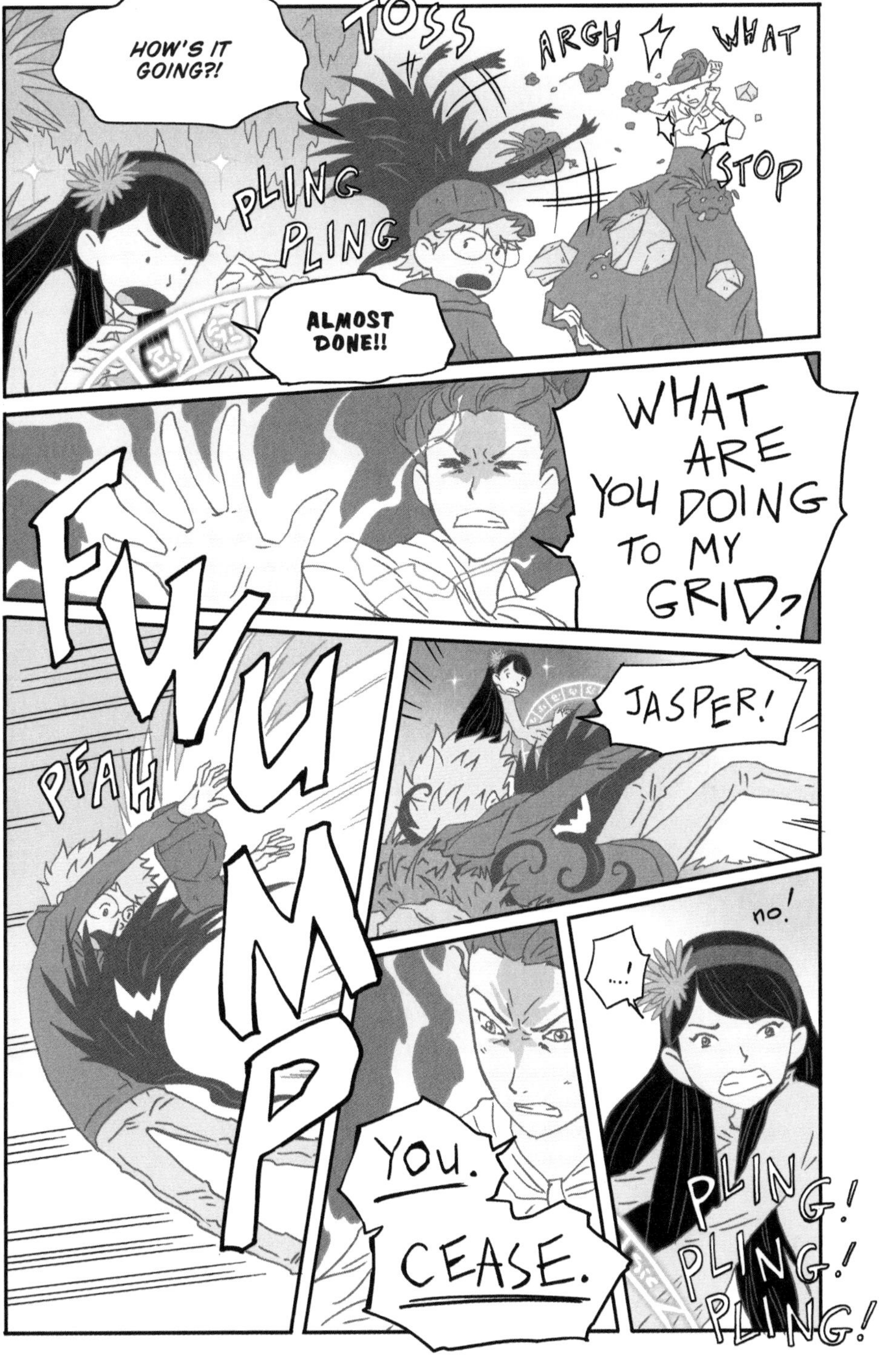
HOW'S IT GOING?!
TOSS
ARGH
WHAT
STOP
PLING
PLING
ALMOST DONE!!
WHAT ARE YOU DOING TO MY GRID?
FWUMP
PFAH
JASPER!
no!
...!
YOU.
CEASE.
PLING!
PLING!
PLING!

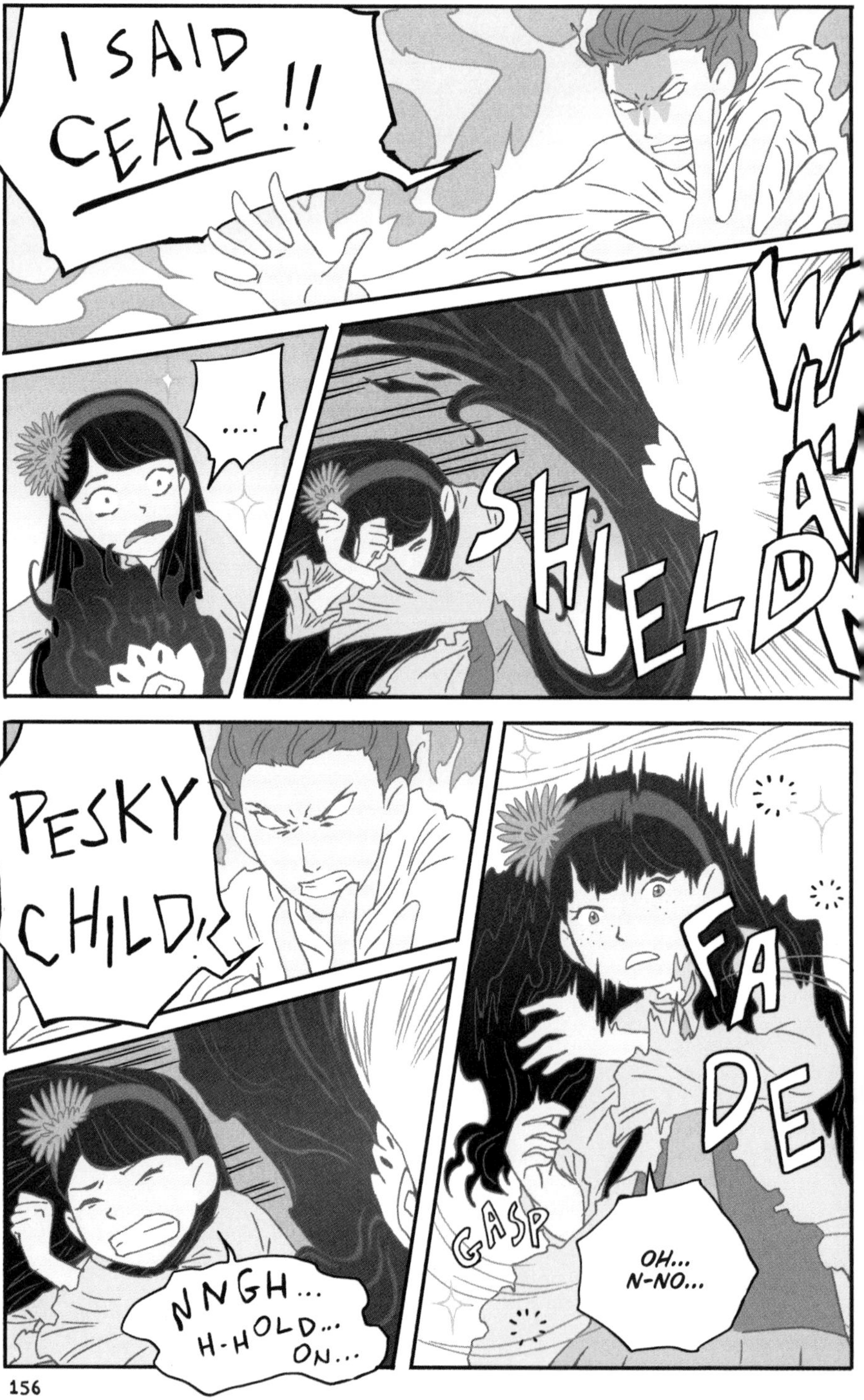
I SAID CEASE!!
...!
SHIELD
WA...
PESKY CHILD!
FADE
GASP
NNGH... H-HOLD... ON...
OH... N-NO...

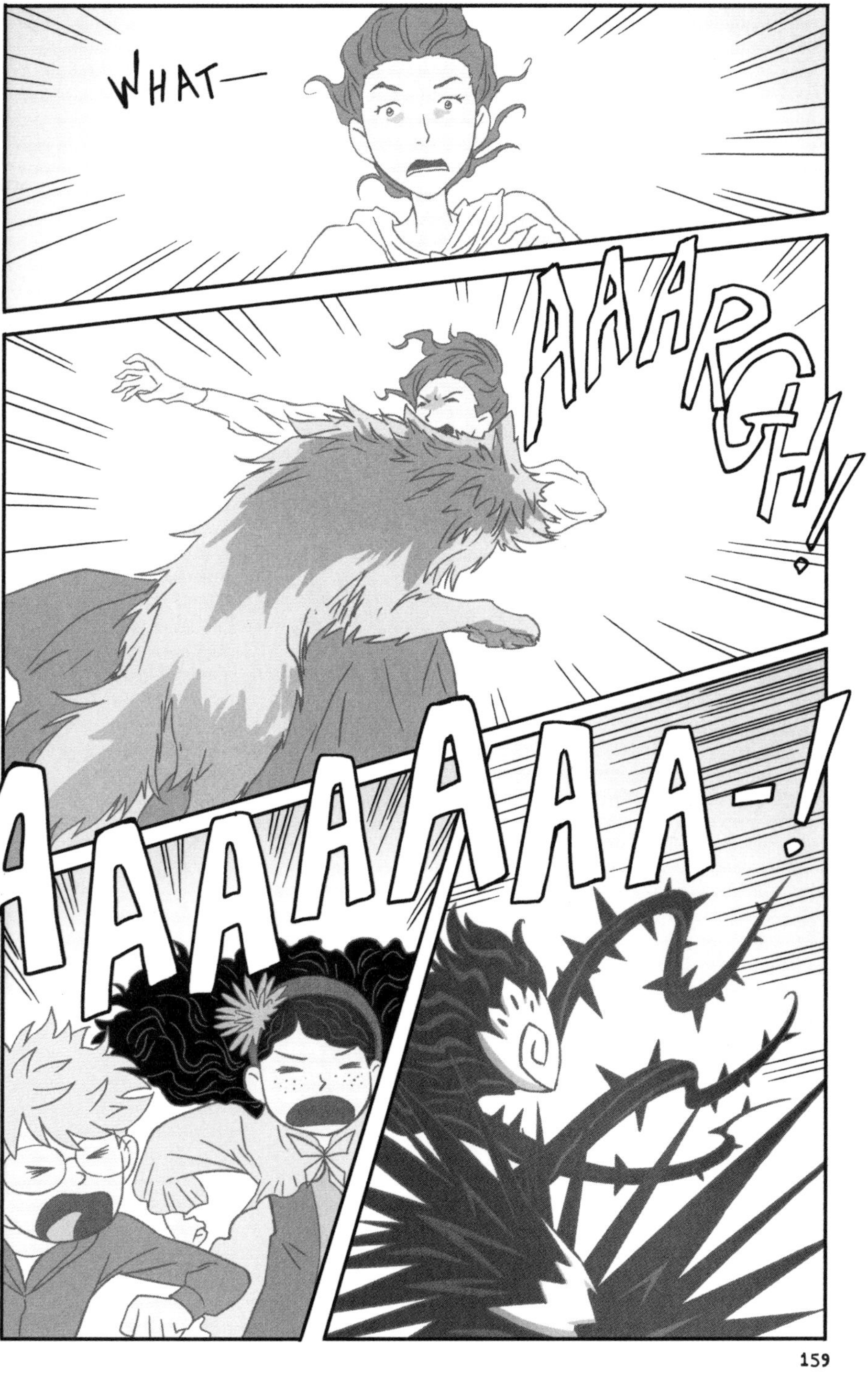
WHAT—
AAARGH!
AAAAAAAA-!

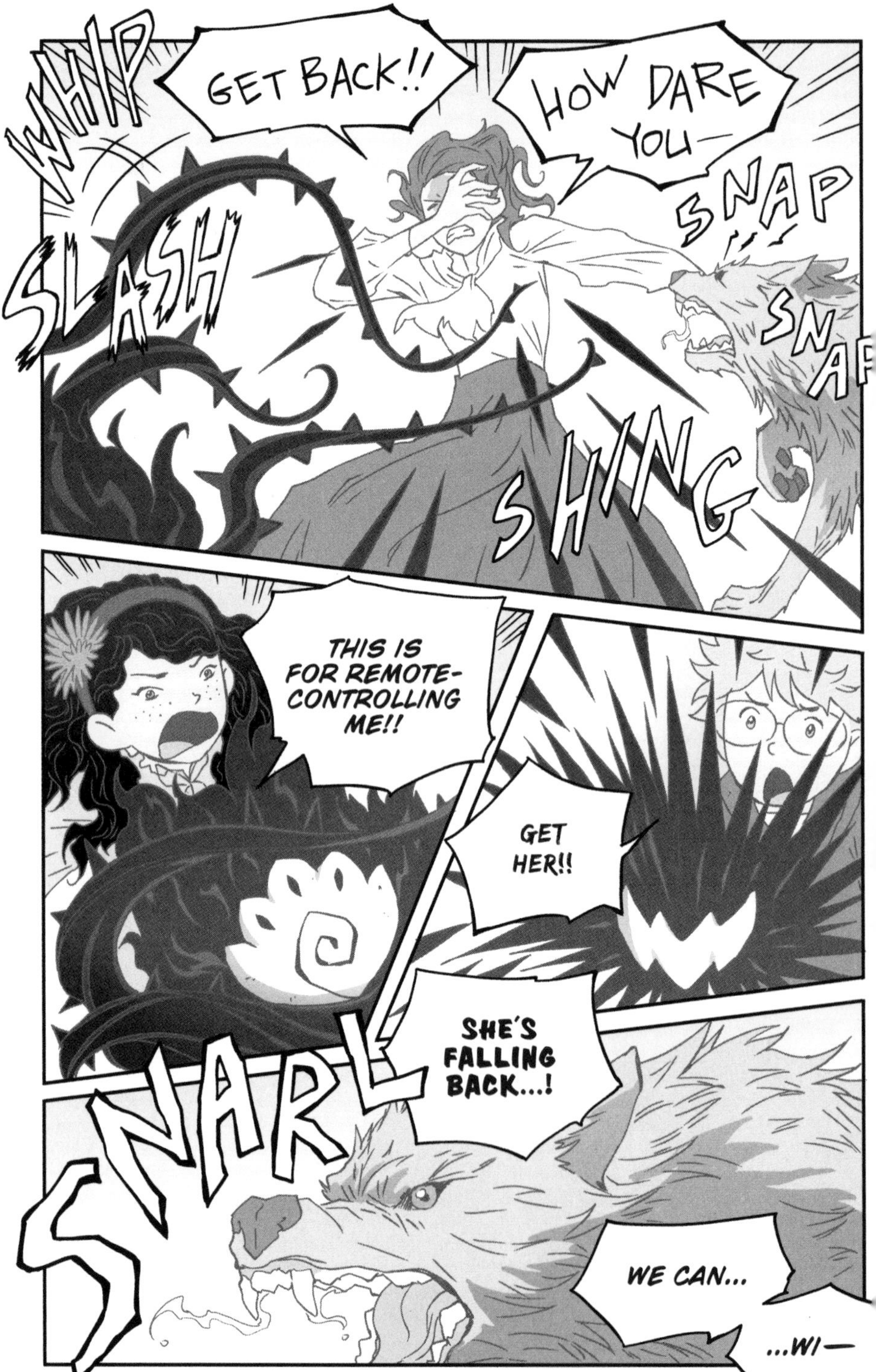
WHIP
GET BACK!!
HOW DARE YOU—
SNAP
SLASH
SNAP
SHING
THIS IS FOR REMOTE-CONTROLLING ME!!
GET HER!!
SNARL
SHE'S FALLING BACK...!
WE CAN...
...WI—

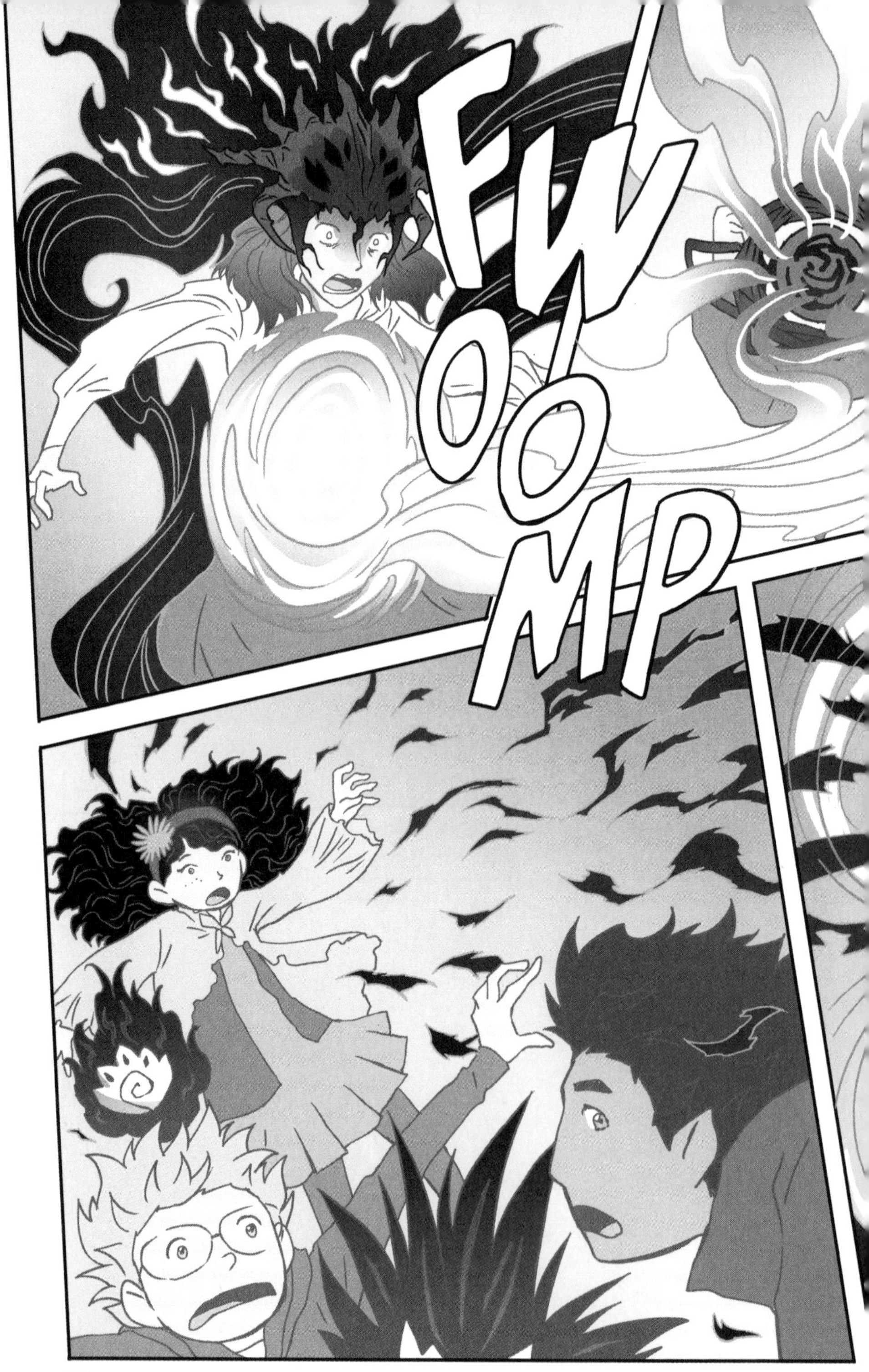
FWOOOMP

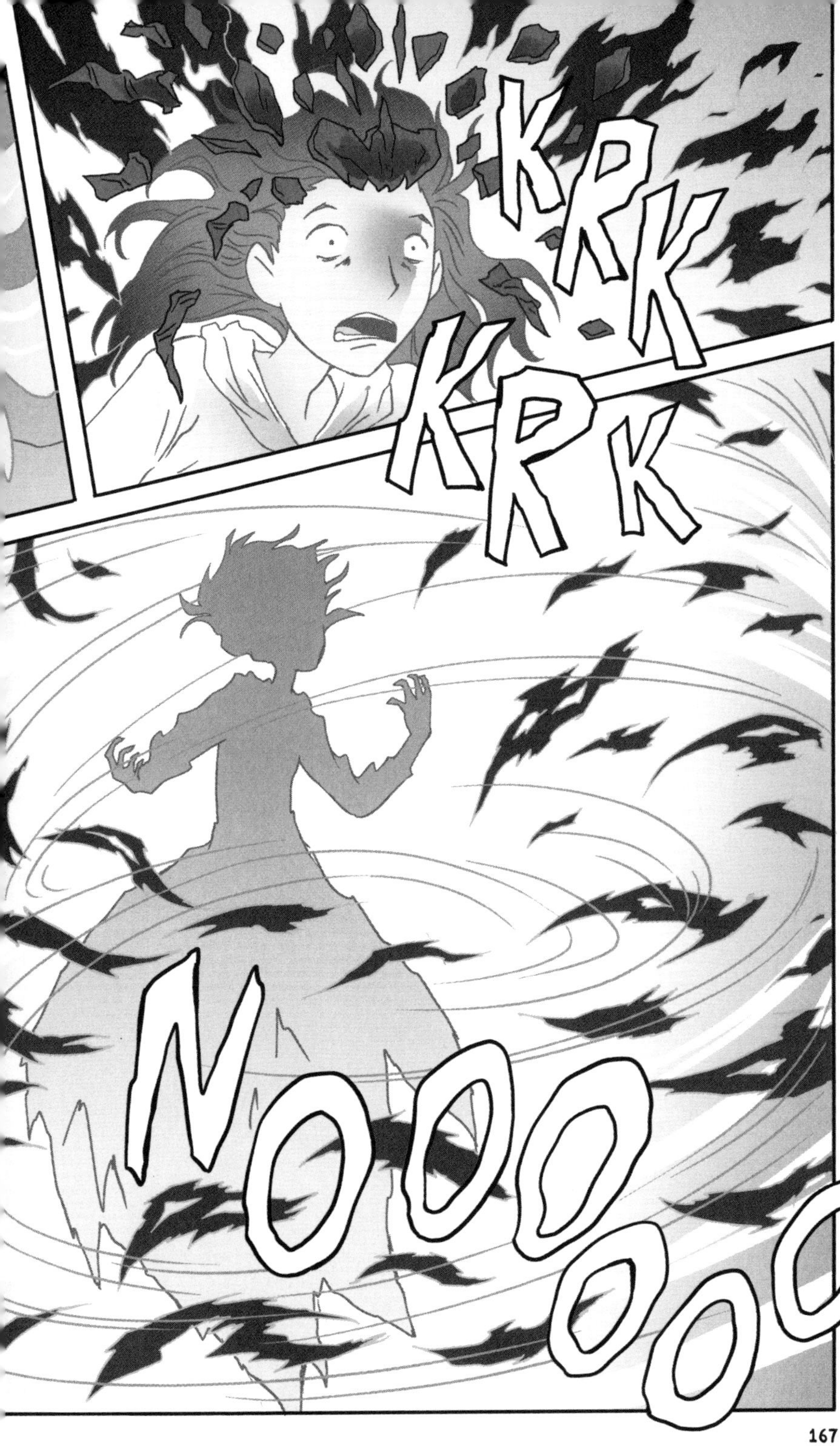
KRRKK
KRK
NOOOOOOOO

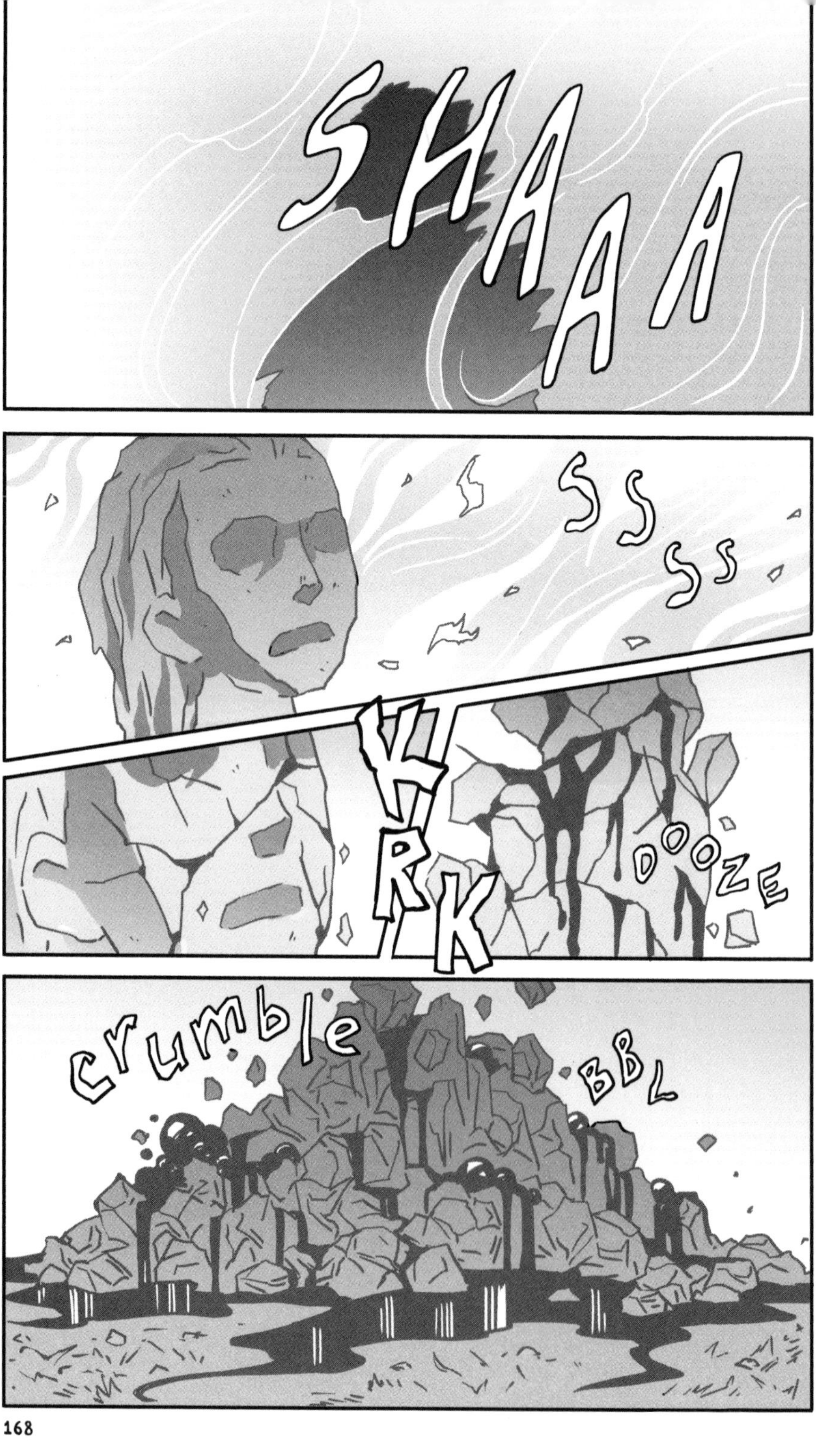
SHAAAA
SSSSS
KRK
DOOZE
crumble
BBL

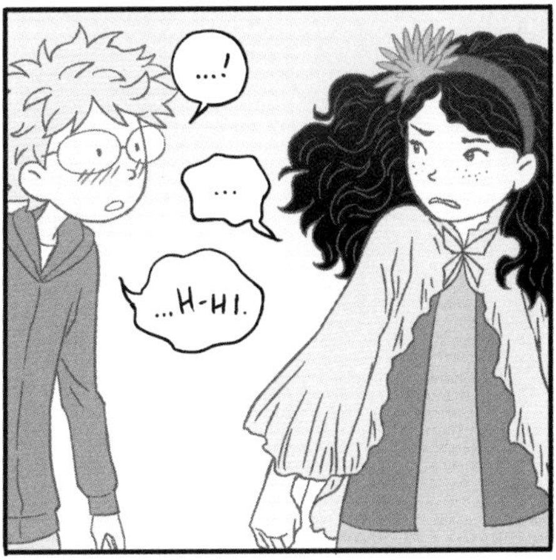
...!
...
...H-HI.

# Epilogue

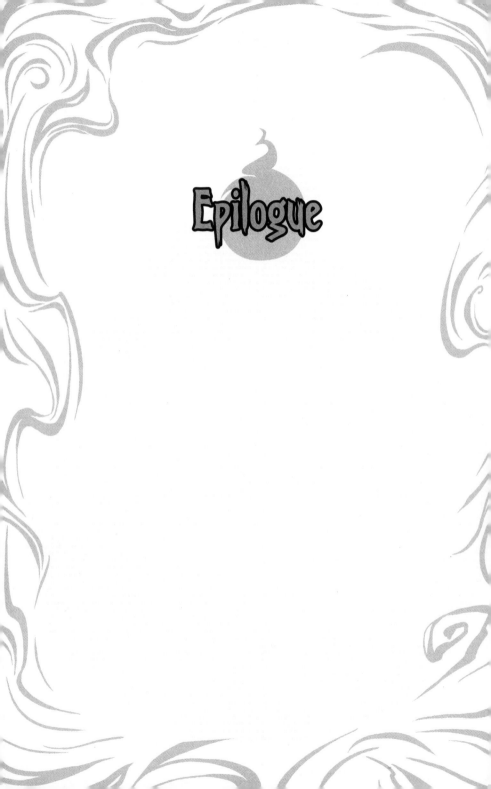

179

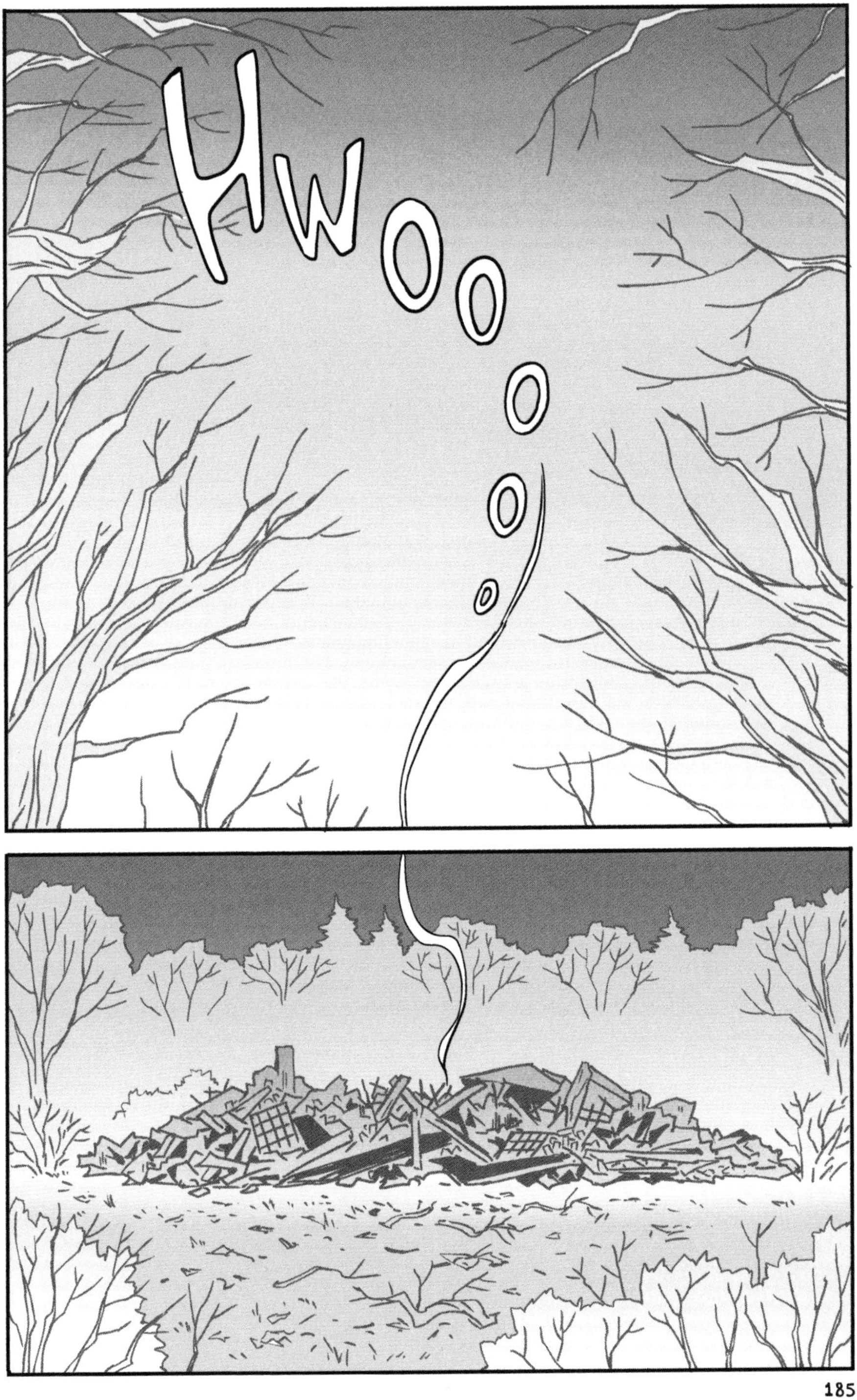
HWOOOOO

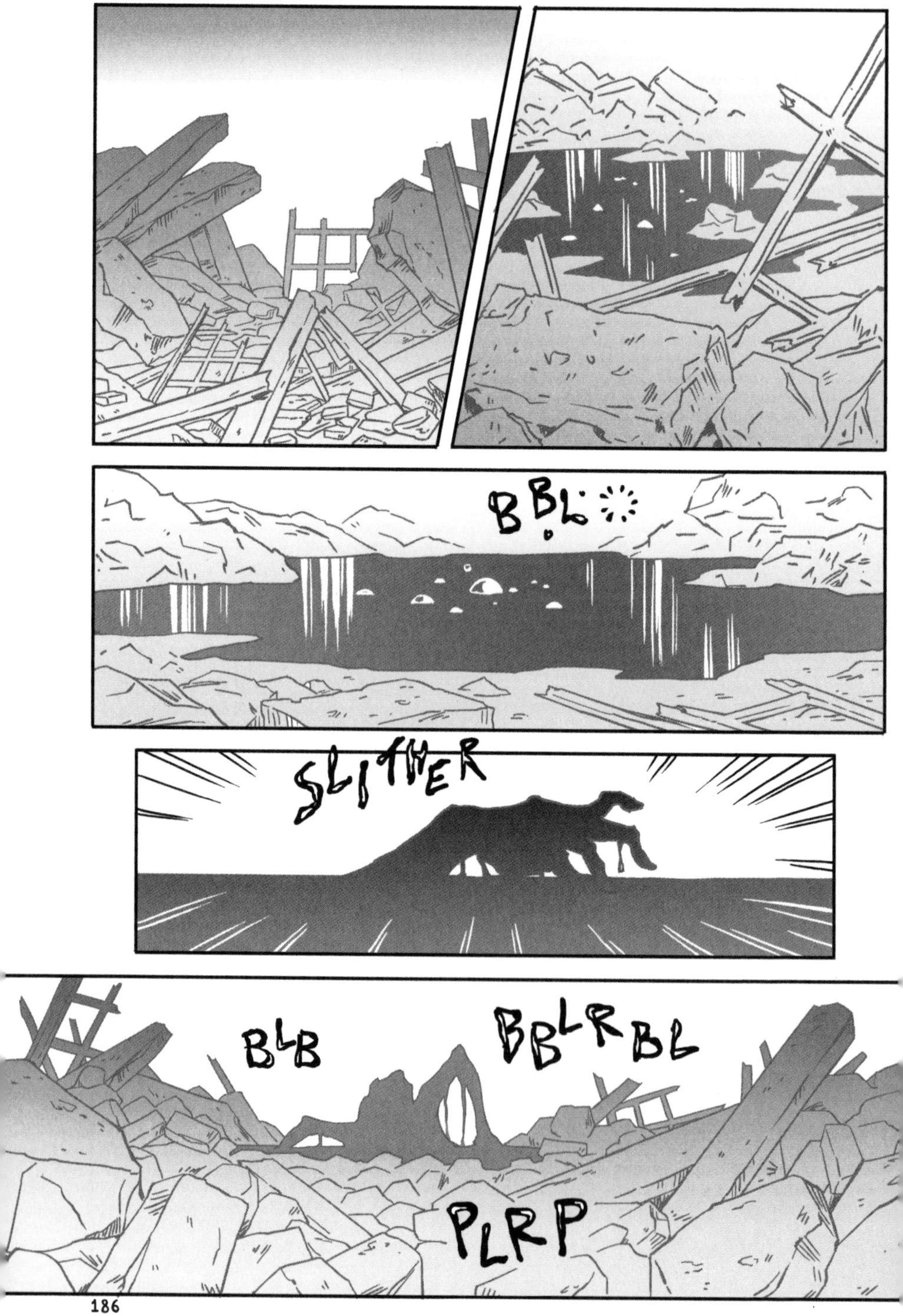
BBL
SLITHER
BLB
BBLRBL
PLRP

THE END
OF BOOK 1.

# FROM the AUTHOR

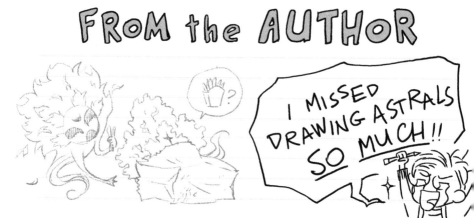

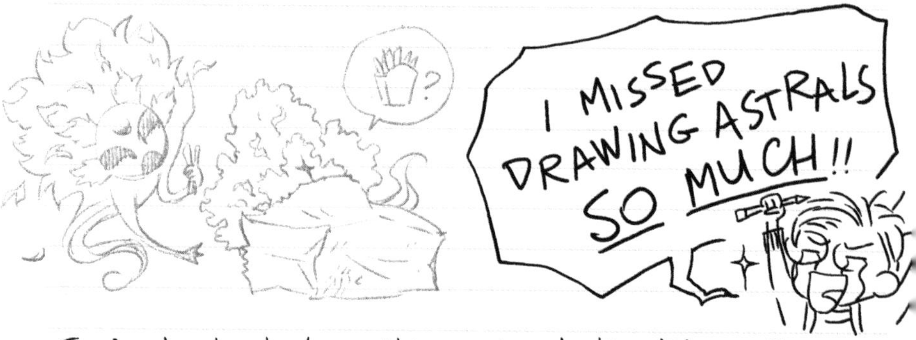
I MISSED DRAWING ASTRALS SO MUCH!!

I first started writing about the Weirn Books world back in 2007 (over a decade ago!! Aaaaa!!) and my favorite thing about it (besides the awesome magic, sharp-witted heroes that make bad life decisions, and a sprawling mysterious world to explore) was ✧ASTRALS✧!! I WANT ONE. Can't wait to get started on the next adventure for Ailis, Na'ya, and their crew. ...Right after I get, like, 10 weeks of sleep (take THAT, Ailis).

Some snapshots from the book production:

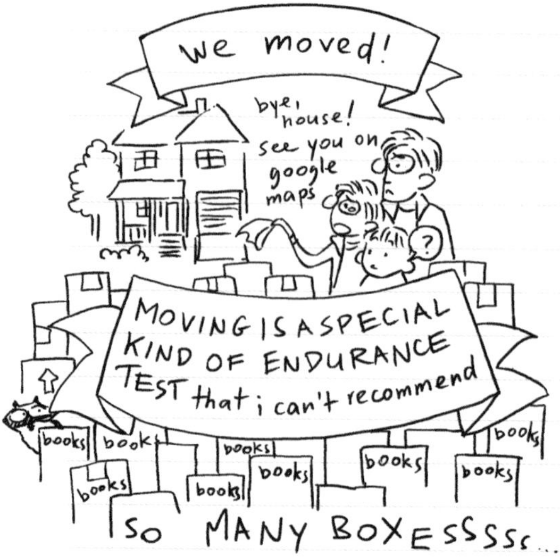
we moved!
bye, house!
see you on google maps
?
MOVING IS A SPECIAL KIND OF ENDURANCE TEST that i can't recommend
books
SO MANY BOXESSSs...

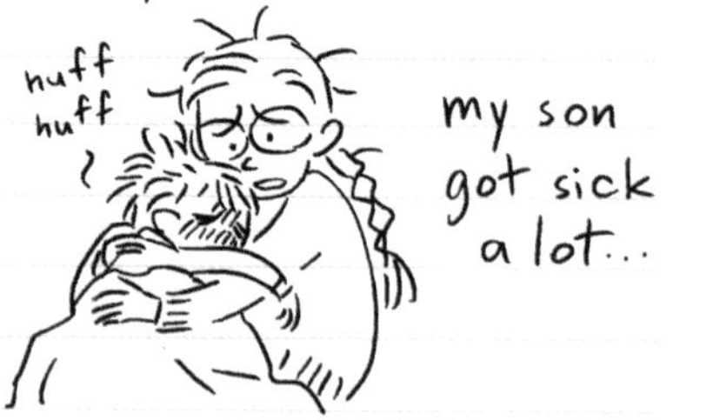
huff huff
my son got sick a lot...

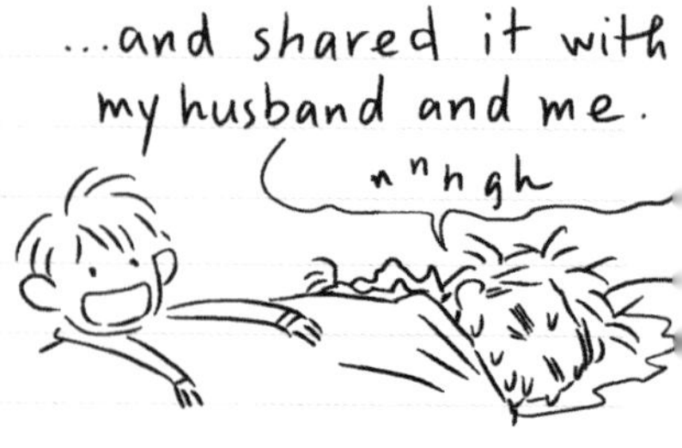
...and shared it with my husband and me.
nnngh

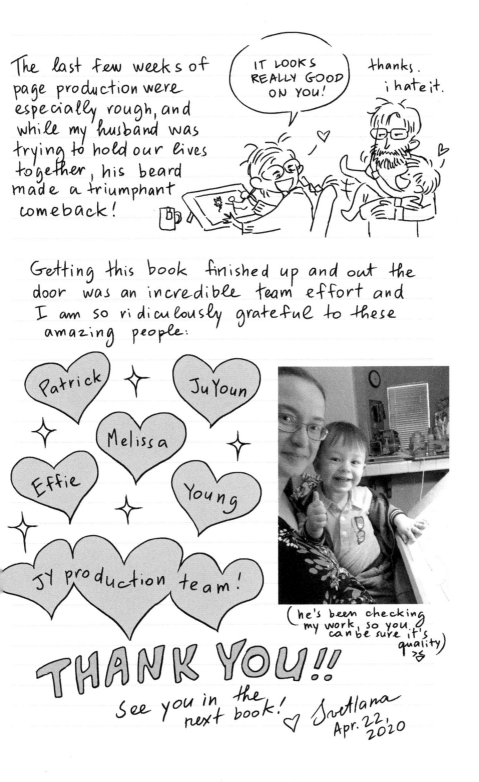

The last few weeks of page production were especially rough, and while my husband was trying to hold our lives together, his beard made a triumphant comeback!

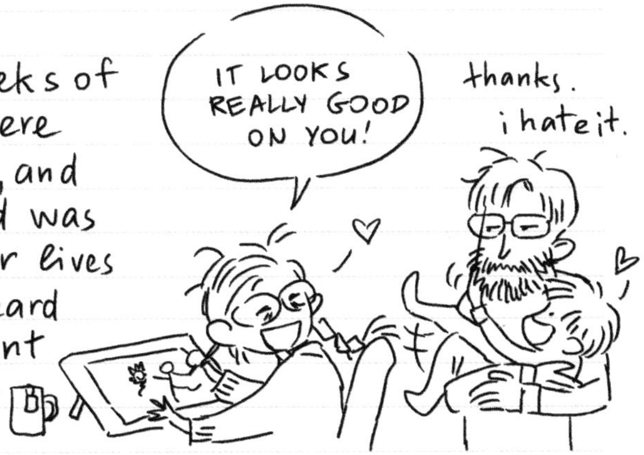
IT LOOKS REALLY GOOD ON YOU!
thanks. i hate it.

Getting this book finished up and out the door was an incredible team effort and I am so ridiculously grateful to these amazing people:

Patrick

JuYoun

Melissa

Effie

Young

JY production team!

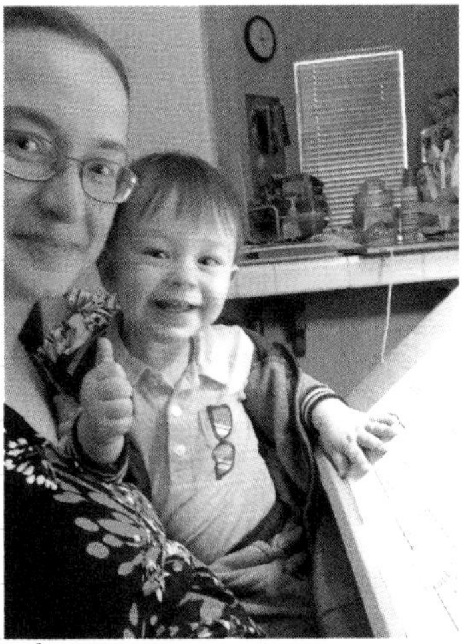

(he's been checking my work, so you can be sure it's quality)

# THANK YOU!!

See you in the next book! ♡ Svetlana

Apr. 22, 2020

# AND FOR READERS WHO'VE GRADUATED FROM MIDDLE SCHOOL—

## Nightschool

### THE WEIRN BOOKS
#### Collector's Edition

Explore the Night Realm once again with NIGHTSCHOOL collector's omnibus editions!

Nightschool answers the age-old question—Where do demons get their diplomas? Schools may lock up for the night, but class is in session for an entirely different set of students. In the Nightschool, vampires, werewolves, vampires, and weirns (a particular breed of witch) learn everything from calculus to spell casting. Alex is a young weirn who has always been homeschooled, but dark forces seem to be drawing her closer to the Nightschool and the mysteries within.

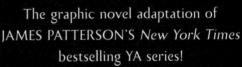

# WITCH & WIZARD

The graphic novel adaptation of JAMES PATTERSON'S *New York Times* bestselling YA series!

**Svetlana Chmakova** was born and raised in Russia until the age of sixteen, when her family immigrated to Canada. After receiving a Classical Animation diploma from Sheridan College, she quickly made a name for herself with graphic novels such as the award-winning urban fantasy *Nightschool: The Weirn Books* and the manga adaptation of *Witch & Wizard* by James Patterson. Her acclaimed Berrybrook Middle School series, which has been nominated for multiple Eisner Awards, has captivated readers of all ages since the publication of its first volume, *Awkward*, in 2015 and has made her one of the most beloved creators in the world of middle grade graphic novels.